# DAVID MARK

# Cold Bones

MULHOLLAND
BOOKS
HODDER

First published in Great Britain in 2019 by Mulholland Books
An imprint of Hodder & Stoughton
An Hachette UK company

1

Copyright © Dead Pretty Ltd 2019

The right of David Mark to be identified as the Author of the Work has been asserted
by him in accordance with the Copyright, Designs and Patents Act 1988.

A CIP catalogue record for this title is available from the British Library

Hardback ISBN 978 1 473 64319 2
eBook ISBN 978 1 473 64318 5

Typeset in Plantin Light by Hewer Text UK Ltd, Edinburgh

Printed and bound in Great Britain by Clays Ltd, Elcograf S.p.A.

Hodder & Stoughton policy is to use papers that are natural, renewable
and recyclable products and made from wood grown in sustainable forests.
The logging and manufacturing processes are expected to conform
to the environmental regulations of the country of origin.

Hodder & Stoughton Ltd
Carmelite House
50 Victoria Embankment
London EC4Y 0DZ

www.hodder.co.uk

To Ruth

*Jafnan er hálfsögð saga ef einn segir . . .*

'Hell hath no limits, nor is circumscribed
In one self place, for where we are is Hell,
And where Hell is there must we ever be.'

—Christopher Marlowe

# Prologue

*Four days before . . .*

He skids on something wet. Something greasy. Something dead. His feet slip out from under him. His shriek of fear is feeble; birdlike. He breaks the worst of his fall with his left hand, jolting his old bones. The blood on his palm blots an impression of plump lips onto the stone.

Desperate, he shuffles his weight, scrabbling at the floor. Kicks out at the darkness as if it were a living thing.

'Please . . . please, stop . . . I'm old!'

He hears himself snivelling, the words popping in bloody spit bubbles.

'I'm just an old man . . .'

He tries to stand. Shifts his weight. The carcass of a bird explodes beneath his boot. The air fills with a sweet foulness and it is all he can do not to throw up as he squints at the streak of feathers and flesh that pattern the broken stones.

He gulps down a breath and wipes the back of his hand through the redness on his brow. There are bloody feathers on the hems of his trousers. He can taste blood. And deeper, like fingers in his throat: the familiar, clammy whisper of rotting flesh.

Scraps of memory: smashed glass and burning paper. He glimpses faces, flickering snapshots. *Pain.* The hoofbeats of hard rain hitting metal. Of metal hitting meat. Of meat hitting stone. He has a memory of bright yellow light: patterns slicing into the blackness; a murmur of steel and the thud of a body striking rock . . .

Remembers.

*Sees.*

Frothing blood and falling snow. The cold: ferocious, as if he were being swaddled with iron chains.

He pictures the girl. Remembers the weight of her in his arms. Scrawny, like an unfed cat; broken ribs shifting inside her skin.

He screws up his eyes. Tries to put the pieces together. Listens, hard. The shifting ocean; water on wood; the kiss of land meeting sea. He looks up. The great oval picture of a raven perched on a harbour wall. Suddenly he knows where he is. The Blake building. St Andrew's Dock. Hull. He returns to himself as if waking from sleep.

He's Gerard Wade.

He's an old man.

An old, broken man.

He's been waiting for this moment for fifty fucking years . . .

'Is it you? It can't . . . we thought you were dead!' screams Gerard, and feels bloody spittle land on his chin. 'Please. I never touched her!'

He has a sudden recollection of the moments before the darkness took him. The postcard. The dark figure beyond the glass. The one who called himself Vidarr . . .

Here, now, it feels as though a great black bird were unfurling its wings within him. He grinds his teeth and feels them rattle in his gums.

He'd been waiting for his pals. His old crewmates. They deserved an explanation. A warning. He'd had enough of keeping secrets. His bones were growing cold. He checked his watch. Checked his phone. Where were they? Napper? Alf? Fat Des?

He'd glared at nothingness and smoked cigarette after cigarette, the glowing embers the only light in this bleak, bitter place. Then the shadows had moved. The air had changed. The shape of a man had stepped towards him; a silhouette cut from black velvet.

Long hair and dead eyes.

A hook in his shimmering hand.

Then it had seemed as if there were iron filings in his nose and old keys in his mouth and he was falling into the whirlpool in his senses; the hook slipping under his ribs as expertly as a filleting knife into the belly of a wriggling cod . . .

Pain shoots and he slides forward, toppling over by inches. He sucks in a breath and begins to wheeze. Opens his eyes. The whole world seems to be vibrating.

His head feels on the verge of splitting apart and one whole side of his body is tingling. He looks down at himself. There is blood on his hands. Thick blood drips down his face.

He reaches out and steadies himself on the wet brick. He forces himself to take a breath and stares out across the black water. On the inky, bloated surface of the Humber it looks as though a billion fish were rising to the surface to feed.

He starts trembling. He can taste bile. He has to breathe slowly to stop himself from retching. Unsought, a memory rises. The reek of mud and rotten timber. The reek of fish guts and blood. Cold air stinging his sinuses.

'I had to . . . it wasn't just me . . . what choice did I—'

He stops gabbling as he feels a sharp, crunching pain in his mouth. A tooth has freed itself from his lower gum, slipping out as easily as a pip slipping free of rotten fruit. He fumbles for something with which to defend himself. Agony rips through him: hot and cold, a perfect burning point of frozen fire. He glances down and sees the hook. The lower half catches the light, glistening silver. The curve is deep within him, sunk into his flesh, curved up beneath the fragile cage of his ribs. He fights for breath and a fit of coughing grips him, tight as pincers. He cannot seem to force any strength into his limbs. He wants to stand up straight and yet he remains where he has found himself: crook-backed, hunched over, peering over the wall as if vomiting into the sea.

He doesn't notice the figure who follows, the creature with the gleaming black braids and the odd, bird-like walk, who cocks his head enquiringly as he moves from shadow to shadow. Doesn't see the man who slowly winds the cord around his gloved hands and reels him in, moving closer with each jerking step.

The man with the black braids is perhaps ten feet away when the cord rises from the broken ground. He can feel the tension in the rope, tied to the hoop at the base of the hook. It's sunk deep. The more his catch wriggles, the further it works itself into his flesh. He seems to enjoy this brief, peaceful pause. Then he tugs on the line in a swift and powerful motion.

The broken, bleeding man comes tumbling back towards him, wet screams bubbling from his mouth.

The man with the braids stays anchored to the spot. Drags his prey across the ground towards him. He hears the creak of bones groaning under pressure; watches, as ribs splinter and skin tears and the hook bursts free in a joyous riot of black and silver.

And *red*. So much beautiful red.

The man who calls himself Vidarr allows himself to smile; the dying man's screams are lost amid the crying of the gulls, and the song of the crows.

# DAY ONE

# I

*9 January, this year*
*Walkington, East Yorkshire*
*9.06 a.m.*

'Off you go, then. Love you.'

'I haven't finished my biscuit.'

'You could eat it while you walk.'

'It's raining. Have you ever had a wet biscuit? It's the worst.'

'It's not raining. It's more like freezing fog.'

'Oh well, that's so much better. I love freezing fog.'

Father and daughter sit in silence for a time, watching ghostly vapour rise from the icy ground. It turns the picture beyond the windscreen into something otherworldly, obscuring the colourful oblongs of the village school as it collects the last of the shivering children like fish into a trawl. They watch as the mist gathers up the silvery breaths of the skiwear-swaddled mums and dads who linger by their cars on this quiet curve of road: gossiping through chattering teeth, hugging themselves with insulated sleeves; a collage of pink noses and sparkling eyes peeking out from great voluminous folds of angora wool and plum-coloured pashmina. None of the grumbling parents seem keen to continue their morning commute; to trust mid-range tyres on roads that shimmer with black ice.

To their right, a harassed-looking businessman is using a credit card to scrape at the windscreen of his hatchback.

'That's going to snap,' mutters McAvoy, wincing in advance.

It does. The businessman's shoulders slump and he looks down disconsolately at the stump of Barclaycard he holds between forefinger and thumb. He trudges back to his open front door. Slams it behind him, hard enough to dislodge the icicles that dangle from the upstairs gutter. Three perfect, translucent daggers plunge to earth. Two shatter as they strike the drive. The other punctures the white flesh of the frozen earth.

In the back seat of the battered silver people-carrier, Lilah McAvoy giggles naughtily. 'Doofus,' she says, then repeats it for emphasis.

In the driving seat, her father endeavours to give his daughter a stern look. He gives up without a fight, unable to catch her in the mirror. Lilah has placed herself in the most awkward position she can find. Every time he shifts his bulk and shuffles around to talk to her, the tatty car starts rocking.

'You'll be late,' he says, cajoling. 'You don't like walking in after everybody else.'

Lilah shrugs. 'Mrs Whatsherface says that she doesn't get angry, just disappointed. I can live with that.'

A misty rain hangs in the air. The car headlamps are on full beam, casting yellow searchlights into the air. Great ferns of ice pattern the windscreens of the vehicles that hunker down in driveways. The water in the bird baths and puddles has been frozen over for days. Uniformed officers are patrolling Beverley Beck, trying to stop teenagers from testing the safety of the sheet ice by throwing younger siblings onto it. The national papers would have called it the Big Chill if it had reached London.

Inside the car, the heater is turned up high. Lilah is luxuriating in the warmth. McAvoy, sticky with sweat, feels like a snowman in a sauna.

'Do you think I look okay?' he asks eventually, gesturing at himself. 'Not too much, is it? I'm an acting detective inspector today.'

'Acting? Do you mean like *pretending*?'

'You're not funny.'

McAvoy's a huge man, all muscles and gristle and scars. He's an easy six feet five with red-brown hair and a full beard, turning grey. His eyes are the soft brown of the exposed earth beneath a fallen tree. He never looks comfortable. Today he has incarcerated himself in a new red and blue checked shirt, his heart sinking when he saw the words 'slim-fit' on the label. He can never relax in slim-fit, forever concerned he will pop a button and cost some poor bystander an eye. His wife, Roisin, insisted he pair the shirt with mauve braces and a deep blue three-piece suit. In one of the hipster pubs in London, McAvoy would be saluted for his style. In East Yorkshire, he fears such affectations may mark him out as a tourist, or a twat.

'I have to go, Lilah . . .'

'I'll come too.'

McAvoy closes his eyes and wonders what the women in his life would make of him if they were to see him in these moments of private struggle with his daughter. Roisin would find it adorable: would grin at him with her most kissable smile and agree with Lilah's suggestion that they give school a miss today and go and do something fun. Trish Pharaoh, his boss and friend, would roll her eyes and tell him he's softer than a sack of dead mice. He's not sure which counsel he would prefer.

He feels fingers tugging his beard. Opens one eye. Lilah is staring into him in that way of hers. He holds her gaze. Fills himself up with it. He loves his family so much that it sometimes threatens to consume him.

'You're such a doofus.' Lilah grins, obeying his instructions to try and use a new word every day. 'I like that word. Has Mammy got a word for "doofus"? Is it a Traveller word?'

McAvoy smiles. 'She has lots of words for "doofus", my love.'

9

'Is that lady looking at us?' asks Lilah. She points towards the school. A woman is standing by an old purple hatchback, peering at McAvoy's car. He suffers a moment's panic. Wonders what he will do if she comes and tells him that he is the worst kind of parent and must be a pretty poor police officer if he can't even get a five-year-old girl to school on time. She comes into focus. Multicoloured coat, battered Doc Marten boots and a woollen hat with flaps that dangle either side of a round, pleasant face. He'd sat next to her at the Christmas concert in Beverley Minster. He can recall a smell of extra-strong mints and gingerbread. She had been the only other parent not taking pictures or recording the event for posterity on an expensive iPad or smartphone. What was her name? Paulette? Paulina? A child in Year 2, as far as he can recall. Little boy. Was it Magnus or Otto? He worries about himself sometimes. There are days when it feels as if the librarian in the great chambers of his mind has retired, leaving the doors and windows open on her way out.

'She is,' says Lilah. 'Look, she's walking over. What have you done?'

McAvoy's eyes widen and he opens in mouth in mock outrage. 'Me? Why is it me? Oh, it's funny, is it? Laughing, are we? Right, come here . . .'

Lilah squeals, wriggling back into her seat as McAvoy grabs her ankle and pretends to chew on her knee. Despite the game, he does it cautiously – Lilah has her mother's tendency to kick out when under attack.

'Quick, lock the doors,' says Lilah, grabbing her bag. 'That's Otto's mum. She smells funny.'

'Everybody smells funny to somebody,' says McAvoy, giving her what he hopes is a firm look. They have had lots of conversations recently about what a person should and shouldn't say about other people's appearances. He has done everything by the book, explaining that it doesn't matter what a person looks like as long as they are decent underneath. Roisin, grinning, had offered a different perspective, suggesting that Lilah had a duty of care: a moral obligation to help those less gorgeous measure up.

'You smell nice,' says Lilah, shrugging. 'You look nice. You are nice.'

McAvoy swallows. He fixes on a smile and slides down the window. The cold air feels delicious on his face.

'You're the policeman,' says the lady. 'Sorry, that sounded rude. Do you remember me? Are you okay? Erm . . .'

'It's police officer, actually,' says Lilah, from the back seat.

'Oh sorry,' says the woman, looking genuinely horrified at having accidentally joined the patriarchy and contributed to centuries of oppression. She puts a hand to her mouth. 'It just sounds right, doesn't it? Policeman. Po-lees-man. Oh goodness, I'm making it worse.'

'How can I help?' asks McAvoy, resisting the urge to tell her not to worry about it. He's long since come to the conclusion that other people don't worry enough.

'I'm not sure,' says the lady, looking flustered.

He considers her. She wears no make-up and her coat appears to have been made from some form of dense hessian. It makes McAvoy think of incense shops and folk festivals. She wears pin badges on the strap of her crumpled school satchel. *Greenpeace. Game of Thrones. Jeremy Corbyn.* He finds himself warming to her. She's scatty, fretting at her cuffs, looking up and down the road as if lost.

'Lilah, can you get yourself to school now? Daddy has to get going.'

Lilah rolls her eyes and shoots a glare at the newcomer who has stolen her daddy's attention. Stops when she catches her father's eye. She smiles and leans across to kiss him on the cheek. A biscuit crumb detaches itself from her lip and disappears into his beard. 'Love you,' she says.

'Love you back. Now, hop it.'

Lilah obliges, climbing from the car and hopping between the ice-covered puddles in the direction of school. McAvoy watches her disappear through the school gates; a perfect splash of colour amid the grey of the day. When she is gone he turns back to the lady at the window. 'Is something wrong?'

She looks at him for an uncomfortably long time. Just stands there, rain on her face, mud on her boots, her gaze intense and yet uncertain. He has seen the look before, has seen people try and talk themselves out of doing something they feel some compulsion to do. He looks at her hands: her index finger picking painfully at the dried skin of her thumb.

'Would you like to get in?' asks McAvoy, glancing at the clock. His first meeting is at ten but he wouldn't be disappointed if he encountered a good reason to put it back.

'Am I holding you up?' she asks breathlessly. 'I am, aren't I? It's fine. It's nothing. Honestly, I'm such a state. How are the kids? One, is it? Oh no, you've got the big lad. Handsome soul. How's the wife? Settling in?'

McAvoy looks at her, fascinated. She appears to be making space in her mind for new software, busily running through some old files to see if they are worth saving. She gives McAvoy a mad grin. 'You are a police officer, yes?'

McAvoy nods. It's one of the few things he knows about himself. 'I'm a sergeant,' he says, with less certainty. 'Detective.'

'You were in the paper,' she says, and McAvoy notices how glassy her eyes have become. She pulls off her hat, revealing short, spiky red hair, shaved close around the ears and neckline to reveal dainty astral tattoos.

'Now and again,' says McAvoy, glancing at the clock. 'Please, do get in . . .'

She wrings out the hat. Closes her eyes. Opens them again and smiles brightly. 'Would you follow me?'

McAvoy raises his eyebrows, surprised at the suddenness of the question. 'Where to?'

'There's a house I pass every day. An old lady lives there. Is it okay to say "old lady"?'

McAvoy waits for more. Gives a nod to get her going again.

'Otto – that's my son – we play this game together,' she says, flinching as a gust of icy wind hits her in the face. 'We know all the houses on our drive in. We make up things about their lives, who lives there, what they do, that kind of thing. It's silly, I know, but . . .'

'It's not silly,' says McAvoy, who does the same thing with his children. 'Are you sure you don't want to get into the warm?'

'There's a cottage off the windy road near Cherry Burton. It's down a little track. We call it the Witch's Cottage, though we probably shouldn't. It's a game, you see. Well, it's cosy and spooky and there's always smoke coming from the chimney. Some mornings we glimpse the lady who lives there. She has chickens, I think. It's nice, seeing this little old person, shuffling about with an old pram for her eggs and her firewood and her feet stuffed in a big pair of workboots. She wears this huge great fur coat, like something from Narnia. We've never spoken to her but she's kind of a happy thing to look at. Is that awful?'

McAvoy shakes his head. 'Seems a nice way to be thought about.'

She grins, breathless, oddly manic in her gratitude. 'Otto drew a picture for her at Christmas. I thought that maybe she was lonely, you see. I'd never seen anybody else there, didn't know if she had any family. I asked in the village and they said she'd been there a few years. Not a recluse by any means but very – what's the word? – self-sufficient. I *ummed* and *aahed* about whether I should say hello and eventually decided that it would be a bit odd, turning up on her doorstep, giving her a picture by a boy she didn't know and telling her we liked watching her. That's right, isn't it?'

McAvoy can empathise with the lady's distress. He's long since stopped understanding the rules about what could be considered good manners and neighbourliness and what tips over into weirdness. He fully expects some day to come to a standstill, inert with indecision, his great hand on a door handle, trying to make up his mind whether he is being chivalrous or misogynistic in holding open a door for the next user.

'And how can the police be of assistance, Mrs . . .?'

'It's Miss,' she says automatically. 'Paulette Skinner. I live in Cherry Burton but Otto was already doing so well at school when I moved and I—'

McAvoy raises a hand to stop her. Unclips his seat belt and opens the door. He climbs from the car and straightens his back, attempting not to loom unnecessarily large in front of Miss Skinner, who seems to be shrinking in the rain.

'Miss Skinner, I'm not—'

'Paulette, please.'

'How can I help?' he asks again. A swirl of gritty rain slaps his face and he gives a hurt look at the air.

'I haven't seen any smoke for days,' blurts out Paulette, grimacing in apology. 'And, well, I saw dead birds. Her chickens, I mean. At least two. If she'd gone away she would have somebody looking after them, wouldn't she? It's hard to see through the trees and the light was dreadful this morning but it looks to me like there are windows open. I'm concerned.' She nods, pleased at having pinpointed the right word. 'I'm concerned for her welfare.'

McAvoy rubs a hand over his face, brushing away the few drops of rain that settle on his beard. He feels almost relieved. There are times in his life that fall into an ethically grey area, when twin principles must war for supremacy and his conscience must be weighed against other practicalities. This is not such a situation. He knows that whatever awaits him at work, the welfare of an elderly lady must take priority. He simply has no choice but to make Bingley wait.

'Do you have a car or do you want to jump in?' asks McAvoy.

Paulette gives a big smile of relief. Her sense of social conscience appears to have been inflating within her. McAvoy's involvement has punctured it as effectively as a javelin.

'Do I need to come too?' she asks. 'I have things to get on with. I just thought if I told you . . .'

McAvoy nods. He understands. She's done her bit. He has often envied people their seemingly effortless ability to wash their hands of complications upon somebody else's involvement. Having spent his life as the 'somebody else', McAvoy sometimes wishes he could do the same.

'What's the address?'

# 2

This is a monochrome place. Sheer cliffs rise from a Bible-black sea, jagged columns of rock holding up a heavy grey sky. The icy rain hits hard here: a maelstrom of needles stabbing tiny perforations into the land's cold white skin. Ravens and gulls scream in the stony grey air.

Detective Superintendent Trish Pharaoh considers the view. She feels as though she has somehow been transplanted from a photograph into its negative.

'Well, Toto,' mutters Pharaoh, addressing the ceramic pony on the windowsill. 'Looks like we're not in fucking Grimsby . . .'

She shivers. Turns her back on the window and surveys her accommodation. A square room with a tatty carpet, low-slung burgundy sofa and a recliner with a missing wheel. Framed cross-stitch on the wall: haycarts and lighthouses bookended with gaudy red flowers in oval frames. Family photographs above a dusty bookcase full of paperbacks: a lopsided gallery of stern patriarchs uncomfortable in Sunday-best; strong hands gripping the square shoulders of grim-faced wives. Pharaoh glares at the portable television, its aerial stuck up in a two-fingered salute. Lets her gaze linger on the coffee table, hunkered down beneath mismatched turrets of paper: page upon page, black on white, white on black, like the beginnings of a migraine.

She looks at her reflection in the darkened glass and turns away before it can upset her.

Pharaoh turns fifty in September. Her kids insist on referring to it as 'half-a-century'. She has never really liked the image that glares back at her from the mirror, despite the admiring glances she has received all her life. She's small and curvy, with intense blue eyes. There is an abundance of physicality to her, her body language extravagant. She wears hooped earrings and big bangles, which clank and tangle as she talks. There is a shade of olive to her colouring that suggests some Mediterranean in her DNA, though Pharaoh has never managed to persuade any of her elderly relatives to admit to some passionate encounter with a Sicilian one enchanted evening. She lives in hope.

She glances at her phone, curses and puts it away again. Moves across the tatty carpet to pick up the top sheet of paper from the pile. It's a printout of an article published by *CrymeLog* magazine in August last year. Spread over two pages, it is illustrated with four pictures, framed in crime-scene tape and laid out to look like insertions in an official police file. The first photograph has been taken on the deck of a trawler: all caps and cigarettes and big broad smiles beneath Brylcreemed hair. One of the men is half out of shot, hand raised to cover his face, the back of his hand a mess of fish guts and illegible blue ink. The picture juts up against a blurred snap of a young woman: prominent nose and angular cheekbones, deep-set eyes and luxuriously thick black hair. The photos accompany a large banner headline:

## WAS TRAGIC ROBERTA THE VICTIM OF SERIAL KILLER?

Halfway down the article is a wonky snap of an old ice factory near Hull Docks – a humble brick construction with a corrugated-metal door. The next shows Roberta Ballantine '*in happier times*', sitting on the grass beneath an expanse of white sky. She's cross-legged, reading.

Pharaoh reads the article again. Hopes that this time she will see something halfway bloody useful.

Those who knew her best have described Roberta Ballantine as a true Jekyll and Hyde character: warring twins trapped in one body.

There are those in the tightly knit fishing community of Hull's Hessle Road who recall Roberta as bookish, smart and eye-catchingly pretty – always happy to lend a helping hand.

Others remember the delinquent she became: a violent and drug-addled runaway who for a time was prime suspect in the grisly death of a relative.

Whichever version they recall, there is no doubt that Roberta's disappearance in 1986 is a mystery that still haunts this run-down port city.

Pharaoh takes a breath. Lights a cigarette. Takes another breath and infinitely prefers it.

Now the questions surrounding her vanishing may soon be answered. With the help of a seasoned investigator, *CrymeLog* has unearthed evidence that suggests Roberta could have been the victim of a serial killer.

Our source is convinced that over the course of three decades, the rapist and killer targeted several vulnerable women around the world, subjecting them to terrible brutality after violating the sanctuary of their homes.

A handful of witnesses and two survivors have claimed that the sick culprit had an obsession with hair, ripping clumps free from their scalp in an act that profilers believe he kept as trophies. Others have spoken of a bizarre and twisted game played by their abductor, altering the angle of the lights and making his victims watch their own slow suffering played out in silhouette on the wall.

The investigator said: 'He thinks he's got away with it. He may have changed his MO. He may not be active. But I am convinced that he cost Roberta her life. I want him to know that somebody knows what he has done, and that they're coming for him.'

Pharaoh reaches for her glass and wonders, briefly, if she would have made a good journalist and decides that she probably wouldn't. She's too good at English.

*CrymeLog* understands that prior to her disappearance, Roberta had told a close friend that she had begun to feel as though she were being watched and followed. But police dismissed such claims when they learned of Roberta's history of mental illness and drug addiction.

'Roberta's life wasn't easy,' said our source. 'Her father Lachlan was a trawlerman, away for weeks at a time. He died when she was still an infant and she was raised by her older brother, Rory. Tragically, he too died at sea. She was just thirteen. She was inconsolable afterwards, always believing he would come back: that he wasn't dead. She continued to live with Rory's widow, Mags, along with Rory's sons. Tragically, Mags had just revealed that she was expecting a child when Rory was lost at sea off the coast of Iceland along with two crewmates.

'Roberta never truly recovered,' our source continued. 'She went from a shy and book-loving girl to somebody whose temper seemed almost beyond her control. She dropped out of school and threw away the jobs that were offered to her by those in the community who wanted to help. She started drinking heavily and in a few years she had gone completely off the rails. While the rest of the family tried to pull together, she simply couldn't cope with her loss. When Rory's widow remarried, her new man became an object of hatred for Roberta. The police were regular attendees at the family home. Roberta would turn up with a knife or matches and petrol, screaming and sobbing. It was heartbreaking to see and must have been terrifying for the two young boys.'

Roberta later took to sleeping rough. Social Services intervened and she was briefly sectioned under the Mental Health Act. Several times she absconded from secure units and would be found among the drug-users who congregated in Piccadilly in the 1970s.

Pharaoh turns the page, sadness creeping over her like damp air.

In June 1981 Mags's new husband, Arthur 'Bowbells' Lowery, was found dead at Hull Docks, where he worked as a 'bobber' – unloading freshly caught fish from the trawlers.

Our source said: 'Roberta detested Arthur Lowery. She hated the thought of him taking her brother's place and she believed he was a bully and a brute who shouldn't be anywhere near her nephews. She said he was dangerous. At the time of his death she was estranged from Mags and the boys but she was still prime suspect when he lost his life. It was a bad way to go.

'Arthur was working below decks on one of the trawlers – a greasy, slimy place known as "the underfoot". The inquest later found that some wooden boards gave way beneath his feet. He fell into a great pool of loose fish roes. The inquest found that his death was the result of suffocation though he had a terrible head wound. Roberta was initially sought for questioning. The police were doing their job and no charges were brought but the experience was very harrowing for her.'

*CrymeLog* understands that Roberta had returned to Hull shortly before Lowery's death. The strain of being questioned caused her to flee to London. She received a police caution in 1981 for soliciting and was hospitalised with septicaemia the following year. Concerned friends found her and helped her back to health. By 1985 she was again living in East Yorkshire and seemed, according to sources, to have turned a corner. She moved into a small flat on Hull's Boulevard and secured part-time work at the Hull Mail. She started working with a local charity providing support for the orphans of lost fishermen and began to write short stories and poems.

On the night of 27 November 1986, Roberta was seen by several witnesses in the Criterion public house. Despite her apparent new sobriety she was drinking heavily. At around 10 p.m. Roberta had an altercation with a group of customers and was told to leave the bar. Witnesses say she staggered away up Division Road towards the docks. She has not been seen since.

Sixteen days after Roberta's disappearance, a courting couple found Roberta's distinctive grey fur coat in a dustbin outside an old ice-making factory near the docks. The coat was stained with blood and speckled with fragments of glass.

At the time of her disappearance, DNA testing was still a fantasy so the blood has never been conclusively identified as Roberta's. Frustratingly, the blood samples taken at the scene have since been lost. One of her nephews, Stephen, is now a successful entrepreneur who owns a logistics and import business. In 2001 he established a charity in her name, giving money to mental health organisations and fishing families in dire straits.

Pharaoh chews her cheek. She strokes the grainy image of Roberta Ballantine with the pad of her thumb.

Our source said: 'The person who took her might think this won't catch up with them but with scientific advances there is always a chance. More importantly, there are people who have stayed quiet for the past thirty years who are feeling a need to unburden themselves. I've spoken to witnesses and I fear that Roberta may have been the last victim of a killer who targeted vulnerable young women. There are cases I've identified in Baltimore, Oslo, Nova Scotia and Le Havre that carry all the hallmarks. These crimes may be decades old but they still deserve our attention.'

Our source has promised that readers of *CrymeLog* will be the first to read exclusive extracts from his book, which is currently without a publisher . . .

Pharaoh picks up her wine glass and runs her tongue around the rim. Looks at her phone. She sucks her teeth and scowls at the window, watching the air change colour; blacks and purples, greens and silvery grey; a bruise on dead flesh.

Eventually she trudges from the room and into the wide, bare hallway. The landlord hadn't been kidding when he advised her that the rental property was 'very basic'. It's a two-bed-roomed, white-painted slab of a place; a joyless collection of right angles and grimy glass, squatting among a dozen facsimiles on the edge of this barren harbour town. She'd been in no position to be picky. Her bosses have become annoyingly strict about using the Humberside Police credit card that represents one of the few benefits of her rank. She's having to pay for things herself then claim it back, which is proving difficult given her eternal lack of funds. She'd been relieved to find that one of her personal credit cards still had a little wiggle room. If it came to it, she could probably get a grand for her car. If all else fails then the medical equipment might be worth a few bob, though her half-dead prick of a husband might be a bit miffed if she flogged the special bed into which he has been sinking ever since the aneurysm that extinguished all traces of the charming, violent man who gave her four children, a big house and a lot of bad memories. His brain had ripped itself apart when the bad investments caught up with him and the bailiffs started arriving. She nurses him out of some vague sense of responsibility, and in the hope that one day he will be well enough for her to beat the shit out of him. The kids treat him like a ghost, a spectre half-heartedly haunting the converted garage.

She sighs, picks up her phone and puts it down again, growling at herself. 'No,' she says. 'Don't fucking call him.'

She takes her last black cigarette and lights it with a cheap yellow lighter. Blows out a perfect ring of smoke and wishes there were somebody here to impress. She glances at the second hand of her watch and tries to take her own pulse. Stops when she realises that she can't feel it and starts to worry that she might be dead.

She jumps as the phone suddenly chirrups into life and glowers at the bits of herself that she can see. She's not a jumpy woman. She hates those flighty, silly sods who shake like a hypothermic terrier whenever the doorbell goes.

'Pharaoh,' she says, her voice loud in the soft silence of the room.

'Excellent name,' says the caller cheerily. 'Sounds from the dial tone like you're abroad. Anywhere nice?'

'I'm sorry, who's this?' asks Pharaoh, grinding her back teeth.

'Sorry, Peter Glover. Editor of *CrymeLog*. You left a message. You're awfully senior to be making your own calls, Detective Superintendent. I'm sorry it's taken this long. What's the time difference where you are? Not disturbing you, am I?'

Pharaoh rummages around in her papers, locating the meagre details she has on the man at the end of the line. He's in his fifties. Used to work for a couple of national broadsheets before falling victim to staffing cuts. He took a decent redundancy and set up a crime magazine and website, indulging in his passion for cold cases, serial killer profiles and the sort of conspiracy theories that get the armchair crime fans dribbling into their cats. His accent marks him out as having come from money.

'No problem,' says Pharaoh, huffing her hair out of her eyes. 'I was wondering whether—'

'Where is it you find yourself?' asks Glover pleasantly.

Pharaoh frowns, unused to being interrupted. 'Mr Glover, I'm looking at an old copy of your magazine. There's a story about a serial killer having a connection to Hull and a missing woman . . .'

There is a pause and Pharaoh fancies she can hear gears changing in Glover's head. 'Bit speculative, that one,' he says, and the chummy tone in his voice sounds a little forced. 'Favour for a pal, I suppose you'd call it. Bit of a space-filler. There's always just enough news to fill the paper, have you ever noticed that? It's not quite the same in specialist mags. Sometimes you need to, shall we say, push the credible – just so you don't leave the reader with three blank pages. What is it you would like to know? I rather hope you're not planning on giving me an ear-bashing.'

Pharaoh takes a moment to consider her approach. Glover may run a magazine with a readership of under 10,000 but he's still a journalist and she fancies she will do better with him onside.

'Long before my time,' she says breezily. 'So you haven't offended me personally. I was intrigued, that's all. That sort of speculation – it doesn't take people long to point the finger at the police. The local paper is bound to pick it up soon. I'm amazed they haven't yet, truth be told.'

'Oh they have,' says Glover, laughing. 'I received an email from one of their feature writers not so long ago, wondering if we could, in their words, "*share resources*". I was a little embarrassed to inform them that we have few resources to share. They wanted to know who our detective was, you see. The chap we quoted so fulsomely. Not an easy thing to provide.'

'Ethical question, is it?' asks Pharaoh, trying not to sneer.

'Oh my goodness no!' says Glover, laughing at the very idea. 'No, sad to say I had no source to give him. The article came from a freelancer. You'll see there's no name on it. Old drinking chum, bit down on his luck. You know the type. I throw him a bone now and then. We'd had a letter from a regular reader, wanting to know if we had ever covered the disappearance of that Ballantine girl. I didn't know the case. It was hardly national news. But you know how it is, when one is asked to provide, one should do one's best.'

'One should,' says Pharaoh, trying not to gag.

'I phoned my pal – he used to know that part of the world quite well. Said we'd pay for a double-page spread. NUJ day rates and forty pence a mile on his fuel allowance.'

'When was this?'

'Early summer?' muses Glover, uncertainly. 'I'll check.

Anyhow, off he went and I forgot about it until he called back and said he was onto something very tasty indeed, that he'd spoken to one of the original investigators and they had this half-baked theory that she was one among many. He was jabbering on like a monkey. I'd have thought he'd had a drink if I didn't know how hard he'd fought to kick the stuff. Ranting about postcards and shadows and people coming back from the dead. I told him to keep at it. It was nice to hear him so enthused. It clearly didn't go the way he first thought. Of course, as you'll see from the article, in terms of actual evidence there's precious little to report. But he stood by his source. Reckoned there was this huge great cover-up and that there would be a hell of a book in it. Silly old duffer has been saying that for the last thirty years but at least when he's on the hunt for a story he has a reason to stay a little more sober than when he's festering in his rat-hole.'

'How did he pitch the story?' asks Pharaoh. The line starts to crackle. She puts a finger in her ear, scowling. 'Did you see his notes? Audio transcripts? You're the editor, after all.'

'I think you may have an elevated idea of what that means.' Glover chuckles. 'My writers write and I let them get on with it. Most of my job is keeping the advertisers happy and trying not to slander anybody. I thought I was on safe ground with Marlowe but he very nearly landed me in it.'

'Marlowe? Does he have a first name?'

'He has many names.' Glover laughs. 'Marlowe's more of a nickname, I think. Way back he was Albert Jonsson but he changed his name as fancy took him . . .' He pauses pointedly. 'Or as circumstances dictated. *Marlowe* suited him. I may have to call him a few other things when he finally gets back in touch. Rather hung me out to dry. Honestly, there was no shortage of angry phone calls and emails when the article came out.' Glover takes a slurp of something, the splosh of liquid audible over the sound of the crackling line. 'They have long memories in Hull,

I'm sure you've noticed. What did we want to be raking over the past for? Did we know how much heartache it caused? All the usual. I'd barely read the piece before we printed it but on reflection I can see there was plenty of vague accusation and nothing in the way of substantiated fact.'

'You contacted him?'

'Of course,' says Glover. 'Asked him, man to man, if this was one of his, shall we say, *slightly more exaggerated yarns*. He was his usual self, giving me hell for what we'd done with his beautiful story. Said we'd hacked the heart out of it, left him looking silly. Said he was onto something that really mattered.' Glover pauses. 'What precisely is it you're after, Detective Superintendent? If you're concerned about the validity of the accusations, you'll note that nobody specific is mentioned. It was just an excuse to print an intriguing tale. Marlowe's old-school, though that's no excuse. The "unnamed detective" thing is very old hat. Should have known better.'

'He wouldn't tell you who he'd got the story from?'

'I don't think he got it from anybody,' says Glover awkwardly. 'He as good as told me that the "copper" was a work of imagination. He'd cobbled it together from a couple of chats he'd had in a bar and an interview with some batty old soul who claimed to be Roberta's friend but who wouldn't even let him quote her.'

'I'd like to see the original story,' says Pharaoh. 'The piece he sent in before your editor chopped it up.'

Glover makes a noise in the back of his throat, a whinge of impending displeasure. 'I don't even know where that would be. Old-school, like I said. He faxed his stories in. Faxed! They'd go to a sub-editor, then on to an inputter at an agency in Dorset and they send an electronic copy. I'll do my best, see if I can't ferret it out. You may be better off just ringing him, though he hasn't the fondest memories of Humberside Police. And you might struggle to track him down. He was furious with me last time we spoke.'

'I would really like to see the original, Mr Glover,' says Pharaoh. 'If your colleagues could try and recall what else the piece might have said, that would be a help too. I'll be back in touch.'

'I do hope this hasn't been a nuisance for you, DSU Pharaoh,' says Glover, an unattractive slick of obsequiousness coating his vowels. 'As I say, it certainly wasn't intended to upset anybody.'

Pharaoh grunts and ends the call. Drops the phone on the sofa, throwing herself back in the chair. She stretches out her arms and rolls her head on her shoulders, listening to the cricks and cracks of cartilage grinding against muscle.

'What are you doing here, you silly cow?'

She asks the question aloud, and it seems to reverberate against the cold, lonely walls.

She wonders, for the thousandth time, whether she is here to solve a crime, protect a friend, or simply hide away for a while.

She looks again at the name on the top page of her notes and the email from the magnificently named *Rannsóknarlögreglumaður* Hildur Minervadottir of Logreglan, the Icelandic Police.

In the early hours of 3 January, a man's body was found on a stretch of storm-lashed beach at the tip of the Skagi Peninsula. He had been in the water for several hours. All identifying features had been rendered useless through immersion in the salt water. One limb was severed at the knee. Birds had pecked at his eyes and begun to strip the flesh from his skin. The local woman who found him was checking his body for some form of identification when she leaned on his chest and a spume of dirty water and crimson blood erupted from his ruined mouth.

He spoke.

One word.

A desperate cry uttered with a tongue all but bitten in two.

'*McAvoy* . . .' he'd said, as he died.

The police found a car abandoned on the cliffs further back down the coast. There was no ID. The only clue was a copy of *CrymeLog*, wedged beneath the driver's seat. The car had been hired at Keflavik Airport forty-eight hours earlier by an English national named Albert Jonsson, immediately after the arrival of his flight from Humberside Airport. He'd selected an automatic due to his prosthetic leg. He'd chatted with the clerk at the rental desk. Said he was writing a book. Told her to google the name 'Russell Chandler' if she wanted to know more about him. She didn't bother. Didn't think about him again until the police came and asked her for CCTV footage and a witness statement.

Minervadottir googled the name immediately and found a convicted criminal: an alcoholic journalist whose taste for whisky had cost him his career and whose addiction to cigarettes had cost him a leg. He'd been arrested for murder a few years back. Eventually it had emerged that Chandler was as much a victim of the real killer as anybody else. The charges were dropped and he wrote a memoir about his association with the real killer. Nobody published it. Nobody gave a damn. He'd gone back to what he knew, drinking and smoking and making ends meet with freelance journalism jobs. Most recently, he'd been working for *CrymeLog*. A few days before, something had persuaded him to fly to Iceland. That decision would cost him his life.

The email from Minervadottir had originally been intended for Detective Sergeant Aector McAvoy. Her *Hector*. Her everything, truth be told. She knows that Roisin owns his heart; that no world exists in which they could ever be together, but the connection between them is a fierce and primal thing and it makes her giddy to know that he thinks of her as his closest friend. They would die for one another, and have frequently had cause to put that claim to the test. Pharaoh knows he has no shortage of enemies and she makes it her business to protect him from as many distractions as she can. He takes things to heart and if she can spare him from unnecessary burdens she is more than willing to do so – even if it means keeping him in the dark about things he would probably rather know about. She had been relieved when she intercepted the email, which had pinged forward into her inbox since McAvoy was out of the office. Pharaoh read it twice. Something had chimed, faintly, in the back of her skull. She'd called the Icelandic officer back and told her that if she needed some assistance, she would be glad to provide it. An hour later, she had booked herself a flight.

Pharaoh crosses back to the window.

A sadness wraps around her and she feels tears pricking at her eyes. She refuses to give in. Swallows painfully, and leans forward with her hands on the windowsill, pressing her forehead against the cold glass. She stares into her own eyes. She allows herself a moment of comfort.

Pictures McAvoy.

Hopes to God the silly sod is keeping out of trouble.

# 3

McAvoy is concentrating hard, gripping the steering wheel like the reins of a skittish horse, willing the tyres to maintain their grip on the slick road. It's all farmland here, a bleak patchwork of muddy squares. There's no snow, but the image beyond the windscreen is patterned with the silvery white of this morning's hard frost.

Through the trees he spots the big white house that Paulette had told him to look out for. She'd scribbled her name and address down for him, adding a mobile number and email details, before bouncing back to her car like Little Red Riding Hood skipping off to see Grandma. McAvoy snatches a glimpse of a grand art deco affair, oblongs and right angles with big square windows. He slows as the headlights pick out a gleaming patch of black ice, changes down to second gear and tries to relax his shoulders. He can feel a headache starting. He stares ahead, concentrating hard. Spots the gap in the trees and glimpses the rectangular property peeking through, and slowly turns the vehicle through a set of crumbling sandstone gate-posts. It feels like driving into a carcass: the tree trunks bending overhead, their tops meeting with each breath of wind, knitting together to form a spindly ribcage that contracts and expands. McAvoy manoeuvres the car down a narrow path. He keeps staring ahead, the trees transforming: black skeletons, slapping their flimsy limbs against the metal and glass.

A dead bird stares back at him from a patch of long, frozen grass, its feathers a hundred shades of brown and gold.

McAvoy suddenly understands why Paulette and her son turned the little one-storey cottage into the setting for make-believe. It's a place that reeks of fairy tales. The walls are the colour of hand-churned butter. It looks like a retirement cake: a gooey approximation of a country cottage, the strokes of the palette knife still visible in the rough icing. Hanging baskets dangle from jet-black hooks set either side of a cherry-red front door. The curtains are drawn across all the windows but they still contrive to give off a cheery air. The roof isn't thatch, but in this light it's hard not to imagine it as such. Hard not to imagine that the gutters taste of gingerbread and that there's a lock on the oven door.

The car rolls to a stop on a large, oval patch of frosty gravel at the front of the house. McAvoy looks through the misty glass. He hopes a light will come on. None does. He climbs from the car and reaches into the back for his long black coat. The air is bitterly cold. He shivers and turns up his collar. It smells of Roisin, all elderberries and lip gloss.

The wind drops and he suddenly becomes aware of the silence. No birdsong. No tyres on tarmac or rustling leaves. He looks again at the cottage and suddenly the jolly image he enjoyed a moment ago is replaced by something more sinister. The door is now an open mouth; the blackened windows eyeholes in a cadaverous face.

McAvoy shakes his head, forcing such nonsense from his mind. There is just enough light to see by. He casts a quick glance around him. A footpath leads from the front door to a little allotment area where he makes out the shape of a small wooden hut. He looks over the neat patch of garden and stops when he sees another sad lump of stiff feathery blackness.

Slowly, feeling like a burglar, he crunches across the frozen ground. He glances at his own reflection in the darkened glass of the front window. Looks away, dissatisfied. Bangs politely. Bangs again. Puts his hands in his pockets and wonders what to do next. He mooches down the path towards the allotment. The soil has been raked into neat furrows and the frost clings to each, making the ground look like a mountain range viewed from above. McAvoy sees another dead bird, flat on its back, feet in the air, as if the corpse had been positioned for comic effect. He turns away from the garden and makes his way to the back of the bungalow. The temperature seems to drop, the darkness becoming denser, as he tries to keep his feet on the slick stones. The spindly branches of a pear tree claw at his face as he pushes past and then he emerges into a small courtyard garden at the rear of the property, low walls and terracotta planters framing a neat patch of grass. A wooden swing sits frozen at the bottom of the garden, where a wrought-iron table and chairs glint.

He tries the back door with the cuff of his coat and isn't sure whether to be pleased or disappointed when the cold metal handle responds to his touch. Cautiously, he pushes open the door, blowing a lungful of air into the icy darkness of the hallway. He steps inside, automatically brushing the muck from his boots on the coarse mat by the door.

'Hello,' he calls into the silence. 'Police. We've had a call from a neighbour . . .'

He finds a light switch on the wall and flicks it on to find himself in a simple, yellow-painted kitchen, cold as an ice-house, sparkling with frost. It shimmers on every surface. Granite worktops and brass utensils, low beams and a small round table set for one. There are dishes by the deep farmhouse-style sink. The lid has been left off the butter dish. There's marmalade on a knife.

McAvoy stands still. Shivers in the freezing air.

He spots a small pile of letters on the worktop. He pulls a pen from his pocket and uses it to leaf through them. They're addressed to a Mrs E. Chappell. Pear Tree Cottage. He glances at the cork board on the wall. A picture in a frame, showing a small, dark-eyed lady with a big smile and long grey hair, one arm around the shoulders of a young man. It looks somehow awkward, and McAvoy thinks of Victorian portraits: of stern, moustachioed Edwardians clapping a proprietorial arm around strapping sons. The image is the only photograph among the great chequerboard of postcards, push-pins glinting in their corners, that have been neatly fastened to the cork tiles. Some are faded, others maintain a more recent glossy sheen. *Auckland. Sydney. Oslo. Le Havre.* He lifts the corner of a loose postcard. There is nothing on the back save an address and a Christian name, neatly etched in a copperplate hand.

Roberta.

McAvoy opens the door to the pantry. Tinned foods, dried pasta, proper old-fashioned vegetable oil. A list of phone numbers is pinned to the back of the door. Landlines, mostly. Spidery handwriting on faded paper. *Alf. Mags. Dentist. Jean. Stephen. Grimur* – an international code jotted down in blue pen.

McAvoy looks at the calendar, covered with one-word notes. He turns back a page to December. It's a much busier month than January, with its three appointments over the past week. '*Doctor's*', '*Hair*' and '*Marlowe home*'. Looking forward, there is nothing.

McAvoy examines the bottom rack of the pantry. A huge bag of chicken feed is wedged into the corner, next to a stack of old phone books and a tower of rusty biscuit tins. He spots a square of colour in the darkness. Squints his eyes and makes out a yellow Post-it note covering the label on a bottle of rat poison. A childish skull and crossbones has been drawn on it in black felt-tip pen.

He turns back to the room. Sniffs the air. It's so cold that it makes his sinuses hurt.

He continues into a wide corridor, the ceiling sagging like a cushion. He pokes his head into what he takes to be the living room. Three-seater sofa, floral pattern and wooden legs. A plump armchair, antimacassars on the arms. A colourful Turkish rug covers most of the grey carpet. There's a walking stick propped against a bookshelf, a cup of tea on a saucer, the liquid frozen solid. An open, lifeless fireplace. A puzzle book is splayed open on the middle cushion. It's a cryptic crossword, barely begun. Only one question has been attempted. The words are in such a spidery hand that he can barely make out the letters. He narrows his eyes.

*M-C-A-V . . .*

*Stop it*, he tells himself. That's a U. Or a Y. He gives a nervous half-laugh, shivering, as the shapes swim and blur.

The wind shrieks down the chimney, its breath icy and unrelenting. The cold is fierce: nipping at his skin, creeping under his clothes, taking his breath away. He shivers as he examines the pictures on the crooked walls. There are photographs in frames on the mantelpiece. A fat, pale-faced baby, gummy grin splitting a grubby face. A tall man in a cloth cap sitting under a tree, squinting into the sun, holding a bottle of something fizzy as the shadow of the picture-taker forms scissors across him. A pretty young woman with dark hair and dark eyes, sitting in the back of a campervan on a sunny day, round sunglasses shielding her eyes as she smiles into the camera lens, puppy fat spilling over the top of tight flared jeans, a book open on her lap. At the other end of the mantelpiece is a square frame containing a black and white snap of a group of young men, hair lacquered, smartly dressed, raising pint pots in a smoky pub.

Slowly, McAvoy turns around. A Victorian birdcage hangs from a wrought-iron hook in the alcove by the window. A china doll sits inside, curly red hair and open eyes, perfect skin and a gingham dress. Below it, a dark wooden cabinet with a Javanese pattern serves as plinth to a collection of ships in bottles. The bottles are a muddy khaki colour and McAvoy has to use the torch on his phone to make out the details. Each of the bottles is mounted on a mahogany rectangle of wood, a brass nameplate screwed to the front. They are vessels from the Blake line. Sidewinder trawlers and three big freezer ships.

McAvoy steps back and the light from the torch picks out a glimmering puddle of ice on the carpet. He changes his position and slowly moves his head. Frost glistens in the light of the torch. Tiny particles of glass twinkle. He counts the bottles. Swings his gaze back to the mantelpiece. The display looks lopsided, the pictures bunched up at one end.

He stands perfectly still. Watches his breath hang in the sparkling air in front of his face. He drinks in the details, the information dropping into him like coins into a slot. He moves through to the bedroom. Sees his reflection in the screen of the small portable TV that sits in the centre of a wooden chest of drawers, a wonky chorus line of china dolls slumped against the side. Old perfume bottles and a bowl of potpourri are arranged on a doily in the middle of the dressing table. The drawers are open, silk blouses and nylons spilling out at the bottom, jewellery above; great beaded snakes twisting into and out of bangles and dangling earrings. A huge wooden wardrobe takes up most of one wall. Reverently, McAvoy opens the doors. He examines the rail of clothes. It's an eclectic mix. Loud, mazily patterned polyester dresses; salmon-pink and powder-blue cardigans; a leather trench coat and a mismatched pile of patched jeans. His hands brush soft fur. A big tattered fur coat has been discarded at the foot of the wardrobe. It's shiny in places, where the fur has rubbed away. A map of tiny stitches runs up the seam. The pockets have been turned out, fluff and boiled sweets, tinfoil and tissues littering the floor beneath.

McAvoy turns away. Looks at the unmade bed; at the indentation left by the slumbering form of Mrs Chappell. He considers the bedside table and the peculiar objects below the unlit lamp. Two books, one black, one blue. *Headscarf Revolutionaries,* by local author Brian Lavery, pushed up incongruously against *In Search of Lost Time* by Marcel Proust. A black, feathery, bulb-shaped object stands on little wire legs on top of the books, a clockwork key protruding from the silky plumes. Beside it is a half-empty jam jar, lid screwed down. McAvoy angles his head and surveys the contents. Grimaces as he makes out a dozen or so cigarette butts, floating in scummy water. The jar has been placed atop a sealed polythene freezer bag. Inside he fancies he can make out a swatch of silk, white circles on red.

He turns away, wondering if he is examining a crime scene or creating one. A low bookcase takes up most of the far wall, the contents lying on their sides or leaning against one another in haphazard triangles. Snow globes twinkle on the top shelf. McAvoy peers at the tiny scenes imprisoned inside the glass. *Rome. Prague. Budapest. Reykjavik. Kissimmee.* Ice glitters on the surface of the water, mirroring the synthetic snow that puddles at the bottom of each miniature.

He crosses back to the hallway, the frost seeming to seep through to his bones. The blue cord carpet is smudged in places, as if muddy boot prints have been inexpertly rubbed away.

Cautiously, McAvoy pushes open the bathroom door. Cold air hits him. His hand knocks against wood and string and he folds his hand around the light-pull. The bulb flares, brilliant and huge, its light bouncing off the frost-covered white walls and the gleaming white tiles, dazzling as it flashes against the frosted glass of the dormer windows, pushed open as far as they will go.

Colours dance in McAvoy's vision and he screws up his face.

He turns his head. Looks at the bathtub: pristine, white,

expensive. It's deeper at one end than the other. It sits on golden talons: sharp claws gripping the carpet.

An old lady's body lies entombed in a perfect block of ice. She looks like a monstrous china doll. Her upper half is a column of pink and blue flesh, rising like a mountain from the frozen water. Her position is unnatural, half twisted. One arm hangs over the side of the tub, the fingers pale and stiff. She stares towards the window, face resting on her arm, throat exposed, long grey hair frozen half in and out of the water. Such a death has gifted her body an odd, elemental beauty. She is almost an ice sculpture; a shimmering, dazzling thing.

McAvoy finds himself staring. He forces himself to look deeper – to see the life extinguished, and not the vessel preserved. He changes his position. Her face is half hidden behind the curtain of hair but he sees enough to glimpse her sadness and to mirror it; to take in the alabaster quality of her aged, wrinkled skin.

McAvoy stands still, blinking. Despite the chill he feels sweat prickle on his back. He closes his eyes. Questions start erupting in his mind. He crouches down. He wants to push her hair behind her ear and see her face properly. His eye is caught by a strange pattern in the frost on the tiles: risen streaks and smears, letters drawn in condensation on a misty window and then rubbed out with a careless hand. Without thinking he takes his phone from his pocket, and starts taking photos, blinking as the flash ricochets off the gleaming walls. He checks the pictures on the screen. Each contains the faint mist of his own breath, snaking into the image like a spirit.

A sensation creeps over him: a strange, unsettling feeling. He realises he is suppressing a shiver – that already, tiny particles of ice are attaching themselves to his clothes, his beard, his hair. He is overcome with the sense that he is looking at something not just tragic, but somehow malicious.

He lowers his head and has to fight the urge to fetch the

dressing gown from the bed and cover her dignity. He glances back at her, taking in new details. She's slim. Her cheeks are sunken. Like old fruit. She wears a simple white band around the middle finger of her right hand. The tips of her fingers are ragged, the nails torn and packed with dust and paint. *She fought*, he realises. Clawed at the wall. He looks at where her skin meets the frozen water; purplish patches spreading on her flesh like bacteria viewed beneath a microscope. There is a tiny graze in her hairline: a perfect drop of red, a jewel upon snow.

He scans the room afresh. A rocking chair sits in the corner by a laundry hamper. Beneath its casters are two lines where the frost has not yet penetrated. He crosses to the chair and cautiously touches his hand to the seat. It's cold, but in this room of sparkling crystal fractals he had expected it to be almost freezing to the touch.

Slowly, he turns back to face the body. Squats down so he is at the level he would be at if he were to sit in the chair. He raises his eyes slowly and takes in the entirety of the scene. His eye is drawn to a tiny splash of blood on the door frame. He stands and inspects it, turning back to the body in the bath. He finds himself thinking of the little pencil marks that Roisin draws on the door frame at home, charting the children's growth. The little patch of red must be at least six feet off the ground. He looks at her again, folded up in the bathtub like a wrinkled foetus. He sits back in the chair. The vantage point is perfect. From here, he could sit and watch an old lady freeze to death without obstacle or interruption. He closes his eyes. Gives a little nod. Lifts his phone to his ear and calls the control room of Humberside Police. The screen is cold against his skin.

'It's McAvoy,' he says. 'I think we've got a murder . . .'

# 4

*St Andrew's Dock, Hull*
*10.16 a.m.*

Napper Acklam leans against the harbour wall, gloved hands squeezing at the rough brick. He looks like a bishop delivering a sermon to the sea.

Napper's seventy-something and looks a hundred years older. He wears alligator-skin shoes with jogging trousers and conceals his Val Doonican sweater beneath a long black cashmere coat. The finer garments have the air of the funeral shroud: fine embroidered silks enveloping a disintegrating corpse. Napper looks as if he died a long time ago and simply refused to lie down. His bald scalp is a mass of weeping sores and crusted scabs. His capped teeth are too big for his mouth. A grapevine of broken blood vessels runs across his sagging, waxy flesh.

Napper stares into the grey air that hangs over the water. Watches the gulls floating above the sucking mud of the River Humber, their wings like big broadsheet pages caught by the gale. He notices the large black bird perched on the handrail of the rusty old trawler that rises and falls on the shifting brown water. He feels as though it were watching him. He holds its gaze. Hocks back a great gob of mucus and spits it expertly towards the bird. It doesn't move.

'Fuck you, then.'

He takes a cigarette from the silver case in his inside pocket, lights it and savours the flavour. It's Turkish, and arrived in Hull via Rotterdam along with ten million of its friends. That little job saved one of Napper's mates nearly £2 million in import duties. They'd done the hard work at the Polish end, stripping out the lorry's cabin and creating a labyrinth of secret compartments within the upholstery and bodywork. It would probably have passed a regular inspection, though it didn't pay to risk it – not when avoidance could be guaranteed through the simple expedient of leaving £200k in used notes at an agreed location and letting Napper and his contacts on the port security team take care of the rest.

The wind lifts the tails of his purple scarf and, as Napper reaches up to smooth himself down, his gaze lingers on the great oblong that stands sentry over this abandoned dock. The old Blake building – a perfect symbol of the industry that it used to serve. Trawling's been dead in the water for nearly half a century. The old offices are little more than a shell now: four storeys of empty window frames and sagging walls. Napper remembers settling day: the cacophony of raised voices, the laughter and curses, so much bustle that it had seemed like the centre of the world. He smiles at a memory. Remembers the tailor from Waistell's meeting him and his boys as they came down the gangplank in their finery, handing over their new suits. He'd had some belters. Half-moon pockets, Spanish waistbands. Powder blues and sunset yellows, string ties and wing-tipped collars. Slick pompadours. Square-toed winkle-pickers, to stand that bit closer to the bar. They'd been fucking rock stars then. If somebody had told him in 1970 that one day the place would look like it had been stepped on by a great fucking bobber boot, he'd have told them they were out of their mind.

The lock gates look as though they are simply staying up out of sheer bloody obstinacy. The timbers are rotten: sinking, inch by inch, into chocolatey sludge, the rusty metal struts half hidden behind hanging tapestries of green slime. Napper feels the freezing air slap against the pinched red skin of his face, and throws his head back and revels in it. He's never minded the cold.

He turns his attention back to the vessel. The *Blake Holst* rises and falls on the shifting water, tied to the sea wall with rope thick as a big man's bicep and elevated on blue inflatable supports. It's been here for more than six months and it's in a worse state than when it arrived. One of Mr Ballantine's ideas. *Stephen*, when he's feeling familiar. Chief exec, majority shareholder and driving force behind Ballantine Holdings PLC. Napper is not an emotional man but he feels some deep and unfathomable affection for his business associate. He's one of the good ones. He gives back. Always happy to put his hand in his pocket to fund church roofs and tennis courts; computers for schools; commemorative sculptures and great gaudy murals celebrating the city's past. Does his bit for the community that made him.

The return of the *Blake Holst* was supposed to be the cherry on the cake.

*A floating museum*, he'd said, when he outlined his grand vision and asked Napper, in that way of his, if he wouldn't mind chipping in with some of the costs. *We can do it for under ten, I reckon. I'll do five, you stick in a couple, we can crowdfund the rest, if we have to. It's a chance to show people what it was really like out there. A tribute to the city's history. For Dad. For all of you . . .*

Napper tried to talk him out of it. Tried to tell him that the city already had the *Arctic Corsair*, safely anchored at the mouth of the River Hull, staffed by old fishermen and overflowing with tourism awards.

Stephen hadn't been deterred. He reckoned that the *Blake Holst* would be a bigger draw than the *Corsair*. Reckoned it would actually sail again; pleasure cruises out into the Humber, up to Spurn Point and back again. *A chance to really feel it*, he'd said. *To experience the life of a trawlerman . . .*

Napper did as he was asked. Drained his overseas accounts and turned a few grubby banknotes into a neat cheque, made out in the name of one of his shell companies. He hadn't begrudged it. He owed the boy, after all.

They'd found the *Blake Holst* in a salvage yard near Tromsø and it had cost a small fortune to have it towed back to the city it last saw in 1976. There hadn't been any kind of fanfare when it chugged back into port. A few articles in the *Hull Mail* and some shipping magazines and not much more. It's been sitting here ever since; more rust than paint: jagged holes in the iron hull. The old boys who promised to help with the repairs are still waiting to get started. Napper keeps trying to assuage their fears.

*Don't worry, lads. A few issues, a few teething troubles, but keep the faith . . .*

The *Holst* wasn't Stephen's first choice. He wanted its sister ship, the *Blake Purcell*, to raise it from the ocean floor and bring it home. Wanted to stand on the gleaming deck of a resurrected craft and imagine what it would have felt like to be his dad, Rory Ballantine. Napper had felt heartbroken for the lad when the wreck surveyors told him it wasn't possible. That it should be left where it had sunk, three nautical miles from the entrance to Isafjordur Bay in Northern Iceland. Divers had been down; the best money could buy. The report was brutal. The cost of refloating it would be more than Stephen had to play with, even before the divorce cleaned him out. Napper couldn't help but feel relieved when Stephen had reluctantly accepted the findings and decided to seek out one of the other vessels from the Blake fleet instead.

Napper pulls his torch from his pocket and lights his way to the metal gateway, caged behind chicken wire and topped with

43

barbed coils. He slips his key into the chunky padlock and walks down the damp wooden gangway. He experiences a moment's déjà vu. His mind floods with memories of stepping aboard countless other trawlers: of taking that breath of cold, brackish air and knowing that the horizon and a fortune in ready cash weren't far away. He feels a fizz of excitement, as if he's young again, then catches a glimpse of his reflection in the smashed glass of the fo'c'sle and laughs at the very idea. He may be wearing expensive threads but he's still a ridiculous thing to look at. He glances around, suddenly certain that he is being watched.

He pulls the phone from his pocket and reads the message one last time. Shakes his head, then throws it, overarm, into the icy waters beyond the stern. He ducks under the rusted metal hatchway and climbs, slowly, down the ladder, pain pulling at his calf muscles. The warm, fetid air of the ship's belly takes him in its embrace. He reaches the metal floor and turns around, eyes adjusting to the gloom. A grin splits his face.

'Fuck me, you two look worse than I do. When did you get so fucking old? Move about a bit. Show me you're still breathing.'

Two men are seated at the low table. Alf and Fat Des. They look cold. Fragile. Old. Napper looks past them, grinning. 'Jesus, are they still here?'

Behind them, a trio of mannequins, dressed in all-weather wet suits and matching ganseys, have been dumped, face-down, into one of the cabin's 'coffin-beds': so-called because of their similarity to a casket. Napper remembers such beds; the stinking wooden womb that held him on so many bitter nights, the ship pitching and rising and screaming beneath the weight of pack ice and the battering of the waves. The mannequins were another of Stephen's bright ideas. He'd bought them from a wholesaler. They'll be exhibits, eventually.

'What were those two old fuckers called in *The Muppets*?' asks Napper, trying again. 'Hotels, wasn't it? Aye, that's them.

44

Waldorf and Statler. Cheer up, you cunts. It's sorted. All done and dusted.'

The bulb in the wind-up lamp on the table casts a buzzing, flickering half-light into the cabin.

'We didn't think you were coming . . .'

'I barely slept last night . . .'

'I can feel it, in my chest – a great bloody weight . . .'

'Is it done, Napper? What did they say?'

Napper sighs, leaning back against the gangway. He wonders if he should tell them everything he saw. Whether he should give voice to the fear that has been pricking away at him. Looks again at the two old men and chooses to be gentle. There is a chance their problems are over, after all. 'Somebody up there likes us, that's all you need to know.'

Alf Howe looks as though he needs a good slug of whisky adding to the cup of tea that is going cold in front of him. His face is an unhealthy grey and sweat greases his waxy features. Alf doesn't drink any more. Had his last pint in 1993: a promise to wife number two as she lay dying in a hospice on the wrong side of the city.

'Stop being a twat, Napper. What's gone on?'

'Journalist weren't there,' says Napper, shrugging. 'Told you he wouldn't be.'

'But what did he say to her? Is he keeping his mouth shut?'

'Doesn't matter now,' says Napper. 'Problem's dealt with.'

'Don't be cryptic, Napper,' says Alf, wheezing. 'You heard what Hopalong said. You saw the article. She's going to tell.'

'Doesn't matter,' mutters Napper. 'Enid's got nowt more to say on the subject. She's gone.'

'Gone?'

'Aye,' says Napper, his voice emotionless. 'The cold weather. Too much for her old bones. Slipped away. It's done with.'

Silence settles on them. Alf turns to his friend, eyes filling up. His breath catches in his throat.

'Poor lass,' he mutters. 'Christ, did she suffer? No, I don't want to know. Don't tell me . . .' His voice changes and a different expression grips his features. 'You saw her? You were there? Jesus, Napper, you didn't . . .'

'Whatever it takes, Alf,' says Napper, looking through him. He blinks hard, pushing back the images that fill his mind. He doesn't want to see them again.

'Her things,' says Alf. 'The papers. All the stuff they said they had . . .'

'I said I would take care of it. It's done. Wherever the fuck Gerard is, he's no threat. And with the old lady gone . . .'

'What about the journalist? Hopalong?' asks the other man, his voice low. 'You know he was getting close.'

'It weren't him we were scared of,' says Alf. 'It's what he said.'

Napper lowers his gaze. Talks to the floor.

'That were a bloody ghost story. He was trying to scare you. Wanted to get a reaction. You all saw.'

'We're old,' says Alf sullenly. 'I should be thinking about grandkids. Playing dominos. I shouldn't be looking over my shoulder . . .'

'They're dead,' says Napper, as kindly as he can. 'All of them.'

'What we did,' mutters Alf, staring at his knuckles as if they're smeared in blood. 'I've started believing in God again, Napper. Started believing in hell . . .'

'There's no such place,' says Napper. Twitches a grin, trying to make the lads laugh the way he used to. 'I suppose there's Grimsby . . .'

'Fuck off,' says Alf, but a glimmer of hope seems to flare in his wet, brown eyes.

Napper looks around him. There are replica lifebelts, overlapping with framed watercolours capturing the likeness of vessels with familiar names. It smells damp, like clothes that have been put away while still wet.

'Is it really all right? I have these nightmares . . . these bloody nightmares . . .'

Napper glances across at Fat Des. His nickname hasn't suited him for years. He caught some nasty infection while working on a pipeline out in Saudi. He still sinks a few pints now and again but he's never put the weight back on.

'She was going ga-ga, Des. She knew it. Even if anybody had believed her it would never have come to court. It was so long ago. Nobody knows what happened in 1986 and the only sods who know what happened in 1970 are in this room. And we're keeping quiet.'

'There's Gerard,' says Des. 'If he's got religion too . . .'

'Gerard's solid, but if you're worrying I'll go and talk to him. He's not answering his phone but I'll knock on his door if I have to. We made a promise to Rory and we're going to bloody keep it, okay? You're old men but you're not meant to be old bloody women.'

Napper looks around again, shaking his head. Glances at the headlines stuck to the walls. Tales of bravery. Arguments over the future of St Andrew's Dock. Rows about whether the intended memorial sculpture is a fitting tribute to the city's lost fishermen, or an ugly abomination better placed at the bottom of the Humber. The *Mail* has certainly had its money's worth.

'I'm off to go tidy up,' he says. 'You can stay as long as you like. Don't lose yourself in memories, though, yeah? It can be dangerous.'

Napper gives his old pals a nod. There's a strange feeling in his chest. He can feel the cancer chewing at him. He can't see the point in telling anybody that he won't see another New Year. Doesn't want sympathy and damn sure doesn't want people telling him that he's had a good innings and outlived better men by half a century. He already knows.

He climbs back up the steps and enjoys the feel of icy air on his face as makes his way back across the rubble-strewn docks to the ruby-red classic car. He pulls his phone from his pocket and looks at the message. It's a text from Mags. She always shows her age when she sends him messages, writing in capital letters as she can't work out how to switch to lower case.

**PLEASE CALL ME. IS IT SAFE?**

Napper rubs his forehead. Wishes things were different. Wishes he was good at something else and that his life had been less consumed with death.

# 5

*Pear Tree Cottage, near Cherry Burton*
*11.54 a.m.*

Frost glistens on the elaborate spider's web that dangles between the gable and the porch of the little yellow hen-house. The spider sits dead in its centre, frozen stiff: legs curled in like hooks.

McAvoy watches, collar turned up over his ears. He finds himself recalling a wildlife documentary he had watched with Fin on Christmas Day. They'd sat together, holding hands, each balancing a tin of sweets on their knees, cellophane wrappers from McAvoy's DVD box set casting an iridescent ripple on the floor. His mind remembers Fin squirming at the sight of the great furry arachnid entombed in a prison of perfect ice. Remembers the chill that crept over him as the cameras captured the creature's inexorable resurrection – those legs twitching like typing fingers, malevolent eyes blinking as it squirmed itself free and stalked away to feed.

'Neck broken,' comes the voice behind him. 'The chicken, not the old lady.'

McAvoy turns. Senior crime scene investigator Reena Parekh is crouching over the body of one of the dead birds. In her white suit, face mask and goggles, she looks for a moment like she's in charge of quality control on a chicken farm.

'Definitely not halal,' says Parekh, pulling down her mask to reveal her cheerful face. She has mocha-coloured skin, almond eyes and sugar-cube teeth, which, according to her online dating profile, makes her a neat fit for men who like their women the same way they like their coffee. 'Oh bugger . . .'

'Do you need some help?' asks McAvoy, moving forward. Parekh's long dark hair is twisted up inside the plastic hood and she struggles with her pen and laptop as she tries to extricate her ponytail. The pen slips from her grasp. She laughs, exasperated with herself. Pulls an evidence bag and a green felt tip from her pocket and slips the pen inside, making a note of the evidence number on her sleeve.

'Well, Reena,' she mutters to herself. 'That was fucking smooth.'

She gives McAvoy a bright smile.

'Shall we just not tell?' she asks. 'I'll pluck, you roast. There's a sack of onions in the kitchen. If we get the oven going it might speed up the great thaw.'

'I'm not feeling hungry,' says McAvoy, looking down at his boots. There are specks of mud on the toes but the damp earth beneath the ice has yet to start splashing up his legs. He doubts the crime scene will remain so well preserved for long. Two forensics vans have already pulled into the driveway and a bored-looking PC is setting up a perimeter and establishing a crime scene log. A uniformed team led by an inspector from Beverley has supplemented the three local detective constables. They're starting on a house-to-house; collecting CCTV from the pubs and the post office and the various security-conscious homeowners in Walkington and Bishop Burton. McAvoy, as acting detective inspector, is nominally in charge, reporting to Acting DCI Iain Dolan. He remembers Lilah's words and can't help thinking that in Pharaoh's absence everybody is simply pretending. Dolan isn't the most inspirational of leaders. He's always coming down with a cold or fighting one off and he has a temper like a jack-in-the-box, erupting seemingly at random in a sudden explosion of directionless madness.

McAvoy feels the cold air playing with his hair, slashing at his face. The air is so bitter it seems to burn where it touches his skin. The ice will melt soon. Tyres and rubber soles will be squelching through thick mud before the forensics team are through, their owners shivering inside coveralls and booties, their shadows looming huge across the fields in the glare of the outside floodlights being erected at the front door and back.

'Sorry it's you again,' says Parekh, looking up at him.

'Me again?'

'Magnet for the weird ones,' she says, smiling once more. She arches her back, groaning. 'All this bending. I must be getting old.'

McAvoy can think of several replies. Decides that all of them are too fraught with peril and elects to say nothing at all.

'You're going to ask me for all sorts of information,' says Parekh, putting her hands in her pockets. 'And I'm going to tell you that it's far too early to say. Then you'll appeal to my better nature and tug at my heartstrings and eventually I'll concede a little ground and give you what I can. Is that about right?'

McAvoy nods, managing a smile. 'The victim is the home-owner, yes? Enid Chappell. Eighty-two on her last birthday. I couldn't see much of her face but I'm confident she matches the photographs.'

'And online,' says Parekh, moving closer and angling her tablet so he can see the screen. '*Hull Daily Mail, Yorkshire Post,* BBC Radio Humberside, *Look North.* Enid Chappell has had plenty to say to each of them. But of course, I'm telling you something you already know.'

McAvoy takes his phone from his pocket. For the past half an hour he has been working the newspaper databases. He finds anecdotes and personal stories more useful in forming a picture of the victim than any amount of cold, hard fact, and there is precious little of that to be found on the PNC or HOLMES systems. He calls up one of the articles. It's from 2006. Enid Chappell is cited as a 'campaigner and activist' and is quoted in a lengthy piece about plans for a permanent memorial to the city's thousands of lost trawlermen. He reads out loud, trying not to let himself feel unsettled by breathing life into words spoken by a dead woman.

*'It's about time we all stopped bickering and put aside our griev- ances. This has been a long time coming. People have heard the statistics so many times that they're immune. But we're talking in the region of 6,000 deaths between the 1840s and the 1970s. Think how many more were affected on land. How many widows and orphans. Worst of all, those left behind have had no focus for their grief. It's not as though they can visit a grave. Men left and never came home and that was that. I was a social worker on Hessle Road and saw first-hand what the fishing industry did to people. A memorial is long overdue.'*

'Sounds like an intelligent lady,' says Parekh. 'Not the sort to get in a bath she couldn't get out of. Not the sort to open all the windows, turn the heater off and throw her mobile phone away.'

'No sign?'

'We'll trace it as soon as we receive the authorisation,' she says, shrugging. 'There's a bill in the kitchen for a mobile phone that covers the period up until 29 December. That's the most recent post we can see. We haven't found her specta- cles, which is unusual considering she's pictured wearing them in several shots online. The bloodspot in the door frame – that's first priority. We'll match it as soon as we can, though the little wound on her hairline looks the most obvious candi- date for that. We might get lucky with the blood-pooling patterns – whether she was carried, whether she had lain somewhere else for a spell. We won't really know much more until she thaws out. I'm using ultraviolet and thermal imaging to try and get a sense of what's inside the ice but it's proving tricky. From the angle of her upper body I think her legs are together, drawn up . . .'

'Like a baby,' says McAvoy quietly.

Parekh nods, her lips a tight line.

McAvoy shivers as a gust of wind rustles the branches of the stark black trees. He watches a sliver of golden sunlight disappear behind black cloud and sparkling grey-white fog.

'Oh knackers, I forgot to say,' mutters Parekh, and McAvoy realises he has been staring into space. 'I had Rikki run a basic Luminol test in the area around the little ice patch in the living room. Good spot, by the way. Ground glass and blood spots and evidence of a serious attempt to get rid of them. Now that might mean that Mrs Chappell broke a glass, cleaned it up and cut her finger but given that you expressed an interest . . .' She shrugs. 'We can conduct the tests in-house but it's expensive. Can you give the word to do it at double-speed?'

'Yes,' he says, surprising himself. 'I mean, it's a priority, isn't it? Of course it is. And the boss will sign off on it when she's back. Any problems, call me.' He grows more confident the longer he speaks. 'Double-time sounds good. Triple-time would be better.'

Parekh nods. Scribbles down a note to herself.

'The ships in the bottles,' says McAvoy, looking away. He breathes out slowly, and his breath freezes on the air. He pulls up the drooping collar of his coat. 'Thirteen of them,' he adds quietly. 'Not the luckiest number.'

Parekh gives him a puzzled look but dutifully glances at her tablet. She pulls up the images. 'Commemorative mementos,' she explains, examining the screen. 'Nameplate on each. Ship's identification number. All part of the Blake fleet. Presented, with thanks, in 1998.'

'By whom? Thanks for what?'

'They're just generally commemorative, I think. Given out by Ballantine Shipping and Logistics at a dinner to celebrate ten years since they purchased Blake, an old trawling company. They were available to buy for a time. Tourist Office, Maritime Museum. I only know this much because you said you wanted it towards the top of the list.'

'Can we match the glass fragments on the floor to the bottles?' he asks, rubbing his knuckle across his eyebrow. One of his scars is throbbing from the cold. 'I know there's a lot to wade through but it might matter ...' He stops, aware he is not explaining himself very well.

'What's your thinking?' asks Parekh, cocking her head.

'There are lots of examples of an interest in the fishing industry,' he mumbles, blushing. 'There's no green in the house.'

'And?'

'Green's bad luck,' he mumbles. 'In the trawling community, some things are accepted as outright fact, and that's the way they feel about green.'

'Maybe she just didn't like green?'

'True.' McAvoy nods, colouring. 'But, well, she covered up the word "rats" on her poisons. They call them "longtails" here, did you know that? The picture on the dresser shows the bar of the Star and Garter pub. That's Hessle Road. Most superstitious people on earth, the fishing community. Thirteen ships in a fleet seems perverse ...' He stops again, shaking his head. 'Maybe it doesn't matter.'

Parekh smiles at him indulgently and writes it down. She lifts the tablet and flicks through a selection of images. One of her CSIs has videoed the entire interior of the house. She plays the video, humming to herself. It's a Disney song, happy and uplifting. The cold air snatches it from her lips.

'Thought this might intrigue you,' says Parekh, stopping the footage. The picture is frozen on a derelict brick building. Large tractor tyres are stacked against a low wall that props up a sagging slate roof. Two rotting wooden doors, set with wrought-iron rings, have been laid face down over a patch of rutted mud.

Parekh touches the computer screen. Jerkily, the image moves, dropping as the wearer of the mounted camera ducks low to avoid the doorway. The interior is dark and looks as though it hasn't been used for a long time. The shell of an old Bedford campervan takes up half of the space. It looks as though it was painted cream and blue before the rust started feasting on its bodywork. At the far end of the room squats a black, pot-bellied stove.

'Where is this?' asks McAvoy.

'Outbuilding a little way towards the trees,' says Parekh. 'I sent Jane down to save you and yours the effort of messing things up with your size twelves.'

'I didn't know it was there.'

'You wouldn't,' says Parekh. 'It's mostly hidden by the trees. Carry on past it and you come out on a little road that leads up to Etton. Middle of nowhere. No cameras. No passing traffic. They could easily have parked there and walked here through the trees. This would be the first thing they saw.'

'That's very good work, Reena,' says McAvoy, impressed.

She grins, pleased. 'It's a new protocol. We access architectural plans, Ordnance Survey blueprints, planning applications. This would have been a workshop, I should imagine. That's a Bedford Dormobile, registered off-road since 1999 and in need of more than a lick of paint. Registered to Enid Chappell since 1967.'

'You've been busy,' says McAvoy, half smiling.

'Not me.' Parekh shrugs. 'Mostly your DCs. They're very good, aren't they?'

McAvoy nods, proud as a dad watching his children shine in a school nativity play.

'That stove,' he says, peering at the screen. 'Looks to have been used more recently than the rest of the place.'

'You're good too.' Parekh grins. 'And you're right. It has.'

She calls up another image. In this one the stove is open.

Scraps of paper lie in a pile of ashes. She zooms in on the top fragment. 'Can you make it out? Looks like a load of squiggles to me, but you could say that about most languages.'

McAvoy examines the slashes and dots, curling sigils, a cuneiform of black ink on charred white paper. Suddenly he realises what he is looking at.

'Shorthand,' he muses. 'Useful skill, certainly. But it's unusual that it would be Teeline and not Pitman, given her age.' He pauses. 'Of course, it depends when she learned. Or if she even wrote it.'

'Thought you'd recognise it,' says Parekh brightly. 'I tell people about you, you know. Only copper I know with a hundred words per minute under their belt. All gibberish to me. Can you read it?'

'Everybody's is different,' says McAvoy, squinting. 'It evolves as you get better. I don't know. I learned years ago. That might be a name. You can see the two tiny lines underneath it – shows it's a capital letter. G, maybe? And the bow-shape. Maybe a W. It could just be a doodle . . .'

'So might everything,' says Parekh. 'What're your thoughts on the dead birds?'

'I just follow the evidence,' says McAvoy automatically. 'No preconceptions.'

'Yeah, but, you know . . .'

'Too many ways to look at it,' he says. 'Do we have a killer who specifically wanted her to die in the bath and didn't want her birds pecking at the road and alerting people she was there? Did she wring their necks because she knew she was going to kill herself and didn't want them left on their own? The two things could be completely unconnected.'

'It's sad whichever way you look at it,' says Parekh.

'I thought you were meant to be unsentimental,' says McAvoy.

'An old lady's died,' says Parekh. 'If that's not sad, what is?'

McAvoy rubs his hand through his beard. He looks at his

phone. There's a voicemail waiting for him from Roisin. He wanted to answer when she rang him earlier but he had been busy talking to one of his colleagues at the Major Crime Unit's new home on the Bransholme estate when her call came through. 'Love you,' she says, as he replays the call. 'Thanks for taking Lilah in. Was she a bugger? Fin's just confessed that he might not be entirely poorly after all. I've said he can stay off anyway, is that okay? We'll do something educational. Honestly, the deceit was eating away at him. Told me he "had to come clean". He's so much like you. Anyways, call me when you can. You looked bloody gorgeous when you left. Love you.'

He hangs up, smiling. Scans the messages in his inbox. There's a progress report from DC Sophie Kirkland. She's made a start on the list of numbers pinned to the door in the kitchen. McAvoy is only halfway through reading it when the phone rings. It's the email's author, anxious for a reply.

'Sarge, it's Sophie. Sorry, I know you're being bombarded. Plenty to tell you. I've been on with the phone company—'

'She's with EE, yes?'

'Yeah, but I mean the landline,' says Kirkland. 'She had the ultra-fast lightstream package. Top-drawer Wi-Fi, which is a bit mad with no computer. Anyway, I've spoken to Kingston Communications. I've had them transfer all calls to her number through to my line and they've emailed over a list of all her recent calls. She last made a call on the third at 01.18 a.m. A pay-as-you-go mobile. We're requesting phone mast details but you know how long those buggers can take.'

'We've rung it?'

'Number unavailable. I'm working my way through the list.'

'Good work.'

'There's more, Sarge. I've just taken a call from the History Centre in Hull. You know the place? Near that nice pub with the Scotch eggs on the bar? Like I said, the victim's calls are coming straight through to me. I spoke to a very nice lady called Sue who was a bit surprised to find herself talking to a copper. She'd been ringing to gently encourage Mrs Chappell to return some papers she may have removed from the archive, if you can imagine it.'

'You can't take papers from the archive,' mutters McAvoy. 'You can pay to make copies, and that's only provided you don't share them with anybody else.'

'That's what Sue just said. Apparently Mrs Chappell's a regular user of the local history unit in Beverley and has started using the Hull one as well. It's bigger. Back copies of the *Hull Mail*. Hull Corporation meeting minutes. Shipping lists. Parish council records and all kinds of births, marriages and deaths. On 20 December Mrs Chappell signed in at the centre to access some documents. Gave them back an hour later, or so Sue thought. She has been trying to get in touch for the past few days to find out if she had made a mistake and "accidentally" put the papers in her bag. Crew lists for dozens of different trawlers – 1965 through to 1971.'

McAvoy processes the information. He hears Parekh clearing her throat, trying to get his attention. 'Sorry, Sophie, just a moment.'

Parekh is watching a live feed from the house. One of her colleagues is examining the bathroom. The image zooms in on the contents of the mirrored cabinet. Among the medications is a strip of tablets in a blister pack.

'Donepezil,' he says. 'That's for . . .'

'Dementia,' finishes Parekh. 'Early stages.'

'Medical records,' says McAvoy, into the phone. 'How are we—'

'If I had an extra pair of hands it would help,' says Kirkland testily.

'Just do your best,' mutters McAvoy. 'Sorry. What else? Is Sue available to give a statement?'

'On it,' says Kirkland. 'Anyway, listen. The phone records. Mrs Chappell has been very busy. Made several calls to a pay-as-you-go mobile in the days leading up to Christmas. Called several local numbers too. Andy's on it.'

McAvoy stays quiet. He can hear her papers rattling and her fingers moving over the keyboard.

'She's a regular user of a Beverley taxi service. I gave them a quick buzz and it seems she always requests the same driver. Ben McKenzie. Lives in Molescroft. I haven't spoken to him direct but the dispatcher says Mrs Chappell's one of his regulars and has been for a couple of years. He was there on New Year's Day.'

'Where has he been taking her?'

'Nothing that sets off alarm bells. Big Tesco at Beverley. Pubs at Etton and South Cave. Couple of trips into Hull. St Andrew's Quay. Christmas shopping at St Stephen's, carol concert at Holy Trinity on the 18th. Pub or two on Hessle Road. I've got an address and phone number for Mr McKenzie. Dispatch lady said Mrs Chappell – sorry, I know it's not confirmed yet but we all bloody know, don't we? – was a good tipper. Polite. Friendly. Bloody shame, isn't it?'

McAvoy turns at a noise behind him. Parekh is using her own chest-mounted camera to film the chicken coop. McAvoy is about to apologise to Kirkland for cutting her off when he realises he has lost the signal and that the line is already dead. It's still an obnoxious, charcoal-coloured day and the bright light of the camera casts an eerie glow on the chicken coop. McAvoy moves out of the way.

'Tyre tracks are unusual,' says Parekh, half to herself. She's examining an image on her screen, uploaded moments before by one of the CSIs. 'Expensive. I'll try and make some sense of it when we're done here.' She looks around, as if seeing the location properly. 'Would have been nice, wouldn't it? Sitting out on a summer's day, watching your chickens, maybe having a drink and reading a book. What we all want, somewhere pretty to end your days.'

McAvoy closes his eyes.

Parekh sighs. She reads out the date, time and log number and focuses the camera. With gloved hands, she wiggles the latch of the chicken coop. Slowly the door swings open. Parekh ducks, angling herself so she can point the recording device into the dark of the coop. From where McAvoy stands, he can see the change that comes over her expression, the way a still-ness enters her posture, as if her joints were stiffening up. She retreats. McAvoy swaps places with her. The inside of the little wooden hen-house looks like something from a slaughterhouse. The walls are a mess of feathers and blood – the ragged, ripped bodies of birds islands in a sea of gore.

'Thoughts?' asks Parekh. 'Fox, maybe?'

'Let's hope so,' says McAvoy.

# 6

Vidarr is remembering. He lies so still that he may as well be dead. He breathes in slowly, the mask filtering the fetid air.

The world moves beneath him. He rises and falls in tandem with the vessel. He prefers to feel ocean beneath him: has spent more time at sea than on land in the long, lonely years since he sailed out onto the river and up towards Spurn Point, watching the city of his birth turn into a dirty grey smudge.

He listens to the men who are about to die. They carp and cry and tell themselves they don't deserve this. He briefly wonders whether they have a right to consider themselves ill-used. He dismisses the thought at once. Reminds himself who he is.

*Vidarr.*

Vengeance.

The silent, unstoppable killer sent forth to avenge an incomparable wrong.

He touches the top of the hook with the gloved tip of his thumb. It's sharp as a knife. He rubs his finger over the twists of braided black cord that mummify his wrists. There is a gap, a sense of nakedness upon his pulse, that both saddens and energises him. He remembers the weight of the old woman in his arms. She had been too weak to fight but she had tried. She'd even said his name. Not Vidarr. Not the name he has chosen for himself. The name of the thing he used to be, before his true destiny, his true blood, was revealed to him.

He hadn't enjoyed hurting her at first. But he found it easier with each finger that broke. Even then, she wouldn't tell. Wouldn't tell him the truth about how deeply she had betrayed him.

Vidarr lets the motion of the water rock him. Finds his mind drifting. He is no stranger to such moments. Sometimes his mind fills with memories that are not his own. Sometimes he pictures things so clearly it is as if he has lived through them. He thinks of Roberta. November 1969. The little house off Road. Rory and his pals, drinking and smoking and setting the world to rights: Mags bustling around them, her platinum-blonde hair cutting through the fog of cigarette smoke like an iceberg. Roberta, leaning in the doorway, bed-headed and lovely. Big Gerard's voice is rising above the din – commanding and unmistakable amid the clink of glasses; the bursts of throaty laughter; the soulful crooning of Roy Orbison drifting from the glossy wooden radiogram that Rory had bought for Mags last time home.

Vidarr is there now. The image so vibrant and fresh that he feels as if he could reach into the memory. He sees them all. Roberta. Mags. Rory. Gerard. Cowboy Mick. Young Billy. Alf, Des and Napper. Billy sitting with his back to the fire, stroking the tiny baby bird that he keeps in his pocket. Alf and Des, arguing over a bottle of crème de menthe. Napper, showing a card trick to Big Gerard. Rory, tickling the back of his wife's knee and making her giggle. They'll all be gone with the morning tide.

Vidarr skips forward. Sees Roberta waking in her cold bedroom with its crimson walls and the violet curtains. She's staring into the dark, fear starting to distort her face. She reaches for the light beside the bed. She never sees who comes for her. The moment that the light spills into the little room, a gloved hand clamps over her eyes, another grips her mouth, and all her senses distil into one sudden terrifying awareness of what is happening. She tries to wriggle free but the hands that press down on her face are utterly unyielding.

The bulb casts a warm light on the red wall. Their shadows become a grotesque puppet show. Roberta's attacker alters his position. He hits her, hard, in the temple. Does it again. When she's still he loops a strand of her hair around his fingers. Tugs, hard. There is a sound like cotton tearing and the hair rips from her scalp. He presses the bloodied roots to his face.

Slowly, his fingers take a new form. He presses his thumbs together, overlapping, like links in a chain. His fingers lengthen, the blades of his hands taking on the shape of wings. Slowly, his hands become a bird. He's mesmerised. Watches as the shape on the wall appears to soar; a perfect replica of a bird in flight. His breathing becomes erratic as the raven on the wall grows in size, doubling, tripling, and he begins to see detail in the feathers: malevolence in the beady eye formed by his conjoined thumbs.

His fingers touch her throat. The wings fold around her neck. Slowly, he starts to squeeze. He shifts his position afresh.

In silence, he takes what he wants.

She is not his first. But she will always be his favourite.

Vidarr lies in the darkness and remembers. Imagines. He fingers the tip of the hook, and smiles.

Listens to the old men, and tells himself that he is a compassionate man. Soon, they will not have to worry any more. Soon, they will be nothing but meat and broken bones.

Here.

*Now.*

Alf Howe and Fat Des eye one another. The lights flicker, causing the shadows to lengthen and dance. Neither wants to leave. Neither particularly wants to stay.

'She deserved better,' says Alf, breaking first. 'She did right by them all. Did right by all of us. She never had to.'

'Don't get maudlin.'

'Says you. There's tears in your eyes too, you old bastard.'

Des puts his hands on the table and pushes himself up, unsteady on his feet. He'll be seventy-six on his next birthday. Has lived longer than he ever expected to.

'You don't think Gerard would tell, do you? I mean, why now? After all this time? We made an agreement. He can say it was him if he wants to but they'll see through him. They'll know it was all of us.'

'But it wasn't us,' snaps Alf. 'Not properly.'

'Police won't think that. Look, Napper will help him see the light. A few quid in his back pocket, eh?'

'When has he ever cared about money? He's only made so much of it because he doesn't give a damn. All that matters is what he promised Rory.'

'But Napper—'

'Des, Napper's a fucking idiot. He always has been. Stephen keeps him like a pet. That Scouser – he wasn't messing about. He knows what happened. Even if Enid's gone, what's to stop him telling the story anyway? He knew stuff even I didn't know. About the currents and where they ended up. Those bodies in Murmansk . . . two not three; if it's them, then why didn't he wash up with them, eh? Why didn't—'

'Stop,' spits Des. 'Please. It was a lifetime ago. One night, one mistake, and it's cast a shadow over my whole life. It might be all right.' He looks at his old friend, beseeching.

Alf slumps in his chair, huddled into his anorak. 'Something's coming. We were never going to take this to the grave.'

'I thought that maybe we'd made up for it,' Des mutters. 'The money we've given to good causes. The people we've helped. That must count for something, mustn't it? I keep trying to pray but the words won't bloody come. I just feel like

I'm talking to myself. There's no sense to any of it, is there? Rory were the best of us and the sea took him and left us useless bastards to pick up the pieces. What were it for, Alf? What were any of it for? Maybe Gerard's right. Maybe we should just tell what happened and take our punishment. We're old. They might not do anything about it.'

'But our families,' says Alf, wiping a bead of moisture from his nose. 'There's a bloody statue of us on the quayside. We'll be remembered as the murdering bastards who kept a secret for fifty years. Can you handle that?'

Des looks down at the tabletop. 'I just want it to be over.'

Alf looks at his friend and feels a wave of compassion. Softens his face, ready to tell him that perhaps he is right. That everything will be okay. He flicks his eyes to the left, catching the faintest trace of movement. The pile of mannequins, stacked like discarded corpses, seems to disassemble. A figure rises, a rippling mass of darkness, lustrous, like spilled oil.

'Des,' croaks Alf. 'Des, behind . . .'

Des turns his head.

A curve of perfect silver catches the light. Des opens his mouth, fear rendering him insensible. The tip of the hook punctures the meat of his lower jaw, ripping up through the soft tissue of his mouth and tongue and bursting through a sudden gaping hole in the side of his face.

For a moment, Alf can do nothing. He stands still as the man with the black braids tugs on the coil of wire that trails from the base of the hook.

Only when the figure yanks on the rope; only when the whole of Des's lower jaw is wrenched free of its moorings – only then does Alf tell himself to move.

The command comes too late. Alf is still rooted to the spot when the man with the braids turns black eyes upon him.

He has a dizzying sense of staring into the past; his gaze fixed on the black, birdlike eyes of a man he used to know.

Alf opens his mouth to speak. No sound emerges. He doesn't even lift his hands. He stands like a puppet, tears trickling down his cheeks, as a noose of braided threads is looped expertly around his scrawny neck.

In the moment before he dies, Alf sees the sea. Black waves and towering cliffs, ravens and crows and gulls. He sees the bloodied figure in the surging water, eyes like stones, blood seeping from his nose, trickling from his ears and criss-crossing the wounds in his ruined face.

At the last, Alf believes in God.

Knows, to his bones, that he has glimpsed the devil.

## 7

*Butterfly Meadows, Molescroft, East Yorkshire*
*12.46 p.m.*

The taxi driver Ben McKenzie lives in a bland, semi-detached house on the new housing development just outside Beverley, ten miles from central Hull. It's been nearly twenty years since the builders finished work on this sprawl of modern homes, but McAvoy knows East Yorkshire well enough to safely assume that the place will be known as the 'new' estate for at least another couple of decades. There are people in Hull who still haven't tried the 'new' bridge across the Humber and it opened in 1981.

'You can pop for a drink if you want to warm yourself through,' says McAvoy, climbing out of the back of the patrol car as it comes to a stop outside the characterless property on the misleadingly titled 'Butterfly Meadows'. A VW Passat is parked on the driveway, tyres not quite bald enough to fail an MOT.

The young, blonde constable gives McAvoy a grateful look. They haven't spoken much on the drive from Cherry Burton but the silence hadn't been awkward. She seemed content to let him stare out of the window, letting his thoughts spool out across the cold, hard landscape beyond the glass. He's not used to being chauffeured but hadn't been given much choice. The forensics team are busy taking shots of the tyres of his own vehicle so they can be ruled out when they start taking plaster casts of the churned-up ground on the driveway. He won't have access to it for another hour or so.

'Can I get you anything?' she asks. 'When do you want picking up?'

'Whenever's convenient,' says McAvoy, blowing on his hands and leaning down so he can talk to her through the open window. 'I appreciate the lift.'

The PC gives him a smile of thanks. 'Tea? Coffee?' she prompts.

A thought occurs to him – a memory of something he watched Pharaoh do at a crime scene when she needed the uniforms to go above and beyond. He reaches into his back pocket and pulls out his wallet. Hands her his credit card. 'Tea, please. Get a round in.'

'You sure?'

He nods. Turns towards the house as he hears the front door opening.

Ben McKenzie stands in the doorway, holding a baby in one arm and a plastic bag in the other. McAvoy knows from a quick PNC check that Enid Chappell's regular cabbie is thirty-eight years old. He looks considerably older. There's a redness to his eyes and a greenish pallor to his skin that McAvoy instantly recognises as the hallmarks of a new parent.

'Mr McKenzie,' says McAvoy. 'We spoke on the phone.'

'Great timing,' says McKenzie, giving an awkward smile. 'The smell's not my doing. Blame Poppy.'

He holds the baby up for inspection. She has the same round face and brown eyes as her father. She is wearing a pink one-piece beneath a hand-knitted, rainbow-coloured cardigan, and seems to feel no obvious embarrassment at being responsible for the extraordinary stench emanating from the Tesco bag in her father's spare hand.

'Gorgeous. How old is she?' asks McAvoy.

'Nine weeks,' says McKenzie. 'I don't remember a time before she came along. It's Mum's day for a breather. You got kids?'

McAvoy nods, smiling without realising it. 'Two. My eldest's ten, daughter's five. They run rings around me, but in a good way.'

'This one's our third,' says McKenzie, looking as though he still isn't entirely sure that he wants children. 'You've come at a good time. She tends to doze off after she's filled her nappy.' He sniffs the air. 'I'm seriously worried about the wife. I mean, she's breast-feeding. That's just from milk! How can a smell like that come from just milk? Can you take her while I go to the bin?'

McAvoy doesn't get the chance to answer. McKenzie thrusts the baby into his hands and pushes past him. 'Go on through,' he shouts over his shoulder. 'Sorry about the mess.'

McAvoy stands on the front step, looking down at the tiny pink creature in his big, cold hands. She looks up at him with curiosity, as if trying to work out who he might be and what he might conceivably be for. She appears to come to the conclusion that despite his size he's probably harmless, and contentedly closes her eyes. McAvoy pushes into the little hallway. Coats of different sizes hang from a set of hooks on the wall and the door won't open all the way because of the huge array of discarded shoes behind it. Two yellow parking tickets in plastic envelopes are stuck to the wall. A letter from school, opened and discarded, makes threats about the importance of topping up Cleo's ParentPay account and warns she will not be getting any more school lunches until the bill is settled.

McAvoy opens the door to his right and enters a chaotically untidy living room. A battered two-seater sofa and mismatched chair take up the majority of the floor space and the carpet is almost invisible beneath an explosion of papers, toys and packaging. A blue playpen full of fluffy toys and splayed DVD cases

69

is wedged up beneath the window. Books lie in a collapsed heap by the fireplace, where an imitation log fire casts a cosy red glow.

'That's got rid of that,' says Mr McKenzie, coming through the door behind him. He picks up a canister of air-freshener from beside the sofa and gives the room a liberal spray. He laughs, a little manic, and throws himself down on the sofa, paying little heed to the bowl of soggy cereal that teeters precariously on the arm. He seems disinclined to take Poppy from McAvoy's arms.

'You said you were a detective, yeah?' he asks. His accent is northern but doesn't contain Hull's flattened vowels. McAvoy presumes that Mrs McKenzie isn't from Hull either. Nobody who pronounces the letter 'o' as 'urr' would name a child Cleo.

'Yes, I'm Detective Sergeant McAvoy,' he says, deciding that he will continue to stand. 'Acting Detective Inspector. I'd shake hands, but I'm holding your baby . . .'

'And a grand job you're doing,' says McKenzie, and he flops his head onto the back of the sofa.

McAvoy alters his expression into something approximating a getting-down-to-business stare. 'Mr McKenzie, as I said on the phone, I'm keen to talk to you about Enid Chappell. She lives in the little cottage off the road to Cherry Burton.'

'Enid,' says Mr McKenzie. 'Aye, grand lass. More cryptic wisdom than a bag of fortune cookies, that one. What's she done? Chained herself to an oak tree in the vicarage or sent a box of dog shit to the parish council? You're not making her life difficult, are you? She's one of the good ones.'

McAvoy hands the baby to Mr McKenzie. He holds her to his chest; his expression changing as he registers the look in McAvoy's eyes.

'Has she died?' he asks, and a look of true remorse ripples across his features. He kisses his daughter's head, holding her closer. 'She has, hasn't she? That's awful.' He rubs his forehead

70

with his palm then pinches the bridge of his nose. If it's a performance, it's a convincing one. 'Accident, was it? She needed help, I told her that. I don't care how tough you are when you're young, age catches up with everybody. Poor lass.'

'I'm afraid that a body was found at the property this morning,' says McAvoy quietly. 'We're awaiting formal identification, but . . .'

McKenzie nods again. Glances at the mess at his feet as if seeing it for the first time. 'Who found her? Was it that mate from up the coast? Or was her fancy man back?'

McAvoy decides to stay quiet and let the taxi driver speak. He wonders how many of his passengers have come to the same conclusion.

'I'm just her cabbie, you know that, yeah? I suppose it was Evelyn sent you to me. Evelyn, the dispatch girl? Yeah, that makes sense. Fuck. *Fuck!* Oh, sorry, Poppy, bad Daddy . . . you're CID?' He rubs his jaw, his thoughts drifting into a shape he can understand. 'So that means there's something not right about it. What can you tell me? Nothing, I bet. It's okay, I understand. What was it? Burglary gone wrong or something? I told her she needed some security. They gave her one of those cords to wear around her neck – you press the orange button in the middle if you need help and the cavalry come running. She wore it for about three days then gave up on it. Said she kept catching herself on door handles and that it made her feel like an old woman.'

McAvoy shifts some papers from the armchair and cautiously lowers himself.

'When did you last see Mrs Chappell?' he asks, looking up as a yellow light illuminates the hoary air beyond the window. He sees the shape of the patrol car. Wonders how long he can allow the PC to wait without being seen as impolite.

'New Year's Day,' says McKenzie automatically. 'Mid-afternoon. Maybe 3 p.m.? I was hung over. Not pissed, before you start. I get a hangover on two beers these bloody days. I wasn't due to work but Evelyn knows there are some regulars I'll always go out for. Enid's one of them.'

'And where did she want to go?'

'She wanted to pop into Hull,' says McKenzie. 'I was relieved it was just a drop-off. Sometimes she'd have me wait for her, which was a bit of a sod as her condition got worse.'

'Her condition?'

Mr McKenzie grimaces. 'She were getting ... well ... confused, I suppose you'd call it. No spring chicken, was she? Eighty-two? Eighty-three? She did her best to hide it but you could tell when she'd had one of her moments. She'd be talking to you clear as anything then she'd lose the signal and you could be a stranger. Could be a bugger when I'd wait for her. She'd come back and not remember that I'd been waiting an hour and then she'd kick off about the bill. Part of me wondered if she were doing it on purpose to get a discount. Wouldn't put it past her.'

McAvoy smiles. He can feel himself warming to Mrs Chappell.

'New Year's, she just wanted the drop-off, like I said. That wasn't unusual. Sometimes she got lifts home from whoever she was meeting. Plenty of friends, our Enid. She was independent. It still pissed her off that she couldn't drive. Was always telling me off for my driving.' A smile chases sorrow across his face. 'Bloody hell I can hear her voice, telling me off.'

'Asking you to slow down?'

'To speed up,' says McKenzie. 'Always reckoned I'd missed a chance to pull out at junctions. Always leaning over and telling me that the accelerator was the pedal on the right.'

'You were her regular driver. How long for?'

'Almost since I started,' he says. 'I've not always been a cabbie. Done all sorts.' He shakes his head again. 'How can I help, mate? Nobody hurt her, did they? I'd hate that.'

McAvoy takes his pad from his pocket. The top page shows his notes, written in a neat hand, black on white. They only makes sense to him, his Teeline shorthand having evolved into something that looks nothing like the series of curls and slashes he was originally taught. He flicks through the pages, seeking a clear, unsullied sheet.

'You know that stuff, do you?' asks McKenzie, squinting at the notebook.

'That stuff?' he asks, not understanding.

'Shorthand, isn't it? Looks indecipherable to me but so does Russian and there are millions of those buggers who seem to understand it. Don't get me started on Chinese . . .'

'I won't,' says McAvoy firmly. 'If we could return to Mrs Chappell.'

'Yeah, sorry,' mutters McKenzie, and strokes his daughter's head with the end of his beard. 'Christ, I'm all over the place. I don't know what to think. There'll be plenty of people upset. She was slowing down of course but she was always up to this and that. Charities and volunteering and handing out food at the soup kitchen. She was giving back, I think. You'll know this already, I'm sure, but when you think where she started . . .'

'Go on,' says McAvoy, his pen making neat, quick strokes on the page.

'What do you need to know? I mean, what do you not know?'

McAvoy looks into McKenzie's eyes for a moment longer than is comfortable. McKenzie looks away, smiling nervously. He wonders whether the cabbie is hiding something important, or is just generally nervous.

'Imagine I know nothing,' says McAvoy, and hears Pharaoh's voice, telling him that it shouldn't be too hard.

McKenzie sits back, sighing, as if this is going to take him a while. 'Been through it, you could tell that. Could have written a book about her life though I doubt any bugger would believe it. She were from Road, you'll know that. Dad were a fisherman

73

but he got hurt and had to become a bobber. Unloading fish from the trawlers, yeah? Hard bloody work. Big hobnails in your boots and a hook in your hand for dragging the kits off the ships. He died when she was young, best I could make out. She told me she'd spent time in an orphanage – the big old place near the bridge. Hesslewood, I think it's called. Big old mansion house. All offices now but it used to be a home for kids from Hessle Road. Dads lost at sea or mums who couldn't cope. I tell you something, when you think about that time, that world . . . for her to become somebody important like that . . .' He whistles, impressed. 'One of the first to do a degree in social services at Hull Uni. From a bloody orphanage to that! Worked for the councils. Hull Corporation. Humberside County. The stories she could tell . . .'

McAvoy's pen hovers over his notepad while he decides whether to steer the ship or let it follow the tide. 'Could you tell me a little about the nature of your association with Mrs Chappell,' he says. 'I understand you were her favoured driver.'

'That's kind of you,' says McKenzie, smiling without showing teeth. 'I suppose I was. Maybe I was just the one daft enough to let her boss me about.'

'She was demanding?'

'Not in a nasty way,' says McKenzie. 'She just asked for stuff that was a bit of a pain. Like, she'd ask you to wait while she went to the doctor's and then she'd pop off to get some shopping and then get talking and by the time she came back, well, dispatch would be giving you earache.'

He smiles, picturing something. 'She could look right batty if you didn't know how clever she was. One morning I turned up and she was wearing this coat she'd found in a charity shop. Huge great leopard print thing five sizes too big for her. She said she knew it was too big but if she didn't wear it now, when was she ever going to? You could tell she'd been a bit of a looker in her day. Like, way back. Before the documentary, even.'

74

McAvoy closes the notebook. 'Documentary, Mr McKenzie?'

'Bloody hell, you don't know much about her, do you?' protests McKenzie, looking distinctly disappointed. He shuffles his position and licks his lips. 'She was a bit of a firebrand when she was younger. She'd worked Hessle Road. When she was a social worker, I mean. You should watch the programme, if you haven't already.'

McAvoy feels his phone vibrate. He ignores it.

'Put in "documentary" and "Bransholme" and "Hull" and scroll through. All about social housing in Hull in the eighties, after the old fishing families were moved up to Bransholme. No jobs. No money. Nowt to do. She was one of the social workers interviewed. You could see she was good at her job. I thought she'd be pleased to see it when I showed her but the screen was too small for her to make it out. Terrible eyes without her glasses. Poor old thing. Anyway, she smiled and made the right noises but I don't think she even knew she was looking at herself. She'd bought herself a computer a few years back but she didn't seem to have much of a clue about technology.' He stops talking, cocking his head at the sound of an engine revving indiscreetly. 'That your lift, is it? I can drive you, if they need to get on their way.'

McAvoy considers the offer, aware that he has plenty more to ask him. Decides he would rather use his imminent departure as an excuse to be less chatty.

'You mentioned she may have had guests?'

McKenzie nods, smiling. 'I think she might have had someone staying over at Christmas. When I asked her if she'd enjoyed the festivities she said "they" had enjoyed a few drinks at home. I liked to tease her, same as she liked to tease me. Asked her if she had a fancy man and she clammed up about it.'

'But you thought somebody had been staying?'

'Aye, I suppose. She had a different smell about her. Funny how you remember stuff, isn't it? She had a fag-smoke sort of smell. Got her nails done by those Vietnamese lasses in Beverley too. Or do I mean Thai? Does it matter?'

'To them, certainly,' says McAvoy drily. 'Did you ever actually see anybody else at the house?'

'Sorry,' says McKenzie, and seems to mean it. 'I'm probably not the best person for you to be talking to. She had that friend up the coast. Atwick way – where the cliff's all crumbling. Took her there once to visit. Had to do a U-turn with two wheels over the edge. I'm sure they'd know more than me. The ladies at the History Centre might be able to help you.'

'I could do with a list of every journey she took with your firm,' says McAvoy quietly. 'I've made the same request at your office but on the off-chance you took the occasional journey privately . . .'

McKenzie flashes a smile, suddenly impish. 'Aye, there may have been one or two. You know how it is. But that's a big ask, innit? I mean, I took her to Tesco, down to Waitrose at Willerby, sometimes down to the Foreshore in Hessle.'

'What did she want down there?' asks McAvoy, looking up.

'Just liked to watch the sea.' McKenzie shrugs. 'She'd just sit. I'd maybe get us both a coffee. She'd watch the water and natter. Like I say, that's how you could tell she was going downhill. She'd repeat herself. Point out old friends who weren't there. Ask me if I could hear stuff that was just in her head. I kept saying she needed to speak to Social Services but she was too bloody proud.' He looks at McAvoy accusingly. 'Your lot didn't exactly cover themselves in glory. Came out of that meeting with a face like thunder.'

McAvoy swallows. 'My lot?'

'Aye, a few months back. Weather was still warm. Took her to the new station at Clough Road. Bloody monstrosity, isn't it? Whoever she was seeing fair took the wind out of her sails. Came out furious. She weren't herself at all. Think I ended up dropping her in one of the pubs on Road. Did her usual trick

'– let me get home then called me back out for her. She'd had a few by the time I found her. Alexander Hotel, I think it was. Some poor barmaid was worried about her. Enid gave her my name and number and said I was her "chauffeur". Crackers, isn't it? Anyway, she deserved better than to be left waiting in the police reception then sent on her merry way. If it weren't for that dark-haired one I think she'd have set the place on fire.'

'Dark-haired one?'

'The one who came down to talk to her when the bigwig was too busy. Only caught a glimpse of her but Enid said she was a decent sort. Bit older than you. Had biker boots on. Big ti—'

McAvoy stops him short, his face suddenly hard. 'I'll need that exact date,' he says, and then glares at his phone, two pink spots of colour on his suddenly pale cheeks. He types in a message to Sophie Kirkland, asking her to check with the desk sergeant at Clough Road. Pinches the bridge of his nose until his thoughts fall silent.

'The last time you saw Mrs Chappell,' he asks, 'what was her mood?'

McKenzie screws up his face. In his arms, Poppy's eyelids flutter. 'Quiet,' he says at last. 'Maybe she knew I had a headache, eh? She certainly wasn't as chatty as usual. Still, she could be that way sometimes. Like I say, she knew she was going a bit, well, doo-lally. That's her word, not mine. She fought it though. Fought it like an enemy. Kept a little pad in her handbag full of things she wasn't to forget. That's where I saw that mad writing. Shorthand, yeah?'

'Would you be able to help me out a little further and jot down anything else that occurs to you?' asks McAvoy, trying to make him feel indispensable. 'An officer will come and take a statement in due course but if you had a few moments to think about anybody you may have seen Mrs Chappell with, or if anything she said to you may have been relevant . . .'

He stands, taking a business card from his shirt pocket and

placing it on the mantelpiece. 'Anything that occurs to you,' he says earnestly. He picks up his phone and starts scrolling through a list of updates, only half listening as McKenzie follows him to the door.

'I'll send you the link to that documentary,' says McKenzie brightly. 'There'll be a funeral, won't there? I'll go. To say thanks, if nothing else. Hope one of her rich pals puts their hand in their pocket. She deserves a good send off. Poor lass . . .'

McAvoy gives Poppy a look. Resists the urge to stroke her head before he leaves.

'Aye,' he mutters, before stepping back into the cold. 'Poor lass.'

# 8

Back outside Mrs Chappell's house, McAvoy looks up at the crumpled clouds, coiled like damp rope. He considers the young constable beside him. Mid-twenties. Slim, but with a gym-hardened physique. Shaved head and a noticeably upturned nose. His teeth chatter against the rim of the mug. McAvoy would swap places with PC Goodwin in a moment. He feels almost nostalgic for the days when he was tasked with standing still and looking official. There were fewer decisions to be made. Fewer judgement calls. He never felt exactly comfortable but he understood that he was doing something necessary, and quite hard to get wrong.

'Going to be a long one,' says Goodwin, making conversation.

'Afraid so,' says McAvoy. 'There'll be some relief for you soon, I think.'

Goodwin takes another swig of coffee. 'You got a next of kin to inform?'

'Working on it,' says McAvoy. 'Mobile phone bill in the kitchen but no sign of the phone. We've requested information. Interesting tyre marks up ahead. Expensive-looking. It certainly seems like she was slowing down.' He looks away, trying to make sense of his suspicions. 'As if she was getting her affairs in order, shall we say. There are things missing, I think. The bin's empty though there hasn't been a recycling pick-up since before the New Year. Where are her Christmas cards? And this talk of going away . . .' He stops, aware he is doing little more than thinking aloud. Shivers a little, as a gust of wind surges up the track from the main road.

'We think it's murder, then?' asks Goodwin, looking a little better for the hot drink. He glances around for somewhere to put the mug and McAvoy takes it from him, as if retrieving a Tippee cup from a toddler.

'Forensics won't commit themselves,' says McAvoy. 'Suspicious, certainly. But no more than that at this stage.'

'You have to hope it's an accident, I suppose,' says Goodwin. 'Or suicide.'

McAvoy angles his head, looking with unexpected sharpness at the PC. 'Hope it's suicide? How so?'

'Getting her affairs in order, like you said. At least it's not so sad then, is it?'

'I'm sorry, Constable?'

Goodwin suddenly looks as if he wishes he hadn't spoken. As if he'd presumed they were two blokes making small talk. He seems to squirm.

'If she's got what she wants, I mean. There's less to feel sad about if this is what she's chosen. Or if she's had a fall, or some-thing.' He shrugs. 'I'd just rather it not be murder.'

McAvoy runs his tongue around the inside of his mouth. He considers it. 'It's sad whichever way you look at it.'

Goodwin looks away. A strong gust of wind hits the trees. The trunks bend, the branches shake: blackbirds and crows squawk and scream into the air. For a moment the sky looks as though it's full of shredded mourning gowns.

'No Pharaoh on this one?' asks Goodwin. 'Met her once. Force of nature, isn't she?'

McAvoy feels the colour rising in his cheeks. Turns his face to the wind in the hope of extinguishing the blush before it consumes him. He nods his head in the direction of the nearest property – a rectangle of white that serves as a canvas for the dark trees.

'Nobody home, according to the DC from Beverley. If you get the chance, could you—'

He stops talking as a set of bright yellow headlamps gleam through the gap in the hedge. A large black BMW X6 turns slowly into the driveway, its tinted windows reflecting McAvoy and Goodwin back at themselves. McAvoy notices his erratic hair and smooths it down, just as the window slides down with an expensive-sounding 'swoosh'. DC Ben Neilsen glowers out from the driving seat. There's a greyness to his skin, as if something has slurped the blood from his jugular. McAvoy notices his hands gripping the steering wheel. He's wearing blue latex gloves. He's sitting on plastic seat covers. A waft of air-freshener and cleaning wipes floats from the warmth of the car's interior. There's a pinkish tinge to his eyes.

'Ben?' he asks, confused. 'You're back in? I thought you'd cleared the compassionate leave.'

'No time for that,' comes a voice from the back of the car. 'Make do with what you've got, that's the mantra. Get in, or at least come round here so I don't have to shout.'

McAvoy glances back at Ben. His jaw is clenched tight. McAvoy peeks past him into the warm, plush interior of the vehicle. Area Commander David Slattery is sitting in the middle seat, reclining against cream leather seats. He's wearing an expensive sailing coat over his uniform. His hair is thinning on top, brushed forward to conceal the receding hairline.

'The gloves?' asks McAvoy.

'Just had her cleaned,' says Slattery, before Neilsen can speak. 'I'm particular about my car. A beauty to drive. I haven't heard a thank you yet.'

'Thanks,' says Neilsen, his voice dry. 'She's a beauty.'

McAvoy removes his hands from the window frame. Neilsen's mother is dying. The family hadn't expected her to see Christmas but she's still hanging on, more than a week into the New Year. Neilsen and his sister have been struggling to care for her and for their father, whose dementia has been getting worse for months. Pharaoh had no problem allowing him to take a few extra days of holiday to be with his mother at the end – whenever that might be.

'I'm not raising my voice any more,' says Slattery, his voice dripping with disdain. 'Come round this side.'

McAvoy takes his time walking around the far side of the vehicle. PC Goodwin is looking away. McAvoy envies him. Envies anybody who can decide what to see and what not to see. He pulls open the door and is about to climb inside when Slattery holds up a hand. 'Show me your boots,' he says tiredly, as if he has been repeating this simple request all morning.

'I'm sorry?' asks McAvoy.

'Don't be,' says Slattery.

McAvoy dutifully lifts each foot for inspection: a horse being inspected by a farrier. Slattery gives a begrudging nod and McAvoy climbs into the vehicle. They sit in silence for almost a minute. Slattery picks specks of lint on his jumper. Retrieves a sheaf of papers from the seat beside him and flicks through. He pulls a pen from his jacket pocket and makes a note. Looks up and gives McAvoy another once-over. Taps his own throat, indicating McAvoy needs to fasten his top button. McAvoy instinctively reaches up and finds it already fastened.

'Get any actual work done while you've been idling about drinking coffee with the uniforms? Can I put this one to bed early? I need it nice and neat. Discovery to charge within twenty-four hours would be a very nice result. I got what you sent through. A little thin, isn't it?'

McAvoy glances up. Sees Neilsen looking at him in the mirror.

'Give me it again, save me looking.'

'Victim's name is Enid Chappell,' says McAvoy, snapping to attention. 'Eighty-two years old in November of last year. Lived here since 1981. Electoral roll shows there was another resident between 1983 and 2002. Maria Winter. Died that year from leukaemia. No other residents since. No children.'

'Yes, yes,' says Slattery impatiently. 'The bit about the Clough Road visit. This McKenzie chap. Seemed to have plenty to say for himself.'

'He was very helpful, sir,' says McAvoy.

'Helpful with what, exactly?' asks Slattery. 'You got every-body very excited when you rang this one in but I must ask precisely why you think this is a matter for Major Crimes and half the uniforms in Beverley? It's terribly sad but terribly sad things happen all the time and the last thing we need is to turn this into a *who's-most-to-blame* public relations issue, wouldn't you agree?'

McAvoy pauses. Understands. 'You were familiar with Mrs Chappell, sir?' he asks, cautiously. 'She came to see you . . .'

'Familiar?' Slattery asks, his voice rising. 'Make your accusa-tion, Detective Sergeant.'

'I make no accusations, sir,' mutters McAvoy, looking down. 'Would you prefer it rephrasing?'

'Contrary to your Mr McKenzie's suggestion, Enid Chappell was not at HQ for a meeting or an interview. She turned up out of the blue with a trolley full of papers and demanded to see me. Me specifically. The duty sergeant tried to take some details but she wouldn't have it. Pulled out a copy of the *Hull Daily Mail* and asked for me by name.'

'You, sir?'

Slattery scowls. 'One of the questionable perks of my rank is being used as the public face of the more sensitive investiga-tions. I had that particular honour with regard to the Russian bodies, or should I say, the bodies in Russia. That was the story in the paper – the one she brandished like it was on fire. My secretary – sorry, my executive assistant – held firm. Knew I was busy. I sent Her Royal Highness to pour oil on the waters but by then this Chappell character had worked herself into such a state that even the sainted Auntie Trish couldn't calm her down. I wouldn't have remembered the incident if I hadn't spotted the mention of it in your report.'

McAvoy looks out of the window, gathering his thoughts. Wonders, for a moment, how it would feel to die here, encased in ice, senses growing numb, life slipping away, memories darkening. He focuses on Slattery's words and tries to slot them into the jumbled picture that is swirling in his mind.

'She met Tri— sorry, she met DSU Pharaoh? When was this, sir? I only filed that report an hour ago. I appreciate you coming here to talk to me about it but at this early stage it's impossible to say whether anything has any relevance.'

'I can't be held personally accountable for every crazy old duffer who turns up with a conspiracy theory, can I? I can't be everywhere . . .' Slattery sags a little.

'What was the case, sir? The article, I mean? You said Russian bodies . . .'

'Get many of them, do we, Sergeant?' snaps Slattery. 'Don't act the innocent with me, you know exactly what I'm talking about.'

'I think you were on leave, Sarge,' mutters Neilsen, from the front seat. 'Murmansk.'

McAvoy frowns. Thinks hard. A scrap of memory flutters down. A story of corpses half a century old. It was the tail end of last summer. He'd taken the family to the Western Highlands. Taken them *home*. He and Roisin and Fin and Lilah, off to stay with Grandad in the small, white-painted crofter's house that looks down from a mountainside onto the mirrored surface of Loch Ewe. It was Roisin's idea. Said that if she could patch things up with McAvoy's father then so could he. Said Lilah and Fin needed to know the land of their blood. He'd enjoyed himself, despite his reservations. It had been a good break. He'd barely even registered the story in the *Hull Daily Mail*.

'Murmansk?' asks McAvoy, squinting with concentration. 'They thought the bodies were from the *Gaul*?'

'The *Purcell*,' says Neilsen, then looks away as Slattery scowls at him for interrupting.

Memories flood in. Towering cliffs and ferocious seas. The saw-toothed edge of a distant Icelandic wilderness. A heroic bosun, lost overboard. McAvoy tries to wring more juice from the memory. Stumbles over the name. Nannatine? Ballantiner? The *Mail* revisited the tragedy every couple of years. He'd just got married, had he not? Or was it something more? A *baby*. He begins to put the pieces into a shape. Rory Ballantine. He'd just learned he was to become a father. There had been other victims. A deckhand and a cabin boy, dashed against rocks while a storm squeezed their ship.

'The Russian authorities asked for our help in identifying some bodies that washed ashore in 1970,' says McAvoy cautiously. 'The villagers who found them buried them and didn't think to tell anybody. They were a little embarrassed about it. All came to nothing though, didn't it?'

'Did it now?' asks Slattery, glancing at his phone, which is beeping on his knee. 'We did our bit right, nobody can say we didn't. A lot of meetings. An awful lot! It's sensitive, like you say.'

'It must have been very trying, sir.'

'Bloody was,' says Slattery, with a nod of something approaching gratitude. 'It doesn't need raking up.'

McAvoy turns to Neilsen, looking for help. 'Sir, there's no suggestion of raking anything up. I sent that briefing note to Acting DCI Dolan because it's important that the team be across everything. I'm learning as I go, sir. Like you say, this is a very early stage of the investigation.'

'I have enough concerns without this, McAvoy,' mutters

Slattery, his tone a little less abrupt. 'Her Majesty, swanning off without so much as a by-your-leave. The head of the Drugs Squad headhunted by the National Crime Agency for some undercover job they can't even tell us about. What do I do? Replace her? With what? Budget cuts here, budget cuts there. Things get missed. But nobody can say that we sent a little old lady home to freeze to death. Nobody.'

'And nobody is saying that, sir,' says McAvoy, beginning to understand his superior's mood. Slattery is relatively new to Humberside Police and was drafted in after an independent report kicked lumps out of Humberside Police over its 'institutional failings'. At his interview, Slattery had famously declared that he could 'do more with less', and promised to improve crime stats fast. The deadline for delivery is fast approaching, and none of his promises look likely to become reality. 'Did DSU Pharaoh get any information that may be relevant, sir? Perhaps I should speak to her directly.'

'None of that,' snaps Slattery. 'You know how it is. You might be jumping up and down desperate to know what it is she's up to but "*need-to-know*" means what it means. She's an experienced officer whose expertise has been requested for an external investigation. It's more than her job's worth to tell you what she's doing and certainly more than mine. You'll just have to make do without her.'

McAvoy watches a muscle begin to tick in his boss's cheek. You don't know where she is, he thinks. And you're worried . . .

'Your victim,' says Slattery, clearing his throat. 'You said she was a social worker. Outspoken on fishing issues. Fuck, aren't they all? I had to ask Ben to turn the radio off on the drive over. Nothing but nostalgia, all this shite about the good old days. Good old days! Six thousand men dead in a century and they talk about it like it was paradise.'

'It was an identity,' says McAvoy softly. 'They were important. They were the last of the hunters.'

'Bollocks. How do you hunt a cod? Sneak up on it? Anyway, if somebody did kill this old girl then it was probably a burglary gone wrong. Some little prick looking for a fix. I've seen it time and again. The Social Services thing probably doesn't matter, though no doubt there'll be some civil servants shitting themselves right about now. Give it a few hours and we'll all be getting phone calls from politicians looking for a bit of currency. I'll handle that side of things.'

McAvoy presses his lips together.

'I know plenty people on Road,' says Neilsen. 'They're bound to know her. They know every bugger.'

'More old duffers?' snaps Slattery. 'Tea and scones and a nice warm fire. I know your game, Neilsen. I'm going to liaise with the press office. Keep me in the loop. Regular updates but not so often that I have to keep steering you, yes? I want to know what we're dealing with. I mean, how certain are the CSIs? You said her fingertips were scratched. How do we know it isn't all just an accident? She slipped in the bath, couldn't get out, tried to escape and died from hypothermia. Very sad. Not as sad as the fact she wasn't found for a week . . .'

'We'll know more when the pathologist is able to examine her,' says McAvoy. 'Obviously with her in situ, it's hard.'

'Like carving a frozen turkey, I should imagine,' snorts Slattery. He grimaces, repelled by the thought. 'You can brief me at 4 p.m. For now, this is an unexplained death. That's all. Ben, you stay here. I'll drive myself back.' He stops. Looks at the pair of them with undisguised disdain. 'Tread lightly, Acting Detective Inspector. I don't want you upsetting the people who can help me – sorry, help us – become the police service that Humberside deserves.'

'There's no such place as Humberside,' says McAvoy, unable to stop himself. 'I can tell you about the history of the boundary changes, if it helps.'

Slattery's cheek suffers a sudden spasm and McAvoy decides

to be quiet. He climbs from the car and back into the cold air. A moment later he hears the driver's door slam and watches Slattery wriggle his bulk through the gap between the front seats. It's like watching a sofa give birth.

McAvoy and Neilsen stand side by side, watching as the big, expensive vehicle reverses back out onto the main road and glides away towards Walkington. Shivering, McAvoy turns to Neilsen, whose whole demeanour puts McAvoy in mind of a marionette with its strings cut. He's not used to seeing his handsome colleague so wrung out.

'How is she?' asks McAvoy at last.

'Mum? She's still fucking dying,' says Neilsen quietly. 'Could be now, could be tomorrow. I didn't want to leave but he said you needed me. He's the boss, I suppose. Pays to show willing.'

'You shouldn't be here,' says McAvoy. 'Your family need you.'

'She might hang on . . .'

McAvoy stares at the gates as if the flash car and its occupant might still be there. Feels something stir in his gut and realises it's something close to temper. He imagines Pharaoh is beside him, what she would say. He has to jerk himself back to alertness when he hears the low buzzing coming from Neilsen's pocket.

'Christ, can I get this?' asks Neilsen, fumbling for his phone. 'It's my sister.'

McAvoy feels the waves of cold grief drift off his friend's frame. Sees the tears in his eyes and admires his courage for letting them fall. 'Sarge, I . . .'

McAvoy nods. 'Of course.' He looks at his phone and types 'Russian bodies', 'Hull' and 'Murmansk' into Google. Like most investigating officers, it's become his go-to database. He prefers to be familiar with the public version of the truth as well as the established facts that are entered into the official police files. He clicks on a story on the *Yorkshire Post* website, dated 12

September, last year, and starts to read. It's ascribed to a 'Grace Hammond' – the moniker traditionally given to any story written by a freelance not a staff reporter.

## DID RUSSIAN VILLAGERS BURY TRAGIC HULL TRAWLERMEN?

Human remains discovered half a century ago in a remote Russian wilderness are thought to be sailors from a doomed British trawler.

Family members of those lost when the *Blake Purcell* was lost in January 1970 have been asked to provide DNA samples after Russian authorities admitted that two bodies were found decades ago.

It was initially thought that the bodies might belong to the *Gaul*, which sank in 1974 during a fierce storm off the coast of Norway with the loss of her thirty-six-man crew.

But tattoos on the body of one of the victims indicate that the men may be from the *Blake Purcell*. Michael Timpson, Rory Ballantine and William Godson were lost in bad weather off Iceland's Skagi Peninsula. The *Blake Purcell* sank after the remaining crew were rescued.

Area Commander David Slattery of Humberside Police said: 'This is a very sensitive situation and compassion has been uppermost in our minds while approaching family members. I admire the way those affected have dealt with this challenging and unexpected development.'

A police press release revealed that the remains were found on the Rybachy Peninsula in the Murmansk region of Russia. It is understood that a local custom was to use rocks to cover the bodies of unknown seafarers, because freezing conditions meant it was impossible to dig proper graves.

Bosun Rory Ballantine had just discovered that his wife was expecting their first child when tragedy struck. His son,

Stephen, is now a successful Hull businessman who has invested heavily in local good causes to honour his father and his lost comrades.

He said last night: 'It's a strange feeling. Part of me wants to know if he really has been lying there all this time – that he was treated decently by men who understood the sea. The other part of me likes the mystery of not knowing. Without a body you always have that whiff of hope. I've tried to measure up to my dad all my life and I've always felt him watching me. This has really come as a shock.'

It is not clear why the discovery was not reported at the time. The Foreign and Commonwealth Office were only told about the remains in July 2012 and have been awaiting a 'suitable opportunity' to begin further inquiries.

McAvoy looks up from the article. Neilsen is talking to Parekh, their body language suggesting a burgeoning intimacy. McAvoy fancies he can see her blushing even through the plastic oversuit. He flicks on to the next article, printed on 23 October.

## POLICE DEFEND 'INSENSITIVE' TACTICS AS DNA TESTS PROVE INCONCLUSIVE

Russian authorities have been accused of orchestrating a cover-up that has heaped fresh grief on the families of Hull fishermen lost at sea almost half a century ago.

Police have revealed that DNA tests performed on bodies found in a remote coastal region of Russia have proven they are not members of the crew of the Hull trawler *Blake Purcell*, which sank in 1970.

The development has left the families of those lost at sea 'devastated' – and there are now calls for the tests to be repeated by British authorities.

Humberside Police had been led to believe that tattoos visible on two bodies suggested they could be fishermen from Hull. Officers had already taken DNA samples from blood relatives of the three men lost off the Skagi Peninsula in Iceland in bad weather.

But senior officers have now revealed that the tests performed by Russian authorities show the remains 'most likely belong to the Northern Russian or Finno-Ugric population'. Police officers had been preparing to travel to assist in the investigation but the force now says that the news from Russia concludes their involvement in the matter.

Sylvia Lyons, 53, had hoped that the tests would conclusively identify the body of her father, deckhand Michael Timpson.

She said: 'I'm devastated and I'm sure the other families are too. It's dragged it all back up again. Why did the police come and get our hopes up? They had me and my two brothers spit into a tube for a DNA match. I don't know what to believe. What if the whole thing is a cover-up? It was like a murder inquiry. Now it turns out it was all for nothing. I don't even remember my dad but his death broke all our hearts.'

Businessman Stephen Ballantine, whose father Rory perished while trying to save teenage crewmate William Godson, said: 'I understand the police have a difficult job. It was the Foreign and Commonwealth Office that pushed it their way and now they have to pick up the pieces. I gave a sample and obviously hoped we would get answers. Now it seems we're back to guessing. It's hit my mother very hard. Without a body you never know how to grieve. She always had this fantasy that one day he would just walk back through the door – that maybe he'd been in some Russian gulag or living a whole other life with some Russian family.'

Area Commander Slattery said: 'We thought long and hard.'

McAvoy jerks his head up at the sound of his name. Parekh is waving him over, angling her tablet to show Neilsen what is happening in the bathroom: huge great metal heaters glowing amber and gold, melting the pack ice that encases Mrs Chappell; a uniformed CSI scooping up the melting ice with large beakers while another takes photographs. McAvoy sees Neilsen stiffen, a sudden rictus gripping him as he stares at the sugarpink corpse. He turns to McAvoy, who crunches across the icy gravel to where his colleagues stand.

'Ben?'

'Look, Sarge,' he says, and it sounds as if his throat is being stepped on. 'Her hands . . .'

McAvoy stares at the screen. Mrs Chappell's fingers are slowly emerging from the ice; the ribs of a sunken galleon exposed by a retreating tide. They stick out at grotesque angles, dislocated and twisted. Somebody has held her old, arthritic fingers, and pulled them clean from their sockets. Somebody has hurt her in a way that McAvoy knows he could not have endured.

He turns to Parekh, who has pulled down her face mask. She swallows, but it doesn't change the expression of revulsion that fills her features.

'She couldn't pull herself out,' says McAvoy softly. 'Couldn't grip the sides.'

'Every resource,' says Parekh, her face taking on a hard look. 'First priority.'

She turns away, muttering. McAvoy barely hears the words that emerge from behind gritted teeth.

*'When you catch him, make sure you hurt him.'*

# 9

*Dog Kennel Lane, Beverley*
*2.57 p.m.*

Neilsen's hands lie splayed on his thighs. His fingers are bent at the top knuckle, his nails pressing through the material of his trousers into the skin of his legs. His shoulders are stiff, his eyes hooded. He sits motionless in the passenger seat, glaring through the fogged-up windscreen, an intensity to his gaze that suggests he is trying to melt the frost from the road.

'Okay, Ben?'

'Fucking peachy.'

It looks to McAvoy as if his colleague has pulled on his suit jacket without removing it from the hanger. McAvoy wishes he could think of something to say to him.

'Coffee?'

Neilsen swivels his eyes. 'Eh?'

'There's a machine in the shop at the village,' says McAvoy, trying again. 'And it'll save uniform a job if we pop in and leave a card or two. There's always a nugget of gossip if you keep your ears open in the queue. I think they do sandwiches.'

'I'm not bothered.'

McAvoy waits for more. Nothing comes. He feels horribly uncomfortable, cold in his belly and fiery hot in his cheeks. It is normally he who prefers silence. He's aware of his reputation for being self-conscious in company. Pharaoh takes the piss out of him for it regularly, telling him that she feels like she is chauffeuring a hideously malformed crash-test dummy whenever he squeezes himself into the passenger seat of her little sports car.

'Do you know Stephen Ballantine?' he asks.

'I know the name,' mutters Neilsen. 'Ask Dad. Get him on the right wavelength, he knows everybody.'

McAvoy doesn't like the quality of the silence in the vehicle. 'You've told your sister you're on your way?'

'Yeah. I'm in trouble for leaving.'

'What's the, um . . . I mean, how long . . .?'

'Today, she thinks,' murmurs Neilsen abruptly, his teeth locked. 'Fading. But they said she was fading a week ago. They should switch the machine off . . . what's she staying for? And Dad's having to live it over and bloody over.' He falls into silence. Shakes his head.

McAvoy concentrates on the road. Hears the vibrations of messages into his inbox as the vehicle crests a slight incline and picks up a 4G signal. His cheeks feel warm enough to stir-fry beef.

'She's still hanging in there,' adds Neilsen, glancing at his phone. 'We can take the scenic route, right enough. Is it better if I'm holding her hand at the last?' He smears the heel of his hand across his nose and cheek. 'I don't even know what I want to happen.'

McAvoy stays quiet, unwilling to make things worse by offering an opinion. He indicates left, turning off the desolate country road and slipping down to second gear as the tyres do battle with a sheet of slick ice. He hears gravel ping and pop against the panels and windscreen, a hail of grit shooting up to strike the underside of the car. The gritters were out early. He makes a mental note to get in touch with the council, find out which crews were on this bleak patch of country road over the last few days. He's already spoken to the uniformed inspector about placing officers at either end of the stretch of road outside

94

Mrs Chappell's property. It would be a huge help to take a name, number and witness statement from every commuter who cruised past the house over the past few days. The inspector claimed there was insufficient manpower. Told him to put up a sign asking witnesses to come forward. He'd thanked her for the advice and sighed.

'When do you think it will thaw?' asks McAvoy, aware that he has now scraped through the bottom of the conversational barrel and into the gunge beneath.

'Sorry, Sarge?'

'The big freeze,' he says, nodding at the sparkling road and the ice and cloud that appear and disappear beneath the headlights of the car. He sits up straighter in the seat, his hair touching the roof of the car, looking into the gloom for potential dangers. Deer live in the little copses of woodland to the left and right. It's a popular spot with dog-walkers and twitchers. He's passed the gates to two farmhouses already. He knows how easily a moment's loss of concentration can snuff out a life.

'Thought you'd like this,' says Neilsen. 'Remind you of home.'

'Home? I live in Hessle.'

'Proper home,' says Neilsen.

'Scotland, you mean?' asks McAvoy, surprised. 'It wasn't like this.' He raises a hand from the wheel and gestures at the stark landscape. He gives a little shrug. 'Maybe it was. I probably remember it differently to how it was.'

'Think you'll ever move back?'

'Back? I left when I was ten. I stopped being a local a long time ago. I haven't really been local anywhere since.'

Neilsen seems to consider this. 'Maybe that's why you're a good copper,' he says. 'You see things as an outsider. You're not blinded by familiarity.' He seems about to say more. Bites his lip.

'Familiarity?'

A flash of temper shows in Neilsen's face. 'I grew up with it,' he says bitterly. 'Fishing. Trawling. Hessle bloody Road. All that City of Culture bullshit celebrating these working-class heroes. It made me sick. Try growing up in a fishing family when there's no fishing industry any more. It left the men empty, you understand that, right? You think it's hard for a footballer to readjust when their career on the pitch is over? That's nothing compared to a trawlerman having to deal with a life on land. They were rock stars, that's the thing of it. Fabulous tailored suits and Teddy boy quiffs, a fortune in their pockets and less than three days to spend it. They worked and they fought and they watched their mates get swallowed by the ocean because it was what they knew and somebody had to fucking do it and it might as well be them. How do you take that attitude into a job as a security guard or a sofa salesman or whatever? How do you teach your kids the right way to live when all you know is how to scrape by and stay alive? And the wives . . . Have you been on one of the Facebook groups? Good Old Hessle Road? All these pictures and photos and memories. All this do-you-remember Dillinger riding a horse into Rayner's and has anybody got a photo of Doris Forrest's Hair Salon for me mam? Some days I understand it – that nostalgia for a time that made sense. Other times it feels like watching a widow cry for the husband who used to beat her up and fuck her sister.'

Neilsen jerks in his seat, lunging forward sharply and scrabbling about in the footwell, retrieving his laptop from the slim leather case at his feet. He opens it up and keys in his password.

'The bodies in Murmansk,' says McAvoy. 'I need to know more than what I can half remember from a newspaper article.'

'Do you?' asks Neilsen. 'I thought Slattery made it pretty clear—'

'Look, Ben, if we join the dots, what have we got? Our victim visits the police brandishing a story about the bodies of fishermen from Hull turning up in Russia. Today, a senior officer belts across East Yorkshire to speak to the investigating officer as soon as he hears about that particular line of inquiry? It doesn't feel right; there's something there.'

'You just didn't like how he spoke about the boss,' says Neilsen, giving a little smile.

McAvoy ignores it. Concentrates on driving. 'The Blake line,' he says at last. 'The ships in the bottles on her windowsill. The patch of frozen water. Thirteen seems an odd number.'

'Thirteen is a bloody odd number,' mutters Neilsen. 'But yes, it is. Superstitions and all that.'

Neilsen fiddles with his expensive computer. Pulls up the images of the living room and zooms in on the nameplates. '*Gamecock. Sidewinder. Freezer.*' He mutters to himself and his hands blur over the keys. 'Blake fleet. Founded in 1876. Different vessels, different classes. Sold in 1997 to a local entrepreneur. There're some links to some business stories about it. I'll have a look at them when we're stopped. Here we are: the ones in the bottles commemorate the Blake ships launched post-war. All named after different composers. *Elgar, Britten, Holst. Pur—*' He stops himself. 'No, that's not there. If she's smashed one, that's it. The *Blake Purcell.* Which places us back with the bodies in Russia. Relevant, do you think? Old people are clumsy, especially the ones with arthritis. I'm not raining on your parade, Sarge, but if you're suggesting Russian spies and secret cover-ups then you're on your own. I don't look good in a hazmat suit.'

McAvoy realises he has been sitting at the junction for over a minute, the indicator ticking like a clock. He moves forward, steering towards the village. 'It's just odd,' he mumbles, wishing he'd stayed quiet. 'Having breakfast, dressed in her nightie, eating her toast. Last confirmed sighting of her alive is 1 January. If the radiators were turned down and the windows opened up on 2 January, then the bottle must have been smashed that day. The water was frozen into the carpet. But where's the glass?

And for that matter, where's her post? We've got some envelopes from the pile that's arrived over the past few days but other stuff you'd expect to find seems to be missing. Her recycling, for instance. It's like somebody has gathered up armfuls of things and left others untouched. Like they were in a rush. But the presence of the chair suggests somebody took their time. And her fingers . . .' He trails off, shaking his head. 'Somebody watched. Hurt her . . .'

Neilsen isn't listening. He's reading the words on the screen. Shaking his head and pursing his lips. 'Fucking ghouls.'

'Sorry?'

'I look after my mum's Facebook account,' he says. 'She's not well enough but she used to like seeing the pictures. Sharing memories. She's had half a dozen posts on her profile from people "sending love".' His voice drips with contempt, his face sneering in a way McAvoy has never witnessed. 'They're ghouls. Just wanting to see if she's kicked the bucket yet.'

'That's not fair,' says McAvoy, unable to help himself. 'She mattered to people. They want her to know that.'

'Good funerals, the Hessle Roaders,' spits Neilsen. 'Always a decent spread. More triangular sandwiches than you can shake a stick at. Chicken legs and vol-au-vents and all the old boys up dancing. Some eighty-year-old auntie singing *Croce-di-Oro* . . .'

'Cross of Gold?'

'Bloody anthem,' mutters Neilsen. 'Bit of Jim Reeves no doubt. People crying and holding hands and saying they wish they'd never moved off Road. They scatter the ashes off the bullnose sometimes. Toss your mortal remains into the one thing you spent your whole life praying would never rob you of those you loved. You been up there recently? The retail park at St Andrew's Dock? It's a waste ground. Looks like a shit-filled back garden languishing behind a nice new house. You should hear my dad go on about it – that's when he remembers what he's angry about.'

Neilsen stops, seemingly too tired and angry to bother any further. He stares at the screen. Taps half-heartedly at some of the messages. 'I wish I knew what I bloody felt.'

'Feel sad,' says McAvoy, as gently as he can. 'Feel angry. There are no right or wrong feelings.'

'Are there not? What if you feel the urge to break into an old woman's house, break her fingers and stick her in a bath full of ice?' He glowers at the road. 'What would make a person do that? What could she have done to deserve that?'

'Maybe it's not about "deserving",' mutters McAvoy. 'Perhaps this was simply how her killer got their kicks.'

Neilsen looks at him accusingly. 'You don't mean that. I can see it in your face. You don't think this is random. Whoever did this, they did it to her. Specifically.'

McAvoy watches the lights dance on the road. Thinks about the letters scribbled in the crossword puzzle. Thinks of ships in bottles and butchered birds.

'Call Sophie,' he says. 'I want to know about her career. About the cases she handled. The people who made threats when she was a social worker. It's a job that provokes hatred. A very personal hatred. She was looking into something that mattered to her. We don't know if it was the bodies in Russia or simply that she saw Slattery's name in the paper and decided he was worth talking to. She met the boss, Ben. I want to know what they said.'

'Bugger Slattery,' suggests Neilsen. 'Call her. She'll answer for you.'

McAvoy watches the road. Feels the weight of his phone in his pocket and wants nothing more than to ring Trish Pharaoh and ask if he's doing things right.

He watches the purple sky fade to black.

Shivers, as at the touch of cold bones.

# 10

*Main Street, Cherry Burton*
*3.36 p.m.*

Cherry Burton isn't much more than a high street with a few little roads leading off: stitches across a rip. There's money here. Big houses and fancy cars; ultra-modern bungalows squatting incongruously among big, black-bricked Edwardian statement homes.

McAvoy brings the people-carrier to a precarious halt outside the little shop on the main road. He's parked behind an old-fashioned Land-Rover, the stickers in its rear window so ancient that they still advertise a car showroom with an old dialling code. A tall figure with bushy hair is sitting in the driver's seat, the engine still running.

'I'll get the drinks,' says McAvoy, grateful to exit the car.

'Sure,' mumbles Neilsen, not looking up. He's lost in the words and pictures that flicker on the screen.

McAvoy's about to close the door when a thought occurs. 'The Facebook sites you mentioned. The Hessle Roaders and the nostalgia groups. Could you search for Enid?'

'Sarge?' asks Neilsen, lifting his gaze from the screen.

'Any mention – by her, about her. I doubt you'll strike lucky first time but you're a bloody wizard on that thing. You can ask Sophie to help, though you run the risk of having your ear chewed off. Just work through the keywords. Try a few variations.'

Neilsen frowns. 'We know Enid wasn't Facebook-savvy. There was no computer.'

'Aye, and no phone,' says McAvoy. 'But we know she had one from the bills, don't we? Mr McKenzie implied she wasn't your typical old lady.'

Neilsen gives a tight smile. His fingers skitter over the keys, images reflecting on the cold, grey canvas of his face.

'No profile,' he says quickly. 'Loads of mentions of a Chappell but that's from posts about the Fishermen's Bethel on Road. I'll have a play, see what pops up.'

McAvoy nods his thanks. He heads into the shop, his hair fluttering as the ceiling-mounted heaters blast him with warm air. He ambles around the shelves, browsing biscuits, crisps, reading the ingredients in packet soups. He doesn't want anything. Doesn't need anything. He's happy to let Neilsen take his time. He finds himself by the newspaper rack. Looks at the titles on offer and decides he would rather go back and read the cup-a-soups. Eventually he picks up a copy of the *Bygones* publication. It comes out once a month: a flimsy collection of old photographs from the *Hull Mail* archive, held together by captions and filler copy that could be boiled down to questions like 'remember this?' and 'weren't it grand?'.

'They're for sale, y'know,' comes a voice behind him. 'You don't have to read it here.'

McAvoy turns. A small, elderly man in a cardigan and dangerously sensible waterproof coat is glaring at him.

'Sorry,' mutters McAvoy. 'I'm not sure . . .'

'I'm trying to get my *Telegraph*,' grumbles the man, nudging McAvoy aside with a jointy arm. 'Evening edition of the *Mail* isn't in yet, either,' he says, tutting. 'Used to get it delivered but of course they can't find the youngsters to do it any more, can they? Idle beggars. Nobody wants to work any more. I asked one little beggar to pick his crisp packet out of my hedge and all I got was abuse. The mouths on them! If I were twenty years younger I'd have thrashed the skin off their backs.'

McAvoy glances towards the counter, seeking support. Behind the till, a round-shouldered, middle-aged woman with a tight perm is busying herself with the vital task of ensuring that all the chewing gum packets face the same way. She looks as though she will continue to do so long after McAvoy and his interrogator have left the shop. He's on his own.

'Oh that's just the last straw,' says the man, face falling, as he looks at the clear plastic tray where the last *Daily Telegraph* used to sit. 'Why don't they ever order enough?'

McAvoy isn't sure he has had the training to answer such a difficult question. He gives the man a once-over. Mid-seventies and ruddy-faced. He looks as though he spends a lot of time writing to newspapers. McAvoy has him pegged as the sort who would like to see the return of National Service and the birch.

He's saved by a sudden gust of wind, accompanied a moment later by the jingling of the bell above the door. He glances towards the entrance. A tall, bushy-haired man in a waxed jacket is closing the door behind him, stamping the snow and dirt off his walking boots.

'Ah,' says the *Telegraph* reader, looking suddenly pleased. 'Vicar! I wanted to talk to you about the issues by the duck pond of an evening. Those youngsters, they make such a racket and I'm sure I smelled furniture polish when I went out to complain. I'm told they use it to get high. Honestly, I ask you.'

The tall man turns to meet Mr Telegraph, exposing the white dog-collar that fastens across his black shirt. He looks to be in his mid-forties. He's wearing a V-neck sweater which strains over an amply upholstered stomach. He closes his eyes for a moment too long as he recognises the small chap marching towards him with all the righteous indignation of a Brit on holiday who'll be damned if they'll pay three euros for a cup of tea that hasn't even been made properly.

'Mr Norman,' he says, a tinge of Ulster in his accent. 'Could we possibly pick this up at a later date? I'm needed.'

'I won't take any more of your time than I have to,' says Mr Norman, waving away the vicar's objections. 'I'm sure you have to go and give one of your talks about hugging drug dealers and giving our leftovers to muggers but this is bloody important.'

McAvoy realises he is still holding the copy of *Bygones*. He flicks through it, not really taking anything in. Looks at a picture of a bearded mayor with his arm around two teenage gymnasts, each holding medals and looking slightly uncomfortable; long socks and scraped-back hair. The caption says the image was taken in 1984. Different times, thinks McAvoy sadly, and puts the magazine back in the rack.

'Honestly, Mr Norman, it's not a good day,' says the vicar. 'I presume you won't have heard.'

'Heard what?' asks Mr Norman, exasperated. He looks at the vicar suspiciously.

'Mrs Chappell,' he says quietly. 'There's been an accident.'

'Tripped over a chicken, has she?' asks Mr Norman, chortling. 'That'll be interesting. Hard to be so bloody pious about animal rights when you're flat on your back with a hen pecking at your eyeball. Ice, was it? Broken hip?'

'She's dead,' says the vicar, without emotion. He looks past Mr Norman, concentrating on nothing. 'Slipped in the bath.'

Mr Norman narrows his eyes, clearly confused. 'Mrs Chappell? Sanctimonious sod? Wouldn't listen to a damn word the parish council had to say about the state of her grass verges or the chickens on the road? What do you mean she's dead? She can't be dead. She doesn't seem the sort.'

'I'm not sure there's another way to put it,' says the vicar wearily. 'I took a call from a parishioner and there's no mistake.'

The door clangs open again and the vicar moves to allow a

woman with red hair, glasses and bright pink cheeks to shiver her way into the shop. She's dressed for an Arctic winter in fleece, parka and padded ski jacket.

'Darryl,' she says, locking eyes with the vicar. 'Did you hear? Mrs Chappell. Isn't it dreadful?'

McAvoy busies himself gazing at the newspaper, trying not to seem as if he is listening. The lady behind the counter finally looks up and moves to the area by the till, raising her eyebrows, hungry for gossip.

'Did I hear you right? What's happened to Mrs Chappell?'

'Dead,' says Mr Norman, suddenly an expert. 'Well, blow me down. I know we didn't see eye to eye, but—'

'I heard there's more to it,' says the fresh-faced woman, nudging the others further into the shop. 'Police up there by the dozen. You know Karen in the house with the apple trees? She heard it from her sister's friend who works in the offices at East Riding Council and apparently they're all in a big panic. A fall, the way I heard it, but you don't know, do you? We had those lawnmower thefts in July and she did go off on her travels now and again. Could have been there for days.'

'You know how she was,' says the shopkeeper, and seems as if she would like to cross herself for taking pleasure in such ghastly tidings. 'So independent! She didn't like people knocking on her door. And she wasn't the lonely sort. I saw her in the Light Dragoon on Boxing Day having a right good chinwag with some ne'er-do-well . . .'

'It's best not to jump the gun,' says the vicar, patting at the air. 'It's a tragedy, no matter any disagreements any of us may have had.'

Mr Norman shoots him a glare. 'I don't hold with all this pretending that somebody is a saint just because they've died. She was a pain in the neck. A right do-gooder.'

'That's a very peculiar insult, Mr Norman.'

'You know what I mean. Bleeding heart. Always rattling a

104

collection tin under your nose. No doubt the fishing lot will be seeing who can buy the biggest wreath.'

'I heard her on the radio once.'

'No doubt, no doubt. Couldn't keep her hands off a good cause.'

'I've still got her magazine,' says the shopkeeper, taking a sharp breath, as if this is one injustice too many. 'Doubt anybody else will want it.'

'You don't think it's something more grisly, do you?' asks the fresh-faced lady. 'Couldn't be, you know, *on purpose*, could it? Last time we spoke was in the library. Before Christmas, certainly. She said she was spending it with a friend. No plans for New Year but she was hoping to get away soon. We chatted for a bit. Then her friend came back.'

'Never short of friends, that one,' chimes in Mr Norman. 'Bleeding hearts.'

'You should be a detective, memory like that,' says the shopkeeper, clearly trying to lighten the mood. She moves to the far end of the till, rummaging behind the shelves. She straightens up, holding a glossy magazine, and flicks through it, shuddering. The publication is bright blue with yellow writing on the cover and a series of lustrous coloured pictures.

McAvoy recognises two of the cover stars as serial killers. He knows this publication. He featured in it once.

'Not exactly bedtime reading, is it? Do you think she was writing a book? Research at the library, crime magazines, that rude bugger with the stick . . .'

'Oh, that sounds like her friend from the library right enough. Old chap. Didn't look well.'

'Not the chap from the Light Dragoon, then. He looked fit as a fiddle, swanky sod. Sorry vicar, excuse my French . . .'

'This friend from the library,' says the vicar. 'The police might want to know who he was. Could you describe him, June?'

'Oh, I don't want any of that,' says the shopkeeper, shivering. 'I'm not one for gossip. But I can picture him clear as a bell. Nasty bugger. Came in to collect a parcel for her a few weeks back. Didn't have the delivery card or any ID and I wouldn't let him have it. They're the rules. He played merry hell with me. He phoned her, right in front of me – put her on to me so she could say it was okay. I didn't like the look of him.'

'You really should tell the police,' says the vicar solemnly. 'What can you remember about him?'

'Old,' muses June. 'Not ancient, but a bit, y'know, careworn. He had a stick. A walking stick with loads of badges on it. I remember because he kept banging it on the floor when he was talking to me and I felt bad that he'd had to walk at all when he was obviously not in the best of health. I said that to Mrs Chappell.'

McAvoy glances at his phone. There's a message from Ben, wondering if he has been kidnapped, and three screengrabs of a message thread, starting on 13 December 2011, on the Good Ol' Hessle Road Facebook group.

Jackie Morris Thanks so much for letting me join your group. My dad was a fisherman who grew up on Hessle Road. He sailed with the Boyd Line for much of his career. He died in 1992 when I was still only young and I would like to know more about him. Him and my mum were on poor terms so I have nobody to ask. His name was Joseph Roskilly. The only story I can find in the newspaper archives is about an incident on a ship called the Persil in 1970. I would love to know more about it. Thanks. xxx

Gary Hendricks I remember Joe well. A lovely family. His mam went to bingo with my mam. He was pals with Rory B and his gang. You're right about the incident on the Percell. Rory and Cowboy Mick (can't remember last name) were lost in heavy seas off Skagi. I think a deckhand went down too. I have a picture of them all somewhere, having a drink in the Criterion. Proper rum bunch but salt of the earth. I sailed with them all in '67 and they were Trojans for work. It was tragic to lose Rory. His missus was pregnant with twins at the time. Anybody else remember when those Skrobs set up the arm-wrestling match in the hospital at Isafjordur? That bloke was the size of a mountain but Big Gerard snapped his wrist and he cried like a girl. Those were the days. Sorry to hear about your dad. X

Christina Merry Oh my goodness, my head is full of images of those buggers! Rory and Gerard were unholy terrors but their hearts were always in the right place. Here's a memory that will put a smile on your faces. There was a family on Westcott Street who fostered children and never had enough money to go around and Rory and Gerard would always be dipping into their pockets to pay for them to have days out here and there or get new clothes. And they didn't like people who were bullies to their kids or their wives. Maybe I shouldn't say it on here but does anybody else remember Big Gerard nailing that bloke's hand to the lock gates after he broke that bain's arm? He was hanging up there and crying like nobody's business and there wasn't a soul would help him down. Some of the bobbers took pity on him in the end. I remember the lady from the social saying that the pair of them thought they were Butch and Sundance but maybe that was a time for cowboys, eh? Sorry to hear about Joe. He was a good-looking lad.

Napper Acklam It wasn't just Gerard nailed that bastard to the lock gates. I held his legs so he'd stop kicking! That's shitty about Joe. He was a grumpy bastard but he was a hard worker. Lost touch after he left the area but sounds like he made a decent age. Nearly met his maker plenty times back in the day. I still owe him a pint or two for what happened on the BP. It were him and Alf that stopped me going the same way as Rory and Mick and young Billy. Pulled me out by my hair, which I didn't thank him for at the time! Raise a glass to his memory for me.

Gary Hendricks Those were the days, eh Napper? Surprised you're still around, you old bugger. Heard you'd got yourself all civilised. You've got me remembering now! What were that young lad's name who went over off Skagi?

Napper Acklam Civilised? That'll be the day. Drop me a line Gary, we might need a bit of extra help getting the Holst ship-shape, if you can still wield a blowtorch.

Calvin Deverill You're right, Gary – the deckie learner was lost too. It were proper tragic. He'd been through some hard times before he came to Hull. I remember the lady from the social asked Rory and Gerard to look out for him. Anybody remember her? She drove a blue and cream bus and looked like a film star. Big pals with Mags Lowery. Mags B, as we knew her. She knew your dad too.

Stuart Highsmith The social lady is still around. Still kicking arse. I saw her on a documentary about Bransholme years ago but she crops up now and again on the radio and in the paper, talking about politics and stuff. Can't have been an easy job, coming to take your bains away. I heard she had that campervan so the kids could sleep on the journey to wherever she was taking them. Wasn't her decision who got taken – she was just doing her job. She used to get her hair done at Nadine's, I think.

Amanda Mongos Hi, this is Amanda from Radio Humberside. Jackie Morris . . . am so sorry to hear of your loss. I interviewed one of the survivors from the Blake Purcell incident a couple of years ago. I'll try and find the audio file and see if there is anything that can help. The 'lady from the social' sometimes volunteers in the Help the Aged shop in Beverley where I'm always popping in to look for books. Her name is Enid Chapel. She might have some memories to share. xx

Amanda Mongos Sorry I've been so long in reply Jackie. I've lost that audio I'm afraid but I know a journalist who may have covered the incident at the time. I'll try and dig out his details and ask him to get in touch, if that's okay. Sorry about Joe. I've seen his photo and he was a good-looking chap. Will DM you. Xx

McAvoy looks up at the sound of a cough – the sort of cough that demands an answer. 'Will you be wanting anything else?' asks June pointedly.

'Detective Sergeant McAvoy,' he says softly. He fishes inside his jacket for his lanyard. Shows it to the chorus of surprised faces, mouths opening. 'Shall we start all that again?'

# 11

*Skagastrond, Iceland*
*4.37 p.m.*

'Have you fed him?' asks Pharaoh without enthusiasm.

'Who?'

'The goldfish, obviously,' she says, a smile threatening the corners of her mouth.

'Oh, I thought you meant Dad.'

'Your dad? You can eat him, love.'

On the laptop screen, Sophia Pharaoh gives her mother a mischievous look. She looks like her mum. Dark hair, blue eyes and tanned skin, though she does her best to cover her complexion with a pale foundation so as to better emphasise her thick black eye make-up. She has a stud in her upper lip and two rings in her eyebrow. Her dreadlocked hair tangles in her dangly silver earrings, all skulls and crosses, and the message on her vest top, visible beneath an open black hoodie, is an instruction for 'haters' to 'go fuck themselves', which her mother considers sound advice.

'Is it cold?' asks Sophia. Behind her, Pharaoh's other three daughters are pretending to be perfect children; heads stopped over homework. Pharaoh knows that as soon as the laptop closes they will go back to their pillow-fight tournament. Pharaoh's money is on her youngest, Amber. She's been known to pad her pillow with a tin of beans.

'Cold?' asks Pharaoh. 'Iceland? No, it's bloody toasty.'

'Do you miss us?' asks Sophia, raising her mug of hot choc-olate to her mouth. A melted marshmallow leaves a creamy splodge on the tip of her nose and Pharaoh feels her heart lurch at the thought of her daughter out there in the world. She loves her so much she's tempted to lock her in a cellar until she dies.

'Miss you loads, love. And those other sods pretending to be angels behind you. How's everything else?'

Sophia rolls her eyes. 'Ro phoned just before you did. We're fed and watered. There'll be baths and bed. No scary movies and no ultimate fighting championships. I told you, I can cope. I'm not a baby any more.'

Pharaoh nods, declining to tell her daughter about the marsh-mallow on her face or the smudge of chocolate on her lips. Behind her, Amber throws her hands in the air, devastated that there will be no mixed martial arts taking place in the living room after they've all pretended to finish their homework.

'I'm just a call away,' says Pharaoh. She wants to reach into the phone and hug her children. They all seem so far away. 'Oh, and Soph, if you speak to Roisin again tonight, keep your lips closed about where I am, yes? Hush-hush, and all that . . .'

'You already said.' Sophia smiles. 'Any message for Aector?'

'Why would there be a message for Hector?' asks Pharaoh, bristling.

'Because he's your mate,' says Sophia sweetly, and Pharaoh feels a sudden heat prickling in her cheeks. 'I doubt he'll call, anyway. Busy with something out Beverley way, I think. Did you hear?'

Pharaoh curses as the picture on the screen freezes: Sophia motionless, eyes half closed, lip drooping as if pulled down by the silver stud. Pharaoh looks at the message on the screen, urging her to rate the quality of the call out of five. She stabs a solitary star into the box and tosses her phone onto the sofa.

She stares up at the ceiling for a while. A patch of coffee-coloured damp is spreading out from the apex of the front window and the near wall. She tries to make a picture out of it; to let it form a shape, cloud-like, in her imagination. A dragon, maybe? A bird? The ruffled edges could be wing-tips, she decides; the mottled patterns a feathered breast. She becomes aware of herself. Feels a moment's embarrassment at being, as her grandfather used to put it, off in fucking la-la land.

She pulls her reports towards her.

'Roberta Ballantine,' she says, under her breath, and drains her glass. 'What on earth happened to you, eh?'

She spends the next half an hour reading through witness statements from the night that Roberta disappeared. Begrudgingly, she starts to realise that the reason Chandler's article was so short on actual facts was because the investigation was lacklustre at best, and dangerously incompetent at worst.

She looks again at the report at the top of the scroll: a pitiful summation of all efforts made by the investigating officers in the twelve months after Roberta was reported missing. The officer in nominal charge was a Detective Inspector Richard Peach. Pharaoh didn't know the name when she started reading. Now she's unlikely to forget it. She feels a desire to track him down and headbutt him in the throat.

```
medical records are incomplete . . . efforts
made by DC Burkeman to secure psychiatric
files from earlier sectioning under the
Mental  Health  Act  had  proven  fruit-
less . . . admission and initial assessment
during hospitalisation for septicaemia in
1981 show high levels of drug dependency
and sexual trauma consistent with having
```

worked as a street prostitute, for which
she was arrested several times . . .

Pharaoh opens up an email and pings a message across to a
former colleague now working as a DI with the National Crime
Agency. Helen Tremberg owes her plenty of favours and now
seems a good time to call one in. Tremberg responds almost
immediately. Tells her she'll do what she can.

Reassured, Pharaoh scans the rest of the document. There's
a list of witness statements at the bottom of the briefing note.
Among those who gave a statement was one Bernard Acklam,
identified by DCI Peach as a 'person of interest' with an exten-
sive criminal record. Pharaoh skims through the file until she
finds Acklam's witness statement. It's short and does not seem
to have been given with much enthusiasm.

I know the family from years back. I fished with Rory
Ballantine, Roberta Ballantine's brother. After Rory's
death at sea in 1970, I have stayed in close contact
with the family and I suppose you could say that I
became something of a surrogate father to his children. I always tried to do my best by Roberta but she
was a troubled person and had lots of problems after
Rory's death. I know she struggled with drug addiction. A lot of people tried to help her and it did seem
like she was getting herself back together.

On the night she was last seen, I had been drinking
with three former crewmates in the Vauxhall Tavern. I
think we may have gone on to other pubs as well but
I had a lot to drink and don't remember much. I was
informed the following day that Roberta Ballantine had
been in the Star and Garter until around 10 p.m. and
then left the pub and headed down Division Road
towards the docks. I have no reason to believe any

harm has come to her and a drinker who overheard her talking with an old schoolfriend, Jean Tatler, said that Roberta had been talking about a fresh start. I presume she has moved back to London. As for the coat and the blood, that could be anybody's. Yes, I do own a part share in that ice factory but it has been derelict for some time. As far as I am aware, the coat used to belong to Rory's wife, Margaret Lowery. It was given to Roberta as a gift but I don't know if she ever wore it or how it came to be at my premises.

Pharaoh flicks through the remaining statements. There's none from any Jean Tatler. The crewmates mentioned by Acklam all say the same thing. They were drinking, didn't see Roberta, and believed she had returned to London to make a fresh start.

Pharaoh feels her eyes start to close. Her thoughts are a rumbling hiss in the centre of her skull; waves disturbing a shingle beach. She shakes her head, angry with the world in general and lazy, judgemental, *can't-be-arsed-to-do-the-job-properly* wankers in particular. She adds Peach's name to the mental list of people that she intends to put up against a wall come the revolution. She's starting to think she will run out of bullets before she runs out of people deserving one.

Drowsily she reaches for her cigarettes and knocks over her wine glass. It rolls off the coffee table and onto the floor, landing by the leather satchel at her feet. She reaches down and picks up the glass before the smudge of red wine can trickle over the lip of the glass and stain the contents of the bag. She pulls out the buff folder from within. Swallows painfully, and opens the thin file.

She looks at the picture on the opening page.

Two bodies, bleached bone-white. Scraps of skin cling to brittle ribs: a broken arm jutting out from beneath a pile of stones, tattered ribbons of clothing patterning faded flesh. The picture was taken in Murmansk in 2012 when the Russian authorities were first informed about the bodies of the English sailors buried beneath the stones. Humberside Police had been tasked with helping the Foreign Office procure DNA samples from blood relatives of men lost at sea in the thirty-six-month period before 1970, when the villagers in Murmansk had found them. It had been a big task and Pharaoh was grateful not to have been a part of it. Barely gave it any thought at all until she was asked to go and mollify an angry old lady who was standing in the reception of Clough Road police station and demanding that Area Commander Slattery come and listen to what she had to say.

Pharaoh starts to read. Falls asleep before she can reach the end of the first paragraph.

As unconsciousness takes her she experiences a moment's perfect memory. Recalls the old woman's face. Long white hair, thin lips, sharp features. Blue eyes, sparkling as if with frost. Pea-green raincoat tied at the neck with a black and yellow scarf. She'd smelled of patchouli and woodsmoke and her fingers were arthritic and all but fused into clubs. She'd struggled with her papers but refused Pharaoh's offers of help. Refused to give her name either. She just thrust the copy of the *Hull Mail* at her and hissed that if the police weren't going to help her she would do it herself.

'*Lies*,' she'd spat, fire seeming to dance on her blue irises. '*Where is he, eh? Where's the one that bloody matters?*'

At the time, Pharaoh had thought the old woman was referring to Slattery. She'd bristled accordingly. Had felt as though her rank and ability and maybe even her gender were being criticised. She'd started to tell the old lady that she would be delighted to listen to her; that she was an experienced detective and could arrange for her to talk to one of her best officers. Pharaoh went to get tea from the machine and by the time she returned the old lady had disappeared out of the double doors. Pharaoh had checked with the desk sergeant. Had she given a name? Any more information? When she went outside, the old woman was gone.

Pharaoh's eyes close. Her fingers continue to twitch at the file on her lap.

As she sleeps, each dream seems to pull her further beneath a frozen sea.

# 12

*The Almshouses on Pickering Road, West Hull*
*6.15 p.m.*

The view through the kitchen window is an unfinished water-colour: the sky a dismal, featureless black. McAvoy finds it unsettling, as if his reality were being somehow erased. He is used to craggy clouds and splintered sunsets: skies that look like crushed elderberries and pulped sloes. Today the sky feels empty, leached of colour. Even the darkness is hiding behind a veil of ash.

A memory rises. He can see his father's bathwater: all sweat and dirt and carbolic soap. For an instant he is a child again. Seven years old. Rough bristles against his skin – the low heat from the peat fire slowly turning his face from pink to crimson. There are tears in his eyes: mud and sheep blood under his nails and on his cheeks. They'd found a ewe in a ravine, two legs broken at horrible angles, an anguished bleating emerging from its bloodied mouth. Duncan hadn't been able to do what was required. It fell to McAvoy to draw his pocket knife across the animal's throat. He'd held the animal like a child as its life-force splashed the snow. They'd walked home in silence. It was Duncan who'd told their father what he'd done. Here, now, he remembers the look in the big man's eyes, sorrow and pride and an aching wish that things were somehow different. Remembers his dad's big, warm hands, massaging soap into his red curls. He realises he will remember that scent until his dying day, will always be able to put himself back in that place, that time, by taking a whiff of peat smoke and coal soap.

He slams the door shut on his memories before they start to consume him.

*'Bastards.'*

McAvoy turns away from the window. Neilsen's dad, Trev, is sitting at the kitchen table with a copy of the *Hull Mail* in one hand and a red pen in the other. He has a mug of tea at his elbow, stewed strong and orange. The remains of a bowl of apple pie and custard is congealing on the circular table. He's lost weight since the last time McAvoy saw him. He's wearing two sweatshirts beneath a padded lumberjack shirt. Grey bristles sprout erratically across his throat and beneath his nose. Neilsen had warned McAvoy not to mention it. *Still likes to shave himself*, he'd confided. *He's shit at it, but he won't let the nurse near him with a blade. Says that's a man's job.*

'Who's that, Mr Neilsen?' asks McAvoy.

'Who's what, lad?'

'Sounded like somebody hadn't impressed you. *Bastards*, you said.'

Trev looks up from the newspaper and glares at McAvoy. His blue eyes wallow in yellow, rheumy tears. He keeps inserting a fingertip into the crevices, pushing his glasses up and down his nose, wetting the tip of his finger as if chalking a snooker cue.

'You're our Ben's mate,' says Trev, smiling in sudden recognition. 'You got a tea? Can we make you a sandwich? There's some bacon about to go off, I think.'

McAvoy holds up his mug. He's already made himself a tea. Made one for Trev, too, who has already recognised him six times in the past twenty minutes. He's running out of things to do. He has fiddled with cups and saucers and knocked up coffees and biscuits for Neilsen and his sister. McAvoy performed his tasks with gusto. He was sweating by the time he carried it all through to the bedroom next door. It felt like entering a mausoleum. He pictures the scene beyond the kitchen wall. Neilsen's mum: parchment skin and grey lips, shrunken inside a floral nightie and encased within two quilts and a rough blanket. The whole house smells of ointment and air-freshener but it's worse in the room where she will die. The curtains are drawn and the only light comes from the pink lava lamp on her bedside table.

*She likes to watch it,* explained Neilsen's older sister, Theresa. *Says it makes her think of goldfish.*

'They say there's more bad weather on the way,' mutters Trev. 'Bad weather? What's good weather, eh? No such thing as bad weather – just the wrong clothes.'

McAvoy gives him a smile. Leans back against the sink. Looks into his mug and considers making another. He's noticed that hot beverages and mobile phones have taken over from cigarettes as ways for people to keep their hands busy and hide their face in awkward situations. He feels uncomfortable, like an intruder. He doesn't know his role. He came in out of sheer good manners and now can't find the right set of words that will allow him to leave. Ben had said he wouldn't be long but the time is ticking on by. McAvoy wishes he could simply stand up and go. He's witnessed grief countless times. He's no stranger to these claustrophobic rooms. But he's always been there as a cop. Here, in the kitchen of the Neilsens' cosy bungalow he doesn't know what he is for. He'd like to go and sit in the living room and flick through the crime magazine he seized from the shop in Cherry Burton or immerse himself in the tapestry of nostalgia on the many Hessle Road social media groups. He doubts he will get a chance until he has typed up the witness statements that he and Ben took from the startled quartet by the newsstand. He doesn't even know if they will be useful for anything more than background detail.

'You'll have seen some storms, I'd imagine,' says McAvoy, trying to make conversation.

'Storms, son?'

'With the fleet, I mean,' says McAvoy. He'd thought he was on safe ground, that he could coax an anecdote out of the old man that would give him time to think of something else to say. Trev looks at him with a vacant expression, as if trying to remember the name of a horse he backed in 1972. Suddenly a grin spreads across his face. 'You're our Ben's mate, aren't you? Bloody hell, look at the size of you. Would you sit down? I feel like you're about to start giving it fee-fi-fum or something.'

McAvoy sits down as instructed. He's already removed his coat and jacket. He wishes he were holding his notepad so he could keep his eyes and hands busy. Wishes Pharaoh were here. She'd have Trev roaring with laughter, flirting and telling him off-colour tales. She'd do what was required without thinking about it. Would know how to keep him busy and distracted while his children say another round of goodbyes to his wife in the next room.

'Another tea, Mr Neilsen?'

'You're a Jock,' says Neilsen brightly. 'Good blokes, the Jocks. Not always the first to buy a round but decent people. What part of Jockland are you from?'

McAvoy rubs a hand over his chin, gathering his beard in a point. Wonders whether he minds being called a Jock. Whether he should make allowances. 'You might know Loch Ewe,' he says. They've had this conversation twice already.

'Sea loch? The Yanks used it during the war? Right up top?'

'Top?'

'Of Scotland, daft lad. Way up.'

McAvoy nods. 'Aye, way up.'

'Peggy and me went to Fort William on a bus trip once. Two distilleries and a shortbread place. Bus broke down on the way back. We ended up standing on the hard shoulder wrapped in blankets – fifty Hull pensioners shivering and singing songs. Best part of the trip, it was. We opened all the presents we'd brought back for the bains. Must have gone through a dozen miniatures of whisky. Good times—' He stops suddenly. McAvoy feels as though he has lost the signal on a radio show – all coherence lost in a blare of static. 'What was I saying? Doctors reckon I'm on the slide. Dementia. They say it like they think I'll bloody forget. Wish I could. That's the one bloody word that keeps pecking away at me like a bloody bird. They can whisper it all they like but I know.' He sags, sinking a little further into the wooden kitchen chair. Repeats, softly: 'I do know.'

McAvoy can hear tears coming from the next room: a soft, rhythmic whispering, like footsteps through dried leaves. He can feel his phone vibrating in his pocket. Knows it would be wrong to answer it. He finds himself remembering Trev the way he was when they first met. Neilsen's auntie and uncle were over from Australia to see the family. Trev had splashed out on a good buffet in the function room at Rayner's. Neilsen hadn't been looking forward to it. Reckoned his every relative would be sharing stories about the good old days and giving him hell about being a pretty boy who'd never found a wife. He'd persuaded a couple of colleagues to show their faces. Andy Daniells and his husband had been a source of great amusement, matching the old fishermen drink for drink and filthy joke for filthy joke. Pharaoh had put a portly, red-faced old sod in a wrist lock when he'd helped himself to one of her curves. McAvoy had stood at the bar, trying to make one pint of dry cider last an hour, awkward and hot, reading the captions on the black and white photographs that covered the wall and trying to make anagrams in his head from the different names on the whisky bottles.

Trev had taken pity on him. Trev had still been a strapping chap, just a couple of years ago. They'd chatted for a good twenty minutes. McAvoy had been struck by the older man's warmth, the way he'd clasped his hand between his palms and looked him in the eye while they talked. He was a good story-teller, a proper pub raconteur. They'd shared a couple of yarns. Talked about Loch Ewe and the merchant navy. Trev had pointed out faces in the monochrome snaps that grinned down from the walls. *Sailed with him*, he'd said, gesturing vaguely. *Must have been in 1968. Loaned him a cowboy book and never got it back. See that sod with the bandy legs? Went down on the* Ross Cleveland. *He were thick as mince but worked like a Trojan. See that bloke chatting up our Linda over there? Baseball cap and a walking stick. Had to have his leg amputated when he came a cropper jumping out some woman's bedroom window when her husband came home. Clung to the windowsill for twenty minutes before he dropped. Bone came right through. Silly bastard. Got himself done for bigamy not long after. Did a few months inside. Reckoned he couldn't bring himself to disappoint her . . .*

'You away with the fairies, lad?' asks Trev. 'Your arse is buzz-ing, by the way. Take the call if you need to.'

McAvoy lets the phone ring and gives Trev his full attention. He tries to concentrate on the man he is rather than the person he used to be. Tries not to imagine their roles being reversed. He has a horrible flash of prophesy: imagining himself in a high-backed chair, grey stubble on a scrawny neck, old sorrow in his eyes, trying to stay focused while his grandchildren look at his old scars and question how such a fragile specimen could ever have chased killers.

'Many corrections?' asks McAvoy, nodding at the newspaper and Trev's red pen. Trev hasn't any interest in the crossword or Sudoku puzzles. He likes to scour the pages for spelling mistakes, grammatical errors and factual inaccuracies. It's a full-time job.

'Like a dead penguin,' says Trev, turning the pages so McAvoy can see. 'Black and white and red all over.'

McAvoy drums his fingers on the tabletop. Behind Trev is a corkboard covered in family photographs. Ben is pictured more frequently than anybody else. He's the youngest of five. His dad's proud of all his offspring but there is no doubting that Ben is his favourite. Trev follows his gaze.

'Some of me up there, I think,' he mutters. 'Back when I were a looker. Our Peg were a bobby-dazzler. There's a picture of her in the living room. I swear, I wouldn't have crawled over her to get to Jayne Mansfield.'

'When were you married?' asks McAvoy, becoming aware of the heat in the room.

'In 1966,' says Trev, without pausing. 'Married on the Saturday and I was gone by Sunday teatime. Three weeks away. Our Audrey was a honeymoon baby, or at least that's what we told her father. Came along seven months after the wedding night. Everybody were happy to play along. Said she'd come early. Come early? She were a nine-pounder. Fattest baby you ever saw.'

'I met your Audrey at Rayner's.'

'Aye, she's never lost the weight. Good heart though. Got one of those jobs I don't really understand. Something to do with selling high-class lightbulbs. Lives in Basildon with a Chinaman called David. Good old traditional Chinese name, that, don't you think? Still, that's the world for you. Nowt against foreigners. There's blokes I drink with who'd send every bugger back where they come from but I don't know how that would help. I'm a Neilsen, for God's sake. Family are from Sweden if you go back four generations. How can you live in a port and dislike foreigners, eh? Me dad, me grandad, me great-grandad, all trawlermen, and every one of us got called Sven from the first day on the docks to the last. That's fishermen for you. Love a nickname, not ones for originality. We were going to call Ben "Sven" just to get it over with but by the time he came along there were no fishing industry left.

He'd have hated life at sea. He's a good lad. Always been a clever one.'

McAvoy smiles. He hopes Trev will stay on this wavelength for a while. Wonders whether he could nudge his memories in a direction that could prove helpful and whether it would be wrong to do so. Promises himself he will steer the conversation somewhere less taxing if Trev seems to be in any distress. 'Ben said you knew Enid Chappell,' he says, keeping it light.

Trev looks puzzled. 'There was a Chappell ran the Fishermen's Bethel. Relative, was she?'

'No, this was a lady who worked for Social Services. You might have seen her name in the paper once or twice.'

Trev rubs a fist against the palm of his other hand, thinking hard. 'There were a woman who used to take the babies away,' he says at length. 'Never had much to do with her meself. Give me a second, it'll come to me. Aye, she drove a van, if you'll believe it. A camper. She'd come out when the police or the corporation decided that the nippers were best off somewhere else. She had a mattress in the back, I think. Cots too. Took them to the orphanage or a foster family or wherever the poor bleeders had been sent. That who you mean?'

McAvoy doesn't answer. He's swirling his thoughts around inside his head. He watches as a blackbird pecks at a coconut shell that hangs from the washing line in the little back garden, dangling in the darkness like a weathered skull.

'Bastards,' says Trev vaguely, looking again at the newspaper. He seems to be on some sort of time-loop: his whole world is skipping like a scratched record.

'Who, Mr Neilsen?' asks McAvoy.

Trev gives the newspaper a back-handed slap. Screws up his face as if he can taste something bitter.

'You lot doing anything about this?' he asks accusingly. 'Had to wait long enough for the thing in the first place and now they're talking about moving it. Did you see the graffiti? We'd have had such a hiding in our day. I'm not one of these buggers who reckons nostalgia isn't what it used to be but some people are too bloody free. Not scared enough. No consequences, that's the thing. Used to be that people were scared of doing things wrong and knew they'd get some reward for doing things right. Nobody gives a damn any more.'

McAvoy angles his head so he can see what it is that has stoked the old man's indignation. The story is illustrated with a picture of the memorial statue to lost fishermen, erected a couple of years back on a patch of waste ground at the old Fish Docks. It's a striking piece: a group of fishermen picked out life-size in rusted steel: quiffs and kitbags, arms around one another's necks, big turn-ups and haunting eyes. It means a lot to the old Hessle Roaders – a focal point for their grief. It commemorates the thousands of men who went to sea and never came home. The bastards in question have daubed splashes of lurid green paint on half a dozen of the faces.

'I'm sorry,' says McAvoy, shaking his head. He feels responsible. He always feels responsible.

'I didn't even like the design but at least it were something,' grumbles Trev.

McAvoy reaches across and takes the newspaper. Scans the article. There's a quote from the landowners and a statement from Humberside Police. He scratches his beard.

'Green, too,' says McAvoy. 'Bad luck.'

'Back in the day they'd have had their shins kicked in and Big Gerard would have nailed their hands to the bloody lock gates.'

'I think I know that name . . .?'

'Him and his mate Rory were the closest we had to a sheriff and his deputy. You wouldn't upset them. Gerard went three rounds with a bare-knuckle gypsy one Hull Fair. Poor sod. Suffered a terrible injury at sea and it knocked him for six, poor bastard. Wouldn't sail after Rory died. Did well as a bookie, though. Dog-track, race-track. Took big bets under the counter, or so they said. Old bloke now, like the rest of us.'

McAvoy looks up from the article.

'Do you remember a surname? For Gerard, I mean.'

'Ask a senile old duffer to remember what he had for breakfast and you'll get a blank look. But 1968 is clear as a bell. Aye, he were Gerard Wade. His mate were Rory Ballantine.'

'That's definitely a name I'm becoming familiar with. Did you fish with them?'

'Once or twice,' mutters Trev, looking at the phone again. 'Gerard had fists like hams. Napper sailed with them too. You know Napper? Big mates with Alf Howe . . .'

'And Rory? I've heard so many different versions of the story.'

Trev settles back in his chair. He looks as though he should be sitting in the bunkroom of a sidewinder, drinking tea from a metal cup and smoking a dog-end. He looks happy, telling a story and remembering a time when his world made some kind of sense.

'He died saving his mates,' says Trev, shaking his head. 'Big sea took them over the side off Skagi and he went in after them. Another fella too. Cowboy Mick. Daft sod thought he was Wyatt Earp but I got on well enough with him. Mick was in the lifeboat when the wind took it. Knocked the deckie into the water. Rory and Gerard went in after him. Only Gerard made it out and there weren't as much of him as before. The other three were lost and the ship went down not long after. Were a bit in the papers about it a while back. Bodies washed up in Russia that might have been them. I had my doubts. Why would the Russians suddenly admit to it now, eh? And there were only two bodies, or so we heard. That's the thing with old secrets, I suppose – when your memory goes, it can be hard to distinguish the truth from the lies. Rory were a good bloke. Bit flash, maybe, but one of the good ones.'

Trev stops, staring past McAvoy at the sky. He lowers his

eyes, as if frightened of looking at the horizon: at the nothing-ness that seems to creep closer.

'Rory's missus were pregnant, too. Can't remember her name though Peg might. She married a right nasty so-and-so not long afterwards. Some mate of Rory's who reckoned he should do right by his pal. Bit handy with his fists, so I heard. I don't reckon his lass had much choice in the matter. Not with a couple of nippers to look out for. He died too, as it happens. Accident on the docks, years back. One of her bains has done pretty well though. I reckon the name must have opened a few doors when he were starting out. He's done his best to repay the debt. Damn fool idea trying to bring the *Purcell* home but it'll be nice to see the *Holst* steaming off towards the horizon again – if it ever bloody happens.'

'Sorry, Trev, you've lost me . . .'

'Ballantine,' he says, as if explaining to a child. 'One of Rory's lads. Stephen, if my memory serves me correctly, though it often fucking doesn't. That bucket of rust down the docks. All his grand plans. You should talk to Napper, if you're interested.'

McAvoy looks up at the sound of an unpleasant, rasping cough, drifting through from the next room.

'Where is she?' asks Trev, looking around him. His legs start moving up and down as if he can't control them. 'You know our Ben?' he asks, eyeing McAvoy accusingly. Recognition suddenly dawns. 'Oh aye, you're his mate. Good boy, our Ben. Baby of the family and sometimes he acts it. Were you asking about Gerard? That big bugger in the sculpture is the spit of him.'

McAvoy looks at the article afresh. One of the figures that has been desecrated has broad shoulders and big hands. His features have been altered so his eyes are huge, perfect circles, like an astonished cod.

'It says here the figures aren't of anybody in particular,' says McAvoy. '*Stylised*, apparently.'

'Aye, so they say,' mutters Trev, scratching at his scalp with both hands. He glances at the image. 'Looks like Rory's crew to me. Would make sense, wouldn't it? His bain owns most of that site. Done his bit to honour his dad's memory, though you never know with that lot whether they're doing it for headlines or heartstrings.'

McAvoy sits back in his chair, wondering whether Trev is telling him something from last week or fifty years ago. Concentrates on what he was saying. Ballantine. He knows the name. A memory surges. He'd been in the waiting room at the health centre on Beverley Road in Hessle, holding Roisin's hand. Lilah was playing with the building blocks, which were sopping wet from the amount of anti-bacterial hand gel that Roisin had slathered them in. They were waiting to hear whether Lilah would require a further operation to repair her eardrum. McAvoy was nervous, his leg jiggling up and down. He was thumbing through the magazines, all country interiors, fly-fishing and year-old *Reader's Digest*s. He'd picked up a copy of a local glossy, free to homes of distinction in the East Riding and a couple of quid to every poor bugger else. There had been a profile on Stephen Ballantine, the fisherman's son who'd become a tycoon and bought the company that used to employ his father.

'You okay, lad? Look like you're shitting a billiard ball. Were you telling me about our Ben? You're his boss, aren't you? He speaks highly of you. Can I make you tea? There's bacon in the fridge, I think . . .'

McAvoy casts an anguished look towards the door. He becomes aware of a faint smell, a subtle colouring of the air that dribbles through from the bedroom. He pictures the scene beyond the kitchen wall. Imagines Neilsen and his sister holding their mum's cold, twisted hands: saying thank-yous, soothing her final moments with fond memories and soft words of gratitude.

He looks up as Neilsen appears in the doorway. His eyes are

red and there are teardrops on his shirt. He manages a smile for his dad.

'You boring the sarge, Dad?'

'Cheeky sod.' Trev smiles indulgently. He seems to light up in the presence of his youngest son. Looks suddenly more comfortable, as if everything has just got better. 'You been in that bathroom, splashing on your Old Spice, have you? Where've you been? Your mate here has to be home for tea, isn't that right? We've been chatting. Your mam shouldn't be long. She's on Road, picking up a few bits.'

Neilsen flashes McAvoy a look. Gives the tiniest shake of his head.

'I'll be in bother if I don't get going,' says McAvoy to the room in general. 'I'll pop back later, Ben. We'll have a kickabout, eh?'

Neilsen's bottom lip gives the tiniest shiver, though whether it is with grief or gratitude, McAvoy couldn't say.

'Only if you're sure,' says Neilsen quietly. 'There's loads to do.'

'You stay,' says McAvoy firmly. 'I'll muddle through. Budget-conscious policing, remember. We do better with what we've got.'

'You seen this in the paper, lad?' asks Trev. 'Bloody vandals down the docks. Once you get on the force you can do something, eh? Bastards need locking up. I've half a mind to call Gerard. He'd nail the bastard's hand to the lock gates, right enough.' He pulls a face. 'Don't tell your mam I said that. She always said that lot were a bad influence. Did all right though, didn't they? Young Stephen, when you think how he started – I wouldn't mind being a few quid behind him. Reckon his dad would be proud, but what dad isn't, eh?' He stops, and again it seems as if he has driven through a tunnel while listening to an analogue radio. 'Sorry, what were we talking about? They tell me I'm going a bit funny. Don't know where I'd be without our lass. She were such a looker. There's a photo in the living room, I think. Or was that at the old house? Where are we at now, our Ben?'

Neilsen wipes his hand across his cheek. McAvoy stands.

'Can you spare the newspaper, Mr Neilsen?'

'It's Trev, lad, like I told you. And aye, you take it. Nowt worth reading anyways. I know more people in the obituaries than the weddings these days.'

McAvoy picks up the paper. Reaches across and offers a hand. Trev takes it, like a child reaching up for the comfort of a parent. 'By heck, you're a big bugger. You should have a go against one of them gypsies at Hull Fair.'

McAvoy's cheeks start to burn.

# 13

McAvoy stops for a moment on the doorstop, angling his head so as not to nudge the pretty hanging basket full of winter blooms. The property overlooks the muddy sands of Hessle Foreshore, three miles upriver from the old docks. Above, the great steel strings of the Humber Bridge cut through the half moon like the blades of an egg-slicer. The fog has shifted a little, allowing a glimpse of the big black sky. A handful of stars wink through the gloom.

Home, he thinks, and strokes his palm against the grainy wood of the front door as if patting a beloved pet. Takes a breath. The air smells of dirty water and freshly dug earth. There's a whiff of snow and diesel. He tries to arrange his face into something appropriate.

He opens the door.

Lilah McAvoy is sitting halfway up the steps, wrapped up in McAvoy's burgundy dressing gown, illuminated by a cone of yellow light that shines down from the sparkling Tiffany lamp on the landing. The robe is so big that her limbs are entirely consumed by the soft, velvety fabric and only a little of her pretty face pokes out. She stands up as soon as she sees him, material puddling on the stairs at her feet and covering up a large patch of the loud floral carpet.

'What sort of a time do you call this?' she asks sternly. She shakes her head and attempts to fold her arms.

McAvoy closes the door behind him. Knocks a picture off the wall as he struggles out of his coat. He picks it up and replaces it on the hook. Gives her his full attention.

'You should be in bed like your brother, young lady.'

'You are in no position to tell me off,' says Lilah, wrinkling her nose. She pulls at her sleeves, trying to extricate her hands.

McAvoy fails in his bid to keep a straight face. He grins and Lilah gives up on her attempt to stay in character. She beams and launches herself at her father, leaping from the stairs as if fired from a cannon. McAvoy plucks her from the air and pulls her into a hug. She wraps herself around him and nuzzles her head against him.

McAvoy opens the door to the living room. Roisin is asleep on the sofa, snuggled up beneath a tartan blanket, mouth slightly parted and a soft smile on her face. She's bathed in the warm, syrupy light that spills from the standard lamp by the sofa, the room's pink walls and eclectic art prints lost in the half darkness. Her eyelids flicker as the draught from the open door disturbs her. She opens one eye. Smiles as she sees him and the burden he carries.

'Well, I do believe there's a gorgeous man in my living room,' she says drowsily. She looks at Lilah, clinging to her father. 'And a wizard, too.' She sits up and kicks off the blanket. She's wearing little shorts and slouchy football socks. On her thighs, a Spirograph of silvery scars pattern her smooth, tanned skin.

'Missed you,' says McAvoy, crossing to her. He bends down, still holding Lilah, and presses his forehead to Roisin's. She kisses him and he tastes chocolate and flavoured tobacco.

'Aye, I can understand that.' Roisin smiles. 'I'm missable. Lovable. Very, very fu—'

He kisses her, stopping the word on her lips. She closes her eyes and her lips move against his as if she is reading from a prayer book. In such moments there is something other-worldly about her; something ethereal.

She stares into him, a blue eye at the end of a telescope. She seems to read some indecipherable language from the inside of his skull. Eventually she blinks, seemingly satisfied. 'Get Harry Snotter off to bed and I'll fix you up. You'll be hungry, no doubt.'

Twenty minutes later, McAvoy is sitting on the sofa with a mug of hot chocolate in his left hand and a colossal banana and chocolate-spread sandwich in his right. His laptop is balanced on his knee.

'There are some horrible feckers out there,' says Roisin, lying back on the floor, her feet up on the sofa, as McAvoy tells her about the day. He sometimes doesn't know how he feels about things until he has talked them over with his wife. 'You'll catch him though. That's what you do.'

McAvoy finishes his sandwich and drains his mug. Puts the crockery down on the carpet and dusts himself down.

'She was a nice lady?' asks Roisin. 'This Enid?'

'It shouldn't make a difference,' says McAvoy, eyes closed. 'But yes, it sounds like she was. She cared. Social worker, charity fundraiser. Bit of a socialist firebrand. Didn't have the easiest of starts – time in an orphanage, no real family, but there was a determination about her. I think I would have liked her. She shouldn't have died on her own like that. That isn't how it should be.'

'The dead birds,' says Roisin, performing an acrobatic backwards roll and standing up, hair tangled with her jewellery. She plonks herself down on the sofa. 'The blood in the hen-house.'

McAvoy hauls himself off the sofa and stands with his back to the warm red glow of the fire: silhouettes dancing like shadow puppets on his skin.

'That smashed bottle,' he says, leaning on the mantelpiece. 'It felt like a piece of a puzzle. And the crossword half done. It all felt wrong.'

133

'You didn't mention a crossword,' says Roisin.

The half-dark of the room hides the blush that warms his cheeks. 'I think I might have been seeing things. The paper was on the sofa. She could barely hold a pencil with her arthritis but she'd scribbled something in one of the boxes.' He pulls a face. 'It almost looked like it spelled out my name.'

'Aector?' she asks, surprised.

'McAvoy,' he says sheepishly. 'Look, I'll show you.' He takes his phone from his trouser pocket and flicks through the pictures he took at the scene. 'It could just as well be anything . . .'

'What's the clue?' asks Roisin, intrigued.

McAvoy holds the phone to the light. '"Enthuse to new bird",' he says, in a voice that suggests the cryptic clue could just as well be written in ancient Aramaic. 'I don't see how that leads anywhere useful. But it felt as though whatever happened, well, it had come out of nowhere. As if a normal day had been interrupted. Then when I heard about the calls she'd made, the talk of going somewhere, the way she'd started drawing away from people; her diary was almost blank after the New Year. And the name *Marlowe* in the calendar. The people in the shop talked about this friend of hers. A troublemaker. Walked with a stick.'

'He'd struggle to lift her then,' points out Roisin. 'You use your legs most when you lift somebody.'

'Then there's the *Blake Purcell*,' mutters McAvoy, retaking his seat beside Roisin. 'I checked all the ships of the line, and that was the commemorative bottle that had been smashed. Smashed so recently that the water was still frozen on the carpet. My name, scribbled on the crossword. And then the name "Marlowe", which seems kind of familiar.'

McAvoy opens the laptop and logs in to the case file. Pulls up the photographs from inside the chicken coop – blood and feathers smeared across the sawdust and frozen earth – and flicks on to the images of the scraps of paper in the log burner.

'It feels like a trail,' says McAvoy. 'Like breadcrumbs for a bird. Is that silly?'

'Crow,' says Roisin, looking pleased with herself. 'Enthuse to new bird. Crow. It's cryptic, isn't it? People crow about stuff, don't they?' Her face falls. 'Have I got that wrong?'

McAvoy stares at her with something close to wonder.

'You'd have got it too,' she says. Then she stops the pretence and allows herself to preen. 'Actually, scrap that. Yes, you're right. I'm fecking awesome, so I am.'

McAvoy looks back at his notes. He feels suddenly over-whelmed by it all. 'She was looking into something,' he says, turning his palms skywards to indicate that he has absolutely no idea what that might be. 'Maybe she found what she was look-ing for and it scared her. She'd been to see the police and we were no help. What if she knew that somebody might come looking? Maybe she hid her papers in the hen-house. Whoever watched her die – they killed her birds. I don't know if it was an act of cruelty or compassion. They'd had their necks pulled. But there is no way that somebody of Mrs Chappell's age and physical frailties could get into the coop. Somebody else went inside. What they found made them angry. They tore the last bird to shreds. If Enid only had a little bit of time – if she needed to leave a message that the killer wouldn't understand . . .'

Roisin rubs her arms, suddenly cold. McAvoy reaches across and picks up the blanket. Wraps her warm and flops back in his seat.

He scratches his beard. He feels as though he has been trying to put together a jigsaw puzzle without any idea of what the finished picture should look like. He lets his thoughts spool backwards, a ball of wool, unravelling – a guide rope into the complications of his own mind. Something is nagging at him: some half-remembered thing . . .

'Your phone,' says Roisin, nodding at his pocket. 'It's vibrat-ing. Answer it or I'm sitting on it. I'm fine with either.'

McAvoy smiles indulgently. He recognises the number and is glad that the CSI boss isn't making a video call.

'Hi, Aector,' says Reena Parekh. She pronounces his name correctly – a slight throaty cough around the first syllable. 'Was that right? I've been practising.'

'Perfect,' he says; his own voice sounds weak, like cordial mixed with too much water. He coughs. 'How's it going?'

'Freezing,' she says, and catches herself. 'Sorry, poor taste. We've broken out every heater we have but it's a battle between getting her thawed out as quickly as possible, and not contaminating the body. I'll be giving talks on the lecture circuit about this one for years to come. The council sent a few suits to see if they can help but your uniforms have sent them away. It's a case of getting access to the forensics without altering anything. We can't speed up the thaw for fear of affecting the skin tissue so it's a very slow process. One thing is certain from the patterns in the ice – she didn't fall asleep in the bathtub while having a lovely soak. This was more of a sportsman's bath. It was already full of ice when she got in. There will have been bitterly cold water sloshing about too but the geometrics of the fractals are absolutely clear. It's sharp. Chipped ice, like you'd use in factories. Far more than you'd store at home. Somebody brought this with them.'

McAvoy frowns. 'Fish van? Meat van? Any vehicle with an automated cooling system would have those facilities. Where are we with the tyre tracks?'

'Hold on, Aector,' says Parekh quietly. He hears it in her voice: a sudden sadness. 'The thermal images have been enhanced. We waited until the thaw was almost done for confirmation.' She breathes out. Sucks in a breath. 'Her ankles were tied together.'

The air in McAvoy's lungs shudders free. He has to stop himself gasping. He feels Roisin's hand stroking at the scarred knuckles of his right hand.

'A length of what we took to be braided cord,' continues Parekh, in his ear. 'Bound tight enough to cut into the flesh. There was some bleeding but the action of the ice on the layers of epidermis prevented much seepage. We took it at first to be twine.'

'But not any more?'

'It's hair. A braid of human hair.'

McAvoy closes his eyes. Roisin presses her face to his shoulder and he leans in so he can smell her hair; soothe himself with the soft scents of burnt sugar and yesterday's shampoo.

'What type of knot?' he asks quietly.

Parekh groans, annoyed with herself. 'Haven't asked that, sorry. I'll add it to the list.'

'Any chance of a match?'

'Slight,' says Parekh, then seems to brighten. 'Slight but not impossible. There may be enough skin cells attached to the root to produce a sample but it requires a more advanced system than we have access to. There's a friend of a friend at a lab in Barking who has the technology but it's not cheap. I can maybe barter him down.'

'Do it,' says McAvoy automatically. He grimaces, questions lining up like bullets. 'Would it be strong enough to bind somebody?'

'There's some form of wax gumming the braids together,' explains Parekh. 'It's more like tarred rope. It was black, we can tell that. All from the same sample.'

'Forensics,' says McAvoy, cutting her off. 'Tell me we've got something, please.'

Parekh takes a breath. He hears the squeak of her chair as she settles back. Can picture her taking off her spectacles and chewing on the stem.

'Partial print,' she says, with the faintest note of triumph in her voice. 'Recovered from the carotid artery, right side.'

'He took her pulse,' says McAvoy automatically. He realises

137

he has been kneading Roisin's scalp, rubbing her dark hair between finger and thumb. He stops.

'Tell me they're on file,' says McAvoy hopefully.

'This should be taking us days, you realise that?' grumbles Parekh. 'I'm going to be torn to shreds at the next budget conference.'

'Reena, please.'

'Bernard "Napper" Acklam,' says Reena. 'DOB 11 June 1942. First conviction for stealing the takings from the Queen's Head on Walker Street. He was eleven at the time. Burglary convictions really pick up after the age of fifteen. Obtaining property by deception got him nineteen months. Served time for assault with a deadly weapon, GBH without a deadly weapon, armed robbery, assisting an offender – that's on four separate occasions – conspiracy to commit fraud, demanding money with menaces – two years in Pentonville for that in 1967 . . .'

'Busy man,' says McAvoy. 'We'll have a file thick as a gravestone, I presume.'

'Not a great deal on the digital archive other than the basics. I've requested the hard case notes from the material archive. I'd put a face mask on, they'll no doubt have gathered plenty dust.'

'What do we know about him?'

'Not much. Your Sophie will no doubt rustle up plenty but all that leapt out at me from the archive was a cross-reference to a suspicious death, early eighties. Arthur Lowery. Found dead in the hold of a trawler. There's a reference number for the inquest.' She hums a little tune, almost masking the sound of pages being turned. 'Acklam's last conviction was in 2001. Broke the ankle of a trackside bookie in Marken Rasen. Served fourteen months. Behaved himself since, or so it seems. Physical description suggests he was a big chap in his day. Over six foot. Maybe he'd still be strong enough to lift her into the bath.'

'Address?' asks McAvoy.

'Church Mount, Sutton. Know it?'

'Expensive,' says McAvoy, glancing around at the small, two-bedroomed fisherman's cottage that drains a third of his salary each month. 'Have you passed this to Sophie?'

'You're in charge, remember,' says Parekh, a smile in her voice. 'I tell you, you tell them, that's how it works.'

McAvoy glances at his watch and wonders about the merits of going straight to see Acklam. He takes a breath and calms himself down. He doesn't know enough. Doesn't want to steam in without performing at least the basics of due diligence.

'Hang on a moment please, Reena,' he says, and flicks through the case files on his phone. His spectacles aren't where he left them and he looks around, mildly frantic. He feels Roisin giggling against him and she looks up, her top lip pulled back and his glasses halfway down his nose.

'The phone numbers,' he says, scrolling through the digital document. 'A landline, I'm sure. I know that name.'

'You were right about the place having been cleaned out,' continues Parekh. 'There are lines in the carpet under the book-shelf dug a good couple of inches into the carpet. The unit isn't that heavy. So the bookshelf is used to holding more books. There's no bin liner in the bin. No rubbish in any of the wheelie bins. There's a kitchen composter out the back for peelings and eggshells and such. You can tell it's been raked through. I'm not here to speculate, that's not particularly scientific, but some-body's been through here looking for something.'

McAvoy tugs the hair beneath his lip. 'Tyre tracks?'

Parekh pauses. 'We may have struck lucky there. Expensive. Very particular. We'll cross-ref those with the DVLA databases and see what we whittle down.'

McAvoy rubs at his forehead, trying to physically push his thoughts into some kind of order.

'You were right about the rocking chair,' says Parekh admir-ingly. 'It's been moved from another room. You can see where

139

the casters dug into the carpet. She'd have struggled to carry it. Would have struggled to do very much, if I'm honest. She was frail. Bathroom cabinet is full of medicine. Heart condition, arthritis, fibromyalgia. She was taking a small dosage of Exelon too.'

'Alzheimer's,' says McAvoy.

'Mild dementia,' says Parekh, clicking her tongue around the word. 'Sophie's chasing up medical records.'

'By the bed,' says McAvoy, a thought occurring. 'The jam jar full of fag-butts.'

'Your guess is as good as mine,' says Parekh. 'Better probably. Maybe she'd been a smoker and used it to keep reminding herself how bloody vile cigarettes are. I had an uncle did something similar. Although that was more to do with earwax and nail-biting. Long story.'

McAvoy frowns. 'Madeleines,' he says, under his breath, as a thought bubbles up. 'Scent memories. A whole story, hidden in your olfactory bulb.'

'You've lost me,' says Parekh, in a way that suggests she's not used to the experience and doesn't really like it.

'Proust's "madeleine moment",' he explains, taking care not to sound like a smart-arse. 'The scent of a single madeleine dipped in tea . . . it's the start of the book. It evokes this whole memory, places him back in another time, lurches him back to childhood. The whole novel takes place from that point.' He sags. 'People use scent to trigger memories. I read about it – how people keep little boxes of specific smells that help to anchor them in a specific time. Enid was a clever person. Perhaps it was something she was trying.'

'Oh. Well, right,' says Parekh, in a way that suggests she has filed this piece of information away in a drawer marked 'irrelevant'. 'Maybe park that one for later, eh?'

As McAvoy begins to politely say he will catch up with her later, she politely shushes him and tells him to hang on. He stays quiet, listening as Parekh has a muffled conversation with one of her team. She's gone more than a minute but when she comes back on the line there is a whisper of heightened enthusiasm to her voice.

'There's something under the nail of her index finger on her right hand. Keep your eye on your screen, it's coming across.'

McAvoy does as instructed. Opens the images as they ping through. He frowns, trying to make it out. Stuck between the pale skin of Enid Chappell's wrinkled fingertip and the pale pastel of the nail, is a fragment of dark fabric, an iridescent sheen to its surface that reminds McAvoy of a bird's throat, or a puddle of spilled petrol. He opens up the accompanying video clip, capturing the way the fragment shimmers when the light changes.

'Tell me what I'm looking at,' says McAvoy.

'Fish skin,' says Parekh simply. 'Treated and tanned by the looks of things. We'll run it through the system, find out what it's from. Don't know if it will help unless you secretly suspect you're looking for a mermaid but it's intriguing, wouldn't you say?'

'I feel like my head's caving in,' mutters McAvoy, and Roisin gives him a pitying look.

'Sorry,' says Parekh. 'Did you get anywhere with that shorthand, by the way?'

McAvoy scratches his beard, realising that it had been on his list of things to do. 'I'll see what sense I can make of it,' he says sheepishly. 'Anything in the hen-house?'

'I never thought I would say this but we're dusting the frozen chickens for prints. The necks were pulled, that's clear.'

'And the mess? The feathers and blood?'

'Somebody pulled too hard,' says Parekh. 'Or hard enough, if a bloodbath was what they were after.'

'So there would have been blood traces on the perpetrator . . .'

'Yep. Your mermaid will definitely have some chicken blood on them. I'll be back in touch when I have more,' says Parekh. 'I do like the way you say "perpetrator". And I must say, it's never dull in this part of the world.'

McAvoy ends the call. Looks at Roisin, curled up at the edge of the sofa. 'Going or staying?' she asks. 'I want to know if it's worth being horny.'

He grins back at her, reaching out and taking her hand in his. 'I'll brief the team first thing. It's an early start.'

'So that means an early night.' Roisin smiles. She lets him pull her to her feet. Leaps up, nimbly, and wraps her legs around his middle.

# 14

*Skagastrond, Skagi Peninsula, Iceland*
*8.16 p.m.*

Pharaoh pulls on her walking boots, grimacing as her bare feet touch the cold, wet fur inside. She only brought two pairs of socks and they both got soaked in the walk to the hire car. They're busy stiffening over the radiator. She fancies she will need to employ a meat mallet to get them back on. She takes her padded coat from the hook and grabs her hat from the top of the pile of boots that cover the dirty floor. She feels the temperature drop as she closes the inner door behind her and steps out into the entranceway. The snow she kicked off earlier hasn't melted yet. The sleeves of her coat are still stiff with frost. She takes the keys from the hook on the wall and uses both hands to yank the front door free from the frame. The cold crashes upon her like a wave. She tries to turn her back to the wind, looks up through the hazy gloom at the great flat-topped mountain that offers this horseshoe bay what little shelter it enjoys.

Christ, she thinks. Are the people who live here just taking the piss? She makes a mental note to ask the question of the witness she's meeting in an hour. She hopes it will get them off on the right foot.

She screws up her face as she picks her way down the steps, taking care to step into the boot prints that she stomped into the soft snow when she arrived. The gale pushes her in several directions at once and for a moment she feels as if she were playing some Victorian parlour game – blindfolded and spun by unseen hands. It is all she can do to keep her feet.

'This is fucking ridiculous,' splutters Pharaoh, eyes wide, half laughing, as she wrenches at the door of the little red hatchback. Ice has formed on the windscreen and around the door frame and it takes a feat of strength to tug it open. She stumbles inside, slamming the door closed behind her. The silence is overwhelming – as if a switch has been flicked. She pulls at the stupid hat, her hair static and wild. She turns on the wipers and winces as they scrape painfully over the icy glass. She's amazed that they even made it this far. She'd hired the Suzuki Swift because it was the cheapest model available but she came to regret the economy during the 170-mile journey from Keflavik Airport. At times it seemed the gale was trying to pick up the little car and hurl it into the mountainside.

Pharaoh takes a breath. There is none of the new-car smell that she had enjoyed for the first hour of the journey. The vehicle now smells of stale coffee and cigarettes, sugar-rich food and her own wet clothes. She turns the key in the ignition. Musty air screams from the blowers, turned up full. She feels out of sorts, struggling to remember whether it's breakfast-time or midnight. She had passed through something approaching daylight for a couple of hours earlier today but that brief spell of hazy illumination seemed like an aberration. When the darkness returned it felt like a restoration of the correct order of things, as though daylight were a charlatan, an impostor not to be trusted.

'I'm sorry about earlier,' says Pharaoh, through gritted teeth, as the satnav erupts into colourful life. 'Let's not mention it again, eh?'

Pharaoh takes the gadget's silence for assent. It was her only company on the long drive and there were several disagreements. There is only one main road in Iceland and it follows the perimeter of the island. Pharaoh had simply pointed the car north and followed everybody else, passing through the European sophistication of Reykjavik inside an hour and on into a landscape that felt like the dark side of the moon. She had convinced herself that the satnav was being pessimistic in its prediction of her arrival time. Had told it so, in no uncertain terms. The phrase 'cynical twat' had been widely employed. Sitting in its black plastic cradle on the windscreen, it manages to exude an air of smugness.

The tyres make a dreadful crunching sound as Pharaoh eases the vehicle forward. The mist on the windscreen is clearing in places but the rain is still coming down hard and she has to curse and squint her way onto the road. It takes her another ten minutes to get herself pointed in the right direction. Even in broad daylight on a sunny day she would struggle to tell the houses apart. In the pitch darkness, buffeted by rain and savaged by the gale, it is only through luck and perseverance that she eventually spots the blurry outline of the elegant white church and realises she has made it to what passes for the centre of Skagastrond.

The lights are still on at the petrol station. It's a cheerful little rectangle of colour against the blackness of the sea and skies. Along with the little supermarket across the road, the petrol station serves as the town's principal pub, restaurant and community centre. She pulls herself out of the car, slams the door and runs through slush and puddles and hard snow into the bright warmth. She gives a mad grin and a gloved thumbs-up to the woman behind the counter. She's a dumpy, half-melted sort; a body made of spheres beneath several strata of madly patterned woolly jumpers; a face that looks like a sock full of socks. Behind her are glossy photographs of the fast food on offer. Pharaoh unzips her coat. It had been an impulse buy in TK Maxx: all synthetic fur and puffy ridges, like a collage made from pieces of sleeping bag. It would have been ideal for a winter spent in Grimsby. In Iceland, it may as well be made of paper.

The woman behind the counter stands still, face inscrutable. Pharaoh approaches the counter.

'You still serving?'

'You are English?' asks the woman. 'How you like Iceland?'

Pharaoh nods, smiling. She's been asked the question a dozen times already. She likes the way that every resident takes their duties as host seriously. Every Icelander she has met is very keen for her to like the place.

'Not sure about the weather,' says Pharaoh. 'I don't think I'll go home with a suntan.'

The woman smiles back. 'Some days are better than others. Don't plan anything, that's the best advice. Hope, but never expect.'

'Quite a dispiriting motto,' muses Pharaoh.

'Concentrate on the "hope",' says the woman, shrugging.

Pharaoh looks up at the menu. 'That price. The decimal point is correct, yes?'

The woman gives a tight grin. Pharaoh ambles along to the edge of the counter, dispiritedly searching for a familiar chocolate bar among the jumble of colours and consonants on the racks. She selects something in a golden wrapper and places it on the counter. She looks around, angling her neck. There must be some bottles somewhere . . .

'Round the corner, by the refrigerator,' says the woman helpfully. 'Alcohol, yes?'

Pharaoh gives her a look, one eye closed, head cocked. Back home, the gesture would have been accompanied by the sound of chairs scraping and the sudden rush of footsteps. A thought occurs to her and she turns back to the woman. She leans on the counter, her manner chummy as a gameshow host. 'A mate of mine said you did some local speciality here. He said I should try some spirit of yours. Can't remember the name.'

146

The cashier closes an eye, as if looking through a telescope. 'Your friend was here a week ago? New Year? We drink everything at New Year. What was it like, the drink?'

'You might remember him,' says Pharaoh, keeping it light. She knows the case file almost off by heart. 'Sixties. Bald. Little goatee beard. Probably not dressed properly, silly bugger.'

The lady's manner changes. Her eyes flick towards the door.

'I might have a picture,' continues Pharaoh.

'Was he English?' asks the lady quietly. 'English like you?' Her manner softens. She leans forward, voice low. 'A man died here. Up the coast road . . .' She stops herself, shivering. 'He fell from the cliffs, they think. One of our customers found him. She tried to save him but he was too cold. He had been in the water too long.'

'Bloody hell,' says Pharaoh, looking shocked. 'That's awful. But no, it couldn't be.'

'No.' The lady smiles, nodding, cautiously at first then more enthusiastically. 'No, no, we get many customers. It will be somebody else's sadness, I'm sure. Too many people still die – they don't listen. I see tourists playing on rocks as the water comes in behind them. They climb down cliffs and into holes or slip on rocks looking for the perfect waterfall or hot spring. We had an American man who scalded himself to death in hot mud because he didn't listen. It's an easy place to hurt yourself – an easy place to disappear.'

'So I'm told,' says Pharaoh. 'I've been doing some reading on the area as it happens. Grim history. Lots of blood. Trolls and witches and magical chests full of gold.'

'We are a strange people,' says the lady proudly. 'Even those who go to church still blame the pixies for their misfortune and many of us still fear the anger of trolls. Not all admit it, of course. We try and be . . . what's the word? Cosmopolitan? But when your child is dying, or your house is ablaze, or your livestock fall sick, that's when you discover what you believe in – not when you're sharing cocktails and talking to your rich friends on the harbourside in Reykjavik.'

Pharaoh finds herself warming to her new acquaintance. She threads her way between the tables and the counter. There is a small grocery section at the far end of the shop: packets of thickly sliced meat and plastic-wrapped joints; a spinning rack of postcards showing the same half-dozen images – Icelandic horses, abandoned farmhouses, the lighthouse at Kalfhamarsvik. In a cubby-hole almost out of sight of the door she finds a shelf full of lagers, spirits and wine. She selects a Merlot and a bottle of vodka with a picture of an Icelandic pony on it. Pharaoh hopes she hasn't picked up some form of equine liniment by mistake. Wonders whether she will still drink it if she has.

There are three tables by the big front window, plastic chairs bolted to the floor. At the nearest, a healthy-looking couple are sharing olives from a pot and splitting a bottle of dry white. At the next, a red-faced, bald-headed man in overalls and a camouflage jacket is pouring strong lager into a coffee cup and reading a book with a picture of a raven on the cover.

Pharaoh selects a large packet of crisps from the rack by the till, settles up and takes her purchases to the table at the far end of the room. She drops her snacks and her bottles on the table. She pours a measure of vodka into a coffee cup and knocks it back. Feels the delicious burn and the golden warmth spreading through her. She pours red wine into the empty cup and opens her crisps. Shoves in a fistful and takes a long swallow of Merlot.

She fiddles with her phone as she eats. There's a good Wi-Fi signal here and there are plenty of messages waiting. No shortage of emails to wade through on her Humberside Police account. Briefing notes, budget queries, holiday entitlements, maternity cover ... she saves all the correspondence about actual investigations until last, treating them like a dessert to look forward to after the dutiful blandness of the main course.

An hour later, she rises to use the bathroom. She splashes cold water on her face and tries to ignore her reflection. When she comes back she begs a notepad and pen from the woman behind the counter, who gives her name as 'Lilja' when Pharaoh finally introduces herself as 'Trish'. She loses herself in paperwork. Jots down dates. Ages. Numbers. Eventually she purchases a new phone cable from the rack by the till and plugs it straight into the wall. Her phone grows warm in her hand. It vibrates several times while she reads. Calls from home. From work. The kids. None from McAvoy.

Eventually, Pharaoh becomes aware of a change in the tone of the air. She looks up. The handsome couple and the camouflaged man have disappeared without goodbyes. Three people now sit together at the table by the door. A man with a black beard and short white hair faces Pharaoh; a vision in huge spectacles and multi-coloured hemp. Across the table his two companions are angled to face each other. Both women. The younger of the two is dressed more conservatively – Canadian Goose puffer jacket thrown over the back of her chair to reveal a sensible woollen jumper and multicoloured neckerchief. Her companion is around Pharaoh's own age but she has the look of a punk who has never given up hope of revolution. Her hair is shaved on both sides to reveal intricate tattoos on her scalp; black and purple dreadlocks are piled atop her crown. She has the footprints of a bird tattooed on her cheekbones and studs puncture her ears, eyebrows, nose and lips. She's dressed in an orange jumpsuit under a black leather jacket and as she sips from a can of lager, Pharaoh feels like a geeky kid standing next to the coolest girl in school. She gives her a nod. A moment later, the stylish punk is standing at her side, smiling nervously, holding out a tattooed left hand, her lager still in her right.

'Hello. I'm Tamsin. I presume you're Trish?'

Pharaoh takes the hand. She feels the hard silver of her rings, the coarse skin of her knuckles. She glances at the hand, the slim wrist; both patterned with the same mesmerising ink: runes and Nordic prose interweaving to form feathers upon her flesh so that it seems her skin ripples as it catches the light. Her fingers are corseted with silver jewellery – a Tree of Life bookended by reflecting skulls and a wolf-head, mouth open.

'You don't look like a Tamsin,' says Pharaoh. She gestures at the seat opposite. 'I thought you'd be a Moon-Unit. Azalea Wildflower, or something. Tamsin. Bit normal, isn't it?'

Tamsin looks at her, a little taken aback. 'I'm in the right place, yes? You're the police officer from England? I hope you didn't think I was being rude when I came in – my friends, they wanted to catch up . . .'

'You're in the right place.' Pharaoh nods, looking up at her. She gestures at her notes as if they are official identity papers. 'Sorry, it was a long drive and I'm a bit out of sorts. I don't know the Icelandic for "discombobulated".'

'Neither do I,' says Tamsin, sitting down. 'But in Canadian it's the same.'

'You're Canadian? I didn't pick up on that.'

'I haven't been home in a while. I speak pretty good Icelandic. A little French.'

'We'll stick with English.' Pharaoh smiles. She puts both hands behind her head and sits back in her chair. 'I'm grateful you came to talk to me. As I explained in my email, you don't have to. You've been through a lot and the last thing you need is to have to go through it again but the man you found – there's a connection to a case at home.'

'I understand,' says Tamsin solemnly. 'I don't have anything to add but I can tell you it all in person.'

'Please.'

Tamsin takes a sip from her drink. Licks her lips. An expression of distaste flickers across her face as she replays the images in her head. 'I'm a photographer, as I told you. I had a residency at the art centre three years ago and never went home.

I'm not one of the resident artists there now but I still exhibit, here and abroad. I feel very at home here. There's something about the wilderness that speaks to me, I suppose.'

Pharaoh smiles encouragingly. Tamsin nods, clearly relieved to be understood.

'My last exhibition was sort of, well . . . out there.' She gives a sudden flash of teeth. 'A bit wacky, you might say. Lots of effects and digital enhancements. It went well, but this time I wanted to go back to what drew me here. Find a way to capture the feeling of this place; to turn a set of emotions and flavours into an actual picture that could be hung on the wall.'

Pharaoh tries to keep her expression warm and open as she fights the urge to tell Tamsin that she'd like her to get to the point. She's interviewed hundreds of witnesses over the years and has found it best to let each tell their stories their own way.

Tamsin pushes on, warming to her favourite subject. 'I know every tourist who comes to Iceland is after a shot of craggy cliffs and spurting geysers and the aurora borealis glinting off the lava field. I thought I could make fun of that while embracing it. A post-modern embracing of the kitsch, if you want it in layman's terms.'

Pharaoh takes a sip of wine. Takes a gulp, too.

'You know that New Year is a big deal here? Iceland comes to a stop. Reykjavik is a controlled riot. Fireworks exploding, everybody drinking like they're guests at a Viking wedding. I was invited to a party in Akureyri and didn't want to miss it but I'd also been told that there was a good chance of the Northern Lights appearing some time around the turn of the year. There was a shot I had in my head – the lighthouse on the headland. It's a magnificent building casting this perfect shadow onto the remains of an old village. Every amateur photographer who comes to this part of the world tries to get it in a new light and I had this image in my head of how it would look emerging from the green lights of the aurora.'

'But you didn't want to miss the party,' says Pharaoh, nodding.

'Well, no,' says Tamsin. She puts her hands together on the table. Pharaoh notices a black bracelet poking out of her sleeve, patterned with scraps of scaly, silvery leather. Tamsin notices the direction of her gaze. 'Cod leather,' she says, by way of explanation. 'Incredibly expensive in the stores in the capital but I have a friend who makes bags and bracelets with the cut-offs for a fraction of the price. They sell them at the Witchcraft Museum and some of the little boutiques between here and Blonduos. Quite popular.'

'You were telling me about how you found the body, Tamsin,' prompts Pharaoh. 'The corpse who spoke to you.'

Tamsin swallows. 'I'd set up a camera. Time-activated. Linked it to my iPhone so I could see the images as they were taken. I set it up early on the thirty-first. The weather was terrible and I was concerned it would be blown away but I managed to secure it under the eaves of the shelter and it seemed pretty secure with a good view across the headland to the lighthouse. I kept checking on it up until a little before midnight.' She chuckles, embarrassed. 'I was a bit out of it from then on. Like I say, we have a drink. A smoke.' She flashes Pharaoh a look. 'Sorry, I forgot, you wouldn't approve.'

'Couldn't give a shit, love. Proceed.'

Tamsin rubs a hand across her mouth. 'I didn't even think about the camera on New Year's Day. I was half drunk, half hung over. It was the next day before I even had the strength to pick up my phone. I got a bit of food down myself and drank some of the strongest coffee you've ever tasted and finally plugged in and had a look at what I'd got.' She stops, reaching into her pocket. She starts flicking through pictures, talking rapidly. 'The lights hadn't been as bright as I'd been promised but there were still some terrific images. The gale was absolutely howling and you got a real sense of movement – the clouds all bunched up at one end and the glare of the lighthouse like another moon in the sky. I felt pretty good about it. Then I saw this.' She angles the phone. 'I thought somebody was playing a trick.'

Pharaoh looks at the image. It's blurry and out of focus. But there is no doubt that the camera has captured a figure, dark as a burnt match, hair flowing out like pondweed. They stand on the snowy headland beneath the lighthouse, arms outstretched; a Christ-like effigy seared onto a canvas of luminescent green and the frothing quicksilver of the sea.

'You get pagans here, I'm told,' says Pharaoh, folding her arms when she notices that the hairs have started to rise. 'Some kind of ceremony.'

'Perhaps,' says Tamsin, looking down. 'Either way I wanted to see. If there was somebody up there they might have taken the camera. That was the last image that it got. I took some painkillers and waited for a gap in the weather and drove up to the cliffs.'

'And this was?'

'Mid-afternoon on the third,' she says. 'There wasn't much light and my friends said I was crazy to go when there was still partying to do but this is important, isn't it? It's not an easy drive. You'll have seen bad roads on the way up here but it gets so much worse as you head north. The cliffs are amazing but frightening too.'

'And you saw a car,' prompts Pharaoh. 'A little red hatchback.'

'Like the one out there,' she says, nodding at the car park. 'Suzuki Swift. It was up there on the clifftop, maybe a mile or so from the lighthouse and the earthworks.'

'You didn't stop?' says Pharaoh, pretending to look at her notes.

'I didn't see any need to. It was pretty dark and it's not that unusual to see a car up on the cliffs and if I'm honest, I didn't have it in my head that there was anything to be worried about.' She shrugs, though not unkindly. 'And maybe I was a bit focused on my camera.'

'Tell me what you found,' says Pharaoh. 'I know it's hard, but . . .'

'I parked where I normally do,' says Tamsin, looking out of the window, her reflection shimmering as the rain beats down upon the hard, white snow. 'The village was pretty much abandoned in the 1930s and really, there are only a few mounds and foundations still in place. Even so, it's popular with tourists. The last farmhouse has been converted into a shelter. They're all over Iceland. Places to escape to if the weather turns or if you're a fisherman who's had to put ashore. It's one of the areas where boats and bodies wash up, you see.'

Pharaoh nods, saying nothing. She glances beneath the table. Checks that her phone is still recording.

'The camera was gone.' Tamsin scowls. 'The twine I'd used to secure it in the eaves had been cut clean through. Whoever was dancing about on the headland had taken themselves a lovely belated Christmas present.' The angry expression fades to sadness and she rubs her cheeks with the heels of her hands. 'I don't know why I walked down to the lighthouse. I suppose I was pissed off and the only place I'd seen the person who stole my camera was down towards the sea. I went to see if, maybe . . .'

'They'd dropped it. They were still there. You wanted to do something. I understand.'

Tamsin nods, her braids becoming untangled. 'It's wild up there. Timeless. Even the lighthouse seems like some ancient monument. And the columns – these big, black basalt columns, stacked together like logs, the sea crashing over them, the sky pressing down. It's beautiful, in a terrible sort of way. I trudged down past all the earthworks and over the snow to where I'd got the picture of the person with the dark hair. And I saw him.' She gulps. Fiddles with her necklace. 'There in the little inlet. On the stones. There were birds overhead. I can see them now. Gulls and crows. A bright orange buoy had washed up. There were green nets, all tangled up. And him. The man.'

Pharaoh reaches across and squeezes Tamsin's hand. Feels the texture of the fish-leather bracelet and banks the information. 'You thought he was dead?' she asks kindly.

'He was dead,' snaps Tamsin. She shakes her head, mumbling an apology. 'Half his face was gone. His leg was missing at the knee, his trouser leg flapping. His skin was white, like he'd been bleached.'

'But you went to check,' says Pharaoh. 'You didn't run back to your car. You were brave. You tried to help.'

'It was automatic,' says Tamsin, brushing over the compliment. 'I did it because that's what I've seen people do. On TV, in films. I ran to the body and bent down. He was face-down. Sort of in the recovery position. The nearer I got the more I saw. There were holes in him. Tiny perforations in his skin. A huge gash in his head . . .'

Pharaoh alters her position so she can look into Tamsin's eyes. 'And you're sure,' she says softly. 'Sure what happened next isn't the result of a hangover and an artistic imagination.'

'No,' splutters Tamsin angrily, slamming her palm down on the table. 'I put my fingers on his neck. He was cold as meat from the freezer. I jerked back as soon as I touched him. And I swear, that's when he shuddered. That's the only way I can describe it. He shuddered as if a current had gone through him. And all this water gushed up, spewing out from the holes in his face and his neck.' She demonstrates, throwing fistfuls of imaginary water into the air. 'I fell backwards, terrified out of my skin. I've never been so frightened in my life.'

'You said he spoke,' whispers Pharaoh. 'In the statement you gave, you said he spoke.'

Tamsin nods, definite in her reply. 'Even over the storm and the waves and the birds, I know what he said. I don't know what it means or how he was alive but it was definite. He barely had any face left but this horrible, strangled sound came out of him. And he said it. He truly did.'

Pharaoh closes her eyes. Looks at her notes and the witness statement Tamsin had given the Icelandic Police a few hours after her gory discovery.

'He said "McAvoy". Like the actor. He said it twice, as if to be sure. Then his body just went still. I'll never unsee that, Detective. It was like watching his soul leave his body. They didn't believe me when I told the local police but what is there for me to gain? I don't know what it means. I don't know who he was. I'm telling you because you said it was important but I don't understand what I've seen or why I've seen it.' She stops, glancing towards the counter, clearly weighing up whether another drink will have medicinal benefits. 'This McAvoy,' she asks quietly. 'Is he a suspect? I mean, it looks like he went into the water and washed up and that's that. I don't see how there could be any foul play. Have they even identified him yet? I sort of feel responsible. Like, maybe I should write to his family or something. What can you actually tell me?'

Pharaoh pushes the vodka bottle across the table and urges Tamsin to help herself. She closes one eye, a headache starting to grind above her left eye. 'The police haven't had the prints back yet,' she says softly, as if imparting a secret to a trusted friend. 'There was no wallet in his clothing. No identifying paperwork, either on his person or in his vehicle.'

'It was definitely his car?' asks Tamsin. 'Suicide or an accident, then . . .'

'The local detectives have done a good job,' Pharaoh says, ignoring the interruption. 'Been through passenger lists, flights and shipping logs. Took a little while but they worked out that Albert Jonsson had several aliases. One of them was Russell Chandler. And Russell Chandler was an awkward sod who nearly cost a friend of mine his life.' Pharaoh sighs. Pushes her hair back and shakes her head. 'He didn't deserve this, though. He was a good investigator. Might have made a decent copper.'

Tamsin pours herself a vodka. Meets Pharaoh's eye and pours her a drink too. They clink glasses.

'What's Icelandic for "cheers"?' asks Pharaoh, stopping her phone from recording.

'*Skal*,' says Tamsin. 'But in Canada, we say "sociable".'

'Fuck off, no you don't.'

'We really do,' says Tamsin apologetically. She swallows her vodka and pours another. They both relax, now the unpleasantness seems to be out of the way. 'Are you going to tell me who this McAvoy is?' she asks.

Pharaoh stops with her glass halfway to her mouth. She feels a little blurry around the edges. Feels a bit tired and a bit pissed and a long way from home. Wonders, for a moment, whether it would be so very terrible to share a confidence with this stranger.

'Sociable,' she says, under her breath. She can't wait to get home and tell him a fact he might not know. 'Fucking hell.'

# 15

*Alfred Gelder Street, Hull*
*10.46 p.m.*

Vidarr is leaning against the damp wood of the boarded-up pub. He doesn't remember coming to a halt at this place. Can't recall what came before. He has grown accustomed to these moments; of returning to himself without any recollection of where he has been.

Vidarr has spent the last half an hour staring at a golden statue in the middle of the road. King William on his horse, splendid and elegant. Black railings and a marble plinth. It looms out of the black air and the grey mist and makes him think of Greek myths and old movies, of Argonauts and gilded calves.

He has a sudden memory. A blanket over his knees, hot chocolate and jam sandwiches on a tray, listening to the gale buffet the campervan – his face only a few inches from the fuzzy pixels of the boxy portable TV. He remembers the sense of sanctuary. Of respite. A friendly hand in his own. Remembers Mam, a bruise on her cheek. His aunt, sitting on the grass. The boy in the mirror, smiling back . . .

He turns his face away from the recollection. Refuses to look too closely. He doesn't want to think about sanctuary in case he remembers what they were fleeing. Doesn't want to remember the blood, or his mam pressing frozen peas to her bruised cheek, or his mirror image, folded in on himself, arms girdling his knees, rocking back and forth in the outdoor toilet.

He licks his teeth. He has smoked one of his cigarettes, his trembling fingers turning colder with each drag. His mouth tastes like his stepfather's: that reek of bile and wet tobacco. He works his jaw in circles, listening to the *click, click, click* as the cartilage snaps against the bone. His jaw has been like this since he was nine. The bad man slammed his face between the refrigerator door and the cold metal frame, squeezing his skull until something snapped and everything went white and orchestral and numb. He had used too much milk, according to the bad man. Deserved everything he fucking got . . .

Despite his promises to himself, Vidarr drifts into memory. Mam sitting on the hard-backed chair at the kitchen table, huffing hair out of her eyes, the oven door open to let some heat into the cold, damp room. Slicing onions. Peeling potatoes . . .

Roberta. Drunk. Drunk, again. Drunk and roaring. Each drink she tipped down her neck was gasoline on a fire. She came through the door like a thunderstorm. Mam had tried to shush her. Pleaded with her. The bad man woke to the sound of smashing glass and screaming. His temper took no rousing. He back-handed Mam so hard that her earring ripped through the earlobe and stuck into the blue ink on the back of his hand.

He took Roberta by the neck. Shook her like a dog with a rat. A light came on in his eyes. He dragged her to the cooker, his fingers about her throat. There was blood on her teeth, puke on her chin and in her hair. He might have just been planning to scare her. Might have left it at that if she'd just kept her mouth shut. Instead she managed to work up enough blood and saliva to spit in his face. He stuffed her head in the oven and held her there, his hand in her dark hair.

Vidarr closes his eyes. He raises his hand to his jaw and feels the splintered bone beneath his stubble and skin. He remembers waking up on the floor, blood dripping from his ear,

159

explosions of black and white, purple and vermilion, turning his vision into a scream. He didn't expect ever to hear such sounds again. Didn't expect to see such terrible things.

Vidarr looks at the length of braided hair around his wrist and feels something stir within him.

Feels the raven unfolding its wings.

He reaches into his pocket and feels the cold, unyielding certainty of the hook.

Smiles, even as the tears freeze against his cheeks.

# DAY TWO

# EMERGENCY CALL – 10 JANUARY,

## 04.23 A.M.

OPERATOR: Police. What's your emergency?

CALLER: *(SOUND OF RUNNING FEET. SHORTNESS OF BREATH)* Christ, I need police. Ambulance ... no, stupid ... it's too late ...

OPERATOR: Sir, can you please state the nature of your—

CALLER: *(FRANTIC)* Of course it's too late. Shit. Sorry ... sorry, I'm at the Fish Docks ...

OPERATOR: Sir, I need you to tell me where you are.

CALLER: *(SOUND DISTORTED)* I just said! Fish Docks. St Andrew's. By the Blake building. My mates—

OPERATOR: I need you to listen to me, sir. Please, take a breath and tell me what's happening.

CALLER: The old trawler on the pontoons by the water. We've been working on doing it up. I came down for my walk and saw the security cage unlocked. Saw blood. They're inside. In the cabin. There's so much blood ... they've been ...

OPERATOR: Sir, are you in immediate danger?

CALLER: *(GASPING FOR BREATH)* I don't bloody know! I didn't even think. Fuck, you can see their bones ...

OPERATOR: What's your name, sir?

CALLER: Norman Michaels. I live at Anlaby Common.

OPERATOR: And the names of the men?

CALLER: Alf Howe. Fat Des Kavanagh. They're old. Old men. Who'd do this? Jesus. Please, send help . . .

OPERATOR: The police are on their way, sir. An ambulance too. I need you to stay on the line until they get there.

CALLER: I can't breathe. My chest . . .

OPERATOR: Mr Michaels? Talk to me . . .

**Call terminated.**

# 16

McAvoy steps out into the frozen morning. Looks up at the bridge, hiding in the low cloud and black air, and frowns across the road at the Humber, its surface rippled with tiny white peaks, sucking and slurping at the muddy shingle.

He licks his lips. Tastes tea and Roisin.

He opens the car door. Gets in and puts the key in the ignition. The readout on the dashboard informs him that the temperature has dropped back below freezing. He stares at the sparkling dust that hangs above the wet, black road. He locks his teeth and closes his eyes. Gives himself ten whole seconds of peace. Then he starts the car, checks the mirror and pulls out into the silence of the morning. Flicks on the radio and hears the last of the news.

*. . . understands that the bodies were discovered aboard the recently rediscovered Hull trawler, Blake Holst, which is being restored by volunteers as part of an ambitious project funded by local shipping boss Stephen Ballantine. We hope to have more information as this story develops . . .*

McAvoy brakes, hard. The tyres screech on the cold road. His phone flies off the seat and strikes the dashboard. He reaches into the footwell, retrieves it and yelps when it starts to ring.

'McAvoy,' he says breathlessly. 'The *Blake Holst*. Who's at the scene? Why did nobody call?'

'I'm calling,' says Area Commander Slattery. 'Get your arse here. And pronto.'

Twenty minutes later, McAvoy is trying to keep his feet while wriggling into a protective blue oversuit and plastic booties and sheathing his big hands in ill-fitting nitrile gloves. The wind coming off the river is brutal and carries with it the scents of the sea: all diesel, brine and slime. McAvoy can barely hear DC Andy Daniells as he chatters away in his ear, using the open boot of the people-carrier as a windbreak. Daniells is already wearing his blue oversuit. He's a plump, fleshy figure in his early thirties and the coveralls make him look a little like a disappointing genie.

'. . . found by one of the volunteers. Norman Michaels. Lives off Anlaby Common. Seventy-six. Wife, three kids. Four grand-children. Used to be a skipper. I reckon he'd struggle to do all this on his own. No blood on him, so unless he'd brought a change of clothes . . .'

McAvoy slams the boot shut and glares across at the outline of the rusty trawler that rises and falls on the shifting sea. The Lord Line building stands sentry across the broken ground, half lost in mist. The old pumping stations glare down over the sunken lock gates, twists of cellophane and silken petals tangled in the coils of barbed wire. He can just about make out the shape of a big orange vessel, anchored at Albert and William Wright Docks. Makes a mental note to get in touch with the security director and request a list of all the vessels currently at anchor, as well as further along the river at King George Dock. There have been some security breaches on the docks over recent months and anybody making their way from a vessel at anchor and heading inland could conceivably have passed this way. There will be security footage, he's certain. The adjacent docks are still bustling with activity as vast amounts of money are poured into offshore wind farms and renewable energy. St Andrew's Dock is only a short walk along the river, though the fortunes of the different quays could not be in starker contrast. St Andrew's Dock is a mausoleum; a crumbling headstone marking the graves of countless men.

'He was here early,' says McAvoy, over the sound of the wind. 'What was he doing?'

'Early riser,' says Daniells, raising his voice. 'Habit of his job. Always up with the lark. Said it's the best part of the day. He likes to see the tide turn and the sun rise. I think he's a bit lost, poor old bugger. They're like that, aren't they, the old fishermen. Haven't known what to do with themselves in fifty years. It's shaken him up good and proper but he's trying to keep it together. We've got him in one of the rooms the CSIs have okayed. I thought you'd want to talk to him yourself.'

McAvoy clanks across the metal floor plates and down the gangway, stepping aboard. There are yellow plastic markers pressed into the soft wood of the deck, identifying rust-red splashes of colour.

'They didn't make any effort to keep out of the blood,' says Daniells, nodding at the markers. 'Should be a decent boot print. They weren't in their right mind, you can see that. Must have been drugged out their mind.'

McAvoy ducks under the metal door and into the cool metal cave of the ship. The quality of the air seems to change as the battering wind is trapped outside. He presses himself to the wall and lets Daniells squeeze past him.

'Down a bit then down the ladder. It's awkward.'

Voices rise from below. Camera lenses flash, a bright white surge cutting through the garish yellow of the forensic scientists' standing lamps. He hears metal clanging on metal and the echo seems to come to him from all directions, bouncing off the metal walls. He grips the handrail and climbs down into the bunkroom. The smell of blood fills his mouth and throat, cutting through the stink of salt water and mildew like a blade.

Both victims have been laid out on the wooden floor of the sleeping quarters. Their torsos have been ripped open and their ribs stick up through a mass of flesh and fabric like the wings of a skeletal bird. The nearest man has had his skull beaten almost flat. The other lies in a crucifix pose. The lower half of his face hangs loose, smeared with black blood, the jawbone grotesquely distended.

Detective Chief Inspector Bronwyn Patten is standing at the back of the room, talking to a white-clad CSI. She spots McAvoy and gives him an incongruously cheerful wave.

'Fucking horrible, isn't it?' she shouts across the bodies. Her words resound off the walls.

McAvoy clanks across the metal plates. He barely takes his eyes off the corpses.

'That one is Alfred Howe,' says DCI Patten, nodding at the corpse with the broken jaw. 'Wallet was in his trousers so no shortage of info on him. Got just shy of eighty quid in his trouser pocket too, so if it's a robbery, they were shit at it. That one's Desmond Kavanagh. Less money but you'll see the big fat gold ring on his forefinger.' She stops talking and gives a bark of laughter. 'Bloody hell, McAvoy, you've gone grey. Slattery's up top getting some air. Rather upset his delicate sensibilities.'

McAvoy considers the DCI. She's in her early fifties and has seen and done just about everything. She's got square shoulders and short blonde hair, a gap in her front teeth and a scar in her eyebrow. There's some lyrical Welsh in her accent. He hasn't worked with her much but Pharaoh has told him she's a good copper who would have become an assistant chief constable by now if she hadn't resisted the advances of a senior officer back when she was still a PC. She'd been the senior officer on call when the 999 came through.

'Any chance of a coffee, Daniells?' she asks, looking past him. 'I don't ask you because you're a junior officer, or because you're a homosexual, or because I'm a woman and you're a man and this is a way to demonstrate the power balance. I ask because you're closest to the door.'

'No problem, guv,' says Daniells from behind his face mask.

'I prefer to be called Bronwyn, actually,' says Patten to McAvoy. 'You okay with McAvoy or should I have a stab at your first name?'

'McAvoy's fine,' he replies, his mouth dry.

'Hell of a time for this to happen,' says Patten, shifting position so that McAvoy can step into the little patch of floor at the rear of the bunkroom. The blood hasn't spilled this far.

'Sorry?'

'With Trish away, I mean. She'd fight for this one and no mistake. You know where she's at or is it all hush-hush?'

McAvoy doesn't answer. Just looks down at the two old men, ripped open and laid out like butchered carcasses in a spreading pool of sticky blood.

'Looks like a major crime to me,' says McAvoy, turning to the DCI. 'We're understaffed but we can take it.'

Patten shrugs. 'You can have it for me, mate, but Slattery's already nodded it to regular CID. Says you're short-staffed as it is. You're dealing with that old lass in the bathtub, aren't you? Christ, that's a bad one. This weather is a killer, right enough. One of our neighbours has been out every night pouring kettles of boiling water into his carp pond and the buggers have still all kicked the bucket. Can fish kick? Forget it, doesn't matter.'

McAvoy squats down, angling his head. He looks at the mass of footprints in the spilled blood. Fights down bile as he considers the thick, clotted blood that dangles from the exposed ribs.

'A hook,' says Patten, following his gaze. 'Possibly a medical implement. Entered under the ribcage and pulled out with enough force to splinter the bone. Incredibly strong or absolutely drugged out of their mind. Pathologist still hasn't made it over from Sheffield but the lead CSI has given a prima facie analysis on both bodies. There's a boot print on that one's jaw. She reckons his face was stepped on as he lay there dying. Strange print. No treads but a clear size nine as if the sole has been wrapped in something.' She nods towards the nearest bunk. 'That thing was pushed into his mouth.'

Patten points to an object by the metal steps. It's the size of a rounders bat, with a pointed end. The thin end looks as though it has been varnished red.

'Is that a fid?' asks McAvoy, squinting. 'The real ones are hard as rock. The wood tends to be lignum vitae.'

'I can tell why Trish likes you,' says Patten. 'Yeah, the old boy said the same. I'd never heard of a fid before. Used for mending sails or stitching ropes or something, isn't it? Thought it was a broken baseball bat myself. We think it was an opportunist weapon for the killer. It was already here, according to the poor old sod who phoned this in. Maybe the hook was too, though we haven't spotted that yet.'

McAvoy turns and considers the remainder of the room. A pile of mannequins in fishermen's clothes are piled into one of the coffin beds. Another lies in an awkward position, leg folded at a grotesque angle, half in and out of the bottom bunk.

'Exhibits,' says Patten. 'They've been storing all sorts of fishing memorabilia here for when they turn this tub of rust into something that might actually float. Can't see it happening myself. Especially not now.'

'Family?' asks McAvoy, considering the ruined bodies.

'Aye.' Patten nods, trying to stay matter-of-fact. 'Family Liaisons will be there once we're at a respectable hour.'

'Either reported as missing?'

Patten shakes her head. 'They were old, not geriatric. Both

widowers but no shortage of children and grandchildren. Mr Michaels next door, he says they were a couple of good lads. Fished together most of their lives. Hung about with some local hero who died the best part of fifty years ago. He were a bit shaky so I didn't push but I thought you might want to have a go. Trish says you're good with the old buggers.'

McAvoy runs his tongue around the inside of his mouth. 'This ship – it's owned by Stephen Ballantine. Stephen is the son of Rory Ballantine. That's the man you're referring to – the bosun who died off Iceland. His name has come up in connection with the Enid Chappell investigation. So has Bernard Acklam. Acklam is a person of interest and it would be helpful to talk to Mr Ballantine.' He stops himself, aware of the sound of footsteps behind him. 'This is one investigation, that's clear,' he continues. 'We can take this on. I'd be glad to work as your number two, Bronwyn. Slattery must see the sense in it.'

'Must I, Detective Sergeant?' comes a voice in McAvoy's ear. He closes his eyes, wishing for a great hole to open up in the rotten boards beneath his feet. He turns, unsure what expression to pull. Finds himself speaking without knowing what words are about to emerge.

'Sir, there is a clear connection between this incident and the death of Enid Chappell. We have hard evidence placing a Bernard Acklam at the cottage in Cherry Burton. Mr Acklam is an associate of Stephen Ballantine, who is responsible for the redevelopment of this vessel and the docklands area.'

'I'm well aware of Mr Ballantine,' says Slattery coldly. 'A true philanthropist. One of the good ones. If he is to be troubled by this ghastly affair then I will handle that myself. As for this wild speculation, I have yet to see anything that gives us cause to believe there is any connection between the two investigations. CID can take this on and you can continue to grub about in the affairs of that poor old woman in the bathtub. What was her name? Edith?'

'Enid, sir. Enid Chappell.'

'Yes. I've still to see any evidence that her death should be treated as murder.'

'Her legs were tied together with human hair, sir,' mutters McAvoy.

'Perhaps she wanted to make sure she couldn't chicken out of a suicide. Stranger things have happened.'

McAvoy wrinkles his brow. 'When, sir? When has a stranger thing than that actually happened?'

'Look, this is a horrible business,' says Slattery, turning to look at the corpses and swallowing hard. 'We don't need internal struggles. Perhaps if Pharaoh were available we could roll this into one investigation but I have to think of resources and it gives us more wiggle room with the budget if they come from separate investigations. You don't have to think about this stuff, McAvoy. I do. Now, I think you would be well advised to go and put together a clear report, outlining what has been done so far and what avenues of investigation the Chappell case will be following.'

'I could use McAvoy,' says Patten flatly. 'There's an old boy next door. Had a bit of a scare when he phoned it in. McAvoy's good with the old boys, I'm told.'

Slattery looks ready to argue but the smell of fresh blood in his nostrils seems to persuade him of the merits of getting back into the fresh air. He relents. 'Talk to the witness, then get yourself back to Bransholme nick. I'll deal with the press personally and I want you to provide written reasons why Mr Ballantine should be troubled before you go and disturb him. You won't be aware of this but Mr Ballantine and I have discussed some very important areas of financial cooperation and, more crucially, I have no doubt this will be a matter of great emotional distress. We all have roles to play within Humberside Police, Sergeant. I hope you understand yours.'

Slattery turns and makes his way back across the boards,

almost colliding with Daniells as he makes his way through from the galley clutching a mug of coffee. 'Morning, sir. Feeling better? I'm sure you'll get your sea legs soon. Never bothered me . . . crime scenes, I mean. Strong constitution, I suppose.'

Patten squeezes McAvoy's arm as Slattery climbs back up the ladder, grumbling darkly all the way. She smiles. 'Let's keep one another informed, eh? I'd like to hear more about the connection. And this Ballantine bloke – anybody who has the area commander shaking like that must be worth talking to. Trish was right, people do either love you or hate you.'

McAvoy lets his gaze drift towards the two dead men, then up to the articles on the wall. He squints as he reads the headline: the tribute to three brave men swallowed by the white sea.

'It's connected,' he mutters. 'She knew something. Stirred something up.'

He reaches into his pocket and pulls out his phone. Scrolls through the list of numbers called by Enid Chappell and makes out the names scribbled onto the log by Sophie Kirkland before she scanned the image and input it into the investigation file. He expands the image on the screen. Finds the number he is looking for and calls it. A moment later, a song resonates in the echoing confines of the bunkroom. Alf Howe's mobile, trilling away to the mournful strains of Rod Stewart.

McAvoy puts the phone back in his pocket. 'She knew him. Called him in the days before she died.'

Patten just nods. 'Send me everything. Quietly.'

# 17

*The map room of the Blake Holst, St Andrew's Dock, Hull 7.04 a.m.*

Norman Michaels looks as though he needs a good slug of whisky adding to the cup of tea that is going cold on the varnished wooden tabletop in front of him. His face is an unnatural grey. His glasses have slipped down his nose, their frames seeming to put a perfect line through his vision. If he notices he doesn't show it. He stares into the milky beige liquid without appearing to see it, barely looking up as McAvoy ducks through the gangway into a small, cream-painted room. Michaels is seated at a low table. A dark-haired female PC has been sitting with him and she gives McAvoy a grateful smile as she excuses herself with a soft, slightly incongruous 'lovely to meet you'. She gives Michaels a squeeze on the shoulder as she leaves.

'Nice girl, that,' says Michaels quietly. 'Family are from down Summergangs Road. Wouldn't fancy her chances of breaking up a scrap if it all kicked off in the Criterion but her heart's in the right place.'

'Wouldn't fancy my chances either,' says McAvoy.

'You're Scottish?' asks Michaels.

'Does it show?'

'I did some time offshore up there,' admits Michaels, staring back into his tea. 'Knew plenty of Jocks on the Gamecock Fleet too. Can I say "Jocks"? No offence meant. I like your lot. Hard workers but a bitch on settling day. You ever been to sea?'

'Just the family fishing boat when I was a boy,' says McAvoy, settling himself into the plastic chair opposite Michaels and slipping out of his wet coat. 'Did some rowing at university but I doubt that counts.'

Michaels looks up. 'You a posh boy, are you? Bet you played union.'

McAvoy smiles. 'I've seen League. Too fast for me. You'll be Rovers.'

'Course I'm bloody Rovers,' says Michaels, rolling his eyes. 'You ever hear the story of when we played FC in the Challenge Cup? Whole bloody city took a bus to London. One city, two teams, and they still play the final at Wembley. I ask you! Some daft bugger strung a banner by the Humber bridge, telling the last person to leave Hull to turn out the lights.'

McAvoy has heard the story before. He's heard most of the stories before. But he'll listen to them a hundred times more if it helps put Norman Michaels at his ease.

'How are you, Mr Michaels?' asks McAvoy, placing his notebook and mobile phone on the table. 'I'm so sorry you had to see what you did.'

Michaels holds McAvoy's gaze. 'I've lost friends before,' he says quietly.

'Doesn't make it easier.'

'I suppose not. It makes it feel more familiar though. I know how it goes. What will come next, what to do to get through it. Still a shock though. Wasn't expecting this when I got up. Poor bastards. Druggies, was it? No, sorry, you can't say.'

McAvoy considers the old trawlerman. A skipper for twenty-seven years. A Hessle Road kid who made it all the way. He volunteers aboard the *Corsair* when he gets the chance. Happy to give up his free time to help put the *Blake Holst* back together too. McAvoy can understand why so many former trawlermen want to stay connected, however loosely, to the industry that defined them. There is a comfort in the familiar. He wonders if he will do the same himself when he retires, whether he will start some meaningless research project down in the archives, popping into community stations for a cup of tea and a yarn, telling the next generation of coppers they would never have cut it in his day. He can't picture it.

McAvoy examines the wall of newspaper clippings behind Michaels. Various appeals for funding. A profile of Rory Ballantine and the son he never met. Anniversary pieces and two-page re-tellings of the same tales of tragedy and bravado he has read about before.

'You have no doubts about the identities of the men you found?' asks McAvoy.

'No doubt,' says Michaels, scratching at the back of his hand. 'Poor bastards. Alf. Fat Des. Christ, whoever did it got bloody lucky. If they'd tried that a few years ago they'd have been torn to bits. Old men now. We all are. Makes you think . . . I tell you, the way the world's going, I don't reckon we should be mourning the dead, we should be bloody jealous.' He closes his eyes. 'Sorry, I'm being a right miserable git. Grandkids got me a mug with Grumpy Old Man written on it last birthday. Cheeky sods.' He takes a breath. 'How can I help? I didn't see anybody. Wish I had.'

To McAvoy, Michaels looks like an actor putting on a mask. He is trying to pull himself together: to be the gruff, matter-of-fact trawler skipper who's seen it all before. McAvoy wishes they'd met under better circumstances. He seems an entertaining sort.

McAvoy makes a show of looking at his notes. In truth, he has the details memorised.

'Tell me about them,' he says quietly. 'Your pals.'

Michaels consider him for a moment. He has intelligent eyes. McAvoy pictures him in the wheelhouse, sitting in the skipper's chair and scanning the horizon.

'I can't say as we were close mates or anything,' says Michaels thoughtfully. 'Not that we weren't either. It's an odd business, fishing. You spend so long crammed in with these lads, sometimes high as kites and sometimes thinking that the next wave is going to kill you all. So there's a bond between you, even when you're having a barney and threatening to kill the next bloke who does something that rubs your fur the wrong way. Alf and Des were good lads. Alf were a decent skipper. They were part of this group of friends – proper characters. I think they thought they were the Magnificent Seven. But there were never much room for an eighth, if you get me.'

McAvoy takes his notepad from his pocket. Ensures that Michaels can see his shorthand notes. He makes no remark. Just stares into his mug and talks in a faraway voice.

'It was always a daft idea. I can't see the *Holst* chugging up and down the Humber. Can't see people flocking to come aboard even if we managed it. You ever been out on the Humber? It takes a while to get your sea legs. An authentic trawling experience?' He shakes his head. 'How could it be authentic? Poor Stephen. He's done bloody well for himself but if you ask me he'd have been happier as a deckie on a sidewinder. The world that made him, it's all gone. Look at what's left. Buildings falling down, docks sliding into the sea. They can put on as many songs and plays about the good old days of Hessle Road as they want but it's never going to bring all that back.'

'You don't agree with Mr Ballantine's plans for the *Holst*?'

'Pipe dream, son. Money to burn. Wants to measure up to this image he has of his old man, and there's nothing wrong with that. Rory were a good bloke, everybody will tell you that and I'm not going to disagree. He was the leader. Told them all what to do. The ones who survived, they were lost for a long time. It's no wonder they filled Stephen's head with all these heroic tales. They turned him into some sort of bloody superman. I don't know if they did Stephen any favours.'

McAvoy sits back in his chair. 'Seven, yes?' He holds up one hand and raises a finger as he counts off the names he knows. 'Rory Ballantine. Alf Howe. Des Cavanagh.'

'Cowboy Mick. Young Billy. They never came back from Iceland. Died alongside Rory. Story's on the wall yonder.'

'Do you know the names of the other two, just for reference?' asks McAvoy cautiously.

'Big Gerard,' says Michaels, nodding. 'Sorry, Gerard Wade. He pops by the *Corsair* every now and again for a cup of tea though he's never been a sociable sort. I think he likes to see how we're spending his money.'

'He contributes?'

'Aye, done well has Big Gerard. Him and Rory were thick as thieves. Gerard half killed himself trying to save him. I don't think he ever got over it. It were Gerard that put Stephen in that posh school. Set him up in business. He'd promised Rory, you see. Told him he'd always look out for his family if anything happened to him.'

McAvoy slides a finger between the buttons of his shirt and scratches the ridged pink skin of the scar across his breastbone. It's starting to throb.

'And number seven?'

Michaels rolls his eyes, pursing his lips to hide his grin. 'You'll know Napper, I'm sure. All the coppers know Napper.'

'That'll be Bernard Acklam.'

'Aye, I suppose. He's just Napper. A walking nightmare but you can't help but like him. Always got his fingers in pies and they usually belong to other people. The fingers, I mean. And the pies, now I think on it. No stranger to a prison cell. Stephen calls him "Uncle Napper", which gives you an idea how things are.'

'Close?'

'It's Napper who got the ball rolling on all this,' says Michaels, gesturing at his surroundings. 'Called in plenty of favours from the sort of people who don't put their hand in their pocket very often. Stephen wanted to do this and that meant Napper was damn well going to make sure it happened. He loves that lad like he's his own.'

Michaels stops, raising his hand to his mouth. 'Don't go thinking I'm buying into gossip, Sergeant. That were a slip of the tongue.'

McAvoy sips his tea. He waits for Michaels to fill the silence.

'There's some spiteful bastards on Road,' says Michaels at last. 'When everybody was wailing and roaring about losing Rory and how it were awful that his wife was left with these bains and his little sister was off her head with grief – always some bastard has to taint it. I never bought into it.'

'There were people who cast doubts on Stephen's parentage?'

'Horrible thing to do if you ask me. Don't forget, we're talking about a community where secrets run from cradle to grave. There are lads as old as me who called some bloke "Dad" for their whole life, and everybody else knows that their mum was having it away with the rent-collector when her man was away at sea. There are people who call their grandmothers "Mum" and their mums their big sister and who've never worked out what everybody else refuses to talk about. That's just the way of it. I was born five months after my mam and dad got married and believe me, I weren't premature.'

McAvoy stops writing. He can hear the CSIs working in the bunkroom, the soft squeak of equipment being wheeled along damp metallic corridors and the drip-drip-drip of condensation tumbling from the rusty ceiling.

'So much sadness in that family,' mutters Michaels. 'The Ballantines. I knew Rory's dad, Lachlan. He were one of twins and the sea got them both. Lachlan trawled up a mine off Norway. His brother, Stuart, was lost overboard near the Faroes. Poor bains. Their dad and their grandad and God knows how many others over the years. Aye, the newspapers had a ball with all that. I remember reading some article on Stephen that went on about how the Ballantines could be forgiven for thinking they'd offended Poseidon. Poseidon! They were just trawlermen. It's a bloody dangerous business. You're lucky one moment and the next you're dead. That's why we're such a superstitious bunch. I've had deckies turn around on their way to the docks and head back home because they've seen a bloke with cross-eyes or realised they've got change in their pockets. No green. No washing clothes on sailing day. No whistling unless you want to whistle up a storm. Don't wave anybody off.' He stops himself. Gives a dry laugh. 'All nonsense, I suppose, but when the ice is building on the rigging and the seas are throwing you about like a cork in a Jacuzzi, none of it seems that daft. It's something to cling to.'

McAvoy looks around. Glances at the headlines stuck to the walls again.

'Rory's up there, somewhere,' says Michaels, jerking a thumb at the wall. 'Story on the *Blake Purcell*. Been stuck to the wall since day one but you can still read it. Reckon the writer thought he was starting a novel but it's not far from the truth.'

McAvoy flicks his eyes back to the clipping. He focuses on the patchy image of the *Blake Purcell*, steaming out of St Andrew's Dock, the low clouds and the smoke from the chimney stack virtually indistinguishable. Inset is a picture of a broad, square-jawed man in a cloth cap, the whites of his eyes unnaturally bright. McAvoy stands and moves towards the wall, the words becoming clearer: the image more precise.

'Can you think of anybody who might want to harm Alf and Des?'

Michaels shakes his head. 'We weren't big mates, like I said. I only popped in because the security gate was open and it didn't look right. I half expected it to be Napper in there with some bit of stuff.'

180

'You weren't concerned for your own safety?' asks McAvoy.

'I'm an old man but I can still kick a burglar in the goolies, don't you worry about me. Napper mentioned that they were putting security cameras in though I don't know if they ever got around to it. You'll be as well asking Stephen about that.'

'They'd had problems before? With security?'

Michaels sucks his lip. Nods. 'Few of us old buggers were having a pint just before Christmas. Des was going for it. Knocking them back like he was catching the morning's tide. He made a bit of a show of himself. Snivelling a bit. Kept saying it weren't fair and that he were an old man. I got the impression somebody had been getting in his ear. Leaning on him a bit. Napper sorted him out. Got him cleaned up and took him home. Brave of Napper if you ask me – you wouldn't want a drunk bloke puking on your nice upholstery. Drives this real vintage beauty, does Napper.'

McAvoy listens to the sound of a muffled conversation outside the hatchway. Slattery? Criticising him, no doubt. Probably taking notes; making loud calls to the top brass, explaining that the reason they haven't put things to bed yet is due to McAvoy's meandering interview technique.

'You'll know all about that night, I presume,' says McAvoy quietly. He's starting to feel as though he has heard the story told too many different ways. 'The night that the crewmen were lost . . .'

'Napper were in his bunk when it happened,' mutters Michaels, and starts to examine the back of his hand. 'The night they lost Rory. He were always happy to talk about it. The journalists sought him out because he'd give them chapter and verse for the price of a couple of pints. He said there was a noise like they had driven a wagon into a wall. Run aground just off Skagi. Radar was completely iced up and it was just bad luck that they hit it. They spent hours huddled together up in the wheelhouse, world getting darker, men getting colder. Radio operator was a good lad. Scottish, actually. Klein, was it? Maybe Klein. He were trying to get a signal out of the wireless. Kept broadcasting, over and over, while the ship started listing, sinking. Skipper gave the order to get into the lifeboats but the instant they threw the first one over the side the rope snapped. Blew away like it were a plastic bag.'

McAvoy swallows. He can taste blood and his headache is starting to squeeze. He closes his eyes as his mind fills with chilling images: pack ice and darkness; the relentless pummelling of the sea.

Michaels looks at McAvoy to check he has his attention. Gives the slightest of nods of appreciation.

'Napper says the lads who hadn't sailed before were nigh-on hysterical. The experienced lads just went quiet. I've seen it. Sometimes all you can do is lay in your bunk and read your book and hope that God doesn't want you dying today. That's it. That's what it comes down to.' Michaels is somewhere else now, describing something only he can see.

'The way Napper told it, the wave picked up the ship like a bath toy and flipped it off the rocks; men tumbling into the sea. Gerard had his head half stoved in. Cowboy Mick took the lifeboat full in the face. Young lad was snatched like there was a fist grabbing him from the deck. Weren't far short of a miracle that any of them made it home. You ever been in water that cold? Can't breathe. Can't think. Poor bastards . . .'

McAvoy turns at the sound of a rapping on the hatchway. Detective Constable Andy Daniells: wide-eyed, wet-faced. 'A word, Sarge? When you've got a moment?'

McAvoy glances at Michaels, who waves a hand. 'I shouldn't be rattling on like this. You've got things to be doing. I told the uniformed lass most of what I know. Like I say, I reckon it were druggies.'

McAvoy hauls himself out of the chair, following Daniells into the gangway. 'Anything?' asks Daniells.

'Better understanding of the victims, if nothing else,' says McAvoy, hating the word even as he says it. He shakes his head, trying to alter his train of thought. He looks at Daniells, who has a pained expression on his round face. 'What is it, Andy?'

'Up top,' says Daniells quietly. 'There's a bit of a ding-dong.'

McAvoy follows him down the gangway towards the stairs. He sees the flash of cameras strobing in the darkness. Puts his foot on the metal stairs and hauls himself up to the deck. The air is so cold it takes his breath away. Daniells points to where two uniformed officers are having an argument with a man in a flat cap. Even from a distance, McAvoy recognises him. He unpeels the blue nitrile gloves, slips them into his pocket and trudges up the gangway towards the fluttering police tape. Ballantine's words carry on the wind.

'...it's my fucking ship, you prick! What do you mean? This is fucking ridiculous! It's my ship on my dock. What's your name?'

As McAvoy approaches, the uniforms shift their position. For a moment a gap appears between them. In the distance, across the broken tarmac and the tumbledown brick buildings, he sees a long, plum-coloured classic car by the Chinese restaurant at the edge of the leisure park. He squints, the cold air playing with his hair and the tails of his coat.

'Mr Ballantine,' says McAvoy, using the voice he reserves for calming angry horses and football supporters. It's firm but reassuring. 'I'm Detective Sergeant McAvoy. Perhaps we should have a wee chat.'

Ballantine stops shouting. His handsome, wolfish face is the colour of old paper and there is a darkness under his eyes. He gives off a smell of whisky and herbal cigarettes. His flat cap is jammed onto a shaved head and there are grey stripes in his black goatee. He wears a designer donkey jacket over black jeans and two silver necklaces glint at his throat. He looks more like a pop star than a property developer.

He looks McAvoy up and down. Scowls nastily.

'Detective fucking Sergeant? That's one up from a plod, isn't it? Where's Slattery? I want to speak to who's in charge. And I want to be allowed aboard my own bloody ship!'

Behind him, one of the uniforms gives McAvoy a look that asks whether it might be possible, just this once, for him to turn a blind eye while they gave this obnoxious bastard a physical education.

'Mr Ballantine, the vessel is now a crime scene. The bodies of two men were discovered here in the early hours of this morning. We are in the initial stages of the investigation but I will be requiring a conversation with you and a number of your associates.'

'Me?' He steps back, affronted. 'Fuck off, I haven't got time for that. And which fucking associates?'

'Mr Ballantine, that language isn't helping anybody,' says McAvoy. 'I appreciate this must be a terrible shock but perhaps if we went and got out of the wind, had a cup of tea and spoke sensibly, we could both answer some questions for the other.'

For a moment, Ballantine seems on the verge of calming down. He looks as though he may see the sense in McAvoy's words. Then he looks past him. His eyes narrow as he sees the two CSIs struggling to carry a corpse in a black body-bag through the dark mouth of the gangway door. McAvoy turns, following his gaze. He spins back to Ballantine, face full of compassion.

'I really am very sorry, Mr Ballantine . . .'

Ballantine's face twists, fury gripping his features. He lashes out with his fist; a haymaker that catches McAvoy full on the jaw. McAvoy looks at him, a little hurt. 'Mr Ballantine, if you do that again I'm going to have to arrest you. Please, I know this is a shock, but—'

Ballantine swings again. McAvoy catches his fist and twists at the wrist, pushing his arm up his back. Ballantine's cheeks burn crimson. He looks like a schoolboy, embarrassed beyond enduring. He writhes and kicks as McAvoy holds him. McAvoy gives his wrist the faintest tug. A screech splits the air.

'Assault! This is assault! He's broken my arm, he's broken my fucking arm!'

One of the uniforms snaps a pair of cuffs on Ballantine's wrists, the sleeves of his donkey jacket bunching up around his forearms. McAvoy sees intricate black ink on tanned skin. A leather strap, patterned with shimmering silver fish scales.

'Stephen Ballantine, I am arresting you—'

'You'll fucking burn for this, you Jock bastard. I play golf with the chief fucking constable!'

McAvoy pushes Ballantine towards the two uniforms, looking around at the sound of running feet. DC Daniells and three other uniforms are tearing towards where McAvoy stands, blood rushing in his ears and a bruise rapidly swelling on his cheek.

'You okay, Sarge?' asks Daniells, out of breath. He glares at Ballantine, who looks ready to do murder.

'It's Des, isn't it!' hisses Ballantine, teeth locked. 'Alf and Des. He's fucking killed them.'

McAvoy nods, his face full of sadness.

Ballantine sags in the constable's arms, folding in on himself as if deflating. He puddles onto the cold black ground. Sobs like an orphaned child.

*Hull Daily Mail*, 5 January 1970

## BRAVE BOSUN LOST IN DRAMATIC RESCUE WAS GOING TO BE A FATHER

*By Neville Greaves, Shipping Correspondent*

TRIBUTES have been paid to 'a prince among men' who perished while attempting to save a crewmate from the freezing Icelandic waters on New Year's Day.

The death of Rory, 23, is the latest tragedy to hit the well-known Ballantine family. His father, uncle and grandfather all died at sea.

Mr Ballantine, of Marmaduke Street, was serving as bosun aboard the freezer trawler *Blake Purcell*, owned by the long-established Hessle Road trawler firm Blakes Ltd, when the tragedy occurred.

He leaves a widow, Margaret, who revealed last night that she is expecting their first child. Mrs Ballantine had relayed the good news to her husband through a coded telegram message just hours before the vessel struck rocks near Grimsey Island, off the Skagi Peninsula in the far north of Iceland, in the early hours of 1 January.

The vessel, already foundering, was trapped on rocks and pummelled by heavy seas. Skipper Malcolm Gill made an emergency Mayday call and ordered the crew to man the lifeboats but the gale made it all but impossible to get any of the rescue vessels into the water. Deckhand Michael Timpson, 42, of Eton Street, Hessle Road, courageously attempted to use his own body to weigh the inflatable down and allow his crewmates to climb aboard. The rope connecting the lifeboat to the *Blake Purcell* snapped and the inflatable was swept away, together with Mr Timpson. Deckie learner William

Godson, 16, was struck by the rescue craft and pitched into the freezing water.

Gerard Wade, 24, was later plucked from the freezing waters by the crew of an Icelandic vessel. He has been transferred to Isafjordur hospital where his condition is critical.

The tattered lifeboat was later found clinging to the basalt columns that form the entranceway to the uninhabited township of Kalfhamarsvik. Mr Timpson's body was not inside. Local rescue workers are still searching for the bodies of his crewmates.

The *Blake Purcell* sank within hours. Those saved by the Icelandic rescue vessel were landed at the tiny fishing village of Skagastrond, where locals provided them with food and dry clothing.

Mrs Ballantine told the *Mail*: 'Rory wouldn't think twice about risking his own life to save one of his friends. He thought the world of Billy and Mick. They were like family to him. I'm trying to take comfort in the fact that at least he knew he was going to be a father. I'll raise his child knowing that their father was a true hero. He was a prince among men.'

At Mr Ballantine's home, his younger sister Roberta, 13, was too distressed to talk to our reporter, refusing to believe the reports that her beloved older brother had perished.

Neighbour Eva Banks, 63, said: 'The Ballantines have known so much heartache. Rory's father Lachlan died in an accident at sea and his grandfather was lost during the war. His uncle, Stuart, was lost overboard in 1945. Rory had worked so hard to become a bosun at such a young age and he'd made a lovely home for his wife and his little sister who doted on him. Him and his pals were such characters. They'd do anything for you, generous to a fault. He and Gerard were inseparable. My prayers are with that poor family.'

Mr Wade was last year awarded a Royal Humane Society

certificate for his part in a previous rescue at sea. He lives with his mother, Kathleen, at 47 Eton Street, Hessle Road.

She said: 'I got a telegram late on New Year's Eve, saying he was sorry he'd left me on my own over the festive season and that he wished he'd stayed home. He would always keep in touch because he knew I worried but he never had to apologise for doing what he was good at. He was a fisherman and he was proud to be one. He and Rory were like brothers. I don't think he even knows that he's gone. It will break his heart.'

Mr Godson had until recently been a resident at Hesslewood Hall, run by the Hull Seamen's and General Orphanage to provide accommodation for the orphan children of seafarers.

He had been lodging for the past seven months in a flat on the Boulevard.

Close friend Enid Chappell, 28, said: 'He was so excited to have been accepted as one of Rory's lads. He and Gerard took him under their wing and he paid them back by being the hardest worker he could be. He was an inquisitive, tenderhearted lad who didn't have the easiest of starts. I can't shake the feeling that in his last moments he would have felt he'd let down the people who had helped him. He won't even have a grave, that's the worst thing. His life was a lonely one until recently and the thought of him adrift, so far from home, breaks my heart.'

Mr Timpson had served more than twenty years in Hull trawlers and was in the *Somerset* when she won the Silver Cod Trophy for the year's record catch by a British trawler. Mr Timpson, who leaves a widow, Iris, two married daughters and a son, was known on the docks by the affectionate nickname 'Cowboy' due to a love of all things Western.

# 18

'Interview commenced at 12.03 p.m.,' says McAvoy, glancing up at the clock on the wall. The red slashes on the digital read-out represent the only real colour in this soulless box. The blue cord carpet and unpleasant yellow strip light somehow contrive to give off an aura of intrinsic greyness. The walls have been painted a shade of white that looks, and quite possibly tastes, like week-old tofu. 'Officers present Detective Sergeant McAvoy and Detective Constable Andrew Daniells.' He looks again at the printed news article in his hands. 'I've been reading about your father. A good man, it seems.'

'You think?' asks Daniells beside him. He has a menthol inhaler up one nostril, his time below decks in the damp hold of the *Blake Holst* having already defeated his immune system.

'Sorry, Andy?'

'Hard to say, isn't it? I mean, what else would they say about him? He'd just died. Hardly going to call him a numpty, are they?'

McAvoy stares across the plastic-topped desk at Stephen Ballantine, who glares back with hard, black eyes.

'You're going to look back on this, McAvoy,' he spits, breathing hard. 'You'll look back on this as the day your whole fucking life changed.'

'Tell me a little about yourself, Mr Ballantine,' says McAvoy, not rising to it. 'I've read the articles but they do tend to put a gloss on things. Difficult upbringing, so I heard. A lot of tragedy in your family.'

'You're rubbing that in my face?'

McAvoy looks hurt. 'I was about to say that you have a lot to be proud of. You're a success. I understand you were a pupil at the Bennington Academy. Scholarship, yes? You must have been quite remarkable.'

'I still am. Ask your bosses. Ask them what I do for this city.'

McAvoy looks again at the man across the desk. He fights with his emotions. Ballantine might well be grieving. He may have lost two men who he'd known all his life. His pet project might be delayed by God knows how many months while police and forensics teams swarm all over it. McAvoy tries to give him the benefit of the doubt. After all, he might not always be like this. There is no evidence that he has done anything at all. He's here because McAvoy was left with no other choice.

'Look at me,' growls Ballantine, gesturing at himself. 'Look at the way you're treating me.'

Ballantine was relieved of his coat and his boots when McAvoy booked him in. They took his jewellery, his necklaces and the leather strap around his wrist. They took his clothes too. He's been given a grey sweatshirt and a pair of supermarket jeans. He looks as though it pains him.

'Mr Ballantine, you understand why you're here, yes?'

'Because I'm successful and you fucking hate it? Because I could buy your house and bulldoze it with the change in my fucking pocket?'

McAvoy can't help but start to feel disappointed. He has heard the word 'philanthropist' used about this man. This working-class boy done good. He tries to appear calm. He knows he's being watched, can feel the eyes drilling into the back of his skull as the interview is relayed to the monitors of the various

CID officers who want a look at the businessman who smacked McAvoy in the face.

'You're quite sure you don't want to wait for your solicitor to arrive?' asks Daniells cheerfully. 'I would, if I were you. This is a very serious matter.'

'Don't speak to me,' spits Ballantine, hugging himself. Steam seems to be rising from his skin. 'I'm talking to this big bastard, not you. You sit quietly, there's a good girl.'

McAvoy glances at Daniells, who waves it off. He's heard far worse.

'Mr Ballantine, I understand you are the partial owner of the *Blake Holst*, currently at anchor on inflatable pontoons at St Andrew's Dock, is that correct?'

'Partial owner? Fuck no. I own the lot.'

McAvoy opens the folder on the table. 'Forgive me. I was under the impression that your associate, Bernard Acklam, has helped source funding from interested parties in the maritime community.'

'Is that how you always talk?' growls Ballantine. 'Do you mean did a few old duffers chuck in a few quid to get the ball rolling? Yeah, they did. But this is my project. Get that?' He looks at the backs of his hands. 'When I find the bastards who did it . . .'

'You'll what, Mr Ballantine?'

He glares back at McAvoy. 'That'd be telling.'

'So tell us,' says Daniells.

'I told you to be quiet, princess.'

Daniells chuckles. 'I'm struggling to know what tone to take with you, Mr Ballantine. On the one hand, you've just lost two very old friends and your vanity project has become a crime scene. That makes me feel for you. On the other, you've punched a police officer in the face and humiliated yourself in front of an awful lot of people. Do I feel sorry for you? I can't make up my mind.'

'Fuck you,' growls Ballantine, teeth locked. 'Humiliated? How?'

'Well, I've heard you hit the sarge here with your best shot. He told you not to do it again. We'll be laughing about that one for a while.'

Ballantine jabs at the air, finger extended, pointing a bullet-wound into the centre of Daniells's head. 'That's not what happened.'

McAvoy clears his throat. Looks back at his papers. 'Mr Ballantine, I want to ask you about Enid Chappell.'

Ballantine glances back at McAvoy. He reaches out and takes a sip of water, glaring over the lip of the plastic cup. 'Auntie Enid? What the fuck for?'

'Auntie? Could you explain your relationship to Mrs Chappell?' asks McAvoy.

Ballantine throws his hands up. 'Is this about Alf and Des or about me smacking you or what? Look, I lost my temper, okay? We both know I'll accept a caution so just get on and fucking offer it. Why are you asking me about Enid?' Anger and bewilderment war in his face as if he were two different people in one skin.

McAvoy scratches his forehead while he thinks. Could he conceivably not know? He thinks about the leather bracelet; the iridescent fish scale. Thinks about the chair, angled towards the bath.

'When did you last see Mrs Chappell?' he asks quietly.

'For fuck's sake, why does it matter?' He looks from one to the other. 'I don't know, just before Christmas, I think. I throw a bit of a do for the old crowd. She came along. Brought me a tin of mints.' A smile twitches his lips. 'She still thinks I'm a bloody nipper.'

'Where was this?'

'Fancy place down Humber Street.' Ballantine shrugs. 'I put a credit card behind the till. It's a bit of a tradition. All the old faces. I make them serve fish and chips. Haddock, not cod. We do things right. Raise a glass to the old days and look forward together.' He stops, rubbing his knuckle across his forehead. 'Des and Alf were there, same as usual.'

McAvoy leans over to Daniells. Whispers in his ear.

'For the benefit of the tape, DC Daniells is leaving the room. The time is 12.14 p.m.'

Ballantine glowers at Daniells as he leaves. Then he flicks his attention back to McAvoy. 'Was it quick?' he asks. His voice softens, and it is suddenly as if an entirely different person is inhabiting his skin. 'Alf and Des. Poor old sods. They shouldn't really have been there at all but I think it was a bit of an escape. They got to remember who they were. Feel the world rocking beneath them. They were who I did it all for, y'know. As a thank you. They've been good to me and mine.'

McAvoy feels wrong-footed. Suddenly he is talking to a reasonable, sensitive man. His whole demeanour has altered. He looks eager to help, horrified by the wretchedness of the world.

'Mrs Chappell,' says McAvoy. 'She was at this gathering.'

'Oh yes,' Ballantine says. 'As I say, it's a private affair for those who have been good to my family. One or two absences but still the usual crowd. My father's old crew.' He stares past McAvoy, smiling at nothing. 'Salt of the earth. Last of the cowboys.'

'I've seen the sculpture,' says McAvoy.

'Do you like it?' asks Ballantine excitedly. 'Stylised, of course. Meant to be your "typical" fishermen. But I think we know who it really is. A suitable tribute, I'm sure you'll agree. The Magnificent Seven, riding on for all eternity.' He starts to hum the theme song from the film. Stops short as a tear escapes his left eye. 'Why are you asking me about Auntie Enid? I know she was on the slide but she hasn't done anything silly, has she? I told her at Christmas, she needs to let me put her somewhere she can be looked after. Too scared of losing her independence, that's her trouble. My mother's the same. Old as Methuselah but won't hear about having any help up there. Don't know which of us is more stubborn.'

'Your mother or Mrs Chappell?'

'My mother or me.' Ballantine laughs. He sits forward, elbows on the table, suddenly conspiratorial. 'We're not talking. Hardly ever bloody talking. I'm nearly twice the age that Rory was when he died, can you believe that? Mam says it's hard. Says it's like watching him age in front of her – seeing the man he'd have been if he hadn't taken that job on the *Purcell*. He should never have sailed. There were enough omens. You ask her, she'll tell you. Roberta dreamed about mirrors the night before they left. She woke up and covered every damn mirror in the house but the bad spirits must have got in anyway. Dad wasn't superstitious. Said they needed the money and that he'd led a charmed life. He'd be fine. Kissed them both and took a taxi to the docks. Can you imagine it? Out there, fighting the seas, the storms, and you get a wireless message from home telling you you're going to be a dad. They had this code. She sent him a wireless message. They'd agreed that if she signed it "Margaret" then she was pregnant and if she signed it "Mags" then she wasn't. So at least he got to know I was on my way. I hope I've done him proud.'

'You seem to have done very well indeed, Mr Ballantine,' says McAvoy, and means it.

'Thank you. I do hope so. Wasn't always easy. Potless for most of my childhood. Dad's old pals did what they could but I think they felt a bit, well, surplus to requirements when Mam married Bowbells.'

'That would be Arthur Lowery,' says McAvoy, consulting his notes.

'Horrible man. The worst. Mam married him for security and he ended up becoming our jailer. It was a blessing when he had the accident.'

194

McAvoy looks at the clipping from the *Hull Mail*, printed out and hastily stuck in his briefing notes as he entered the interview room. 'Horrible way to go. Open verdict, I see.'

'That's a technicality,' explains Ballantine. 'No doubt about it. Floor gave way and he drowned. Can't say we grieved. An insurance payout came through and it helped Uncle Gerard pay for me to go to a good school. It was hard, being away from what I knew, but it made me what I am. Then obviously when Uncle Gerard decided to invest in me, well, it all took off. Haven't looked back since.'

McAvoy feels as though he is listening to a motivational speech. He forces himself to focus. 'Mrs Chappell,' he says again. 'Your aunt, you say?'

'Oh, not really.' Ballantine smiles warmly. 'She was very good to my real aunt. Roberta. You'll know about Roberta, I'm sure. I established a benevolent trust in her memory. We've done a lot of good things in her name. She was another victim of the sea, in her way. It calls to us, the Ballantines. It's in our blood.'

'I've been reading about her,' says McAvoy, looking at his notes. 'No body. Still listed as a missing person. A hard life, it seems.'

Ballantine nods. 'Enid was her social worker. Mine too, I suppose, though I was only a bain. Roberta went off the rails completely after Father died. Enid did her best by her for a long time. Even went looking for her in London when she disappeared after Bowbells died. Brought her back, cleaned her up, got her a job. But there was a sadness in her. I think she gave herself to the sea.' He looks at McAvoy, suddenly intense. 'I don't think we'll ever know.'

McAvoy pauses. His tea has gone cold. He wishes he'd had more time to prepare.

'Bernard Acklam,' he says.

'Napper.'

'A character, by all accounts. Quite the criminal record.'

195

'And a good man, underneath it all.'

'The classic car that Mr Acklam drives,' says McAvoy softly, glancing at the latest email from Reena Parekh. 'The tyres match prints that were left in the snow at Mrs Chappell's home.'

'And?' asks Ballantine, bemused. 'They've known each other fifty years. So what?'

'Mr Ballantine, do you know anybody who would wish Mrs Chappell harm?'

'Auntie Enid? Plenty of people. She had a mouth on her. But no, not now. She's losing it. What harm could she be to anyone? I don't think she can tell what's fact and what's fantasy.'

McAvoy doesn't change his expression.

'She's okay, isn't she?' asks Ballantine, sitting forward. 'There hasn't been an accident or anything? I'd feel awful. I sort of feel responsible for all of them. And with Alf and Des . . .' He looks into his lap. His shoulders stiffen. When he raises his head there is a darkness in his eyes; his brows knitting together above malevolent eyes.

'Stop talking,' growls Ballantine. 'Stop asking him.'

'I'm sorry, Mr Ballantine?' McAvoy glances towards the door, distracted by the sound of raised voices. He glances back at Stephen, trying to work out whether he really might not know about Enid's death. Could he simply not have been informed? The look in Stephen's eyes stops the words in his throat. He feels as though he is looking at a completely different man.

'Leave it, you cunt. Leave him be.'

McAvoy sits back in his chair. 'Stephen, there are a lot of questions to answer but if you want a break then—'

The door swings open and Area Commander Slattery stamps into the room, DC Daniells behind him.

'Sir, we're in the middle of an interview . . .'

Slattery looks at him with a face that could curdle milk. Turns on his heel and addresses Ballantine. 'Stephen, on behalf of

196

Humberside Police I would like to extend my sincerest condolences.'

'Sir, Mr Ballantine has been arrested for striking an officer.'

A thin, rakish man with curly blond hair is standing in the doorway. 'I understand you dislocated my client's arm,' he says.

'And who are you?'

'Adrian Warriner,' he says, holding out a business card between two pale fingers. 'My client will be accompanying me to visit his private physician. It is possible that we can chalk today's tragic events down to heated tempers and the unpleasantness of the situation. But we shall be taking photographs of my client's injuries and if there is any permanent damage we will of course be requiring compensation and will not hesitate to demand an inquiry into the conduct of your officer. Mr Ballantine, if you would follow me.'

McAvoy starts to stand. Slattery shakes his head. 'Another time, eh Stephen?' he says, fawning, as Ballantine pushes his chair back and languidly stands. He keeps his eyes on McAvoy, an ugly smile on his handsome face.

'It's not Stephen,' he says, under his breath.

'Mr Ballantine, yes, of course, and if I could reiterate my sincere apologies.'

'This is wrong, sir,' sputters McAvoy, his face turning red. 'This is a murder investigation.'

'And we wish you the very best of luck with it,' says Warriner, as Ballantine joins him in the doorway. 'Let's get your clothes, eh? What else did they take? Jewellery? This is a gross breach of my client's rights. You can rest assured you will be hearing from us.'

Slattery follows the two men from the room. As Ballantine passes Daniells, squeezed together in the doorway, he leans forward. Whispers in his ear. A look of revulsion flickers across Daniells's face and he takes a step back. He moves to follow the retreating figures as they disappear down the corridor. McAvoy takes him by the forearm.

'What did he say?' asks McAvoy.

'He licked me,' stammers Daniells, pulling his sleeve over his hand and using the cuff to clean out his ear and neck. 'He fucking licked me!'

McAvoy stares up at the ceiling at where the video camera is recording every movement and word. Checks the clock and closes his eyes.

'Interview terminated at 12.56 p.m.'

# 19

*Clough Road Police Station, Hull*
*2.06 p.m.*

Slattery has his back to McAvoy, staring out of the big glass window at the little retail park across the busy road. They're on the third floor. The windows are toughened glass, though nobody knows for certain whether that is to protect the police staff within, or to discourage senior officers from throwing themselves head-first into the car park.

McAvoy is sitting in a big brown leather chair in front of Slattery's antique wooden desk. It's topped with green leather and studded with gold pins and looks big enough for a game of snooker. He keeps looking over his shoulder at the little rectangular door and wondering how on earth the delivery team managed to get it up here. Wonders whether Slattery paid for it himself. Whether he bought any of the oil paintings that hang on the pale-blue walls in gilded frames. Gun dogs and vintage prints of old racehorses and lithographs showing hirsute academics discussing philosophy by lamplight. One of the walls has been covered with a wallpaper that recreates the effect of mahogany wood panelling. There's a drinks cabinet in the shape of a globe beside the tall, leathery plant in the corner of the room. McAvoy feels like he's been summoned to a private room at a gentlemen's club. He wonders how much this is going to hurt.

'I hate this city,' mutters Slattery disconsolately. He has his hands behind his back, as if handcuffed. 'I hate this view.'

'Would you like me to draw the curtains, sir?' asks McAvoy, keen to be helpful.

'Shut up,' says Slattery quietly. He turns from the window, rubbing his head, and drops into the seat across the desk. He keeps his gaze fixed on McAvoy, only glancing away as he fiddles with his desk drawers. He removes a bottle of Bombay Sapphire and pours a small measure into a crystal tumbler. McAvoy glances behind him at the drinks cabinet.

'For visitors,' explains Slattery. 'Too far away for me.' He raises the glass to his lips. Breathes it in. Then puts it back on the desk and glances at his computer, pushed off to the far end of the table. He clicks through a couple of emails and makes an unpleasant noise as he unsticks his tongue from the roof of his mouth, a slurping sound that makes McAvoy think of blocked drains.

'Mr Ballantine, sir,' says McAvoy, eager to get this over with. 'You saw the interview? That's a dangerous man.'

'I saw a man under extreme emotional pressure,' says Slattery coldly. 'I saw a pillar of the community being treated like a rapist.'

'He assaulted a police officer, sir.'

'You're okay, aren't you? You've had worse.'

'That's hardly the point, sir. He knows all three victims. He has a temper, we've seen that.'

'Three victims?' asks Slattery archly. 'I understand you are investigating the unexplained death of one Enid Chappell. I distinctly remember asking DI Patten to head up the inquiries into the *Blake Holst*. Team player, DI Patten. A solid, reliable career officer. She's with the son of Des Kavanagh right now. She's running that investigation. And you're not a part of it.'

McAvoy sits forward in his chair. 'Sir, is there something I'm not aware of? You must see that these investigations should be linked.'

Slattery sits forward too and looks at McAvoy with disdain. 'Detective Sergeant McAvoy, at this moment there are hundreds of things going on within Humberside Police that you're not aware of. You're not aware of them because you are a detective sergeant. You may be an acting detective inspector but that does not make you privy to every scrap of information in every single case. I, on the other hand, am area commander. Let me tell you a few of the things that I told Humberside Police Authority when they asked me to apply for this position. I was a chief superintendent in overall command of CID with Dorset Police. I will be confirmed as assistant chief constable as soon as the year-end financial reports are completed. I have degrees in sociology and criminology, the latter from Cambridge. I have twenty-three years of service under my belt. I transformed community policing at my last posting and I intend to be chief constable within the next three years. You,' he says quietly, 'are something of an enigma. You have been asked to move up to detective inspector on several occasions and declined. You have been put forward for the fast-track senior officer scheme and repeatedly withdrawn. You were nominated for the Queen's Police Medal on three occasions and asked for the nomination to be withdrawn. You designed a crime database for Humberside Police that, if patented in the private sector, would have set you up for life. You confuse me. I don't like being confused. That's why I stick to the unequivocal. I give instructions, those instructions are followed. Everybody seems to understand this basic concept. You, however, appear to need a reason for my decisions.'

McAvoy grips the arms of the chair. Looks down at his shoes. Looks up again. 'Is DCI Patten treating Stephen Ballantine as a suspect, sir?'

'Everybody is a suspect, McAvoy.'

'So she will be talking to him. Requesting phone records. Bank statements. Checking alibis.'

'DCI Patten is already making considerable progress,' growls Slattery. 'According to Kavanagh's son, his father had been acting differently recently. He'd received a postcard that unnerved him. His son, Thomas, remembered it because the image on the postcard showed the area of Iceland where his father's old ship was sunk. According to Thomas, his father was also visited some weeks ago by a gentleman who walked with a stick and who left him most upset. We have a sketch artist with him now. And you will be astonished to hear, Detective Sergeant, that a postcard just like the one that so unnerved Mr Kavanagh was found folded in the back pocket of the jeans worn by Mr Howe when he was killed. If it transpires that this horrible incident wasn't the work of drug addicts seeking an easy target, I would say we have an excellent suspect. And I would say, as I have done twice before, that you need to respect the chain of command, do the job you have been given, and stop muddying the waters. Do I make myself clear?'

McAvoy licks his lips. He flicks his gaze towards the window and the squally grey air. He can see the orange lights of a department store; can just about make out the big rotating take-away cup that spins the sparkling mist above the drive-thru coffee chain. He glances at his watch. If he's going to get screamed at, he decides now would be the ideal time.

'I admire him too, sir,' says McAvoy softly. 'Mr Ballantine. He's clearly done very well. I admire what he has done for the city and the way he tries to honour the dad he never knew. It's inspirational. Tragic and inspirational. But I don't admire him so much that I'm willing to let him murder an old lady in her own home or butcher two elderly men on a fishing trawler.'

'And you believe he's capable of that, do you?' asks Slattery, his back teeth clamping together.

'We're all capable, sir,' says McAvoy. 'Capable of anything in the right circumstances.'

'And in what circumstances would this much admired tycoon murder a woman he referred to as Auntie Enid?'

'I don't know, sir. But there were peculiarities at the crime scene. The smashed trawler-in-a-bottle. It has a significance, I'm sure of it. If she had a visitor and things began to get nasty, if she knew she was going to be ransacked – she might have tried to leave a trail.'

Slattery shakes his head. He seems to deflate, as if the effort of being such an arsehole has exhausted him. 'Those bloody bodies,' he mutters.

'Sir?'

'Murmansk. The bloody Russians.' He sags further, looking sullen. He gives McAvoy a once-over, as if checking whether this is a safe place to deposit his burdens. Realises that it is. 'You'll be aware that I was tasked with procuring samples from the blood relatives of the trawlermen lost at sea between 1966 and 1971? Of course, it took long enough for anybody in authority to act on what the Russians told them. I'd imagine that's pretty standard – it takes a while to tell which way the wind is blowing. Politics, and all that.'

'Yes, sir.'

'A thankless task. We couldn't win whatever we did. The Foreign Office dumped that one on me and all I could do was try and run an efficient operation. We contacted the relatives by letter. Explained the situation as clearly and honestly as we could. We sent family liaison officers and some of our very best people to procure the samples. I personally went to see Stephen because I knew how much this would mean to him. We met at his offices down at the Marina – great glass monstrosity of a thing. He was the man I knew from the magazines and the TV interviews. Smartly dressed, charming, eloquent. Eager to help. We sat and chatted and then I asked him to provide the sample. A change came over him.'

McAvoy thinks back to the interview room and the way Stephen had seemed to flick wildly between two personalities.

'He was sobbing. A grown man sobbing right there in front of me. I said I knew it must be hard, but that at least this would finally give some closure. He said he couldn't do it. He didn't want to know the truth. Wouldn't give the sample at first.'

McAvoy rubs his bruised face with his left hand. His superior officer's demeanour has changed as noticeably as that of the man he is describing. He looks as though he has wanted to talk about this for some time.

'It left me in a situation, McAvoy. A bad one. The Foreign Office wanted answers, the other families had done their bit. What could I do? Things slip through the net if you'll pardon the pun. As far as the information I had went, there were no other blood relatives to ask and we were pretty damn sure from the tattoos that one of the men was Mick Timpson. It had always seemed quite clear that these were men from the *Purcell*.'

'The cabin boy? William . . .'

'Billy Godson, yes,' says Slattery. 'He was in care homes all his life. Horrible, horrible childhood. Orphanages and foster families and then at fourteen he gets a chance to become a deckie learner with the crew of likely lads. He'd just found some happiness, some stability, when this happened. No blood relatives, McAvoy. What was I to do? Three days later his solicitor came to see me. Stephen's solicitor – the slimy bastard you met downstairs. He explained how hard his client was finding things and could I see my way clear to leaving the mystery, as it were, unsolved. In return, he would continue to assist our partner agencies with high-profile investigations. He'd keep an ear open, as it were.'

McAvoy sticks his tongue in his cheek, his mind racing ahead. 'You told the press the Russians had made a mistake. That these bodies weren't from the *Purcell*.'

'Foreign Office didn't mind. I get the impression that the Russians don't do anything without thinking a few steps ahead. That's why they're good at chess. Maybe they were playing some game with the Home Office. Maybe not. But they seemed confident that the bodies belonged to our boys. The sample given by Timpson's son confirmed it. "Cowboy Mick" washed up there, battered almost unrecognisable. You wouldn't know his face from the pictures. But you'd know what was left of his tattoos.'

'But you haven't told his family?'

'It was a pragmatic decision,' says Slattery glumly. 'I don't like it but that's the duty of rank. Ballantine is an asset. If you had some hard evidence then that would be different but all you have is the faintest of connections and an intrinsic dislike of the man because of the way he spoke to you at the crime scene.'

'That's not true, sir,' mutters McAvoy. 'I swear, I'm just following the evidence.'

'You have no evidence, Sergeant,' says Slattery, putting his hands on the desk. 'What you have is a whiff of a suspicion.'

'You think he would tell,' says McAvoy, exasperated. 'Tell people about the deal with him that denied closure for the family of Mick Timpson.'

'No, Sergeant. That is not what I fear. I fear you making an arse of yourself and me, as line manager for CID, looking like a prick as a consequence. It's very important to me that you understand this. Stay away from Stephen Ballantine.'

McAvoy starts to stand.

'You get that? Crystal clear? Ringing like a bell? Concentrate on your frozen lady and leave the rest to DCI Patten. You are a good police officer, McAvoy. If you would just bend a little I'm sure you and I could have a very successful partnership.'

To his horror, McAvoy realises that Slattery is extending his hand. He wants them to seal whatever arrangement he thinks they have just made. It feels as though there are hot stones in his lungs. He reaches out. His big hand closes over Slattery's clammy palm. McAvoy has taught himself not to grip too hard. He has a tendency to crush bones. Slattery squeezes McAvoy's hand, his right arm starting to shake with the amount of effort he puts into the grip. McAvoy flexes. Enjoys the look of discomfort that crosses Slattery's face. He lets go. Gives the faintest of nods.

He's almost out of the room when Slattery calls him. As he looks back, Slattery is holding up a folder. Even from across the room, McAvoy can see it's his own personnel file. 'Interesting reading, Sergeant. No shortage of skeletons in your closet.' He gives a sharp smile. 'Do pass on my regards to your family.'

McAvoy leaves without another word.

# 20

*Skagastrond, Skagi Peninsula, Iceland*
*3.06 p.m.*

Pharaoh wakes at the deep end of the bed. She dozed off in the shallows but the 45-degree gradient had quickly proven too much. Each time she turned over she had slithered a little further down the sagging mattress: a skier in a slow-motion fall. She comes to in pain, tangled in woollen blankets and with half of the bedsheet twisted around her legs. She fell asleep fully dressed but has managed to remove both boots and one leg of her jeans in the five hours since she staggered into the bedroom. She runs her tongue around her mouth. Her lips are cracked. She winces as she pushes herself free of the covers. Sore head, sour gut, tired limbs. She scowls into the darkness, opens her mouth as wide as it will go and hears a loud crack, like a log popping in a fire, as she releases some of the tension in her jaw.

The air in the bedroom is cold, like the air in front of an open freezer. She clears her throat and resists the urge to cough. Coughing is something that smokers do and she has never been a conformist. She feels a sudden urge to pee and decides to fight that too. She fumbles about with the lamp on the bedside table and gives an audible sigh of relief as she finds the button, the tassels on the old-fashioned lampshade tickling the back of her hand. She squints as a soft, golden light spills into the room. She's back in the holiday rental. Flock wallpaper and melamine wardrobes, cord carpet and a closet full of somebody else's clothes. She huddles in on herself and lets it hit her: her morning dip; this flood of sadness crashing over her and through her. She glances at the cold, untouched pillow on the far side of the bed.

Pharaoh nods and gets herself together. It doesn't take her long. She undresses properly, refits the sheet and gulps down a glass of water. She rummages in her travel bag, rumpled and unemptied by the bed, until she finds a packet of ibuprofen. She swallows two. Takes her morning anti-depressant and another pill to ease her gastric reflux. The doctor keeps talking to her about going for tests. Changing her lifestyle. Taking things a little easier . . .

She finds her phone, plugged in to a travel adaptor sticking out of a socket by the radiator. She touches the surface of the heater. It's freezing to the touch at the top and scalding at the bottom. She wraps herself in a bedsheet, heading for the small, boxy kitchen. The strip light on the ceiling flickers into life as she presses the switch. For a moment she sees her own reflection in the big window above the sink. She crosses the floor and pulls down the blind – partly to prevent her neighbours from seeing her but more to spare herself the sight. She considers the room, with its ancient electric oven, stinking fridge and cupboards crammed full of packets, tins, bottles and Tupperware. It's tatty but not unpleasant. She could make it nice. Splash a coat of bright paint on the walls and put down a couple of rag-rugs. A new bed, a sofa, some black and white photographs . . . she could double the landlord's takings at a stroke. She opens the cupboards and frowns at the mass of unfamiliar labels. Finds a jar and whittles down the list of possible contents to olives, cornichons and puffin-hearts. Puts it back.

The owner said that she was welcome to help herself. She does so. Opens a tin of peaches and pours half the contents into a bowl. She sips the juice from the can; a metallic flavour insinuating itself into the sensual sweetness of the syrup. She looks in the fridge and sees a pot she recognises. Tips half a tub of skyr onto the peaches. Spoons some into her mouth and pulls a face. She isn't sure whether she finds it unpleasant or merely dull, but her body seems to feel better for the unexpected appearance of vitamins in her system and she finishes the bowl. She makes tea in a stripy mug. Sniffs the milk and decides it can't be any worse than the skyr.

She walks back to bed, sipping her tea and feeling a little more alive. Decides to be kind to herself and makes a detour to the bathroom. She pees in the dark, sipping her tea and feeling the cold air snake under the door to chill her bare legs. When she returns to the bedroom she opens the curtains. Dark outside, though she's no idea what that might mean in terms of the time. She turns her phone back on. She settles down among the bedclothes. Notifications start beeping through. Pharaoh is content to listen and not look. *Ping-ping-ping*, like the bell on a busy reception desk. She'll get to them eventually. A little smile creeps onto her face as memories flood back. She listens to her voicemails and sends a text to her daughters, telling them she misses them, loves them, and has bought them some amazing presents. By the time she gets home, she hopes all the claims will be true.

She picks up her laptop and reaches down to the floor for her coat. There are fistfuls of paper in the pockets: drunken questions and notes. She smooths the crumpled leaves on her knees and opens up a search engine. Licks her lips.

Types 'murder' 'Le Havre' 'Baltimore'. Recoils as the screen fills with a ream of homicides from the US. She streamlines the search criteria. Starts to type in different keywords from the *CrymeLog* article. Loses herself in police work. She finds it inconceivable that Chandler could just make up the article. She has no doubt that he could embellish and exaggerate to the point of near fantasy but she has an inkling that he would base his stories on some nugget of fact. Somebody put the idea in his head. Somebody got him thinking that Roberta Ballantine was one of many. Pharaoh doesn't yet know what she believes about the old journalist's death but she finds it hard to imagine that he came all this way for nothing. He was seeking answers.

She starts to read. Newspaper reports on homicide after homicide. None mentions Hull. None mentions Roberta.

After fifteen minutes of hammering at the keys, Pharaoh spots an article that looks a little more promising. A headline guaranteed to twang the heartstrings: a retired detective sergeant from the Baltimore Police promising to never stop looking for the man who assaulted 'tragic' Marcia Delacroix in 1985. She reads the piece again. Ugly things were done to the fifteen-year-old girl with the long dark hair and the big round spectacles. Somebody broke into her home. Woke her. Raped her. Would have killed her too if her father hadn't been sent home early from his shift at the docks. He left her there bleeding and escaped through a window. Witnesses remember seeing a male of average height and average build watching the house in the days before the incident. He had dark hair and dark eyes. They couldn't offer much more. Nobody was caught. Police didn't even get close to a suspect. Marcia took her own life in 2002. Her father died last year. Detective Sergeant Thomson Kidman, now retired, told the *Baltimore Sun* that he had made a promise to Linwood Delacroix before he succumbed to cancer. Told him he would keep looking and never give up.

It doesn't take Pharaoh long to find the contact details for Kidman. He has a website advertising his services as a motivational speaker and consultant in police procedure. She checks the time difference. It's mid-morning in Baltimore, though she isn't sure whether it's tomorrow or today.

'This is Kiddo,' comes a soft, Irish-tinged accent. 'What you need?'

'Mr Kidman.'

'Kiddo, please.'

'My name is Detective Superintendent Trish Pharaoh. I run the Major Crimes Unit with Humberside Police.'

'Humberside? Yorkshire, yeah?'

She smiles. 'There are complicated boundary lines. I won't bore you.'

'Bore away,' he says. 'I'm sitting watching the ass-end of a sixteen-wheeler. It ain't moved in the last seven hours and I doubt it's going to move any time soon. Keep me awake. Whaddya need?'

'It's about Marcia Delacroix,' she says, her eyes flicking over his résumé on his no-frills website. Forty-five years as a cop, left the academy in 1971, turned down a dozen different promotions so he could stay at a rank that allowed him to work the streets. Seven former commanders attended his retirement party, where the Drug Enforcement Agency presented him with the Legion of Merit medal, making him just the seventh officer in the department's history to receive the honour. He works in private security now and gives lectures at schools and colleges all over the South Baltimore district where he grew up, and where his four children still live within a ten-minute walk. Pharaoh thinks he sounds too good to be true, though she knows another sergeant of whom the same could well be said.

'That was bad,' says Kidman flatly. 'I've seen a lot. Seen things that fill my head with hot fucking snakes. Marcia's the one that chews at me. It had the longest reach, y'know? Cast the longest shadow. How can I help?'

Pharaoh sits up a little straighter. Clicks her pen against her teeth. 'Have you heard of a true crime magazine called *CrymeLog*?'

He chuckles wryly. 'I knew he wasn't a fucking cop.'

'I'm sorry?'

'The guy with the accent,' says Kiddo. 'He called me last fall. That's where I know the name. Humberside . . . Yorkshire. Said he had a case that showed all the hallmarks of having been carried out by the same person who hurt Marcia. I'm retired and I don't have a problem with talking about old cases. He never said he was a cop but he didn't say he wasn't when I pushed him. Either way, I told him that whoever attacked Marcia will be an old geezer by now. There hasn't been an attack with his MO since 2002. I think rapists stop once they need Viagra, don't you?'

Pharaoh stays quiet, hoping he'll fill the silence. He obliges.

'Sorry, that was crude. I spend my time with boys at the gun range and sometimes I forget who I'm talking to. My wife gives me hell for it. Like I say, the guy who called me, he had seen the article in the *Sun*. After Linwood died. The *Sun* sent a reporter to the funeral and they recognised me. I gave a soundbite.'

'You mentioned other cases,' says Pharaoh. 'Oslo. Le Havre. Nova Scotia.'

'Hull too, according to your guy. Said his case was from a long time ago. That this was one last chance to get answers.'

'The victim, Roberta Ballantine. She's been missing since 1986.'

'So he said, though the attack happened long before that. She was still a girl. I asked him to send me details but he never did. I only remember it because Marcia's the case that I carry with me.'

Pharaoh consults her notes. She'd presumed that the article referred to the night of Roberta's disappearance. She skims it again and realises that it never states so directly.

'Can you tell me about Marcia?' she asks.

He sighs. She can hear him settle back in his seat; the rustle of his collar catching the mouthpiece of the phone.

'Pretty,' he says at last. 'Sweet. Bit of an innocent, according to her friends. Her dad was a longshoreman. Union guy. Well liked. Influential. Marcia was his only daughter and he doted on her. Everybody liked her. Home was just the two of them. Mom passed away when she was young. January 1976, Linwood comes home from work and goes to his daughter's room to check on her. She's half dead in her bed, bruises on her windpipe, blood running down her face where he's torn her hair at the roots. Goes out of his fucking mind. I was first on the scene. We're trying to bring her round but she can barely speak. She's hysterical, hallucinating, fighting us both. They took her to the hospital but it was months before she got home. I tried to make some sense of what happened but the guy was like a fucking ghost. We think he woke her up. Don't know how he got in or how he got out, but—'

'You think? She never gave a statement?'

'Hard to get much out of her,' says Kidman quietly. 'She started trying to block it out as soon as she was released. Drinking. Drugs. He took everything from her. It half killed her father. Half killed me too. I couldn't leave it alone . . . you know that feeling? Looking at the crime scene photos night after night.'

'You found something?' asks Pharaoh, spotting the change in his tone.

'Maybe. Maybe I've been wrong this whole time. But I looked at the photos we took and some that had been taken by a friend when she'd had a sleepover there a few months before the attack. The lamp was on the wrong side of her vanity table. The picture on her wall had been removed. My partner didn't think it mattered but it goddamn did to me. It matched up with something she said when she was on the psych ward. About the birds. The big black raven looking down on her. He needed space to make his shadows.'

'I don't understand,' says Pharaoh.

'Neither did I. Not for a long time. I was playing with my granddaughter, years later, when it hit me. We were playing shadow puppets. Rabbits, dogs, spiders . . . giggling together and casting pictures on the wall. You ever make a bird with your hands? Lock your thumbs together and make wings with your arms. That's a stranglehold. It matched the injuries on her thorax perfectly.'

'Bit of a leap,' says Pharaoh, hoping she doesn't cause offence.

'You're not the first to say it.' Kiddo laughs. 'My major told me I was insane. But I had a feeling. Kept at it, more of a hobby than an investigation. I looked for cases nationwide with similar char-acteristics. Young girl. Dark hair, ripped out by the roots. The same type of strangulation injuries. Got so many matches it would break your heart. I chopped them down until I had a handful that might be connected to Marcia. Three deaths. One who survived when the attack was interrupted. Brianna Garcia. Happened in 1991. She gave a better description than Marcia. Spoke about the long braids in his hair. A mask he wore, like something from a horror film. And the fucking shadows on the wall.'

Pharaoh realises she is stroking her thumb against her neck. She has a sudden image of her daughters. Dark-haired. Beautiful. Alone . . .

'They were all near ports. Which meant this thing might be global. And the chances of catching him had gone from slim to none. You know ports, right? There are men from all over the world, in and out like wasps from a nest. I had to tell Linwood we were probably never going to get answers but he wouldn't have it. Made me swear to keep looking. Him and his friends kept the case alive. They made a nuisance of themselves, rough-ing up every damn weirdo in the district, going through the records of who was in port on the night of the attack. Kept bringing reams of paperwork, shipping lists, all these goddamn records. Wouldn't let it rest.'

'Would you?' asks Pharaoh.

'Fuck, no.' He sighs. 'Maybe I gave him too much. He trusted me. Believed the theory. I swear, him and his pals must have spoken to every seaman and stevedore who came through the port, eyes and ears open for gossip, snippets, anything. He heard about a couple of similar cases. Other ports. One in Le Havre – the girl survived. Woke up to find him strangling her. She said the man who took her hair wore a mask. That it – and I swear I ain't making this up – it "rippled like a mermaid's tail". Like my major told me, you can't build a case on that. I kept at it. I think I'll always keep at it. It broke my heart that Linwood died without knowing.' He stops, a little out of breath. 'The guy I spoke to. He's a journalist, right?'

'Sort of,' says Pharaoh, clicking her teeth together as she thinks. 'He told you about our connection, yes? Hull, late sixties, early seventies . . .'

'It's possible she was one of his first,' says Kidman. 'But if he was hurting people in the eighties and nineties then he was either real old when he ended or real young when he started. Your guy sounded like he was fishing. Causing problems, is he? Hope you're not too rough on him, I kind of liked him. I liked the way he lied.'

Pharaoh doesn't reply. She hears the sound of tyres on snow. Her head is fizzing; Alka-Seltzer dropped in a glass.

'You never got close to a suspect?' she asks.

'Closest we got was way back at the start,' says Kidman. 'The night before the attack on Marcia a security guard caught a guy trying to leave the port without signing out. I'm not saying security is perfect down there but the guard caught this guy right in the act of slipping under the wire. Couldn't do nothing, could he? Gave him a talking-to and took him back to his ship. It was a bulk carrier out of Iceland. The *Corvus*. He went back aboard meek as a lamb and the security guy let it be. He only came forward weeks later when Linwood and his boys asked him to remember anything unusual in the days before Marcia's attack. He remembered the guy.'

'He matched the description?'

'Hell no, that was the problem. This guy was pretty goddamn distinctive. One eye was glass.'

215

'*Corvus*,' mutters Pharaoh. 'You followed up?'

'Tried. Followed a paper trail that would give you a nose-bleed. It had been sold on by then. New owners registered in Cambodia. But I got hold of the previous owners in the end. The *Corvus* had been transporting salted cod to the Mediterranean then wooden furniture and Madeira wines to the US. Mid-size crew. Names didn't mean much to me. Nothing flagged. I've got a copy of the crew list. Got shipping plans going back to 1969.'

'Could you send it to me?' asks Pharaoh. She allows a little charm to enter her voice. 'You know what, it would be such a help if you could send me all of it.'

'Honey, I've got crates and crates of it. If I send you it all you'll drown in info. Let me see if I can pick out a few choice pages. The crew lists shouldn't be hard to find. Your buddy – the reporter – he asked for the same thing.'

'You obliged?'

'I'm an obliging guy. I'll phone my wife. Ask her to send you a few things.'

'She sounds an obliging lady,' says Pharaoh with a smile.

'I am fucking blessed.'

Pharaoh thanks him. Gives her email address and ends the call. She slumps back against the headboard and retreats into her own thoughts. *Corvus*, she mutters, as documents start to flood her inbox.

It takes her a while to register the noise. She can hear a banging: a muffled thumping of a gloved fist on wood. She decides to ignore it.

The banging comes again. Somebody is hammering at the door. Pharaoh takes her false tooth from the glass of water on the nightstand and slips it into place. It still tastes of wine and cigarettes. From the open suitcase at the foot of the bed she removes a pair of black leggings and a baggy wool jumper. She dresses herself as she makes her way to the door, grateful for the warmth of the fresh clothes as the chill of the corridor nips at her flesh. She smooths herself down and ruffles her hair. Takes a breath of fresh, cold breeze and pulls at the door. It's frozen into the frame and Pharaoh has to tug the handle with both hands to get it open.

'For fuck's sake,' she grunts, as she pulls the door open and clatters backwards into the hall.

On the doorstep stands a huge man in blue and yellow Icelandic police uniform: waterproofs, fluffy hat, boots and overcoat all dripping with snow.

He steps aside. Behind him stands a young woman. She wears the same overcoat but is wearing jeans and high boots. Against the plummy blackness of the sky, her blonde hair seems ghostly and the blueness of her eyes makes Pharaoh think of frozen lagoons and ice caves. She's slim and attractive and Pharaoh dislikes her on sight.

The officer puts her hands on her hips. Her coat opens and Pharaoh spots the gun in a holster at her hip. It's clear the feeling is mutual.

'Ah,' says Pharaoh. 'What an unexpected delight.'

## 21

*Bransholme Police Station, Goodhart Road, Hull*
*4.02 p.m.*

It's more than fifty years since Hull's civic leaders opened the Bransholme estate – their endeavours fuelled by the same spirit of post-war social conscience that had led to the creation of the National Health Service. They believed that the city's hard-working men and women deserved homes with back gardens and hot running water. They wanted to finish the work that the Luftwaffe had begun and tear down the slums that surrounded the docks. They bought a huge swathe of land to the north of the city and laid out ambitious plans for a new way of life. What they created was more akin to a new town than an estate: a peculiar melding of boggy farmland and urban utilitarianism. Over the course of a decade they produced a vast sprawl of back-to-front, chimneyless houses and bleak maisonettes, huddling together around grassy verges the size of cricket pitches. The roads were traffic calmed and speed-humped, looping back on themselves as if lost. The urban planners had wanted to create a new community: a place of inspiration and space, greenery and neighbourliness and emblematic of a new dawn.

Fishing families left Hessle Road in abundance, attracted by the idea of being a part of something new and intoxicated by promises that this new town would be free of the poverty that had so blighted the streets they used to call home. Within a decade of its grand opening, the fishing industry died. The thousands of men, women and children who moved to the new estate found themselves out of work. Worse, they found themselves trapped. There was nothing to do on Bransholme for those with no money. No jobs to be found in a city without a manufacturing base. Nowhere to go for the bored teens, the isolated pensioners, the young mums trying to make their little homes into a paradise on a budget of bugger all. Bransholme became Hull's problem estate – a place of high crime, low employment and little hope. Worse, it became a punchline. Men and women thrown on the scrapheap by the death of the fishing industry were once again the victims of cruel circumstance. Many council tenants begged to be allowed back to the familiarity of their old neighbourhoods. Most were denied. The houses they used to call home had been razed to the ground. Those who stayed became its defenders; spiky, combative community activists desperate to show the rest of Hull they were wrong to bracket their estate as a den of iniquity. It's been rebranded time and again. Endless urban renaissance specialists have squabbled for shares of the government cash set aside to help regenerate estates like this one. The results have been mixed. There's still graffiti on the boarded-up shops, but now it's spelled correctly. Bransholme is still a far from sought-after address but the residents can at least take comfort in the knowledge that their estate is no worse than anywhere else.

McAvoy has an inkling of how the residents feel. He and the last scraps of Pharaoh's team were dumped at Bransholme nick a year ago, occupying the top floor of a dull brick building painted a nasty shade of forest green. It looks like a cross between a Victorian prison and a discount motel. It's a cold, drab environment with stained ceiling tiles and a carpet so dirty that the occasional visitor from forensics has been tempted to take samples. A whiteboard occupies one full wall and an old, boxy TV flickers in tandem with the strip lights overhead, each one patterned with the outlines of dead spiders and bluebottles within. McAvoy's desk is at the far end of the room. He's the only member of staff who can tolerate the cold wind that blows through the gap where the window fails to meet the frame. He stopped keeping his files on the windowsill when the damp started to turn them the colour of used teabags. If he cranes his neck, he can make out the shopping centre, all sharp angles and cold glass, its blue-red lights casting lurid shadows onto the icy surface of the road.

His colleagues often joke that the North Point Centre has everything a human being could ask for. Within a stone's throw of his office he can access a minor injuries unit, two doctors' surgeries, a pub, a bookie's, a shopping mall, a funeral parlour and a Gregg's. He knows of at least two women nearby who supplement their income by welcoming gentleman callers between school runs. It's all sex and drugs and sausage rolls. The window beside his own desk looks directly onto a catalogue superstore: a joyless jamboree of leatherette sofas, widescreen TVs and the sort of ceramic hair straighteners that tend to double as a sandwich toaster after their owner's third bottle of sparkling wine. He's bumped into plenty of coppers browsing the aisles during their lunch breaks, trying not to be tempted by offers from one or two of the less morally straitjacketed consumers to acquire similar goods for half the price, provided no questions are asked.

'And that was when? 1983? Right, '84. Well, of course, if you could locate the documentation it would be a huge help.'

McAvoy, a large purple bruise between his beard and his left eye, has been glaring out of the window for twenty minutes, his stare falling just short of turning the glass back into sand. The screensaver has eclipsed the documents on his computer screen: a picture of a giant bumble-bee sitting on a thistle on a sunny day. He didn't choose the image but it strikes him as strangely apt. His head is full of half-formed pictures. There's an itching just below his skin: a prickly heat demanding attention. He knows what needs to be done, how to investigate the murders of Alf Howe and Desmond Kavanagh. They should be rolled up into the Enid Chappell investigation. Pharaoh would have found a way to make it happen, he tells himself. Pharaoh would have got her way. He chews on his cheek, furious with himself.

'No, no, that's incredibly helpful. I realise how hard this must be for you . . .'

McAvoy turns away from the window at the sound of DC Sophie Kirkland's voice. She has a strong Hull accent – every 'no' a 'nurr'; occasionally given to moaning about never seeing *hurm* due to shifts straying beyond the *narn* to *farv*. She taps away at her keyboard, mobile phone tucked between her chin and shoulder, talking quietly over the chatter of the other officers who mill around, tapping at keyboards, printing out reports, sending messages warning that this might be a late one. Kirkland's desk juts up against McAvoy's own and he has discovered that no matter how far down in his chair he slouches, her head is forever visible over the top of her monitor. As such, Kirkland has grown used to spending her whole day under accidental observation. She claims to find it reassuring, but over the past few months he has noticed her chair getting subtly higher and her monitor rising higher on her desk, elevated by stacks of box files. He confidently expects to look up some day and see her staring down at him like a deity on a cloud.

'That's been so helpful,' says Kirkland brightly. 'Yes, please. Of course. Thanks so much.' She puts the phone on the desk.

Cautiously, McAvoy looks across the top of the monitor. She's flushed; her round face slightly pink, eyes sparkling behind cat-eye spectacles. Her marshmallow cheeks clash with the red and black lumberjack shirt she wears beneath a dark green cord jacket. She's one of the youngest members of the MIT, not due to hit thirty for another few months. She's always struck McAvoy as hyper and sorrowful in equal measure, given to fits of enthusiasm followed by periods of maudlin navel-gazing. She falls in love every few weeks, falling out just as fast. She likes the virgin press of each new heart; the ripe flush of absolute infatuation. Anything less leaves her bored.

'She was shaken up,' says Kirkland, nodding to herself. 'Put a brave face on but you could tell it had really frozen her marrow. Some temper there too. She's in her late sixties but I wouldn't fancy kicking my football into her back garden. I reckon it would come back with a knitting needle through it.'

For the past half an hour, Kirkland has been chatting to a retired social worker by the name of Fiona Wall. She worked with Enid Chappell in the late eighties and early nineties, when the unitary authorities were arguing about where to draw the boundary lines and whether there really was a place called Humberside. A phone number registered to Mrs Wall had made repeated calls to Mrs Chappell's landline from New Year's Eve onwards, increasing in frequency by the day. The last had been made while forensics were still at the house. The details had been passed to the team and Kirkland had been tasked with filling in some of the blanks about Mrs Chappell's life. The task of informing her about Mrs Chappell's death had also fallen to Kirkland, though she had been under instructions to keep details vague. As per Slattery's instructions, the cause of death was 'uncertain', not 'suspicious'. McAvoy presumed that anybody who had spent time as a social worker would be able to read between the lines.

'They were friends?' asks McAvoy.

'Going back years, yes,' says Kirkland, nodding. 'She's younger than the victim – sorry, Mrs Chappell – but they worked together in the eighties. I've found a documentary online – Mrs Wall showing the camera crew around this estate. Doesn't look much bloody different, to be honest. She didn't pull her punches then, doesn't now. Said Enid was a bloody good person but a bit of a handful as a colleague. Tended to go her own way.'

'I have a statement from an East Riding councillor that says much the same thing,' says McAvoy with a nod.

'She did what needed to be done, even when it wasn't always by the book,' says Kirkland, reading her notes. 'She'd done damn well for a foundling. Honestly, what a word! That was how she referred to herself, by all accounts.'

'Mrs Wall?'

'No, keep up. Mrs Chappell. Her mum died when she was young and her dad was away at sea most of the time so she spent a lot of her childhood in Hesslewood Hall. Big stately home near the bridge, though of course there was no bridge there then. It provided homes for the orphans and the like from fishing families. She wanted to make a difference when she got older and by God she did that. Got into university and never stopped fighting all the way to the end. She was asked to stand for parliament on a few occasions but she always laughed it off. Said there were too many skeletons in her closet.'

McAvoy rubs his beard, scribbling notes on his pad. 'I think we'd have got on,' he says.

'You get on with everybody.' Kirkland laughs, stuffing crisps in her mouth. 'Apart from the people who try to kill you.' She glances at her notes. 'Apparently she had a really good relationship with the Hessle Road fishing community. Worked for Hull Corporation from 1966. Mrs Wall is sending over some photographs. She was a bit notorious at one time. Bought herself the most noticeable vehicle she could – that campervan in the outbuilding, by the sounds of it. Didn't hide away. She wanted people to be on their guard all the time so they always did right by their kids. The stories Mrs Wall told! She turned up at one house early on to follow up on a report about a toddler being neglected and the lady of the house told her that it wasn't even their baby. She was here when we moved in so we just kept her!

That's what she said. Record-keeping was a nightmare. There were home births never registered, mums begging doctors to put different dates on deliveries so their blokes never did the maths about conception times. But for all that she said Hessle Road was a place to be treasured. The people there would give you their last brass farthing and if they'd already spent it, they'd know a bloke who could nick you another.'

McAvoy stays quiet.

'Enid was retired a long while,' says Kirkland. 'Jacked it in back in 1993. They asked her to stay on to mentor young social workers but she said the job wasn't the same one she'd signed up for. Too much paperwork and form-filling. Too much scrutiny, that's what Mrs Wall says. Enid was good with people. She could get the teenage mums to talk. Could put the fear of God into dads who let their fists do the talking. She knew how to get a drug dealer to stop selling to one of her clients who was trying to get clean. But none of it sounded good in an official report. She went into voluntary work. She was on the board of a charity as well, set up by a certain businessman who's always in the papers. Ballantine.'

McAvoy rubs his cheekbone with his knuckle. 'We have to box a little clever with that one,' he says. 'Good lawyer, powerful friends . . .'

'The Roberta Ballantine Foundation,' says Kirkland. 'Registered charity. Enid was a trustee. You'll never guess who else was.'

'Try me.'

'Alf Howe. Desmond Kavanagh. Gerard Wade. Bernard Acklam. How can the brass be running this as separate investigations? It's clear there's a link.'

'We'll just have to make the best of it,' says McAvoy, brooding.

'Aye, well, I'll send you the details on the charity. I googled it but the website is just a holding page. Mrs Wall couldn't shed much more light on it but it's got a decent turnover according to the public accounts. Done a lot of good. Paid for emergency housing and educational materials, a refuge for battered spouses. I saw the way Ballantine was in the interview. Can't make up my mind if he's a decent bloke or a raving fucking psychopath.'

'Did you ask her about Mrs Chappell's companion? Her house guest?'

'I did, and it came as a bit of a surprise to her. She'd presumed that anybody staying with Enid would be female. Never one for gentlemen, apparently. Mrs Wall suggested she favoured women. Maybe she kept herself to herself, eh?'

McAvoy massages his scalp. 'Recent movements?'

'She hadn't seen as much of her in recent months,' says Kirkland. 'She definitely wasn't as sharp as she used to be – those are Mrs Wall's words. She'd call her sometimes, they'd have a chat and then ten minutes later she'd ring back and start the same conversation again. Age comes to us all – Mrs Wall's words again – but it was sad to see Enid on the slide.'

McAvoy waits for more and notices a slight smile twitch across Kirkland's face. She likes having his attention. She's made him wait for something good, he can tell.

'Last time they spoke she told Mrs Wall she was planning a holiday with "a friend". She was quite enigmatic about it. Sounded very excited. Mrs Wall was a bit concerned as the last time they'd met she certainly hadn't seemed up to going away in the middle of winter.'

'Some winter sun, might do her good . . .'

'No, she said she was going to see the Northern Lights. It was on her bucket list, apparently. Said it was time to start putting her affairs in order.'

McAvoy cocks his head. He gives a nod of appreciation. 'There's more, I can see it.'

'She asked her if she wouldn't mind looking after her chickens,' says Kirkland, her lips still curved in an affectionate smile.

'Mrs Wall said she would try and help but that it wasn't really her area of expertise. Said she never liked birds, which just made Enid laugh. Turns out Enid was obsessed with them. She was never allowed a budgie when she was a girl because apparently they're bad luck.'

'Get to the punchline, Sophie,' he says quietly.

'She was very insistent,' says Kirkland. 'Told Mrs Wall that she really did need to look in the hen-house. Made her promise. Mrs Wall called her on Christmas Day to wish her a merry Christmas. A man answered. Slightly Scouse, that was all I could get. He'd had a few drinks. Passed the phone to Enid and she'd had a few as well. Told her she would be in touch when she got back. That was it. Mrs Wall's been trying to get in touch with her ever since.' Kirkland sits back in her chair, raising her hands behind her head, sweat patches showing beneath her arms. She notices, and slowly lowers her arms.

McAvoy settles into silence. Broods on all he knows. The more he learns about Enid Chappell's life, the more he laments her death.

'Roberta Ballantine,' he says at last. 'There's a connection there, I know it. If Enid's been looking into her death, stirring up trouble, perhaps somebody wanted to silence her. I want to know more about Roberta. As a person, I mean. There must be people who remember her. Schoolmates. Teachers. Neighbours. Have a root around. Liaise with Ben and see what crops up on the Facebook groups. It wouldn't hurt to set up a false profile, ask a few questions, see who comes out of the woodwork. I know it's a big ask, but . . .'

'I'm on it,' says Kirkland firmly. She glances up towards the incident board, where McAvoy has secured a picture of Mrs Chappell as she was in life: vibrant and vital, her eyes sparkling and her mouth turned up in an attractive smile. He needs the team to fix the image in their mind; to be aware of the person for whom they seek justice.

'Sarge? I think this one's worth a look.'

McAvoy turns from his computer screen and into the jovial, fleshy face of DC Andy Daniells. He doesn't look well. He's dark beneath his eyes and sweat is oozing out of every pore, as if somebody were giving CPR to a saturated sponge.

'Andy? Jings, what's wrong?'

'Early prognosis would suggest Black Death, Sarge,' says Daniells. 'Just don't breathe in anywhere near me. Or touch anything I've touched. In the event that I don't pull through, I want you to sing at my funeral. Fucking Ballantine. I swear, he's freaked my immune system out. Who does that? I feel bloody violated.' He stops and grins. 'And please, say "jings" again. It's so sweet.'

'How about *help ma boab*? You know that one?' He finds himself chuckling. Daniells always makes him laugh. 'Best I can offer is a Lucozade,' he says, rummaging in his pocket for change for the vending machine. 'God, sit down before you fall down.'

Daniells gratefully eases himself into a battered blue swivel chair, resting his arm on a pile of papers. He sniffs: a rattling, outrageous sound that turns McAvoy's stomach.

'Should you still be here, Andy? We all appreciate going above and beyond but not if you drop dead.'

'I'm a trouper,' says Daniells, his voice thick with catarrh.

McAvoy adjusts his position. 'You said you had something?'

Daniells nods. 'I've been going through the phone numbers,' he says. 'Sophie and me divided them up. The 01964 number that's in use a lot belongs to a Margaret Aspinall, of Cliff Road, Atwick. Up the coast. I managed to get through. Very frail, nervous soul and it half broke my heart to tell her that her friend was dead. She wanted to know what had happened. How it had happened. She asked me if it had happened on her holidays. When I told her she'd died at home and that she'd been there on her own for a few days, that was when the tears came. I couldn't get much sense out of her after that. I asked if I could pop up and see her and I think she said yes, though it was hard to tell. I'm looking into her background but I thought it might be one that you wanted to help with? You're better with little old ladies than I am.'

McAvoy keeps his face inscrutable. Turns his chair and looks through the papers on his desk. He finds the list of phone numbers. Mrs Aspinall's number is one of the lines that Mrs Chappell most regularly called. He takes his pen from his shirt pocket and underlines the pay-as-you-go mobile number. It appears within half an hour of each call between Mrs Chappell and Mrs Aspinall. He sucks his lip, thinking hard. He types the unregistered number into Google.

'Shit,' says Daniells quickly. 'Sarge, I never even thought . . .'

Midway down the first page is a website called WriteStuff. com – one of several UK networks established for media free-lancers seeking work. The glossy website claims to be a one-stop shop for creative professionals eager to demonstrate their skills and showcase their portfolio. The home page is littered with testimonials from recruiters and members alike, all claiming that nothing in the known universe could possibly be as effective as paying a few quid for a year's membership. McAvoy types the number in to the search field. It brings up a grainy thumbnail image of a Parker pen wrapped in crime-scene tape. It advertises the services of Marlowe Media. He clicks the link. Reads the paragraph that accompanies the badly drawn image of a private investigator in a raincoat, holding a magnifying glass. McAvoy smiles instinctively. He gets the impression that somebody, somewhere, has been taking the piss.

*Award-winning editor, journalist, writer. I edit and ghost-write books, magazines, reports, blogs and articles. Recent clients span architecture, oil and gas, management consulting, construction, high-tech and economic development. Organisations from around the world use me to create high-impact content campaigns that*

*demonstrate thought leadership in mature, crowded B2B markets.*
*I have twenty-five years' experience in professional and business*
*press and newspapers.*

McAvoy turns back to Daniells. 'You've rung it?'

'Switched off,' he says.

McAvoy stares sullenly out of the window. Something is
nagging at him but he can't quite grab its tail. He frowns. The
fog has given way to a mizzling sleet which makes the view
beyond the glass so miserable that if it were a TV show, he
would be tempted to put his boot through the screen.

'That's bloody odd,' says Kirkland, from behind her monitor.
She slams the phone back into the cradle and looks accusingly
at McAvoy. 'The hard copies of the investigation file,' she says.
'Roberta Ballantine's disappearance. I've been on to the archive
asking for the case file to be sent over and apparently it's already
been signed out.'

'By whom?'

'The boss,' says Kirkland. 'Signed it out on 2 January.'

'The boss?' asks Daniells.

'Pharaoh, of course,' says Kirkland. She narrows her eyes at
McAvoy. 'Is something going on? You must know.'

McAvoy stands, pulling on his coat. Tries to look as if he is
on top of things.

'Up the coast, you said,' he mutters to Daniells. 'We need a
better understanding of her movements. Mrs Chappell. They
all knew each other, I'm certain of it. And this holiday she was
going on – why didn't it happen? Your Mrs Aspinall may be on
her own, upset – needing somebody to talk to.' He stops, aware
he is only talking so that he doesn't lapse into catatonia. 'Did I
see your pick-up in the car park?'

'Yeah, but Stefan's really funny about—'

'Come on,' says McAvoy, aware that he is about to erupt into
a crimson blush if he has to face Kirkland's harsh glare for
another minute more. She presumes that he's sworn to secrecy:

229

playing it coy. Can't imagine that he's every bit in the dark as the rest of them. He trudges to the door, Daniells wriggling into his puffer jacket, picking up his notebook, gathering papers and trying to inhale a snort of nasal spray all at the same time.

'You do know . . .' whispers Daniells: germs and hot breath in his ear. 'What's she up to?'

McAvoy wonders if tapping the side of his nose would make him seem like a dickhead. Decides that it would.

He bangs through the door and down the stairs and out into the darkening air.

# 22

*A1035, East Yorkshire*
*5.06 p.m.*

McAvoy and Daniells head north, the big fat tyres of the pick-up truck throwing up slush and spray, pushing into a darkness that closes around them like blood clotting around a wound. The outskirts of the Bransholme estate disappear as they head into farmland: black fields dotted with patchy hedgerows and the occasional copse of trees, their branches transformed into grasping, sinister apparitions. They pass through a straggle of little villages with names that still reek of their medieval origins: *Wawne, Meaux, Routh*, tumbledown farmhouses and chunky white cottages looming out of the darkness like passing ships. Daniells clears his throat as they swing right onto the coastal road. On summer days it's consistently snarled up and even on cold winter evenings it's usually nose to tail at rush hour. This evening it's quiet, and Daniells is able to flick the headlights to full beam, casting toppled pyramids of yellowy light into the sparkling, grey-black night. Ice still gleams on the wet road. It's hard to see where the horizon meets the sky.

Margaret Aspinall's house sits at what has recently become the very end of Cliff Road. It used to be the middle, but the eroding coastline has claimed the bungalows, chalets and farm-houses that used to act as a buffer between her back garden and the encroaching sea. The property is unlikely to have won any awards for innovative architecture. It looks like a triangle sitting on top of a square, set back from the road behind a low brick wall. Towards the back a flap of tarpaulin swells and curtsies on the gale, veiling the entrance to an old barn with a curving, corrugated roof.

Daniells starts to slow down as McAvoy sits forward in his seat. He cranes his neck, peering through the misted window.

'Bloody hell, it's the edge of the world . . .'

A few car lengths ahead, the road simply disappears, its edges sheared as neatly as if a giant set of jaws have taken a bite out of the land. McAvoy steps from the car. Feels the wet air slap his face and licks the salty air from his lips. He walks tentatively towards the edge of the precipice and leans forward, peering into the blackness. He can just make out the frothy white line where the sea hits the sand. Mud and boulders slope away beneath him. Slowly his eyes adjust. The darkness takes on new shapes. He can decipher pipes and electricity points sticking out of the ground. Holiday-makers used to park caravans where now there is only cold, empty air.

'Lovely spot,' says Daniells. 'Shame. What are they doing about it?'

'They?'

'Council, or whoever. Must be something they can do.'

McAvoy thinks of several things to say and decides none of them are worth giving breath. He just gives Daniells a little smile and gestures towards the house. 'Come on. She might have a Lemsip.'

Mrs Aspinall is waiting at the front door as they approach the house – a pinkish apparition in the mouth of the door, lit from behind by the soft glow of the hallway. She doesn't seem to get any taller the nearer they get. She's a good few inches under five feet tall; gently rounded at the edges. She'd be smaller still if not for the mounds of peroxide curls that adorn her head like a hat. She wears a salmon-pink cardigan over a matching jumper, neat blue trousers with a crisp seam. Her feet are snug in mauve slippers, embroidered with thistles. She smiles, then catches herself and stops. She seems unsure how to act. Different expressions wrestle in the doughy battleground of her pleasant face.

'Mrs Aspinall? I'm Aector McAvoy. It's good of you to see us.'

'You're Scottish,' she says, her voice thin and pained: a smoker's vibrato. 'That's good. Did you say you were an actor?'

'Aector,' he says again. 'You can call me Hector, if you prefer. I'm a detective sergeant. This is my colleague, Andy.'

'Nice to meet you in person, Mrs Aspinall,' says Daniells. 'I won't shake your hand. Think I've got something ghastly.'

'Are you the one I spoke to?' She peers at them both, sizing them up. 'You look like your voice,' she says to Daniells, then turns back to McAvoy. 'It's a bungalow. You might not fit. Don't be banging your head. Shall we go into the kitchen? There's tea, if you want it.'

'Lovely, if it's no trouble,' says McAvoy. 'Shall we take our boots off?'

Mrs Aspinall smiles, in a way that says she appreciates the gesture. Screws up her face as if shrugging with her cheeks. She doesn't care.

The hallway smells of cigarette smoke and air-freshener. The heat is stifling. Mrs Aspinall leads them down a corridor with a low ceiling and into a comfortable square kitchen: a drop-leaf table and four chairs pushed up against the scorching radiator; sugar bowl and milk jug, newspapers and letters dotted around a glass ashtray overflowing with grimy stubs. Vintage Formica units line the low, pale-blue walls. A haze of cigarette smoke hovers around the artexed ceiling. The floor is cushioned with a loud linoleum that clashes wonderfully with the marigold and avocado curtains. They frame a large, double-glazed window which, in daylight, would afford magnificent views of the disappearing clifftop and rolling sea. The darkness has instead turned the glass into a mirror. McAvoy sees himself as he ducks under the doorway, notes the difference in size between himself and the tiny lady who points him to a chair and starts filling the kettle. Framed cross-stitch pictures hang in rectangular and oval frames. A poinsettia, its red leaves turning brown at the edges, sits on the windowsill, bookended by pictures of two smiling children, gap-toothed and goofy, smiling for the camera amid waves of silk. A watercolour of a trawler, steaming out of the lock gates, takes pride of place above the radiator. McAvoy lets his gaze linger for a moment. He closes his eyes and tries to summon up a picture from his memory. He feels as though he has seen Mrs Aspinall before.

'Lovely place,' says Daniells, sitting down. He keeps raising his hand to his nose, blotting the dew-drop of mucus that continually threatens to fall. 'Would you mind if I used your bathroom? If I don't blow my nose I think I'm going to drown.'

Mrs Aspinall turns from the kettle. 'First left,' she says. 'I can do you a toddy, if you like. You'll sleep for a week but you'll feel better when you wake up.'

Daniells gives McAvoy a beseeching look. McAvoy shakes his head apologetically. He knows Pharaoh would be fine with it. He also knows he's not Pharaoh. Daniells pouts then vanishes to the bathroom. A moment later they are treated to what sounds a lot like a bin lorry reversing over a brass band.

'Poor lad,' says Mrs Aspinall, motherly. 'I do a good toddy as well. I'm sure you do them better, being Scottish and whatnot.'

'I'm not much of a drinker,' says McAvoy, wondering what to make of the 'whatnot'. 'I'm told that cloves make the difference.'

'They do.' Mrs Aspinall smiles. 'I enjoy a nip of the whisky, now and again. Keeps out the cold. Enid didn't mind a drop or two, when we were putting the world to rights . . .'

Her voice falters. She puts her hands down on the worktop

and turns away. McAvoy wants to stand. To put a hand on her squared shoulders and tell her he is sorry for her loss. He forces himself to stay in his seat.

Mrs Aspinall blinks back tears. Recovers herself and gives him a penetrating look. 'It's all true, I take it. She's not upped sticks and moved to Panama and not told anybody? I mean, have you seen her? Are you sure?'

McAvoy's head fills with images of yesterday's grim discovery: the pale, frozen body of Enid Chappell secured in pack ice in her bathtub, hair dangling like curtains towards the glittering floor. 'I'm very sorry, Mrs Aspinall. There's no mistake.'

She nods, her lips a tight line. 'They said on the radio there were questions to be answered. That it was "unexplained". It's a bit vague. I mean, did she slip and bump her head or something? I told her time and again that she were getting too old to be living the way she did but she were so independent. Wouldn't let anybody interfere.'

McAvoy pulls his phone from his pocket and places it on the table, microphone facing up. Retrieves his notebook and pen. Mrs Aspinall places a mug of tea in front of him and sits down opposite. McAvoy puts in a spoonful of sugar. She doesn't look up as Daniells appears at the door. He crosses to the sink and picks up the spare mug. Turns his back on the room and squints into the darkness.

'You were friends a long time?' asks McAvoy.

'Most of my life,' says Mrs Aspinall. She sips her tea. She settles back in her chair and retrieves a silver cigarette tin from her cardigan pocket. She opens it with a click. Removes a cigarette and places it between her lips. In her left hand she holds a gold lighter, its buffed surface worn smooth by years of being caressed by her fingers and thumbs. She breathes deep as she lights the cigarette. Blows out a little cloud of smoke that drifts upwards to join the ragged nimbus around the ceiling light. She seems instantly more comfortable, as if she has made sense of this environment. She's in her kitchen, chatting with a nice young man, drinking tea and having a smoke.

'Mrs Aspinall?'

'Call me Mags, please.'

'You were telling me about Enid . . .'

She smiles. 'Brain like a library. First woman to do the new social services degree at the University of Hull. Well, her and one other, but she were in the first intake so that's still good, eh? Her family were Hessle Roaders. Life wasn't easy for her, but it weren't for many people, not back then. She made the most of her opportunities. Got into one of them good girl schools on a scholarship and sailed through her exams. Apparently she could have gone to one of the fancy ones down south but she chose Hull because she was a bit of a home bird and wanted to do some good in an area that she already knew. Brave, if you ask me.'

McAvoy looks up from his notes and realises she is watching his pen move across the page. She gives the tiniest smile at his indecipherable notes.

'She'd have made a good politician if she'd been allowed to pick and choose the policies she thought were important. Never very good at towing the line, our Enid. Her conscience were too big to let herself off with a lie. I had to stop her listening to the radio phone-ins when we were in the car. She'd get so cross, roaring at the callers and the presenter, asking them what was wrong with them. I think she despaired a bit, about how things are getting. She always did the right thing, you see, or what she thought was right. Amazing that she held onto that despite all those years in the job. She saw some horrible things. Had to do some pretty horrible things too. There were some nasty buggers who used to call her the Pied Piper, as if she were getting a thrill out of taking bains from their families. She saved lives, that's what she did.' She sucks the last of the cigarette down to the filter and immediately lights another. Her hand shakes and the light of the flame shimmers on her tear-filled eyes. 'She did a lot of good by my family. She was a good friend to all of us.'

'I know this is hard, but can you think of anybody who might have wanted to hurt Enid? Any enemies?'

Mrs Aspinall shoots him a hard look, the age and infirmity seeming to vanish for a moment. 'Kill her, you mean? Aye, plenty. But not now. Not as an old lady.' She seems to realise the enormity of the question. Her lip trembles and she pulls her cardigan around herself. 'Unexplained means "killed", does it? Who would do that? She was old. She was just an old lady, same as me.'

Daniells moves forward, about to put his hand on her shoulder. McAvoy flicks him a look. He would love nothing more than to offer comfort but right now he needs her like this. Needs her to tell him everything; to give him a full picture of her dead friend while still in a muddle of emotion. He doesn't need the sanitised biography, offered like a eulogy and with the negative aspects removed. He needs it all.

'Not now?' he says, repeating her words. 'You mean she's had enemies before?'

'Of course she bloody has,' says Mrs Aspinall, looking flustered. She pulls a handkerchief from her sleeve and dabs her eyes, the tip of her cigarette dangerously close to her peroxide curls. 'She were from the Social, wasn't she? To some people she was the enemy. Those who knew her realised that she was their ally.'

'How did you meet?' asks McAvoy, trying to keep his tone light.

'A good woman, more or less,' mutters Mrs Aspinall in a far-away voice. 'She was there to lend a hand. To keep an eye on people. To make sure that "poor" never turned into "neglected". Those who lost their kids had plenty of warnings. She did right by me and mine. Saw me through some bad times . . .'

She stops herself. Wraps her hands around her mug.

237

'You'll have heard about my first husband,' she says flatly. 'Died at sea. I were pregnant.'

McAvoy frowns, making connections. Feels his guts turn to ice as his entire imagination pictures all the ways in which Area Commander Slattery is going to go berserk, and Stephen Ballantine is going to destroy him. He's sitting here with his *mum*.

'You were married to Rory Ballantine,' says McAvoy, enunciating each word carefully. He turns to Daniells and gives him a hard look. The DC looks pained. He'd had no time for a background check. 'A good man, I'm told,' says McAvoy, horribly uncomfortable. He's replaying each syllable of Stephen Ballantine's threats.

'Best man I've known,' says Mrs Aspinall, and a tear cuts a channel of white skin through the rouge on her cheeks. 'Childhood sweethearts, more or less, though childhood ended a damn sight sooner in those days. When Rory's dad died we took his little sister in. The Social needed to check she were being looked after properly. Enid were our care worker. We struck lucky.'

'You got on?' asks McAvoy, floundering.

Mrs Aspinall cocks her head, birdlike, and gives a lopsided smile. 'She were like a colour telly in a black and white world,' she says. 'Same as my Rory. Same as all the fishermen. Characters. She was one of us but she weren't one of us, if you follow me. She was glamorous. Dressed how she wanted and didn't seem scared of anybody. I'm from Road. We're all strong women. But she never seemed in the least bit afraid of doing what she had to do. She'd march into the busiest, roughest pub and pull a bloke out by the ear if she was concerned for one of his nippers. She'd park herself in the hair salon and give mums what for while they were having their hair set if they hadn't been pulling their weight. She tried to help, you see. She wanted what was best for the kids.'

'She never had children of her own?' asks Daniells.

Mrs Aspinall pauses for a beat too long. 'She took some in, now and again. When they had nowhere else to go. Bought that campervan just so the bains had somewhere to sleep if there was nowhere willing to offer a bed for the night. Couldn't do that now, could you? Probably couldn't do it then. But she did, and we respected her for it.'

McAvoy drains his tea. It's gone cold. 'It must have been unbearable,' he says. 'When Rory was lost. Baby on the way, no source of income.'

'Hardest time of my life,' says Mrs Aspinall. 'I don't think the person I was before he died and the person I became after it would even recognise one another. Roberta and me – we were broken. That's the only way to say it. Broken. Enid was a miracle worker. She managed to negotiate a payment from one of the benevolent associations. A hardship grant. Enough to keep the house going. Rory's mates would have helped more, if they could, but what happened on the ship, it changed all of them. He was their leader. I think his mates felt it all as much as I did. Gerard was in hospital for weeks, up in some out-of-the-way place in Iceland. Enid was there through all of it. There for me all my life . . .'

'I understand that you remarried,' says McAvoy softly.

Mrs Aspinall tenses her jaw. 'I thought the bains needed a father. I thought anybody willing to take on another man's kids must be decent. Arthur played the part all right. He showed his true colours before the honeymoon was out but by then he was my husband and we were always taught that it were a mother's job to keep the family together. Where would we go, me, Roberta and the bains?' She shakes her head, eyes wide, reliving the horror of the situation she found herself in. 'I was numb. I wanted to be at the bottom of the ocean with my Rory and instead I was trapped – tied up in the promises I'd made him that I'd keep her safe, be a good mum, keep his memory alive—'

'Sorry, can I just ask something?' interrupts Daniells, sitting forward. 'Stephen Ballantine is your son? He's worth millions. I'm not trying to be horrible but shouldn't you be in a mansion house somewhere?'

If Mrs Aspinall is hurt, she doesn't show it. 'All I ever wanted was a little house on a clifftop,' she says. 'I've got happy memories of this place. My little family. Enid's old camper parked out there. We used to come here. Escape Road for a bit. It belonged to a friend of Enid's. Arthur's death gave me another reason to be cheerful. Bastard was well insured. I bought my little patch of paradise. This is my place and I'm beholden to nobody. If it falls into the sea then it falls into the bloody sea. I don't need any bugger to tell me that they could give me something better with the change from their pocket.'

Mrs Aspinall glances out of the window towards the blackness of the sea. The temper goes out of her voice. 'It'll hit him hard,' she says. 'Stephen. About Enid, I mean. It'll hit a lot of people.'

'Have you listened to the news today, Mrs Aspinall?' asks McAvoy kindly. 'About the *Blake Holst*?'

'Silly bloody idea, that one,' says Mrs Aspinall, dabbing her eyes. 'Thinks he's got money to burn. My own fault, I suppose. Built his dad up to be a superhero so it's no surprise he's always trying to live up to him. All the lads have chipped in to help. They'd do anything for him. They have long memories. They loved his dad.'

McAvoy's words turn to dust on his tongue. He can't find the courage to tell her about the bloodied bodies and the horrors in the hold.

'It would be helpful to speak to Gerard Wade,' says McAvoy. 'I understand he and Rory were especially close. And Enid had been trying to make contact with him . . .'

'Funny bugger our Gerard,' says Mrs Aspinall. 'Made a mint but never seemed to enjoy a penny of it. He gave Stephen a good leg-up though. Always did the right thing. He's got a place in West Ella. I've never seen it myself. Invitations must have been lost in the post, eh?' Tears fill her eyes and she dabs at her cheeks afresh. 'It's just all so horrible . . .'

McAvoy reaches out and closes his hand over hers. She jerks back as if she has touched a hot surface. 'Sorry,' she mutters. 'Sorry, you made me jump.'

'Forgive me,' says McAvoy, scratching awkwardly at his hair. He wonders what she has endured to cause her to flinch so violently at human contact. 'Mr Lowery died at the docks, I understand.'

Mrs Aspinall lights another cigarette, her fingers shaking. McAvoy senses a storm is coming.

'Horrible,' she mutters, still shaking. 'Some boards gave way when he was working on one of the trawlers. I didn't grieve for him.' She flashes him a look of defiance. 'I hated him, if I'm honest. He was a horrible man and he died in a horrible way and I sat through the funeral feeling like I'd just won the pools.'

Silence creeps into the room. For a long while there is nothing but the sound of the sea, rolling and sucking and moving forward in inches. McAvoy glances at the darkened glass and has to resist the urge to shiver, despite the warmth of the room.

'Do you have any photographs of Enid?' he says. 'It would help. Jog people's memories, you know. Show her as she was.'

Mrs Aspinall frowns, tears still falling. 'On the dresser,' she says coldly. 'By my bed.'

McAvoy looks at Daniells, who moves through the fog of smoke towards the door. He returns moments later, holding a picture in a silver frame. It shows Enid, Mrs Aspinall and a dark-haired, pale-faced young woman. They are sitting on the roof of a campervan: silvery sea, wildflowers and damp grass, bright yellow sun shining. Enid is smiling, a neckerchief at her throat. Mrs Aspinall is dressed in a poppy-coloured T-shirt and a mini-skirt, her hair loose and unkempt. He peers at the dark-haired girl. Holds up the picture, poker-still.

'Roberta Ballantine,' says McAvoy. 'I've seen another picture of this day. At Enid's. A different angle. I didn't realise.'

'We don't talk about Roberta,' says Mrs Aspinall. 'It's too hard. It doesn't matter how many nosy sods come knocking on my door and asking their questions, I don't know what happened. She vanished. Maybe she's having the time of her life somewhere, laughing at those of us who grieve. You ever think of that? I told her. Told the pair of them. Let it be.'

McAvoy pinches the bridge of his nose, feeling himself losing control. 'You must be very proud of Stephen,' he says cautiously.

'I'm proud of both my boys,' she replies automatically.

McAvoy stops. He remembers Slattery telling him about the blood relatives of Rory Ballantine. Stephen had declined to give a sample. He tries to recall the original article he read about Hull's working-class hero. Had there been mention of a brother?

'I'm sorry, Mrs Aspinall? I do recall a mention of a twin but there's nothing in the case files.'

'Shows what you know,' she says, a little unpleasantly. 'Rory left me with twin boys. A widow, with two bouncing boys to bring up. His little sister too.'

McAvoy thinks again about the bodies in the cold Russian ground. The brothers' DNA would be identical. Did Slattery not know about Stephen's brother, or had he declined to track him down for fear of upsetting Stephen?

'What's your other son's name, Mrs Aspinall?'

'Thomas,' she says. 'Thomas Rory.'

'And where is he now?'

She laughs, as if the question is ludicrous. 'Had his father's blood, that one. Went to sea as soon as he was old enough. Barely been back since.'

'Do they see much of each other?' asks McAvoy. 'Would you perhaps have contact details for him?'

'Why?' asks Mrs Aspinall sharply. 'We got put through the

wringer by your lot when Roberta did her vanishing act. Same when Bowbells died at the docks. You've always had it in for us. Even now, with Stephen doing all he does for this city, you still have to keep digging away at us.'

Mrs Aspinall picks up her clunky handbag from the floor beside her and starts rummaging inside for a tissue. Pulls out her purse. Mints. A little address book and a gold pen. Two lipsticks and an Agatha Christie paperback. She has little bags of ten-pence pieces and pound coins. She makes a mountain of them on the tabletop. 'I like the amusements,' she says, pulling a tissue from a packet and blowing her nose. 'No law against it, is there?' She starts putting the items back in the bag. As she picks up the paperback he spots a square of card being used as a bookmark. It slithers halfway out of the pages. He sees black basalt columns and hard white seas.

'Friend been on their travels?' asks McAvoy.

'Sorry?'

He nods at the postcard. She tucks it back between the pages. 'I just pick up the first thing that's lying about. I don't like turning the pages over.'

'Do you mind if I have a look?' he asks. 'I'm thinking about somewhere to take the kids.'

'You have children?' she asks, softening slightly.

'A boy and a girl. Ten and five.'

'They'd love it there, I reckon,' says Mrs Aspinall. 'Skagi. It's nicer than it sounds, even when you consider what it means to me and mine. Miles and miles of nothing. Stephen took me, years ago. That's where it happened, you see. Little island just off the headland. Where the *Blake Purcell* went down. Where Rory went into the water.' She swallows painfully. 'We were both choked up. We laid flowers. I poured a bottle of his favourite tipple into the water. We both had a good old chat with him. Anybody passing would have thought we were mad. No chance of that. Completely abandoned. I was scared to death on those roads. It was important though. We had to see it. Had to say goodbye.'

'Did your other son go with you?'

'Tommy? No. He's had his problems, has Tommy. I think there's some jealousy there, if I'm honest. I mean, Stephen's done so well.'

'Tommy not so much?'

'He's made some bad decisions. He's fine at sea – not so good at land. Stephen's tried to help him time and again but he's very proud. It's not easy seeing somebody doing so well in life while you're stuck in the bowels of some stinking ship and trying to stay on top of your debts. They've always been competitive. I suppose I should have seen it coming. You split up twins and raise them differently – it will always have an impact.'

'Stephen went to a very good school, I understand.'

'Scholarship,' says Mrs Aspinall. 'Still cost the earth but we managed.'

'And Thomas?'

Mrs Aspinall lights another cigarette. 'Didn't get in. Went to a state school off Road. Was good enough for his dad, that's what I told him. He was still my bain and I was just as proud of him as I was of his brother. They drifted apart from then on. Twins, drifting apart. Can you believe it? It was a full-time job stopping them coming to blows. Tommy had problems with my second husband as well. He never took to him. Treated Stephen okay but Tommy always seemed to bug him. There were incidents.'

McAvoy reaches across and takes the postcard. 'There's no stamp,' he says. 'No message.'

'No? I picked it up with the post on the step and didn't give it a thought.' She doesn't meet McAvoy's eye as she talks.

'Mrs Aspinall, who might have sent you this?'

'Some silly sod, no doubt,' she says warily. 'Honestly, my head's starting to hurt with all these questions. Why can't people

244

leave the past buried? That's what I told Stephen when you lot were raking about in all our muck, asking him to spit in tubes and talking about Rory's body and making it all horrible when things were fine as they were. It's been fifty years and I still feel like he's about to come through the door. Why do they want to take that away from us, eh?'

'I'd like to talk to you about Napper Acklam,' begins McAvoy.

The old lady holds up a hand. Her gold rings sparkle. She shakes her head. She's had enough.

'All the same,' she grumbles. 'All want to rake it up. To mess things up. When they're tidy . . . when they're pretty.'

'Mrs Aspinall, who else has been asking questions? What accusations are you referring to?'

'I'm tired,' snaps Mrs Aspinall. Her eyes become glassy; damp pebbles dropped in snow. 'I don't feel very well. I want you to go.'

'Mrs Aspinall, I don't think you realise—'

'I've got a bad heart. My friend has died and you're here trying to put pressure on me. When my Stephen hears what you've been saying . . . he's a rich man, you know that, don't you? Done well. Done so well.' She dissolves into sobs, sucking the knuckle of her thumb.

'Sarge,' says Daniells softly. He glances at the door. 'That'll do, eh?'

For a moment McAvoy feels like tearing a strip off his junior colleague, a sudden urge to tell him that this is important: that an old lady has had her life extinguished and that justice is worth a few tears. Instantly he feels ashamed. Sees what he could so easily become. He presses the back of his hand to his head as if battling a migraine. 'I'm sorry,' he says. Repeats it as he stands, the chair scraping across the lino. He fumbles in his pocket for a card. Leaves it on the table. 'When you're ready,' he says quietly.

Mrs Aspinall looks up at him, tiny and pink, blue-eyed and

245

fragile. He stares down: a huge presence casting a great shadow across her tiny frame. He leaves without saying another word.

The man who calls himself Vidarr watches them leave. He feels exhilarated. Feels as though his blood were on fire.

The image of the big man with the red hair and the kind eyes stays burned on his memory long after the truck has departed.

He feels an intrinsic hatred for him; a loathing that feels like flame and wriggling maggots beneath his flesh. He doesn't remember meeting the man before. Can't recall how he has wronged him. But he knows that the big man has seen blood-shed. Has seen death.

Vidarr longs to test himself against the big man. Hurting the old men has been too easy. He is dangerously close to having killed all the people he set out to hurt. He wonders what he should do when his work is done. He has grown to like killing.

He looks at the dark mass of the clifftop beyond the little house. The last time he came here the girl had still been buried beneath the earth. The dirt has been disturbed since. The things that lurk beneath the surface have been taken; their graves dese-crated. He hears his father's voice.

*'She was my favourite. We were so perfect for one another. They took her from me. Took you. I tried for so long to find a replace-ment; another Roberta. But the bird never feasted so hungrily. Look at their braids, son. Look at the tresses of the ones who failed to satisfy the raven. You see it, I know you do. You worshipped at the wrong altar. You are my son. My blood. Let yourself be the thing you always longed to be. Find them. Hurt them. Make your father proud . . .'*

He wonders whether he is strong enough to split the big man's ribs. Wonders how his heart will feel in his hand.

Vidarr slides back into the shadow. In his pocket, he fingers the tip of the hook. Scrapes the dried blood with his nail, and raises the tip to his nose. He breathes in and smells the blood of the men who did him wrong.

He looks around him at the lights of the city: neon and gold sparkling against the cold black air. A lot has changed but so much remains the same. He can find his way back to Road just through the smell of the air and the direction of the wind. He smiles in anticipation of what awaits him there. Hopes that the next one will fight a little harder.

He is so very pleased to be home.

# 23

*Skagastrond, Skagi Peninsula, Iceland*
*7.03 p.m.*

Pharaoh stares out through the glass. Everything seems too white, too dark. The snow makes her think of autopsies she has witnessed: the pale, bloated skin of drowning victims. She stares up, through the clouds and circling birds and towards the absolute blackness of the mountain. She turns her cigarette so that it faces palm inwards. Turns back to the two Icelandic police officers. The big man had told her his name was Thor, though his surname was beyond her. The two officers have spent the best part of the afternoon using her holiday home as a makeshift office, dragging in computers and printers and wireless routers from the car, chatting into mobile phones and making video conference calls with superiors back in Reykjavik. It's too cold and stormy to drive back. Apparently, Pharaoh has been the cause of some consternation at HQ. They are being very polite, but after hours of being talked about rather than to, Pharaoh's patience is close to snapping. She's opened a bottle of red and made herself a sandwich containing what might be the remains of last night's pizza. She's got a mouthful of soggy carbohydrates when the blonde officer finally closes her laptop with the air of a virtuoso pianist at the keys of a Steinway grand.

'All sorted,' says Minervadottir, with a poor attempt at a smile.

'You're fucking thorough,' mutters Pharaoh. 'My brain's hurting.'

'My colleagues have been working very hard to keep me abreast of all developments in this case, and the many others for which I am responsible.'

'You're responsible, are you? Going to arrest yourself?'

Minervadottir ignores her. Continues with the speech she has clearly been rehearsing in her head. 'My superiors are pleased at the zeal with which you have approached witnesses, ignored established procedure and neglected to work within the investigation unit which you previously claimed would benefit from your specific expertise. They would like me to pass on their thanks, while encouraging you, from this point on, to consider an alternative working practice.'

'That was a mouthful,' says Pharaoh, swallowing crusts, tomato sauce and a mouthful of Merlot. 'Didn't look easy to say.'

'Can you say it in Icelandic?'

'I can only say "skyr", and that's not much use. Not unless you're trying to explain to a paramedic what you've just thrown up.'

'You asked to be involved in this investigation,' says Minervadottir icily. 'Now, can we please begin to cooperate?'

Pharaoh sighs, tired and not anywhere near drunk enough to be belligerent. 'What do you know about the *Blake Purcell*?' she asks at last.

Minervadottir glances at her junior colleague. They talk briefly in Icelandic. She moves her fingers over the keyboard of her laptop and taps at the screen.

'An English trawler,' she says finally. 'It sank off Isafjordur Bay in 1970. The hulk's still there. There are fishermen here who curse it. They still snag their nets. There was talk of trying to refloat it – some salvage operation paid for by an English businessman. The report said it was impossible. So we are stuck with it.'

'Very good,' says Pharaoh, impressed. 'Why do you know all that?'

Minervadottir licks her lips. 'When a foreigner's body is found in a remote patch of your district, do you not make it your business to know everything of interest in the area?'

'Yes, I do,' says Pharaoh sweetly. 'But I doubt I'd know the names of every Icelandic fishing vessel that ever sank off Spurn Point.'

'Perhaps not,' concedes Minervadottir. 'We have a database of all maritime fatalities; an accurate map of wreck sites and tide patterns. It helps with the search for bodies, which is one of the less pleasant parts of our job. When we recovered the car and found the magazine ... well, the *Blake Purcell*'s name caught my eyes and the rest I read online. What is the relevance?'

Pharaoh grinds out her cigarette. 'The man,' she says. 'The body. Do you have the ID?'

'Our lab has yet to provide the report,' says Minervadottir, with an edge to her voice. 'But I have been able to give the forensic team a little push in the right direction. We both know who we are referring to. Albert Jonsson was Russell Chandler. Russell Chandler was a witness in a trial in England. That trial spoke of the work done by Detective Sergeant McAvoy, and the recommendation that he receive the Queen's Police Medal. That makes Mr Chandler's final words extremely interesting. That is why I contacted your department for assistance.' Minervadottir looks her up and down. 'And here you are.'

Pharaoh smiles, opening her hands as if having performed a conjuring trick. She suddenly realises she has misjudged the Icelandic officer. Considers how she would feel if the roles were reversed and comes to the conclusion that she should really start playing more nicely.

'That's good work,' she says, nodding. 'Seriously, I'm impressed.'

Minervadottir gives a curt nod. 'I believe we both share the same rather insane theory. This Mr Chandler believed he had identified some kind of serial attacker – the man from his ridiculous magazine article. He came here seeking answers. He underestimated the weather and fell from the cliffs like so many other foolish tourists. Had he not managed to mutter a name, he would have been chalked up as another victim of the Icelandic winter. Instead, here you are.'

'Yeah, lucky you,' says Pharaoh. She glances at the big man. 'You don't say much. What's your take on it? Why was an English journalist up here in the dead of winter? Why did a local artist get a picture of a figure out at the lighthouse?'

He turns to his superior officer. They exchange a few words. At length, she pulls a plastic evidence bag from an inside pocket. Inside is a squat black telephone.

'Please don't think we came up here just for you,' says Minervadottir, holding the bag out to Pharaoh as if she has won a goldfish at the fair. 'This was found this morning by the engineer visiting the lighthouse at Kalfhamarsvik. It is encrypted, as you see. We charged it up on the drive but it will take some time to ascertain if it belongs to our victim.'

Pharaoh holds the bag up to the light. She turns to Minervadottir. Flashes her best smile. 'Look, I've been a terrible host. I'll put the kettle on. Have my next fag outside, yeah? There's information to be shared. We're all police officers. I've got a few ideas to run by you and no doubt you want to use the Wi-Fi and get some paperwork completed. Let's start again, eh?'

Minervadottir holds her gaze for a moment. She glances at the dark, unwelcoming sky beyond the window. 'Might I trouble you for a cigarette?' she asks at last.

Pharaoh grins and throws her the packet. She heads to the kitchen and starts jangling pots and pans. Reaches into the fridge. Opens the milk and pours it onto her jeans and then the floor. 'Fuck!' she shouts. 'I've got no bloody luck. Bit of a spill-age. I'm frigging soaked. Look, I've got to . . .'

She darts to the bathroom and locks the door behind her. Wriggles out of her jeans. Sets the shower running, all hiss and steam. Pulls the phone from her pocket and slides it free of the plastic bag. She fancies that Minervadottir would have agreed to let her try and unlock it, but until she knows precisely what secrets it may contain, she would rather not risk exposing its contents to anybody.

'Right, Patricia,' she mutters to herself. 'Let's see how clever you really bloody are.'

Pharaoh sits with her back to the bathroom door. Despite the lock, she suspects that if Thor were to give it a push she would end up at the far side of the room. But the position gives her a vague feeling of privacy. She peeked out a few moments ago. The big cop is sitting in the living room, reading one of the paperback novels from the rickety bookshelf. Minervadottir is in the kitchen, sitting at the table and trying to persuade her laptop to connect to the non-existent Wi-Fi.

The tatty bath towel she found in the airing cupboard isn't big enough to fasten so she has draped it over herself like a tablecloth. She has her knees drawn up, and there is gooseflesh on her skin despite the humidity in the small bathroom.

She looks at the phone. It's waiting for a password. She doesn't know how many chances she'll get before it locks itself for good and she doesn't want to jump in without a plan. She pictures Russ Chandler. Journalist. Drunk. Aspiring writer. Sixty-something and never stayed anywhere long. She fancies that he wouldn't use a birth date. He'd want something personal. Something memorable. Something significant. She has an idea. She jots twenty-six letters onto the steamed-up glass of the bathroom cabinet. Works her way through the alphabet, circling numbers and types the resulting figures into the keypad.

13-3-1-22-15-25

There is a pause, then the screen turns green. The word HELLO appears in the centre. Pharaoh gives a tight smile. She takes off the towel and smears the letters away. Then she crosses back to the door and slides back down to the floor. She works her way through the contacts first. There aren't as many as she had expected. The first is from Advantis, a debt collection agency for Her Majesty's Revenue and Customs. There is an asterisk next to it, and the words 'do not answer'. She scrolls through. **Adele. Alf. Andrew**. The names become a blur as she skims through them. McAvoy's entry contains his last three mobile phone numbers as well as his direct line at work, his two email addresses and an extra number that Pharaoh doesn't recognise. It's a landline. She sucks her cheek, thinking hard. Her grip on the phone tightens as she realises that Chandler even has a number for McAvoy's father, up on the family croft a couple of miles inland from Loch Ewe in the Western Highlands. She looks at the activity log attached to the contact. Reads through the various emails that Chandler has written and not sent. They're not much more than notes; heartfelt scribblings. Were they written on paper they would have been rolled into balls and thrown over his shoulder. They drip with apology, with profound regret.

*I don't know what I am . . .*

*Such a cunt . . .*

*You were caught up in something that I could never have foreseen . . .*

*I need to make it right . . .*

She skims on through the contacts to her own name and rubs a hand across her forehead as she spots the contact details attached to her file. Recognises Sophia's number. Her Facebook profile. A private email address that Pharaoh used during a previous investigation. She bites down on her lip. He was a good journalist, she knows that much about him. Thorough.

Diligent. Admirably dishonest . . .

She grinds her teeth. Looks at the numbers dialled most recently. There are several with Hull area codes. She wonders if she should call and decides that the reception is too patchy to try. She opens up the recent emails.

A low, rumbling voice emanates from beyond the door. 'You okay? I've tidied up the mess.'

'Be out in a bit,' shouts Pharaoh, as brightly as she can. She navigates her way back to the home screen. Skims through the handful of photographs. The phone's camera is woeful and the images are blurred, as if viewed through cataracts. She opens the documents folder. Four files. She opens the one marked 'Roberta'. Reads the top paragraph and smiles as she recognises the first draft of the article that appeared in *CrymeLog*. The next file contains a list of numbers and dates. They begin in 1985 and continue up to the present day – a list of ships and years. She wipes the fog from the screen.

'Fuck!'

Pharaoh drops the phone as it suddenly chirrups into life. It lands screen up, connected to a number with a Hull dialling code. She reaches out for it, unsure whether to speak, but she loses the signal before she has to make a decision. She finds herself short of breath, panting and perspiring and telling herself to calm the fuck down.

There is a file called *Vidarr*.

**Medical notes: head injury. Partial deafness. Talipes (club foot). Evidence of long-term abuse: physical, not sexual. Aggression, aimed primarily at sibling. Extreme intelligence but lacking in social skills. Bond with aunt but endless conflict with mother, stepfather. Expelled from three schools. Aggressive, frequently disappeared from home. 1983, death of Bowbells. Hysterical at funeral. First meeting with X, '86? RB, attacked at**

**ice-house. Blood and glass. Gerard? Clifftop property in Atwick. Merchant Navy record incomplete. Cadet to deck officer. Capable but poor disciplinary record. Incidents of violence. '93, Sri Lanka. Questioned for attack on local woman. Security officer aboard MV *Excellence*. Trained in submersibles. Leaves the Aspen over falsification of documents. Visa difficulties, Gibraltar, '02. Postcards stop at this time. '05–'07, brief time ashore, resident in Southampton. Signs on as deck officer, Iceland-reg. Trail cold since April '09.**

Pharaoh uses her own phone to take a picture of the garbled notes, hoping that, given time, they will make more sense. She hears Thor, pacing around outside. The last file is a list of names. A crew list. The name 'Ballantine' has been typed in bold. She scrolls to the bottom of the document. Feels like she's staring into a man's mind; the complex machinery of a journalist making connections.

**Kalfhamarsvik. Ravens? GB. Videy. Rag. Le Havre. Hair motif. Speak to Mags. Enid to introduce. Talk to Napper while SB away. <u>Torfadalsvatn</u>. Latitudinal line with Atwick? Bobber boots and wound to soft palate. Wreck site. FB Good Ol' Hessle Road.**

She opens the memory display on the phone's home screen. A selection of sound files saved on the microphone function take up a huge chunk of the data allowance.

Pharaoh sucks her teeth. Her head is spinning. It's too hot in the bathroom. Too clammy and close. She feels a pain in her chest and she slams the palm of her hand against it, praying for indigestion rather than a heart attack. She climbs to her feet and splashes cold water on her face. She pulls her jeans off the radiator, still damp at the front but scorching at the back. She grabs her vest and sweater from the back of the door and ties her hair back with a sodden band from around her wrist. A smear of roll-on deodorant and a squirt of Issy Miyake. She slips the phone back into her pocket, takes a breath and opens the door. Thor's waiting outside. She's about to apologise for keeping him waiting when she realises that the look in his eye is not irritation, but concern. He's been sitting here worrying about her. She finds herself tongue-tied, her words falling over one another. She casts an appraising glance. He's bigger than McAvoy. A little broader in the shoulder. Not so handsome a face but not so many scars either. Same sad, mournful eyes.

'I thought you'd drowned,' says Minervadottir, emerging from behind him.

'You could have buggered off,' says Pharaoh. 'I'd miss you but I'd get over it.'

'That would be my preference,' says Minervadottir, as Pharaoh crouches down and starts pulling on her socks. She's suddenly embarrassed at her chipped nail varnish, her size 4 feet, the hem of little black hairs sprouting from her ankles. She concentrates on the past few moments. Makes a decision.

'What are your instructions?' she asks, grunting, as she puts on her left sock upside down. 'Keep me out of mischief or help me?'

'A little of both. It would help if we knew your suspicions.'

Pharaoh finds a pair of earrings in her jeans pocket. They're simple silver hoops, a present from her daughters on her last birthday. They turn her earlobes green but they mean a lot to her. She slips them in. 'The place with the lighthouse, half an hour up the road. Basalt columns. You know it?'

It's Thor who answers. 'It's beautiful. Bleak, but beautiful.'

'Best combination,' says Pharaoh. She meets his gaze. 'Could I get there in the Swift?'

'That little car? No way. Why do you want to go there?'

'That's where his car was,' says Pharaoh. 'Makes sense to see it.'

'No it doesn't, it makes sense to stay here and compare notes.'

'You could take me,' says Pharaoh. 'I could talk on the way.'

'We're not a taxi service,' says Minervadottir, pulling a face.

'You will go anyway,' says Thor quietly. 'You will go in that silly car.'

'Don't dith the Thuzuki,' mutters Pharaoh. She reaches out a hand and Thor takes it. His hands are huge and warm. He pulls her up like she weighs nothing.

'We'll come back in the morning. We can show you where his car was,' says Thor. 'I don't know what good it will do you. The lighthouse. There's nothing much beyond.'

Pharaoh looks out into the darkness. Her voice is soft as snow when she speaks.

'Yes, there is.'

# 24

*Wawne Road, Meaux, East Yorkshire*
*7.06 p.m.*

The truck's brash headlights are the only illumination on this cold, dark tunnel of road. The fog hangs in the blackness, a tangled mesh of silvery white. McAvoy feels as though he could scoop handfuls of sky into his palm.

They're still twenty minutes away from Bransholme station. Voicemails and message notifications start pinging on McAvoy's phone as soon as they enter something approaching civilisation. McAvoy is putting them in order when the device chirrups into life. He spots Neilsen's number and answers at once.

'Ben . . . how's your mum?'

'Still with us,' he says, and his tone suggests he has other things on his mind. 'Look, I've been talking to Dad. He's not so bad at the moment. He's in with Mum now. I don't think he knows he's saying goodbye but he knows she's not well and he's doing his best to make her feel better. She's drifting in and out but she still managed a smile or two.'

McAvoy says nothing, aware that he can contribute nothing. He wonders how his own exit will look, and feel.

'We've been sat here for an age,' says Neilsen, a slight catch in his throat. 'Just talking. I think you've jogged something in his memory. He was on about the *Blake Purcell*. Kept talking about Big Gerard. Rory. Some bloke called Napper. Well, I've had nowt to do other than sit and look at Mam and Dad and Shirley and the carers and I thought I'd be useful. Went through the Facebook group looking for anything or anyone that might have a connection to Mrs Chappell. That comment about her being "big mates" with Mags Lowery. Well, I've looked into her and she's still local. Her name's Aspinall now. Went back to her maiden name in 1988, a few years after hubbie number two died in an accident at the docks. Lives up Atwick way.'

McAvoy can't decide if he should let Neilsen continue or ask him to put it in an email and send it over. The last thing he wants to do is tell him he already knows.

'That's great, Ben. Look, you really should be concentrating on—'

'Sorry, Sarge, I don't want to butt in but listen, this is important. I mentioned Arthur Lowery – her second husband – to my dad and he said he were a right nasty bastard. Got what was coming to him, which could mean anything. But given what he'd said about this Gerard I managed to get a few more details. Gerard Martin Wade. Born 1947. Did three stints inside before he was twenty-one. Real tearaway. Suffered terrible injuries when the *Purcell* went down. Bought a track licence in 1973 – bookie at the greyhound races – and made some serious money. He invested in a couple of vessels that were all but knackered and then made a fortune when the government offered decommissioning money. Reading between the lines, it was this Mr Wade who backed Ballantine when he dropped out of university. Helped him buy the Blake line. Hell of a way to honour his old mate, eh? That sort of gesture – well, what else might he do for him? It got me thinking, if this Arthur Lowery's death wasn't an accident, if this Gerard bloke did it, well—' He stops himself.

'I'm listening,' says McAvoy cautiously.

'I logged on to the investigation database and saw what Sophie had been working through. The contacts list? Well, look,

I don't know what it means, not in terms of Mrs Chappell, or whether it means anything at all, in fact. But Mr Wade. He lives up at West Ella. Huge house. He's one to talk to about the bodies on the *Holst*. They were crewmates. Enid had called him.'

'See what you can find,' says McAvoy, concentrating over the hum of the tyres on the cold road. 'Recent movements. Current whereabouts. Let me know what you find.' He glances to his left and sees the jagged black V of a crow, a slash of charcoal on the mounds of grey cloud. He feels a chill tickling the scarred skin of his chest.

The phone makes a chirruping sound and McAvoy glances down at the screen. Kirkland is ringing through.

'Sorry, Ben, can I just take this? I'll be back. Sophie. Sorry, how are you?'

'I'm fucking starving, Sarge, but don't worry about that,' barks Kirkland, who has heard the sound of the tyres on the wet road and altered her volume accordingly. 'Anyway, Enid's mobile phone has been pinged. We've followed its trail along the masts. It only left her property yesterday morning, not long before you arrived: 7.04 a.m. Country roads through Raywell, Ellerker, Welton, North Ferriby, down the A63 past the docks. Stopped there for eighteen minutes. At 8.34 a.m. it's on Hessle Road. Back to the docks. Then it disappears.'

'CCTV,' says McAvoy automatically.

'We're working on it. But we picked up a specific vehicle through the number plate recognition software. You'll remember the tyres. I've been sitting here watching four bloody screens and going boss-eyed but the vehicle belonging to Bernard Acklam – y'know, Napper – it flashes up on an ANPR check in four locations that would match the journey of her phone.'

'How clear is the shot of the driver?'

'We've got a great shot of him coming down Clive Sullivan Way and he looks geriatric. He's not exactly blending in, either. Bright yellow suit, face like a sack of screwdrivers. Good enough shot to run through facial recognition software, if it's in the budget.'

'The boss would say that it was,' says McAvoy, aware that Kirkland has no doubt already decided to do what she thinks best.

'Could take some time, according to Reena Parekh. She's got a report coming your way in the next half-hour. The PME is scheduled for first thing but she's been able to take preliminary swabs and samples.'

'And?' asks McAvoy.

'Makes me sad to think about it,' says Kirkland, her voice dropping. 'Doesn't matter, does it? Not really. But she died a virgin. Makes me want to cry.'

McAvoy doesn't know how to reply. Why was she known as 'Mrs' when it seemed unlikely she had married? Was it just presumption? Did it make a difference? 'Good work,' he says automatically. 'How did you get on with the pay-as-you-go?'

'The one that belonged to this Marlowe you found online, yes? I keep ringing it. Different provider, different phone masts, but the last location we can identify for certain was on the M18, 30 December, near the Scunthorpe roundabout. If the phone's gone out of the window that may be the last we see. Do you want me to send uniforms down Hessle Road, keep an eye out for Enid's phone? It's a long shot, but . . .'

'May be worth a saunter around the docks,' muses McAvoy. 'Ask a uniform to follow the trail, where possible. Might strike lucky.'

'No problem, Sarge,' says Kirkland, pressing on. She coughs and he hears her take a swig of something fizzy. 'I've spoken to Sue again, at the History Centre. They've got old copies of the *Hull Mail* on microfiche. She can dig them out for you.'

'Thanks, Sophie,' he says. 'If you could send me her number I'll make arrangements.'

'I've been trying the other trustees,' says Kirkland, before he can end the call. 'I wasn't sure how you wanted to deal with Mr Acklam, considering the, y'know, political nature of it.'

'Do you mean Area Commander Slattery's instruction not to go anywhere near him? I think we can safely expand that to include those connected with him.'

'Yeah.'

'The fingerprints, the car – they're good but they're not critical. We need to have something firm before we can pick him up. Concrete. Something Slattery can't brush off. Park it for now.'

McAvoy sighs. It hurts where Ballantine hit him. Hurts even worse in the pit of his gut; the place that gnaws at him and won't let him sleep until he knows he's done the right thing, no matter what the cost.

'What do I tell Slattery?' asks Kirkland. 'I mean, if he asks where you are?'

McAvoy lets the breeze cool his forehead. 'Tell him we've gone fishing.'

# 25

*Freetown Way, Hull*
*7.23 p.m.*

Daniells parks the truck on the paved area beneath the curving glass roof of Hull's History Centre, drawing glances from the drinkers who huddle outside the Old English Gentleman. It's one of Hull's prettier pubs: a big, reassuring rectangle of a place that serves, more or less in its entirety, as Hull's theatre district.

McAvoy stares out through the rain-jewelled windows of the truck, trying to work out what the hell he's got involved in. He doesn't truly know what he suspects. He's not given to gut instinct or intuition but something has felt terribly wrong about this investigation from the start. He wonders whether it was his own name, half completed in the crossword puzzle, that made it all feel so personal, so oddly familiar. He wishes, more than anything, that he could simply ask Mrs Chappell what she had been up to in those weeks before her death. Whether he is right in his suspicions that she and her friend had somehow identified a serial killer.

He glares at the pub, his thoughts grinding against one another. The pub interior looks as inviting as the façade: all imitation gaslights and creamy lace drapes, parted like the stage curtains to reveal a scattering of drinkers dotted around the wooden bar. Behind the bar a short, immaculately dressed man with a large moustache is chatting to two mismatched customers, drying brandy glasses on a white apron like a saloon-keeper in a cowboy film.

He turns back to the archive building where two figures are silhouetted in the light from the open door. One is tall, with long, straggly grey hair and dirty spectacles, a sizeable beer-belly straining at a Hull Libraries T-shirt like a space-hopper in a bin liner. His companion is younger and considerably more glamorous. She has big eyelashes and luxuriant dark hair, tied up in a knot and precariously secured with a Biro and a felt-tip pen. She gives the two officers a smile as she approaches.

'Would you be Sergeant McAvoy? I'm Sue Whittle.'

'Thanks for going out of your way to see us, Ms Whittle,' says McAvoy, shaking her hand. Her palm is soft and warm, slightly damp.

She gestures towards the History Centre and the man who stands sentry at its open door. 'This is Martyn. He's an archivist as well.'

'All rather exciting, isn't it?' asks Martyn, a little giddy. His accent is Mancunian. He manages to give off the air of a roadie from a metal band, from the roots of his patchouli-smelling hair down to the Tippexed toes of his steel-capped boots. He has taken the time and trouble to paint the word 'Dead' on his left boot, and 'Head' on the right.

Martyn leads them into the warm embrace of the reception area, locking the door behind them. There are two wooden high-backed chairs and two low stools with round, shabby cushions. McAvoy and Daniells take the stools.

'I appreciate you giving up your evening, Ms Whittle.'

'Sue, please.'

'Sue. Thank you. And it's Martyn . . .?'

'Wilde. Like Oscar.'

'And you're a librarian, I understand?' says Daniells to Sue.

'No, I'm a senior archivist. Not as senior as Martyn here but he won't live for ever.'

Martyn nudges her with a pointy elbow. There's a pleasant camaraderie between them and McAvoy wonders for a moment how he would fare in their line of work. He imagines himself wheeling a cart, loaded high with old manuscripts and text-books, helping students and genealogists with their queries and delving into dusty old tomes for nuggets of forgotten informa-tion: a treasure hunter seeking a speck of gold. The pleasure of being contractually obligated to tell people to 'shush'. He can think of worse ways to spend a life.

'I'm sorry to have landed this on you,' says McAvoy. 'You'll have heard about Mrs Chappell . . . and about the incident on board the trawler at St Andrew's. We're trying to put a picture together of Mrs Chappell's movements in recent days. You spoke with Sophie about some papers.'

'It's horrible,' says Martyn, looking down at his boots. 'She was so full of life.'

Sue shuffles her papers. Closes her eyes for a second too long. 'Sophie, sorry, DC Kirkland – she gave me a start when she answered Mrs Chappell's phone. She's explained this to you already, I presume? That I was ringing to enquire about some documents that she had been examining?'

'Yes,' says McAvoy. 'There had been some, shall we say, inaccuracies.'

Sue smiles, grateful for the choice of wording. 'There were some papers missing from one of the files she'd been examin-ing. People can be scatter-brained, can't they? It was Martyn who noticed. I rang her to point out that she might have, you know, had a moment. She did say she dithered a little, now and then.'

'I'm aware she was in the early stages of dementia,' says McAvoy. 'Could you perhaps tell me how you first came to know her?'

'Through the library,' says Sue, palms open. 'She used to come in to central now and again. Sometimes she was invited to exhibitions and new displays. She was involved in lots of charities, you see, and the main library has a lot of events. She was a bit of a character, with her big coat and her crazy outfits. I liked her a lot. It must have been not far off a year ago that I first had a chat with her. Alec's exhibition. The Hessle Road one.'

McAvoy nods. He remembers it well. Alec Gill's exhibition capturing Hessle Road in the 1970s had been hugely popular. They were candid black and white snaps, images of children with grubby faces and gap-toothed smiles, playing with tin soldiers on rubble-strewn street corners; tattooed old men with flat caps and spectacles as thick as the bottom of their pint glasses. They immortalised the housemaids with their aprons, scrubbing front steps until they gleamed; women in overalls and boots, their big hair trapped beneath headscarves. Images of shopkeepers leaning in the doorways of shops long since shuttered and bulldozed. Men on the docks, arms around donkey-jacketed shoulders, backs to the sea. It had been a powerful, oddly emotional exhibition, made doubly eerie by the presence of many of the photographer's subjects. Each framed picture became a magic mirror, reflecting a distorted, cruelly aged facsimile of the original. Shrivelled, arthritic pensioners stopped and smiled in front of monochrome depictions of themselves as they used to be. Men with bald patches laughed as they saw themselves sitting astride motorbikes in bell-bottomed flares and hippy tresses.

'Mrs Chappell was there at the opening,' explains Martyn. 'I don't know whether she was in any of the pictures but she was part of that scene, right enough.'

'I recognised her when she came in a few months back,' adds Sue. 'That coat was rather distinctive. She said that she had been using the archives at the Treasure House in Beverley because it was more convenient but that they didn't really hold what she was after.'

'And that was?' prompts McAvoy.

'All this,' says Sue, pointing at her paperwork. 'Social Services documentation from the days of Hull Corporation. Old copies of the *Hull Mail* on microfiche. The records from Hesslewood Hall. Trawler logs. Shipping registers. It was a big undertaking.'

'That's our speciality, of course,' says Martyn, flicking his long hair behind his ears as if he's a model in a shampoo advert. 'That's what this place is for. A complete archive of local history, all under one roof. If we haven't got it, it doesn't exist – or it's sealed until such time as we're allowed to share the contents.'

'And you have a record, yes? Everything that she examined in recent months?'

Sue glances at Martyn. 'Not precisely, no. If it had been that easy I could have said all this to your DC this morning. You see, we have records of everything she signed out for study but only up until the end of November. After that, it's more patchy.'

McAvoy looks to Martyn, correctly guessing that he will want to explain any inefficiency or malpractice. 'Her friend started accompanying her,' he says. 'She said that he was her carer though I must admit that seemed unlikely, given how infirm he looked. But he was a rather trickier character. We'd find him examining folders that he hadn't signed the forms for. As you can imagine, we operate on trust in many cases. If you're going to make copies of things you sign the correct form, pay the fee and we have a record. It's a simple system. He seemed content to help himself, picking out folders from the stacks as if he were browsing the shelves in a newsagent's.'

'This gentleman,' says McAvoy. 'Can you describe him?'

The two archivists nod. 'We were talking about him before you came in,' says Martyn. 'Obviously nobody gets into the archive without signing in so we have a record of the names and details and the various dates he visited the archive with Mrs Chappell. Walked with a stick. I'd say he was at least sixty.

Looked rather shrivelled, as if he'd been big and lost weight.'

'He had a bit of a beard,' adds Sue. 'There were badges on his walking stick.'

'The name,' says McAvoy.

'There was a trace of Liverpudlian in the accent,' adds Martyn.

'He gave his name as Sam Marlowe,' says Sue. 'Address the same as Mrs Chappell's. We had no reason to doubt it.'

McAvoy feels shards of ice slip beneath his skin. He experiences a sudden explosion of memory. Sees himself, sitting on a bench in the grounds of a stately home. Sees the man at his side, smoking an unfiltered cig and drinking whisky from the bottle. Russ Chandler. Russ fucking Chandler. A freelance journalist and jobbing researcher. A failed novelist. A one-legged alcoholic; angry and bile-filled, spending his latest expenses claim on a month in a drying-out clinic, soaking up other men's stories; their pain . . .

'Hesslewood Hall,' says McAvoy, under his breath. 'I know that name.'

'It seems a horrible word in this day and age but it was an orphanage,' says Sue, looking at McAvoy's face with concern.

He has to give himself a little shake before he tunes back in to what the archivist is saying. He nods politely, even as he starts logging in to the police database, cursing under his breath. He should have known. *Should have fucking known!*

'We get some former residents who come in to see the records,' continues Martyn. 'Some are looking for answers about their own pasts. Some were adopted and are searching for the names of their real parents. We have to disappoint a lot of people. The more confidential information is sealed for ninety-nine years. To trace your family origins you need to go through certain channels. Certain procedures.'

'That used to be the case, at least,' chips in Sue. 'Social media has changed all that. Never mind getting counselling and making sure you know what you're letting yourself in for. Nowadays people go on the first social media page that fits whatever snippets of info they have about their past and ask anybody who knows who they really are to get in touch. As an archivist I find it all horribly inaccurate. As a person, I find it all rather . . . wrong, I suppose.'

McAvoy twitches in his seat as a great red warning message flashes up on the screen of his phone. All inquiries regarding Russell Chandler, or his pseudonym Albert Jonsson, should be directed to Detective Superintendent Patricia Pharaoh.

Sue shakes McAvoy's arm and hands him a sheaf of documents.

'This is what she wanted,' she explains. 'On 4 December Mrs Chappell requested access to all files relating to Hesslewood Hall between 1963 and 1966. She paid the flat fee that allowed her to make copies of whatever she saw fit, having signed a disclaimer promising that they would not be shared. That's standard. As I say, the names of the children and such, they're kept out of the public domain, but . . .'

'But the pictures in the *Hull Mail*, for example . . .' adds Martyn.

'The photographic archive has lots of images. Children smiling for the camera. Sports days. Charity events. Football matches and rugby matches. There're no names in the captions but if you were looking for a face you knew . . .'

McAvoy swallows. He feels like there's something stuck in his throat.

'What was missing?' he asks. 'What did they help themselves to?'

'I've spent the best part of the past two days going through every file that she signed out over the past few months,' says Sue. 'That was why I rang her and ended up speaking to Sophie. There are crew records missing. The Blake fleet. Trips between the end of January 1965 and the end of January 1971.' She

269

shakes her head, appalled. 'She must have made some kind of mistake. Or her "carer" did. He was a nuisance, I can tell you that. We'll certainly be beefing up our security.'

'You have CCTV, I presume,' says McAvoy. He wants confirmation. Needs to see Chandler's face with his own eyes. He's squeezing his phone as if trying to massage a heart.

'It's an outside security firm but we've requested the footage as a matter of standard practice,' says Martyn. 'Stealing from an archive is serious.'

McAvoy looks at him with hard eyes. 'I think the authorities may have to forgo the pleasure of locking Mrs Chappell away,' he says.

'Of course, of course,' stammers Martyn, embarrassed. 'Sorry, I meant . . . well, whoever her companion was, he must be worth your time. And if there is to be some comeback, then he would be the first person for us to speak to.'

'This man,' says Sue, to McAvoy. 'Is he, what, a suspect? I know you can't tell me how Mrs Chappell died, but there seemed something between them. Like they were friends. More than that, even. I don't know. They were on the same team, is what I mean. I figured they were writing a book or something. We get so many writers in, all really focused on whatever their project might be. And she really was a character. That's why I suggested her for the memories project in the first place.'

McAvoy stops writing and looks up. 'I'm sorry?'

'Martyn runs it,' says Sue. 'We got some grant money. We wanted to get people's oral histories down. It's not much more than a couple of volunteers with cameras but it means that there's a human record of what life was like at key points in Hull's history. We started it a couple of years back. Mrs Chappell seemed such a neat fit.'

McAvoy looks to Martyn, waiting for more. 'Well, she would have been ideal, of course,' he says apologetically. 'I think we were just a little late. Her memories weren't all that they could have been and she was more than a little confused about dates. She clammed up as soon as the camera was on her. It was a real shame. We ended up with unusable footage.'

'Did you film at her home?' asks McAvoy. In his pocket his phone vibrates. Distractedly he pulls it from his pocket. Reena Parekh has called twice. There's a text message from Sophie Kirkland, urging him to open her recent email. He does so, trying to concentrate. Kirkland has tracked down a schoolmate of Roberta Ballantine's. She lives in a high-rise on the Thornton estate. Works part-time at the Star and Garter. Starts a shift tomorrow at eleven. He swallows the information. Turns his attention back to Martyn. 'Mrs Chappell,' he repeats. 'Did you film her at home?'

'No, we didn't have the resources,' says Martyn. 'Most of the filming was done down Road. It made for a more atmospheric piece. She was pretty nimble on her feet, happy to go to all the old locations – Rayner's, the old entrance to the subway, down to the docks. As soon as the cameras were rolling she seemed to get second thoughts. You can imagine my surprise when Sue told me she was here doing a history project. From what she told me on the day, she couldn't remember what she'd had for breakfast if it wasn't for her Post-it notes.'

Sue gives Martyn a sharp look. 'Do you still have that footage? Don't you think it might be helpful?'

'There was no footage,' says Martyn, bristling. 'Not of any use. I deleted it when we called it a day. To be honest, I don't think she even remembered doing it. When I saw her again at the archive it was like she was meeting a stranger. Maybe one clip made the final edit. A panning shot, I think. Looking all dreamy, staring out across the old docks. We played it to the backers and they loved it but' – he glances up again, distracted – 'most of the interviews, all the ex-trawlermen and fishwives, they gave us all the "*wasn't it marvellous?*", but the little we had from Mrs Chappell was just sad.'

'The backers?' asks McAvoy.

'Ballantine Holdings Ltd,' explains Martyn. 'They invest heavily in projects like these. He's very much a modern-day philanthropist, our Mr Ballantine.'

McAvoy pulls on his lower lip, considering. 'I want it all,' he says. 'All the footage you have.'

'It's important?'

McAvoy nods his head.

He closes his notebook and shakes hands with the two archivists, leaving a business card with both. He leaves Daniells to chat and finds a quieter corner of the atrium where he can return Parekh's call.

'Hector,' she says breathlessly.

'What have we got?' he asks, leaning forward to press his forehead against the cool glass.

'The hair braid Mrs Chappell was tied up with,' she says, and her voice is quiet and clipped, as if she doesn't have much time. 'We'll have extracted enough skin tissue from within the braid to provide a partial DNA profile before the morning. I can already tell you with certainty it wasn't cut from the scalp. It was pulled. The roots are woven into the braid. All black, no dyes. It's been braided like a dreadlock, two loops across, two loops down. Think of a Viking's beard and you get the idea.'

'Thanks, Reena,' says McAvoy. He hears the tiredness in his own voice. He wants to go home, to fall asleep somewhere safe.

'There's more,' she says, her voice dropping even lower. 'I heard you'd been bumped sideways on this one. I'm not involved with the two bodies on the boat but Professor Garvin has just completed the post-mortem exam. We've had to wait for Mrs Chappell. The two obvious murder victims take priority.'

'What can you tell me?' he asks.

'Cause of death for victim one is impossible to ascertain. The injuries were simply too catastrophic to say which killed him. Victim two, same rib-splitting injuries but he was still alive when somebody stepped on his jaw and wrenched his mouth open. Stabbed him in the throat with the wooden implement from the memorabilia stash. A fid, is it? This was a frenzied attack. You want somebody utterly powered by rage.'

'A different flavour of crime to the murder of Mrs Chappell,' says McAvoy, swallowing hard. He looks through his own reflection and into the cold night air, past the locked gates of the old fire station and to where the road curves up towards the city centre. He sees a couple, hunched over, holding hands, as the icy wind tugs their features into grimaces. He wonders if they have any idea what kind of world they live in, what they would think if they knew what somebody had done to two old trawlermen and a retired social worker. He envies them their obliviousness.

'Apart from the injuries to her fingers I would have said there is no obvious connection at all,' says Parekh. He can hear her intake of breath: the energy creeping into her voice.

'What else is there, Reena?'

'Alfred Howe was strangled with a cord before he was butchered. The cord left imprints on his skin. The pattern matches the braid wrapped around Enid's ankles. At the moment, that information hasn't gone further up the food chain and no doubt when it does reach Area Commander Slattery he'll take his sweet time deciding what to do with it. I thought you might want to know now.'

McAvoy steps back from the glass. Daniells is waiting for him. He wants to go and find Napper Acklam. Wants to put a tail on Stephen Ballantine. Wants to ring Pharaoh for an explanation, and go knock on the door of Roberta Ballantine's old schoolfriend. He looks at the clock above the reception desk, at Daniells's tired, unhealthy complexion. Feels the tiredness creeping over him.

'Home,' says McAvoy. 'My brain is fried.'

Daniells sags, relief seeping out of him. 'Glad it's not just me,' he says. 'I have no fucking clue what is going on. Sorry for swearing.'

They walk through the cold air to the truck. It takes McAvoy a moment to register that his phone is ringing. He answers it without looking at the number. Stops still as Area Commander Slattery's voice growls in his left ear.

'I told you, McAvoy. I made it clear.'

'Sir, I—'

'Don't come in tomorrow. Don't go near Stephen Ballantine or his family. I want you to think very carefully about how you want your future to go. Don't say a word, McAvoy. And if you call Her Majesty to whine like a little bitch then I swear you will regret it until your final breath.'

# 26

*Division Road, Hull*
*10.16 p.m.*

Napper rubs his finger on the screen, caressing the pained, frozen features of a woman who used to matter. He shakes his head. *What a fucking waste.*

He ignores the phone when it rings. Mags won't stop bugging him. She's always been a demanding sod but she was a looker back in the day. Rory adored her, and Napper adored Rory, so he's never allowed himself to lose his temper with her and tell her to sort out her own bloody problems, much as he would have liked to. He's done terrible things in Rory's name. In his private moments he sometimes finds himself wondering if he has lived his entire life the wrong way. If he has spent half a century protecting a secret that nobody else gives a damn about.

He looks at the cigarette burning down to nothing in the ashtray of his expensive vintage car. He's not the sort to cry but there's a nasty gritty feeling in his eyes and the tumours in his lungs seem to be moving about. He keeps thinking about his pals. Fat Des and Alf. He can't stop thinking about how scared they looked when he left them. He wonders if it hurt. It's a ridiculous question. Of course it fucking hurt. They were torn apart, ripped to bits.

Napper lets the tide carry his memories. For a moment he is

twenty-six again: shivering in the icy prison of the fish room in the hold of the *Blake Purcell*. Cowboy Mick is hanging from a hook, his face a mass of bruises and blood. Rory is squatting down low, trembling, a bottle of whisky in his hand and a long braid of dark hair dangling from his right. There are tears on his cheeks. Napper has his arm around young Billy, feeling the poor little sod tremble through his gansey and duck-suit. Gerard is thumping his great fists into Cowboy's ribs. They can hear the sound of bones breaking over the churning of the engines and the howling of the storm.

It was Billy who found the braid of dark hair in Cowboy's washbag. Billy who asked him, in front of everybody, where he had got it. Billy who asked the rest of the lads if they remembered that night, a few weeks back, when Roberta came downstairs during the party before they shipped out. They were gone for three weeks. When they came back, Rory had asked Roberta what had happened to her lovely hair. There was a great patch missing and an ugly wound in her hairline. The new hair was growing back white. She said she'd caught it in something. That it didn't matter.

Mick had gone for Billy. Told the young lad he was doing nowt but stirring up mischief. Slapped him, for his troubles. Gave him another when he started to enjoy it. That was when Rory came bursting in, a huge stupid smile all over his handsome face. 'She's pregnant,' he said. 'Mags. Twins, she reckons. Fucking twins!'

Then he saw the braid of hair. Saw his pals, trying to drag Mick off young Billy. That quick brain of his worked it out at once. Everything about him changed. He looked at Mick and it had seemed to Napper that the air between them crackled with power. Mick didn't even get a chance to protest. Rory whispered in Gerard's ear and a moment later Cowboy was on his back, a front tooth twisted inwards, blood running into his beard. They took him to the fish room. Asked him questions.

When he refused to answer, they asked again. They'd broken all his fingers before the storm came in. They hadn't intended it to go so far. None of them had. It was Billy who brought them to their senses. Billy who asked the question that none of the others had asked themselves. What are we going to do with him?

Rory had been bundling his broken body into the lifeboat when the *Purcell* hit the rocks. Soon, it didn't matter what they had done to the man who hurt Rory's little sister. For the next few hours they were all fighting for their lives. Rory lost his. Billy too. The sea took the best of them. Des, Napper, Gerard and Alf all made it home. Bowbells too, and he never went back. Took a job as a bobber, on shore. They made a pact to look out for Rory's children. Agreed to keep Roberta safe. And then Mags fucked everything up by marrying that Cockney bastard and turning the other cheek while he knocked the stuffing out of her and her bains. Napper let it go on longer than he should have. By the time he killed Bowbells, he had already let Rory down. He made a new vow. Pledged he would never fall short again. He was there for Rory's lads from then on. Helped pay for their schooling. Set Stephen up in business; got Tommy a good berth at sea. Tried to help Roberta, even when she wouldn't help herself. He tidied up their messes for them, even while that little voice at the back of his head told him again and again that in his attempt to do the right thing, he'd allowed those he cared about to commit endless wrongs.

He thinks of Enid, dead in the bathtub. He'd sat and watched for hours, trying to decide what to do. Gerard was going to tell. Her journalist friend had tugged away at Gerard's conscience until he couldn't take it. He was going to hand himself in and admit to what they did in the fish room of the *Blake Purcell*, tell the police about what happened to Roberta. Napper couldn't allow it. Too many people had too much to lose. He wanted Enid to see sense. It was too late for that. Poor old soul was already dead: white skin and blue lips and pain etched all over her face. He'd taken a little while to get himself together. Sat in the rocking chair and thought about how to proceed. It was an opportunity, wasn't it? A chance to truly bury the past. He didn't know if anybody was coming for him and his old pals but he knew that the most important thing was to destroy anything that linked her death to the happenings on the *Purcell*. He gutted the place. He took every last scrap of paper; all her printouts and folders and research books and her phone. Pulled every Post-it note from the wall. Crunched over broken glass and looked down at the tiny ship beside his boot. He'd felt his world shift – as if he were staring with Godlike eyes at the bloody violence being committed within. He'd picked it up and put it in his pocket, thrown it into the Humber along with Enid's phone. He still needs to burn her papers and get rid of the fragile, terrible things in the boot of his car. It had been easier to dig the grave in 1986 than it was to dig it up again. The ground was frozen solid. He'd needed a pick to break through the hard crust of earth, his feet only three or four steps away from the oblivion of the cliff edge. He wishes he could have left them there. He can feel her nearness, still see her flimsy bones emerging from the hard, black dirt.

The phone rings again and he switches it off. He doesn't want to talk to anybody. Not the big copper or Trev Neilsen's pretty-boy son. Not even Stephen. It will be a while before he feels like talking to him again. Napper's not the sort to carry a grudge but he feels a little damn unappreciated. He's spent half a century keeping Rory's lads safe. He expects better. Expects a bit more of a thank you.

He puts the phone away, slips the car into gear, and eases into the traffic. An air of melancholy blooms inside him as turns left onto Hessle Road. Up past the discount stores and hair salons and the gaudy takeaways with their iron shutters. Past Boyes' department store and the bakery: matronly women flogging cheese straws to young mums and fat babies and bitch-ing about the weather.

He turns left at the Star and Garter and cruises past a board-ed-up warehouse until he reaches the old ice-house. The name has been weathered down to a series of smudges and sigils but Napper knows what it's supposed to say. It's been out of busi-ness for the best part of a decade but the generator still works and the ice machine can be coaxed into life after a few taps with a hammer. If the walls could talk, Napper would have a lot to worry about.

Napper glances up to check that the security cameras are still deactivated. Satisfied, he climbs from the car. He looks at the jumble of papers, folders and photographs that surround the wooden trunk in the centre of the boot. He tries not to touch it as he gathers up the documents, fumbling with the key for the padlock that secures the heavy metal doors. He tries not to look too closely at the papers. Doesn't want to see himself as he was then or to look into the face of the poor bastards lost to the sea these past fifty years. To see Billy as he was in case he finds himself picturing the thing he became in those last terrible moments – blood spilling from his eyes, his ears, his nose, his head pitched into the gnashing teeth of the ocean, his cries for help lost beneath the roar of the waves and the scream of the gulls.

He picks up the last of the papers. Gathers up the laptop. He feels the weight of the lighter in his pocket and sighs, slowly, as if accepting what must come next. The feeling settles in his chest like falling snow. He stops himself thinking of Enid – of the cold, stiff thing in the bathtub. He has a flash of irritation at what she had brought upon herself. At what she had forced them to do.

He fumbles with the lock and slides the doors open. He takes three steps into the gloom. The cold black air wraps itself around him like a wet veil.

The blow to the back of his knee cripples him instantly, his patella shattering from the impact and his old, fragile shinbone snapping beneath the sudden weight. He spills forward, dropping papers, photographs, photocopies of crew lists and notepads full of neat blue ink. The pain rolls up and through him. He opens his mouth to roar with the agony of it and the next blow takes him in the mouth. When the club comes down again it shatters his left arm at the wrist. His eyes roll back in his head as he falls onto his back and stares up at the figure above him. Black hair. Black eyes. A shimmering silhouette, like the shadow of a shark.

He sees the last of the light glint off the metal hook in a black-gloved hand. Feels it puncture his skin and slide between his ribs, slipping into his flesh as easy as a filleting knife through the belly of a fish.

The shutters clang shut. The light dies.

Soon, so will Napper.

By then, death will be the thing he wants most in the world.

# 27

*Skagastrond, Iceland*
*11.59 p.m.*

Pharaoh's head is spinning. Her throat feels as though somebody were standing on it. She looks at the ashtray where her
cigarette has burned down to a grey dog turd, curling, unsmoked,
over the lip. She looks at the phone: the little rectangle that serves
as a flimsy casket for the words of a dead man. Wonders how far
the Icelandic cops will get back towards their HQ before they
notice it's missing. She pins her hopes on the fact that in her
experience, coppers are well-intentioned, but deeply fallible.

Six files. Six transcripts. Each branded with initials and dates.

DK 0610

*Are you the one who's been calling me? Look, mate, I don't*
*want to be rude but I've talked about all this before. It was a*
*long time ago. You're being a bit of a nuisance. There's no big*
*conspiracy. It happens, y'know? Bad things happen to good*
*people. I know Enid means well but you're on a fool's errand.*
*Don't come round here again, okay? I don't want to be a twat*
*about it but if you come here again you'll regret it.*

AH 0610

*Before you start I've already spoken to Fat Des and he says*
*you've been bothering him. What's any of it to do with you? I*

*loved that lass. We all did. I don't let myself think of her dead. You're just stirring things up. What is there to gain other than making people feel bad? I don't care what you think you know, you're wrong.*

## GW 0710

*Can I get you a proper drink? Something a bit stronger? No? Look, Mr Marlowe, I don't know what to say to you. It was fifty years ago. I saw him go into the water. He's dead and the terrible thing he did died with him. It was different, you must see that. You can't be much shy of my age. You know how the rules were then. The things he did, he deserved what he got. All these other ones, America and Norway and such – it's make-believe. There's no way. He'd have come for us by now if he'd somehow survived. Why wait all this time? There's no way, Mr Marlowe. Whatever Enid thinks, she's wrong.*

## EC 0710

*You can come in but I don't know what help I'll be. The doctors say I'm going doo-lally. Yes, I live alone. Is that thing recording? Who are you going to play it to? You did well to find me but I suppose that's what you're paid for. Marlowe, you say? Like in the detective books? Sit yourself down. You like them? Presents from Stephen. He's my godson, or at least, the next best thing. He runs a shipping company. His father was a fisherman though you'll know that already. Sorry, I think I went off there. Was it Mr Marlowe, you said? Like the detective books? If you want tea you can help yourself! Oh yes, that's one of my favourite pictures. Used to belong to Roberta. You'll know about Roberta, of course. Such a waste. Sorry, I can't remember your name. Yes, Marlowe. Like in the detective books. We let her down, that one. Should have seen it but it was all behind closed doors. You accept what they tell you. You'd* have kids not registered, others with mums who were really their sisters and sisters who were their mums. It was a mine-field. Roberta could have been something, I know that. Could have been a writer or an artist or anything. The things that happened. She never told and I never pushed. Not until it was too late and she was already on those horrible drugs. I tried to make amends. She buried it all and I let them.

Sorry, could you pass me the puzzle book? I do the cross-words. Can barely hold a pen but I answer the questions in my head. Roberta was better at it than me. That's why you're here, isn't it? Well, if you're looking for answers you're a bit late. My memory's a big Swiss cheese. There are days when I feel like giving up and saying that's that, had a good innings, time to just slip away. But how do you switch yourself off, eh? I don't know if I'm ready to go. I don't know what I think when it comes to Roberta. She lived with me for a little while. We were all very close. That's why I quit the Social Services. It had all changed. You couldn't have that kind of relationship any more – it's all about ticking boxes. They think of the parents as the client and not the child. That's not right, is it? Everybody turned on Roberta after Bowbells died. Des. Alf. Gerard. Napper. Oh you've spoken to them, have you? You've done well. Aye, Napper wouldn't be joking with a threat like that. I'd steer clear.

Look, even if I wanted to help you, I can barely remember what I had for breakfast. All that stuff, those memories, they're leaking. I've been trying, I promise you. Ever since you first called. I even read an article about how to stop yourself losing the pictures in your head. Sounds barmy but it's all about smells. Scents, I mean. And what good's that? Where do I buy her shampoo, her cigarettes; that wet-dog smell of her big fur coat? And even if I could find it all, would I want to? I've got some of her things in the guest room. All

*her writings and drawings and the postcards he used to send.*
*Who? Her Rory, of course. Come with me, I'll show you.*

Pharaoh refills her wine. Plays back the fourth recording and feels wasps moving beneath her skin. Skips on.

SB 0910

*No you can't. This is private property. You're lucky I've let you this close to me without calling my uncle. If you come here again you'll fucking regret it. Do you think I need this in my life? I've done more in Roberta's name than she would ever have done in her own and you're still hounding me? I was nowhere near Division Road. Nor Rayner's. Nor the fucking ice factory. She got pissed, changed her mind about the life she wanted and pissed off to God knows where. And what if she's dead? Does that help my mother? You think I need all that wailing and caterwauling and telling everybody how this has brought it all back? Her poor sainted Rory. Have I not done enough? The silly old cow's an embarrassment as it is. If you print a word of this my solicitor will tie you up in so many layers of red tape you'll feel like a fucking mummy. Don't come near me or my family. Fucking Scousers . . .*

TB 1110

*How did you find me? No it's not, you don't have to say that. No, it's just temporary. Did Stephen send you? I don't need his fucking help. St Stephen, self-made man. What a fucking joke. Do you drink? Are you buying? Oh, do you like it? That one's Fenrir. He's the wolf that kills Odin during Ragnarok. I've always been interested in that sort of stuff. That's how I pick my ships. Horses too. Anything to do with the Norse gods. I'd write a book about it but I'm not really very good at that stuff. Sorry, I'm rattling on. Are you okay? Those badges on your stick – you've travelled? Yeah, always happiest at sea. I just fuck things up when I'm on land. I like the horizon. Room to breathe. Nobody in your face telling you what you should be or what you could have been. Fucking Stephen. I told him last time, I don't need anything. Not his money or his charity. He's Rory's heir, isn't he? Not me. All of Rory's good blood went into him, I reckon. I got whatever came from Mags, which isn't anything good. Used to turn a blind eye to what that bastard did to me. Can you see that scar? Wait until I tell you. You're buying, yeah? I could maybe spare some time. Are you recording me? You can't record me . . .*

Pharaoh feels her eyes closing. The laptop is just out of reach. Her phone is ringing but her eyes are too blurry to make out the number. She's beginning to understand how Russell Chandler found himself in this bleak and beautiful wilderness. She starts to scribble a note to herself – the name of the old lady she met back at Clough Road. The lady who had demanded to speak to Area Commander Slattery about the bodies in Russia. Pharaoh knows she is getting closer to some kind of truth.

She drains her wine, a drip of red running from the corner of her mouth, staining the skin of her neck. Her eyes close and she gives in to sleep.

*Tomorrow*, she tells herself, and her mind fills with the image of home.

# DAY THREE

# 28

*Hessle Foreshore*
*1.11 p.m.*

A place of muddy whiteness. Sugar and salt and dirt: all squashed between the concrete slabs of land and sky.

A small white house with a red front door.

A people-carrier, parked as if the owner would have liked to use it as a wrecking ball. On the main road are a further three vehicles, snuggled up tightly in the shadow of the great steel bridge. The rain falls as if the sky has opened a sluice.

Aector McAvoy is sitting in his armchair, hot chocolate now cold, looking at his phone every fourteen seconds and jiggling his leg as if trying to provide enough kinetic energy to power the house.

'He can't stop you doing your job, Aector. Well, maybe he can. But feck him. Do the right thing.'

'I don't know what the right thing is,' he mutters.

Roisin smiles at him indulgently. 'Whatever you choose, that's the right thing.'

He looks at her, lying on the sofa in a purple tracksuit, each toenail painted a different colour. She'd been excited when McAvoy revealed that he was taking an unexpected day off. She had realised by mid-morning that if she was going to have any fun she was first going to have to work out who killed Enid Chappell, Desmond Kavanagh and Alfred Howe. She was also going to have to murder some bloke called Slattery. So far, she's pleased with her progress.

'Call her,' she says.

'I can't.'

'Why not? Because he's threatened you? Feck him. You're a fecking hero and he's some fly-by-night who's trying to have a dick measuring contest with you, and we both know he's not going to win that one.'

He looks at the carpet mournfully. 'I don't even know what I think.'

'Yes, you do. You just don't know if you want to believe it.'

McAvoy glances at the fire. Watches the shadows creep up and down the wall. 'I don't know where she is,' he protests feebly.

'Sophia said she packed for cold weather.' Roisin shrugs. 'I didn't know they did thermals in her size. Can't be easy getting a fleece to do up over boobs like that.'

'Roisin,' he says, more plea than remonstration.

'I'm teasing,' she says. 'And don't look at me like that. You know Sophia talks to me. She's a bit miffed herself, to be honest, left to look after three little sisters so her mum can bugger off on a ski trip.'

McAvoy frowns. 'Ski trip?'

'That's what Sophia said. Hang on, I'll get my phone and check my messages.'

McAvoy scratches his beard. He lets his thoughts spool backwards, a ball of wool, unravelling – a guide rope into the complications of his own mind. Something is nagging at him: some half-remembered thing. He retraces his steps in his head, trying to pinpoint what he has forgotten to examine properly. He sags as he remembers his visit to Mr McKenzie's scruffy house on Butterfly Meadows. He'd mentioned a documentary. The memory sparks another – Martyn talking about the oral histories project and the 'backers' being delighted with the

290

footage. He opens a search engine on his computer. He finds the programme without much difficulty. Some 60,000 previous viewers have already watched the hour-long programme. There are eleven pages of comments underneath. He scans through them. All nostalgia and sentimentality and 'those were the bloody days'. He presses 'play' and a blare of tinny synth-pop blurts from the speaker. He watches as a group of twenty-some-things, drainpipe jeans and white trainers, cluster around the entrance to the shopping centre, exchanging hard-edged banter with the security guards. The voiceover sets the scene. One of the most deprived areas in Europe. No work. No prospects. No hope. McAvoy finds himself becoming depressed just watching. He skips forward, stopping at random. A lady in a loud jumper and bright blue eye shadow is driving around a labyrinth of identical closes. The caption identifies her as Fiona Wall, part of the area's team of social workers. She's talking to the camera, her Hull accent dialled down a little.

*They don't always settle. They don't, I suppose, fully unpack. It was built with the best of intentions but the decline of the fishing industry hit the city as hard as the Luftwaffe did thirty years before. This is a different community. People who spent their whole lives on Hessle Road have had to readjust to a new way of life. The amenities they've been given have in some ways become a millstone. If they were cold they used to at least be able to gather wood and make a fire in the grate. With an electric fire, if you don't pay the bill you go cold. People go days without seeing one another and the young people don't see much of a future.*

McAvoy skips the film forward.

'Is that your old lady? Back when she was young?' asks Roisin, returning with her phone.

McAvoy glances at the screen. His concentration has drifted

and he has scrolled the programme on to past the halfway point. He finds himself looking at a shot of an attractive middle-aged woman, her dark hair secured beneath a white visor. She's slim, with blue eyes and a bold smile. She wears a white tennis T-shirt underneath a turquoise shell-suit top and is talking to a group of teenage girls in a sports hall. There's no information on the screen but the voiceover talks about the 'volunteers' who give up their own time to help the locals learn 'valuable life skills'. She addresses the camera as if it's an intrusion, spinning back to talk to the youngsters midway through her interview.

*We can't knock the place down. It's done. They've built it now. People live here and we have to get on and make the best of it. It might not be paradise but what the people outside this city don't realise is that we're the ones allowed to make fun of it. Nobody else. Every time you act like you're hopeless, as if you're the thing that they tell you that you are – every time you do that, they win. Do you like people judging you because of where you're from? No? Well, why not make where you're from into something better, eh? Hessle Road was a place of poverty but people were proud of it. They want to think of you as glue-sniffers and teenage mums. Dole-scroungers sponging up benefits. That's what they think of you – don't think of yourself like that. That may be where you start but it doesn't have to be where you finish. Why not be proud to be from Bransholme? Why not be all you can be?*

The camera pulls away and McAvoy finds himself caught mid-smile, enjoying the controlled power of her words. 'Yeah, that's her; her colleague said she was a bit of a firebrand.'

He stops himself as the camera pans out. Sitting at the back of the sports hall, feet pulled up, arms around her knees, sits a young woman. She's mid-twenties though there's a darkness under her eyes that makes her look older. She's wearing combat trousers and steel-capped boots, a wrinkled polo neck and a tartan shirt. She's wrapped in a matted grey fur coat, shiny where the fur has scraped off. She has dark hair though there's a wisp of tufty white at the front, a whisper of bog-cotton against dark peat. Either side of her sit two teenage boys. They look similar but far from identical. Knotty frames and wolfish faces. Short dark hair. Matching checked shirts and stonewashed blue jeans. One of them waves as they acknowledge the camera and the other slaps their hand down, too cool for such tomfoolery. Between them, Roberta Ballantine fiddles with her hair, smiling nervously to reveal yellowed teeth; two gaps in the bottom row. She waves and her top rides up, revealing the faint tracery of stretch marks; silvery skin, like sand kissed by the tide.

Stretch marks.

He calls Kirkland.

'Sarge, what's going on? Are you suspended or something? Did you go and see Ballantine's mum? His solicitor is here going bloody mental. What's—'

'The childhood friend of Roberta Ballantine,' says McAvoy quietly. 'Jean something-or-other. Has anybody spoken to her yet?'

'I don't think anybody else cares about that, Sarge,' says Kirkland, as gently as she can.

'I'm going. Quietly.'

He rubs his brow. Pulls on his coat. Turns to say goodbye to Roisin and realises she's fallen asleep. He takes off his coat and drapes it over her. She opens one eye. 'Don't be a fecking eejit. It's pouring. Love you.'

He kisses her. Puts his coat back on.

He steps out into a ferocious rain and dares it to hit him harder.

He's been ordered to stay away from anything to do with Stephen Ballantine.

But he's not sure Stephen Ballantine truly exists.

# 29

*Clifftop road on the Skagi Peninsula*
*2.06 p.m.*

Pharaoh tries not to look at the view beyond the windscreen. She feels as if she's being driven directly into the centre of a collapsing star. The world beyond the glass is black and silver, like the display on a broken TV. The wind is blowing loose snow and splintered ice across the road so that the concrete takes on the appearance of liquid. She concentrates on the files on her lap. She's wriggled out of her coat and is holding it between her knees; the snow from her hood slowly melting into the manila folder.

The phone line is crackly and keeps cutting out. It's hard to hear everything that Detective Inspector Helen Tremberg of the National Crime Agency is bellowing into her ear but she picks up enough to confirm her suspicions.

'... really didn't want to play ball but I leaned on him a bit ... yeah, all in storage, massive great underground barn of a place ... poor DC stuck there for seven hours ... yeah, admitted '81 Septicaemia. Next of kin listed as Enid Chappell. Gynaecological exam showed that she had previously given birth ... no, nothing else, just the name of the medicine and a request for a psych consult ... that all you wanted? I'll get it across to you.'

Pharaoh thanks her and ends the call. She puts her phone on her knee and lets the information marry with what she already knows. She picks up the phone again. Seeks a number for an Enid Chappell: a former Hull social worker and one-time resident of the children's home where William Godson spent some of his childhood. It's still publicly listed. She's already worked out who the other voices on the tape belong to. She needs numbers for Des Kavanagh, Alf Howe, Gerard Wade. She'll get to them in time. She wants to speak to the old lady first. She needs to break the news that the journalist who became her friend, who helped her sift through her own memories and to cling to the fading whisper of Roberta's memory, has paid for it with his life. She knows this will be hard. Wishes she could turn to McAvoy and ask him to do it instead. He's good with the old ones.

She calls the number, wondering whether she would be better served waiting until the car comes to a halt. Braces herself. 'Mrs Chappell, my name's Trish Pharaoh and—'

She nearly drops the phone when Sophie Kirkland answers. 'Boss? Boss, is that you? Where are you? Fuck, have you heard from the sarge? It's going mental here. How did you get this number?'

Twenty minutes later, Pharaoh is rubbing her forehead, pissed off with herself and everybody else.

*The poor bastard's been chasing shadows!* Chasing a trail she never intended to leave. Enid Chappell is dead. The man who was helping her – Russell Chandler – is dead. Two old trawlermen, dead on the *Blake Holst*. Sophie's having no luck in finding Gerard Wade. Napper Acklam is missing. Area Commander Slattery has all but suspended the acting head of Major Crimes and Rory Ballantine's son has some weird split personality that caused him to punch McAvoy in the face and lick Andy Daniells on the chops. Her insides bubble.

She feels Minervadottir's eyes upon her in the mirror.

'Cards on the table,' says Pharaoh. 'You know that phrase? It means we stop dicking around.'

Minervadottir nods, turning around and angling the mirror back to where it belongs. Thor glances at Pharaoh, his eyes gentle. She tries to return it but gets thrown against the door as he swerves around a huge pothole in the road. To their left the sea crashes relentlessly at the towering black cliffs. The wind rushing by the window is a low, mournful drone, broken only by the crying of the gulls.

'Just like the postcard,' mutters Minervadottir, nodding at the view.

'Sorry, love?'

'Your Chandler. The postcard in his car – it showed this exact place.'

Pharaoh pushes her hair behind her ear. 'Postcard?'

'The list of items recovered from the rental car – the magazine, the postcard.' Minervadottir plays with her phone, frustrated. Her face falls. 'Yes, this was mentioned in the initial report – a postcard showing the lighthouse, it was beneath the mat in the passenger seat. My apologies, I don't know why this was not in the inventory we sent you.'

'Poor bastard,' says Pharaoh, lighting a cigarette. Her blue eyes sparkle. She suddenly feels very tired. For a moment she imagines how Chandler must have felt – believing he was coming closer to the truth, to a form of redemption, only to realise he had been manipulated all along – lured to this dismal place to be buried with his secrets. She decides the time has come to share everything she knows. 'Listen to this,' she says, and calls up the files on Chandler's phone.

'You kept it!' growls Minervadottir, looking at the phone with angry eyes.

'And you were too busy showing off to ask for it back,' says Pharaoh. 'Don't get upset. It was worth it.'

She begins to read them aloud.

'Password was McAvoy,' she mutters, by way of explanation, when she finally comes to a stop.

There is a long silence inside the vehicle. 'What do you think happened here?' asks Thor quietly.

'I'm not sure yet. But Chandler made it happen. He didn't mean to but one of the people he spoke to on that recording – what he told them changed everything. They became somebody else. Did terrible things.'

Pharaoh feels the car start to slow down and grabs the door handle as they lurch to the left, bumping over mounds of ice and snow. They roll to a halt ten feet from the cliff-edge. Pharaoh turns her back on the thick black line where the land stops and the fall begins.

'Here,' says Thor, in the driving seat. 'The car was here.' He points along the road. 'The lighthouse,' he says. 'Kalfhamarsvik.'

The car shifts as he moves, reaching over to the seat behind Minervadottir and retrieving the laptop. He opens it and flicks through a file of images, black and white; a body laid out on the sea wall against a slate-grey sky; a face, half eaten by birds and sea-life; teeth and bone leering out from beneath a mask of tattered flesh.

'You two – you know your mythology?'

'We're Icelandic,' says Minervadottir. 'We were raised on the sagas.'

Pharaoh shows them Chandler's notes. 'Vidarr,' she says. 'Tell me what I don't know.'

Minervadottir and Thor share a look and speak quickly in their own language. 'Vidarr is Odin's son,' she says. 'In the legends. At Ragnarok – the end of the world – Odin is killed by the great wolf. His son, Vidarr, avenges him. He makes a great book from the scraps of leather discarded by shoemakers all over the world and uses it to stamp on Fenrir's jaw and stab through into his heart. He is the god of vengeance.'

Pharaoh scowls and sifts through her notes, muttering to herself. 'The god of fucking vengeance. What I wouldn't give for somebody stabbing somebody else because they're fucking drunk . . .'

'These stories – they matter to people. If your killer believes themselves to be Vidarr they won't stop until they take a blood revenge on everybody who has wronged them.'

'You're full of helpful nuggets you, aren't you?' She glowers at Minervadottir. 'What was he doing up here? It can't just be the fact that it's close to where the ship sank. Have you got a decent map on that thing? There must be some kind of land-mark – something that drew him here.'

'Only the lighthouse and the village,' says Minervadottir. 'There are two farms further ahead but they are uninhabited. The light-house is automated – the engineer visits sporadically. Tourists come, they take photographs. The only time we get called up here is when a hiker gets lost or a polar bear drifts ashore.'

'Just show me the map please,' says Pharaoh angrily.

Thor takes the tablet from his colleague and hands it across. She thanks him with a nod. 'This is where he was found,' says Thor, touching a curve of coastline with his big, pale finger. 'Here, a little further on – that is where Mr Timpson's body was found.'

'The buildings,' says Pharaoh, gesturing at the screen. 'There are farmhouses marked here.'

'Empty, as I said. The villagers left in the 1930s. The last inhabitant at Hvalreki died in the 1970s. That is just a ruin.'

Pharaoh runs her finger over the screen. 'Tell me about the people who lived there.'

'Why?' asks Minervadottir, losing patience. 'Do you expect me to know everything about every house?'

'You knew enough to find your way to me with nothing more than a magazine and a dying name,' says Pharaoh. 'You knew about the *Purcell*. Your head's full of information, love. You checked this place out the second you heard there was a body on your patch, I know you did.'

A tiny smile flickers across Thor's face. He suppresses it. Minervadottir turns away, veiling her face lest she betray any trace of pride.

'Arnaldur Ragnarsson,' says Minervadottir. 'His family were the last to farm here. It is still registered in his name but the land and the shell of the house – they have no value. There are houses like this one all over Iceland, nothing but walls and broken roofs. Ragnarsson was old and his son did not wish to become a farmer.'

'Where did you get your information?' asks Pharaoh.

'One of the last inhabitants of the village,' says Minervadottir. 'He gave a statement to the local police some years ago. He knew little of Mr Ragnarsson, despite being neighbours for so many years. But when electricity came to Skagi, he attempted to persuade the authorities to extend the coverage as far as his own farm, at the tip of the peninsula. He believed he would have a more persuasive case if he brought his neighbours on board. He visited Hvalreki and found it abandoned. He presumed his neighbour had simply left, as many do, but he did his duty and informed the constable from Blonduos when next they met. A report was taken.'

'And what was done?' asks Pharaoh. 'Was he located?'

'We have a report from his son, Vilmar, from 1976. A letter in our files, sent from the cargo ship where he was a crewman. It is a touching communication. His father was half blind. He was troubled with bronchial pain. Vilmar had agreed with his decision to move to their summer residence nearer the capital. It was too late. While Vilmar secured work at sea, Mr Ragnarsson did little but drink himself insensible and sadly, that caused the accident that led to his death. We have his medical notes. The District Physician signed the death certificate. He was discovered by a neighbour at their new home outside Kopavogur, not far from the capital.'

'What's the significance of that location?'

'None,' says Thor, beside her. 'But it is attractive. Good for the lungs. Convenient for the sea. People do retire there.'

'Cause of death?'

Minervadottir flicks through her notes, two pink spots appearing in her perfect white cheeks. 'He fell while in a drunken stupor. Banged his head and did not get up. He had been dead for some time and due to the heat in the property, the body was mostly liquid by the time it was discovered. Vilmar sent money to pay for the funeral and a cremation.'

Pharaoh licks her lips. 'The farm,' she says. 'What does it mean?'

Thor smiles. 'It is a good word. It means a gift of the sea – the carcass of a whale, washing up during a time of hunger. We use it instead of "Godsend".'

Pharaoh sits back in her chair and screws up her eyes. She can almost see a full picture. Can almost make sense of it. 'Is it far?' she asks quietly. 'Just a look. Just to see what Chandler saw.'

'Your phone is ringing,' says Thor, nodding at her pocket.

Pharaoh looks at the screen. Her heart clenches, her mouth dry. A number she knows by heart. She opens the door and steps into the gale, unwilling to talk to him inside the confines of the car. The wind tugs at her hair. She hears the waves crash against the rocks and stares across the snow-covered blackness at the miles and miles of nothing beyond. The ocean and the distant, jagged mass of island that sank its teeth into the *Blake Purcell*.

# 30

*Hessle Road, Hull*
*4.06 p.m.*

The clouds have folded in on themselves. The raindrops are the size of boiled sweets, tumbling in their millions to strike gutters, brickwork, cobbles. The bin liners outside the foods-of-the-world buffet are overflowing: and a smear of crushed leftovers and soggy cardboard leaks into the teeming drains.

Stephen Ballantine dares the gale to hit him harder. He glares, shoulders squared, as he stomps down Hessle Road, head back, coat unfastened; shirt and jacket stained almost black. He takes a breath and catches a whiff of rotting crops over the muddy air of the nearby river.

Stephen's been drinking since this morning. He woke up in the passenger seat of his fancy car, parked up near the ice-house. It was the first place he bought when he came into money. Eighteen years old and already taking the steps towards owning an empire. Rory's son. The best of the Ballantine boys. The heir to the prince of the city. The ice factory hadn't cost much. The docks were already dying, the fishing industry already sunk. He saw a chance to buy old-established businesses at bargain-basement prices. A chance to diversify. He's bought and sold countless local firms in the years since. Still owns the ice factory. He's nostalgic like that. Just like Mum, up there on the coast, unable to leave her little patch of paradise; her reasons for staying deep in the crumbling earth.

There's a cold misery in Stephen's gut. He's always felt a loneliness; the emptiness of the solitary twin. To share a womb; to be pressed up close against your doppelganger: to feel their every movement. He is half a thing; a divided soul. He feels his twin's absence more keenly now than ever before. Sometimes it feels as though he has absorbed his sibling; peculiar feelings and unnerving impulses taking control. He bites down on his cheek. Thinks of Tommy. Not identical, but close enough.

He steps into the doorway of the student flats as a police car glides past, lights flashing but silent, pitching rain-splintered spotlights into the gathering dusk. Checks his phone so that he has something to do with his hands. A message from Mum.

Not for the first time, Stephen wonders whether he was born too late. If he'd slithered out of his mother fifteen years earlier he'd have had a different life. A simpler, harder life. He wonders how he would have fared as one of his dad's lads. One of Rory's crew. He indulges in the fantasy. An alternative life. He could have joined the crew of a trawler; two weeks away, two days home; his kids conceived during drunken fumbles after a night in Rayner's, gradually filling a two-up, two-down off Hessle Road with a succession of pale, bare-legged kids; fighting the elements during eighteen-hour shifts, sliding his gutting knife into the belly of fat silver cod with hands that felt like blocks of stone; one eye on the horizon, watching the ice and snow double then triple the weight of their vessel . . . only ever one big wave away from turning turtle and sinking beneath the waves.

He looks across at the Star and Garter. Rayner's, to its friends. When had he last popped in? Summer? He'd been handing over a big cardboard cheque, smiling for the camera and telling some pretty thing from the *Hull Daily Mail* that whichever local charity he was helping today was a cause particularly close to his heart.

He thinks about the big man who had humiliated him. The Jock. His brother would have loved to meet him, he's sure of that. Tommy. Silly sod. Always nose deep in a book: lost in fantasy. It was no wonder Bowbells had hated him. He was just too fucking meek. There was something delightful about hurting him; like holding a bird in your hand and squeezing until the bones splinter and crack. Stephen feels bad looking back. He should have let Napper and Gerard step in sooner. But Stephen liked watching Bowbells hurt his brother. Tommy was always Roberta's favourite. She'd wipe his nose and dry his eyes and cuddle him like he was a baby. She swore she'd kill him if he ever touched him again. Stephen saved her the trouble. He told Uncle Napper that Bowbells had started touching him. Soon, Bowbells was dead. Gerard fixed it for the two boys to apply to go to boarding school – a chance to become something decent in memory of their dad. Stephen got in. Tommy didn't. It was a shame, but what could you do? If Tommy had been a little less trusting, a little less feeble, Stephen would never have been able to switch their exam papers. It might have been Stephen who buggered off to the sea at sixteen and fucked up his life. Instead, he's heir to the throne. He's the prince of the city. He's . . .

He realises his walk has brought him back to the old warehouse district. To the old ice-house. The place where it started. He has a memory of that night, thirty-odd years ago. Roberta blubbing and sobbing and saying she had something to tell them. Something important. Stephen didn't like it there, in the cold and the dark, with dust on his posh school blazer. He'd said that whatever it was, he didn't care. She'd tried to make him stay. Said this was about who they were. What they were. He hadn't wanted to hear it. He put his hand over her mouth. Told her to stop. Pushed his brother to the ground and kicked him bloody. Banged Roberta's head off the floor until the lights went out in her eyes. He'd felt nothing. When Tommy woke up, there was blood on his hands. Stephen was sobbing.

*You've killed her,* he said. *Look what you've done . . .*

He stares at the ice factory. He still sees it each night in his dreams. He has made something of himself but he knows that only half of him is worth anything at all. The other is grotesque: ugly, a thing of absolute darkness . . .

He feels his thoughts colliding; fracturing and splintering. His whole body starts to shake. His legs begin to buckle as the lies untangle themselves. He pushes himself away from the door and staggers down the empty street, the smell of salt air growing stronger in his nostrils. Feels the wind and swirling rain.

He looks up as a shape appears from the darkness. Black eyes. A shimmering, iridescent mask. Long black braids. The figure holds a hook in one black-gloved hand. He raises his hands to his face and drags away his second skin, a shimmering mass of leather and scales. Stephen stares into the face of the man who used to call him 'brother'.

He sobs. Calls for help until the word becomes a nonsense. Calls for his father, for Rory, the prince of the city. Calls for him until the name becomes mere sound catching the wind, skittering through the damp streets, billowing up and over the great double doors of the lock gates, before disappearing towards the sea.

# 31

*The Star and Garter, Division Road, Hull*
*4.25 p.m.*

'Still damp out, I see,' says the barmaid. 'Snow, fog, bloody ice.
Now it's pissing it down. There was sunshine an hour ago.
Maybe you missed it.'

'Story of my life,' says McAvoy. He glances around. Takes in
the red walls and the varnished wooden floor, criss-crossed
with muddy footprints. He can hear the tinny sound of country
and western bleeding from a speaker.

McAvoy surveys himself in the mirror behind the spirits.
He's pale and the darkness beneath his eyes makes his face look
leaner; harsher.

'Just the one,' he says, surveying the brass tap. No real ales
but a decent dry cider. This way, he can tell himself he's not
here as part of the investigation. This way, he's a bloke on his
day off, having a pint and chatting to the bar staff. If she happens
to be the childhood friend of Roberta Ballantine, that's just
pure coincidence . . .

The barmaid pulls a glass from the dishwasher, steam billowing out like smoke, and runs it under the tap to cool it down.
She glances at him and holds up a finger, urging patience, and
starts rummaging under the bar. She hands him a dry beer
towel as he slips out of his coat and drapes it on the bar stool.
Tieless, wrinkled, he barely recognises himself. He dries his

hair, his face, inhaling a musk of spilled ale and wood polish. Hands the towel back and takes a sip of his drink. It's good. Cold and refreshing. It hits his stomach like ice. He realises how hungry he is. How cold. There's pain in his chest, across his arm, across his shoulders. His mind is fizzing with connections and theories.

He sips his drink and lets the warmth of the bar seep into his aching limbs. He likes Rayner's. Likes knowing he is drinking in a place where the city's legends were created and their stories shared. A fisherman's pub. Rough and raucous. They served trawlermen their first pint when they got home and their last before they left. He's seen old photos and it hasn't changed much in the last half century. If the regulars could be persuaded to dress as they had in 1968 it could easily serve as a museum.

He looks at his phone. Missed calls from Slattery and two from a number he doesn't recognise. He puts it back in his pocket without unlocking it.

'Any good news for us?' asks Jean, her face already twisting into an expression of pre-emptive dissatisfaction. 'Bloody horrible what's happened down the docks.' She's small. Late fifties. A skin-tone that speaks of too much Marbella sunshine and a lake of white wine. She's wearing leggings and a black vest; a wedding ring on a gold chain around her neck. She looks beguiling when she smiles, though it doesn't happen often. Last time he was here, Jean explained she had been a barmaid for most of her life. Seen it all, done it all, bandaged lacerations with the T-shirt. She's never shied away from booting out trou- blemakers or demonstrating to drunken Romeos what she is capable of if they overstep their boundaries.

McAvoy looks around the faded, peeling pub. At a table by the window, two men in bright blue jeans and knock-off Ralph Lauren T-shirts are sitting side by side playing with mobile phones. McAvoy can't tell if they are together, or whether they are strangers who are both secretly seething that their fashion style has been copied. Neither looked up as McAvoy entered the bar. The other drinker did. He's an old man. Big flat ears filled with coarse grey tufts. Thinning strands of yellow-white hair scraped back over a greasy, mottled head; the lines left by the comb still visible, like rakings in a Zen garden. He wears a grey suit over a V-neck pullover, shirt and tie. The collar of the shirt is threadbare where it has rubbed against the stubble of his jawline. He's reading a copy of the *Hull Mail*, though McAvoy notes that his eyes aren't moving over the words. Instead, he's making a display of being occupied, listening in while seeming engrossed.

'I presume the gossips have got it right for once,' says Jean. 'Fat Des. Alf Howe. Druggies, wasn't it?'

'Why are you asking me?'

'You're a copper, aren't you?'

'How do you know that?'

Jean shrugs. 'Sixth sense.'

'Okay then,' he says. 'Let's test your powers. Why am I here?'

'I should imagine it'll be to do with Roberta,' she says.

McAvoy nods. 'I'm investigating the death of Enid Chappell.'

Jean sniffs, sadness flooding her features. 'Bloody shame,' she says, nodding. 'Weren't a bad sort, for a social worker. Tried, if you know what I mean. Did her best by Roberta though that weren't always easy. What was it you were wanting to know?'

McAvoy wonders if he knows the answer. 'She was looking into something,' he says carefully. 'Local history. Something from her past. I wondered if you knew what that might be.'

Jean leans in, her breasts squishing against the bar and wrinkling at the cleavage. McAvoy makes sure he doesn't look. 'I think you may be barking up the wrong tree with that idea,' she says quietly. 'Enid were going a bit funny. She was just trying to sort out her own memories, I think. She and that friend of hers, they were visiting old places, seeing things that might help her stay a bit more . . . well, y'know . . . connected. Did the Hessle

Road tour a few times. Still bright as a button, you could tell that, but she would, well, lose her place, I guess. She'd be sipping her port and lemon and chatting away and then she'd be batting at the air as if she were being attacked by bees. We get plenty of old sods in here so everybody was kind to her. That pal of hers glared holes in anybody who looked like they might laugh.'

'Her friend,' says McAvoy. 'Can you describe him?'

'Old. Walked with a limp. Bit unhealthy looking. Started on the orange squash but looked at the whiskies like he was a diabetic and they dispensed insulin.'

'You have a very good memory, Jean.'

'Barmaid's job. Nice to remember people's names and what they drink. I'm good with faces. His name was Marlowe, before you ask. Enid introduced him as such. It might have been a nickname though. He glowered at her when she said it and she laughed.'

'Do you remember the last time she was in?'

'Around Christmas, I reckon. We've got days and days of CCTV on the system, if it's any use to you. I wouldn't fancy going through it myself but it's yours if you want it.'

McAvoy smiles warmly.

'You're a sweetie, aren't you? Must be horrible, seeing the things you see.'

McAvoy nods. 'The day you get used to it is the day you're supposed to quit. That's what my boss says.'

Jean shrugs. 'Must be nice to have the luxury. Most people just go to work and play the Lottery and hope that the people they love don't suffer.'

McAvoy raises his glass in her honour. 'Do you mean I over-think things?'

'I'm sure your wife loves you despite it.'

'How do you know I'm married?'

'Call yourself a copper?' scoffs Jean. 'The ring's a giveaway, you plonker.'

Jean waves as one of the Ralph Laurens clatters out of the double doors.

A gust of cold wind raises the hairs on McAvoy's neck. He finds himself wondering how many men had tottered drunkenly away from Rayner's and onto ships that never made it home.

'You must be one of the chivalrous souls, I bet. Maybe you'd have fitted in on Road. Don't go thinking fishermen aren't romantic. My dad used to send flowers to me mam every time they had a row. Used to buy her a new dress or a fur coat each time he was on shore. The second he was back at sea Mam would be pawning it to pay for food. It was a mad life.'

'Your dad was a trawlerman?' he asks, pretending to look surprised.

Jean rolls her eyes. 'I bet Sherlock Holmes is shitting himself with you hot on his heels.'

'You're a hard woman,' says McAvoy, looking hurt.

'Aw, look at you – you're like a big toddler. I'm only playing with you. I just mean it's not exactly rocket science, is it? Everybody from round here was from a fishing family.'

'The Ballantines,' prompts McAvoy. 'They suffered a lot of sadness.'

'More than most,' says Jean. She checks the level of the liquids in the glasses of her customers and comes to a decision. 'Just a second,' she says. It takes her more than five minutes but when she returns she's holding a burgundy folder and a black coffee in a floral cup. She lays the album on the bar top and flicks through until she finds a black and white photograph. McAvoy recognises Rory Ballantine and his mates, squashed in together in a little square living room with a floral carpet and mustard-coloured walls. Mags Ballantine, sitting on her man's knee, his fingers playing with her peroxide-blonde curls. The rest crowd in behind, all Teddy boy quiffs and bell-bottom trousers and eyes that look ready for adventure. Roberta

Ballantine sits squashed up between Cowboy Mick and William Godson. She's maybe thirteen and looks even younger. Her hair is thick and dark, like her brother's. She's smiling for the camera, centre of attention. She's wearing pyjamas and her hair's messed up at the back. It looks as though she's come downstairs midway through a party.

'Who took this?' asks McAvoy.

'Arthur Lowery,' says Jean. 'Blokes called him Bowbells.'

'The man who drowned at the docks? Who married Rory's widow?'

'You know a lot, don't you?' asks Jean. 'Aye, he were pals with them all. Didn't sail on the *Purcell*. Septic hand, I think. Worked out well for him. Not so much for Rory.'

'You knew Rory?'

'Oh yes, Roberta was my friend. Much cleverer than me and not easy to get on with but I was there often enough. She had a good life for a while. After her dad died Rory stepped up and took her to live with him and Mags. He sent her brothers and sisters off to relatives but he wanted Roberta with him. She adored him. Broke her heart when he didn't come home.'

'And with Mags expecting too,' says McAvoy conversationally.

Jean looks away. Sips her coffee. 'It was a comfort to Mags, I think. To know that at least she'd given Rory a bain, even if he never got to see him.'

'Twins, wasn't it? Stephen and Tommy? Stephen's done very well for himself.'

Jean closes the book and puts it behind her. She sits down on her stool and looks at McAvoy, arms folded. 'Why don't you just ask me?'

'Ask you . . .'

'Ask me whether those bains were Roberta's.'

McAvoy sips his cider. 'Were they?' he asks quietly. 'Are they?'

Jean sighs and it seems to come from deep inside her. 'The copper who investigated her disappearance – Peach, that was his name – he asked the same thing. Plenty of people know secrets about one another in this part of the world. Plenty of "brothers" who are two foot different in height. Lasses pushing their "little sister" around in a pram and you all know that she's just come back from nine months staying with her auntie up the coast. You turn a blind eye.'

'Except when there's a missing persons inquiry,' says McAvoy.

'Aye. Peach asked me the same questions you are, though not in such a nice way.'

'What did you tell him?'

'I said that yes, after Rory died, Roberta and Mags went away. Convalescence, we called it. They went up the coast. A friend had a caravan up there. And when she came back, Mags had her nippers in tow. Rory's boys. Stephen and Thomas. And that was that.'

'You suspect that they were Roberta's?'

Jean scratches her arms, suddenly cold. 'I was in here the night she disappeared,' she says. 'We hadn't seen much of each other over the years but I still thought she was my pal. People said horrible things about her after Bowbells died. And she was in and out of that hospital, got into drugs. Enid – you know she was her social worker – she was up and down the country in that daft old campervan of hers, picking her up, bringing her back, trying and trying to save her from herself. She'd almost got the job done too. Had a nice job, little place of her own, got herself cleaned up.' Jean lowers her eyes. 'I think that was the problem. The haze lifted. She started to remember. My fella – husband number one, I call him – he didn't like me hanging about with her and in those days you still had to pretend to do what your bloke said. I maybe wasn't there for her. We had a couple of drinks in the few weeks before she vanished and she was talking about shadows and birds and the night her hair got ripped out.'

'I'm sorry?'

'She had this white streak in her hair. There was a clump pulled out when she was young and it grew back white.'

'When did that happen?' asks McAvoy.

'Few weeks before Rory was lost,' answers Jean sharply.

McAvoy finishes his drink. He'd like another but daren't risk it. 'Jean, you seem like you would be a better detective than I am. Tell me, honestly, what you think happened to Roberta.'

Jean holds his gaze. A fine mist clouds her eyes and she blinks back the tears. 'Whatever she remembered, she was going to tell. And I think there were people who would have done anything to make sure she didn't.' She glances in the direction of the docks. 'He's done everything to measure up to his dad. Can you imagine? To find that out? The world thinking you're this boarding-school posh boy making his tragic daddy proud and it turns out you're the son of whichever nasty bastard raped your so-called aunt.'

McAvoy considers her. 'This all seems very fresh in your mind. Almost as if you've been waiting to tell somebody.'

Jean shrugs. 'That pal of Enid's. He asked me if I would give an interview about Roberta. Wanted to know what I remembered. Whether the police had been leaned on to hush anything up. Whether I believed Roberta was still alive.'

'What did you tell him?' asks McAvoy.

'Not a word,' she says sadly. 'He never came back in. I'd got myself in a bit of a lather, as it happens. I'd spent so long not saying anything, you see. Rory's pals, Napper and Gerard, they could be a bit handy with their fists. They'd made it clear that it wasn't appreciated – talking. That it was best to just stay quiet. But they're old now, aren't they? I heard Napper's not got long left and Gerard's got religion so I can't see any repercussions. I had my heart in my mouth the other day when I saw him going past.'

'Napper?'

'Yeah, on his way down to the docks.'

'And this was?'

'Morning before last,' says Jean. 'He'll have been heading to see the lads no doubt. Probably shifting Gerard's car.'

'Sorry . . .'

'Old Ken who drinks in here. He goes fishing at the docks. Says Gerard's Range Rover's parked outside the Chinese. Sorry, can I say Chinese? You know the place. Been there since middle of last week. Still, he can afford it, eh?'

McAvoy holds up a hand to ask for a moment. He sends a text to Andy Daniells. Gets a ping back a moment later.

Jean suddenly looks worried. 'When I say Napper was going towards the ship . . . don't go thinking what you're thinking. He wouldn't do that. I mean, they're his pals. He wouldn't.'

McAvoy looks at his phone. The mobile phone registered to Gerard Wade has been in the same place for the last six days. Before the battery died, it was still receiving signals from a telecommunications tower that could pinpoint its location more or less exactly. It was on the second floor of the abandoned Blake building on the fish docks.

'I've enjoyed talking to you, Jean,' says McAvoy, putting the drink down on the bar. He heads for the exit and stops. Heads back to where she stands. 'They're not even brothers, are they? That's why he wouldn't spit in the tube. He doesn't want to know.'

Jean starts picking at the tabletop. 'I think Roberta thought he would be pleased,' she mutters. 'To know the truth. That she was his mum, not his aunt.'

'Which one?' asks McAvoy, his voice a whisper. 'Which one of the boys is hers?'

Jean's lip trembles. She gets it back under control. 'She didn't know. They took the baby away at once. She was still out of it – didn't know what was real and what was hallucination.'

313

He reaches into the pocket of his trousers and removes his phone. Presses the screen. Fourteen missed calls and a trio of voicemails. He listens to the first.

McAvoy balls his fists. Looks at the last message: a number he recognises but can't quite place.

**Call me at once. Trish.**

McAvoy suddenly realises where he knows the number from. He saw it on the list of phones dialled by Enid Chappell. He found it on a list of freelance journalists, offering the services of a reporter and researcher.

It's the phone number of Russell Chandler.

# 32

*Kalfhamarsvik, Skagi Peninsula, Iceland*
*6.43 p.m.*

Icy rain drums on the roof of the car. Droplets of water run down the glass, turning to ice on the bitter air. Steam rises from the bonnet of the 4x4; ribbons and curls of soft smoke, drifting upwards to lose themselves in the swirling clouds.

'Hector,' says Pharaoh, under her breath.

The big police car has come to a stop on the barren strip of land. The lighthouse is an exclamation mark on the headland; a column of white rising from the snow-covered ground, throwing a yellowy light onto the scattered earthworks and toppled brick walls of the abandoned town. She has her back turned on her companions.

She speaks quietly. Briefs him on why she is here. Tells him about Russ Chandler and his dying words. Listens as he speaks of Enid Chappell's body, entombed in a block of ice. About Russ Chandler: journalist turned investigator, who had stumbled upon half a century's worth of secrets and hidden bones.

'Hector, I'm so fucking sorry. There's so much I have to tell you about – I was trying to keep you safe.' She growls, shaking her head, furious with herself. 'Not "safe". I thought you might be in the frame, somehow. You have so many enemies. I thought if I could just . . . spare you. Not put you through it . . . tidy it up. I should have done things differently.'

She hears him breathing.

'Did he suffer?' asks McAvoy quietly. 'Russ?'

'I think he did, yes.'

'He said my name.'

'It was his password. That will be why Enid wrote it in the crossword. She didn't have any time. When her attacker appeared, all she could do was leave a trail. Russ had told her about you.'

She pauses. 'What about Enid? Why did he hurt her, do you think? Why the hair?'

'A way to use Roberta against her. A way to be extra cruel. He got frustrated with her. Maybe he wanted answers and she couldn't remember. Or she simply wouldn't tell and he hurt her to break her. Either way he wanted her to suffer. The chipped ice – he carried it there with him, I'm sure of it. Knew what he was going to do.'

'The chicken coop?'

'He's out of his mind, Trish. Unhinged. That's why this has looked so erratic – a profiler would mark it down as the work of two people. Controlled one moment, frenzied the next.'

'You're going to arrest Ballantine?'

'I think I'd like to arrest everybody,' says McAvoy. 'But what do you think my chances are of getting a conviction?'

'Where are you now?'

'I'm going to look for the phone. Gerard's phone. It might contain something real. Something I can show Slattery.'

'If we'd just listened to her when she came in,' mutters Pharaoh. 'She knew something was wrong. When she read about the bodies in Murmansk. Two bodies. Three missing men. What if, eh? What if she and Russ really had found a rapist and killer who never stopped doing what he began with Roberta. Do you think Enid had any idea what she was stirring up?'

'She was losing her senses,' says McAvoy softly. 'Had to leave herself notes to remind herself what was important. She didn't know what was made up and what wasn't. She needed to find out for sure. She agreed to help him so she could put her mind at rest. Roberta Ballantine. The boys. Chandler came along at just the right time. He printed that article to cause a reaction. He got one.'

'Tell me,' says Pharaoh, inching down the window and letting the blisteringly cold air turn the sweat upon her skin to a fine layer of ice.

'She spoke to Chandler. Early on 3 January. Whatever he'd found out, he was passing it on. It was already too late by then. The killer was on his way.'

'Vidarr,' she whispers.

'Vidarr?' asks McAvoy, sounding puzzled. 'That's the Norse god of vengeance. Born to avenge the death of Odin – to kill the wolf that slew him. Where did you hear that name?' She hears him playing with his phone. 'There's a ship at Albert Wright Dock with that name. Cambodian registered. I can request crew lists.'

'Chandler's notes. He's got records of Vidarr's movements going back to 1986. He stumbled onto something. Onto some- one. Christ, he wrote that piece to flush him out. Ruffled all those feathers to see if he could bring him out of hiding.'

Pharaoh opens the car door. The wind grabs it from her hand. Pushes it back against the hinges. The car shakes and she gasps for breath, hair and rain and wind in her mouth, and then Thor is pulling her clear, slamming the door shut.

'There!' he shouts, pointing across the headland. 'The cove. With the black stones. The body was found there.'

Pharaoh turns her back on the wind. Minervadottir appears in front of her. She gestures for her to follow, wind tugging at her clothes. Pharaoh presses the phone to her face but she can barely hear anything over the roar of the sea and the song of the gale. 'I have to go!' she screams, and her own voice is lost on the wind. 'I'll call you back!'

She ends the call and turns into the wind. Her feet slip on the snow-covered ground and she tumbles to one knee. Thor pulls her up. She grabs his arm and he turns them both into the wind, using his huge bulk to shield her from the onslaught. Minervadottir, better used to such conditions, squats low as she powers through the gale, the glow of the lighthouse casting great black slashes onto the hard ground.

Pharaoh trudges forward, gasping for breath. The inside of her skull feels as though it has been filled with broken glass and white noise. She flicks a glance back over her shoulder. Winces at the explosion of spume and foam; the sea sucking back in upon itself, clawing back loose stones and dead birds from the beach: an endless cycle.

The rain stings her features, tugs at her clothes, hurling itself at her exposed inches of flesh. She loses any sense of which direction she is travelling in; mounds of brick and earth rise on both sides; thick grass awnings drape over toppled foundations where the houses have sunk into the earth. She glances up as a light shines in her face, blinking rapidly. She catches a glimpse of the rescue hut, out on the headland. She's standing where the black, crow-like figure was captured on the artist's camera. Minervadottir's ghostly face appears at her side and Pharaoh feels terribly disorientated, as if the world were spinning around her.

There is a tug at her sleeve and suddenly Thor is pulling her into the shelter of a tumbledown building, his blue waterproof coat smearing against her cheek. She smells him: a warm fire-side on a cold day. She looks around her, Minervadottir's torch throwing circles into the darkness. She makes sense of her surroundings. She's standing in the porch of the last inhabited farm of Kalfhamarsvik. This is Hvalreki. A week ago, Russ Chandler stood here. He sought answers to a mystery fifty years old. Those answers cost him his life.

'Inside,' she shouts, gesturing further into the darkness. She smells kelp and brackish air, diesel oil and cinders.

'Detective Superintendent!' says Minervadottir. 'There's nothing here. This is dangerous!'

She reaches out, mud and crumbling wood giving way under her fingers. Thor shines his torch into the darkness. She glimpses broken bottles. Empty food cans. A couch, ripped open at its centre, springs sticking out like the workings of a broken clock.

'Tourists!' says Thor in her ear. 'Students! People looking for peace.'

Pharaoh pushes further inside. The ground is soggy under-foot. Frozen puddles form mirrored stepping stones in the darkness. She glimpses clumps of pornographic magazines. Solvent cans. An empty demijohn, label scratched off the surface. She reaches out again, low to the ground. Her feet crunch over broken glass. Smashed ceramics. She sees the remains of a kitchen table, legs blackened, half folded in on itself.

'Pharaoh!' yells Minervadottir. 'Enough!'

Pharaoh ignores her. Switches on the torch on her own phone. Slices white lines in the darkness. Turns back towards the door.

Sees him.

He's not much more than a shadow; a silhouette of absolute darkness, hiding in the black like a shape cut from black card. Long tresses of hair catch the light as he leaps forward, a bird striking prey.

'Behind you!' shouts Pharaoh, as he lunges at Minervadottir.

He pushes her aside, black eyes fixed on Pharaoh. She glimpses the ruination of his face. The scars and rips and tears in his cheek. The ugly trench of flapping skin where his eye should be.

He grabs a fistful of Pharaoh's hair and she tumbles. His feet go out from under him and he falls back; Pharaoh on top of him, her attacker on top of her, fists in her hair, bloodied face pressed against hers.

And then they are crashing through rotten wood and broken

boards and tumbling into the place beneath. The place that, for half a century, a Hull fisherman has called home.

The impact takes the breath from Pharaoh's lungs. She coughs, pain in every cell. Looks up just in time to see the black-clad man close his hands around her throat: thumbs interlocking, fingers becoming wings, squeezing the breath from her.

She reaches up and grabs at his hair, hanging low. Yanks as if ringing a bell.

He screeches, birdlike, head thrown back, and Pharaoh feels the hair rip free from the scalp.

She hits him, hard. There's nothing fancy about it. Just puts as much force into her right arm as she can, jabbing upwards from where she lies on a mound of wood and stone and man. She hits him again and he slithers back, hair still in her fist. More tresses come free. And then Thor is rising from the ground, pushing her aside, wrapping his huge arms around the man and pinning him to the ground. Pharaoh falls back, panting, dirt and blood on her face. Looks up into Minervadottir's pale, shocked face. She takes a breath. Wriggles forward through the dark. Thor shifts his bulk and she shines her torch in the face of her attacker. He shudders in the light. One eye is nothing but crusted black blood. There are stab wounds in his face and neck. Chandler had gone down fighting.

Slowly, she angles the torch. Takes it in. His trophy room. The place he has kept his curls of long, dark hair, each taken from a different girl.

'Hello, Billy,' she says.

Pharaoh sits with her back against the wall. Thor and Minervadottir have him cuffed between them. His head lolls, hair hanging over his face like pondweed. There's not much meat on him. He's skinny. Fragile.

Pharaoh has lit the only oil lamp that didn't disintegrate

when Thor smashed through the rotten timbers and into the cellar beneath. She surveys the room. The walls are painted the colour of mushroom soup and there are stains on the threadbare carpet, its once gaudy checks and zigzags trampled and shuffled into a nondescript mulch. An assortment of ornaments and paperwork is scattered haphazardly on the shelves of a 1970s dresser: tacky china figurines and age-mottled landscapes; greens and browns muddling together beneath the grimy glass. Teetering towers of paperbacks buttress the walls of the alcove by the doorway. Pharaoh scans the titles. Crime novels, mostly. A couple of red-leather hardbacks: waterways of England; ghost tales of Yorkshire; Fishermen's Memories; memoirs of a journeyman boxer by Russ Chandler.

She raises the lamp. There's another door beyond. Painfully, she starts to stand.

'*Stöðva*,' mutters Billy. 'Stop,' he repeats.

Pharaoh realises she's been holding her breath. She lets out a lungful of air and then breathes in, wrinkling her nostrils. It catches in her throat. The place smells of disinfectant; the high, acrid tang of chemicals masking the reek of urine.

'He found you,' she says flatly. 'Chandler. How?'

He shakes his head. 'You give him too much credit. I found him. The article in the magazine – so many lies. I laid a trail. Brought him here. I wanted to know what he knew. He told me, gladly. Recounted all my glories. Reminded me of so many happy times. He smelled of death. He was dying. Happy to tell me what would be coming for me.' He swivels his head, good eye glaring up at Thor. 'You must be the man he spoke of. This McAvoy.'

'No,' says Pharaoh. 'This is Thor. He's a local cop. So's the lady on your left. McAvoy's home, in Hull. He's still going to stop you.'

'Stop me?' asks Billy, raising his face. 'You have me. What are you trying to stop? I'm an old man. My wounds are infected. I have been dying for a long time. Too weak to indulge my pleasures.'

Pharaoh stands up and walks to the far end of the chamber. There's another door, bolted from her side. She slides it open. The bedroom contains a single bed: the stripy quilt twisted around a stained, off-white sheet. The bathroom is cold and damp; dead flies stuck in a cobweb next to the bare bulb. A leather strap hangs from a nail by the mirrored cabinet; badger-hair shaving brush propped next to the tooth mug; denture grip and a splayed toothbrush poking out of an inch of dirty water. There is a wig stand by a cracked mirror. A wooden plank studded with nails, loose hairs tangled around their base. Lethal-looking fish hooks stick out from a long strip of plasticine. Loose threads pattern the enamel of the basin. She looks down at the floor. Dried blood. A fountain pen, thick gobbets of crimson crusted to its point. She angles the light again. Behind her, Billy watches her shadow on the wall. She squats down and sees it, absurd and tragic; kicked under the bed like a broken piece of furniture. She returns to Minervadottir. 'Gloves?' she says, and the detective obliges. Pharaoh goes back to the bedroom and pulls the false limb from the shadows. Chandler's shoe and sock still clothe the prosthetic foot. Grimacing, she looks inside. She recalls a conversation with McAvoy, years ago, about the journalist with the false limb and his special hiding place. She slides her finger around the smooth plastic and gives a grunt of satisfaction when the panel clicks open. She reaches in and slides out the thick, creamy scroll. She read both sides before she calls McAvoy.

'He's here,' says Pharaoh, when he answers. 'Billy. Chandler was right. He survived. Took the identity of the farmer's son. Killed the old man and got himself a new life. Sailed the seven seas and took his pleasures where he wanted.'

She stops, unable to hear him. His voice is distant. Patchy.

'Where are you?' she asks. 'Hector?'

She looks back at Billy, trying to imagine those first moments, frozen and bloodied and somehow alive, clawing himself up the black beach. Rory's blood, Gerard's blood, all washed away by the frozen sea. Finding shelter. Finding a boy, around his own age. Warmth. Comfort. A new beginning. She looks at the pictures on the wall. Feels sick as she drinks in the picture of shabby normalcy: the pictures of home, the landmarks and watercolours; the snowglobes on the low table, the picture of the two boys in the frame. Pharaoh snatches it up. She turns to Billy. He's smiling. Even through the blood and the pain, he's grinning as if he's won first prize.

'The journalist,' he says. 'I saw what was left of him. He did this to me but it did him no good. You don't get far with one leg. Not here. Not on the ice. It takes something special to survive here.'

Pharaoh raises the phone to her ear. 'Hector, I can barely hear you. Where are you?'

'Docks,' shouts McAvoy in her ear. 'Gerard's phone . . . uniforms . . . reports of a disturbance . . .'

Pharaoh crosses to Billy. Squats down in front of him. She holds up the picture of the two boys. 'Which one?' spits Pharaoh. 'Which one's yours?'

'It doesn't matter,' says Billy. 'Enid didn't know. Roberta didn't know. Only Mags knows which one is Rory's seed and which is mine. After the article …well, one of them chose to seek me out. To come to the place where I was reborn. He's my heir. I'm too old. He has his instructions.'

'Enid,' growls Pharaoh, teeth locked. 'Why? Why that way?'

'She had to know how it felt,' he hisses. 'To be plunged into water so cold that it seems to burn the skin. I saw it, in his final moments. The realisation. I took the braid from his hand and he knew that it was me. That he'd killed his friend for nothing. Roberta was mine. My favourite . . .'

Billy's voice has grown louder, as if he were speaking to

somebody in another room. He stares past her, at the pictures on the table. She changes her angle and squats down. Picks up a small music box, black feathers and a silver key. There is a microphone transmitter on its base; a fisheye lens concealed beneath the feathers.

Pharaoh throws the table to one side. Searches beneath the rubble. 'Where?' she hisses, into Billy's missing eye. 'You wanted to watch, didn't you? And your boy – he wanted to make his daddy happy.'

She stuffs her hands into the pockets of his black coat. Pulls out a sleek black phone.

On the screen, a man in a black mask stares at her, hair lustrous, face a mass of leather and scales. He's framed against a smashed window: six white rectangles and spikes of jagged glass. She sees the shape of a big man behind him, beard and grey-flecked hair.

'Hector,' she says, raising the phone to her ear. 'Hector, for fuck's sake!'

'Trish?' he asks, just as McAvoy's phone goes dead.

'Do it!' screams Billy behind her. '*Vertu sonur föður þins!*'

She watches the man with the black braids and the silver hook.

Watches him make his father proud.

Watches McAvoy crash through the broken window frames and tumble into the darkness beneath.

# 33

*Blake Line Building, St Andrew's Dock, Hull*
*8.08 p.m.*

McAvoy lies on the ground like a discarded toy, his coat spilling out around him. He thinks he's alone. Feels alone. Hasn't seen any of the anglers who use this spot after dark. No Travellers parked up on the area of hard-standing by the main road. No rat-faced teens slinking under the metal shutters to rub each other in the dark and suck aerosols from polythene bags.

He realises he is looking at the world from a crooked angle. Blinks, painfully, until things make some kind of sense. He grinds his teeth. It feels as if a bomb has gone off inside the carefully ordered library of his mind. He screws up his face, trying to focus.

A flash of memory. A shape.

The gleam of something cold and hard. The sensation of falling. Glass in his face and hair.

He hears sirens. They cut through everything else – a sharp, precise scalpel-slash of a sound.

McAvoy clamps his teeth together. He becomes aware of the pain in his head. The sirens are getting louder. He is staring past the gaudy illumination of the Chinese restaurant, up towards furniture shops and burger bars, electrical stores and the petrol station. The Humber Bridge is a series of charcoal slashes on the grey-black paper of the sky. He tries to stand.

Topples forward. Half turns and looks up into the black eyes of the man he came to find.

*Vidarr.*

His face is a mask of rippling silver-black leather. His hands are clad in black. Long dark braids hang down to his shoulders.

'You don't have to,' grunts McAvoy. 'It doesn't need to be like this.'

The man strides forward and kicks McAvoy in the ribs. It feels as though his whole skeleton vibrates with the impact. He catches a glimpse of the great black boot as it slams into his guts, again, again. He tries to roll to his feet but the other man is too strong. He slams his fist into McAvoy's jaw. Takes a handful of his beard and stuffs his other hand into McAvoy's mouth, trying to wrench his jaw apart. There is nothing in his eyes.

McAvoy feels the man's weight on his chest and the tearing, popping agony as the hinge of his jaw begins to creak . . .

His hands close around a piece of broken brick. He swings, desperately. Feels the rock strike bone. The pressure eases for a mere heartbeat and McAvoy drops the brick. Swings again: a fist this time. Slams both hands into his attacker's chest and pitches him back onto the dark ground.

Dizzy, half-blind, McAvoy struggles to his feet. Vidarr moves more quickly. Skips through the darkness and launches himself at where McAvoy teeters, clumsily, on the sea wall.

For a moment it feels as though the world is coming apart like damp paper, and he pitches forward, only half registering the sudden flood of hot wetness on his collar. He sees the water. Black coffee and quicksilver. He lurches forward, feels the sea wall against his ribs, his hip, as if the ground were trying to push him into the ocean, and then he is slithering down hexagonal stones, tumbling down the sloping wall and into the water.

The cold is agony. He cannot tell whether his eyes are open or closed. He takes a desperate gulp and chokes as water floods inside him. He kicks desperately, feels the toes of his boots catch the wall. He pushes against the slimy surface but cannot find the strength to propel himself upwards. He reaches out, frantic, clawing at the water as if it were a net he could climb. For a moment he fancies that the water has taken on a human shape; that it has been transformed into a pale and phosphorescent assemblage of limbs . . .

And now he is encircling his hands around the corpse that eddies on the waves, rising and falling with each movement of the water. The arms are taut and elongated, bound at the elbows with a wire that eats into the puffy white skin. One hand is missing, flesh and bone cut clean through. The water is so dark that it is only as McAvoy pushes past the figure, close enough to kiss, that he is able to take in any details. The man is naked. Elaborate patterns have been carved upon alabaster skin.

McAvoy breaks the surface and grabs frantically for the sea wall. The first sound is the screaming of gulls, raucous and dreadful. He hears the slap of water against stone. He tries to speak but the rank brown sludge of the estuary floods his mouth and he has to fight to keep above the surface.

He feels himself go under again, as if there were weights tied about his ankles: hands clawing at his clothes. He tips his head back. Tries to shout. Turns himself over and feels the body bounce against his torso. Instinctively he lashes out. Pushes the corpse away with hands that do not feel like his own.

Spears of torchlight cast distorted polka dots onto the surging surface of the water. He tries to focus on the light, his teeth chattering, fingers numb. He is shivering, fading, unable to tell his body what to do, and then it feels as if somebody were dragging at his coat, pulling him away from his anchorage at the wall, and he is thrashing wildly, certain that the corpse is reaching out for him. He feels the meaty impact of his fist hitting bone.

*People will come*, he tells himself.

He can see his breath rising, drifting upwards through the

dark, and as his hands fasten around some solid part of the corpse's remaining tissue, he feels a tug, as of a fishing wire snapping beneath the strain. The body rises up. McAvoy looks into the empty eye sockets. Glimpses metal. Four silver streaks winking out from the stone circle of his mouth, tiny harpoons forming a cage . . .

*Napper.*

He drags himself upwards, claws his way up the bare brick, tearing skin, ripping nails. And then he is spilling onto the hard ground like a cod released from a trawl, puking up brown water and gasping for breath. He tries to raise his head and collapses back, suddenly aware of the colossal pain that runs from his head down into his shoulders and back.

'Bodies,' he says into the darkness. 'Down there. . .'

The world turns purple and then black as he slithers back towards the floor. He finds himself staring at the lock gates. Two great wooden and iron doors, topped by a rickety walkway.

A hand has been fastened to the rotten wood. It looks like a dying flower, the fingers becoming petals, slowly closing. It seems to writhe as sudden flaring searchlights project a rippling flower of yellow light. The light glints on metal. The head of the nail protrudes from the palm like a jewel.

*Napper.*

McAvoy feels a great sadness bloom inside him. Blood and dirty water, upon his lips, his tongue, his throat. He smells it. Rust and old machinery, iron and blood.

The darkness closes over him like the mouth of a shark.

# 34

*St Andrew's Dock, Hull*
*9.14 p.m.*

McAvoy jerks awake. The pain grabs him from both inside and out. His skeleton seems to have been jarred loose.

Uncertainly, he tries to focus. He sees lumps and blurs and twists of ragged grey. He hears voices. Sirens. Slowly, like a face in fire, the haze becomes something familiar. He raises his hand to his face. His knuckles are grazed. He turns his hand and looks at his soft, clean palms.

Memories come together like quicksilver. St Andrew's Quay. Stephen Ballantine. Hard rain. He'd lifted the metal sheeting and slithered into darkness, his nostrils filling with the smell of brick dust and iron. He'd fumbled for his phone, the light of the screen casting a sickly green illumination into the shadows. He remembers rubble and graffiti, old bottles and cans. A broken lift-shaft; a metal cage. He recollects dead birds at his feet – the stink of them, the taste climbing into his mouth. And then he was moving over shattered rock, up stairs, slipping on feathers, on birdshit. Swung the light on his torch at the great picture on the crumbling wall. A raven. The symbol of the Blake Line; a portent of the gathering dark. He'd heard the sound of sudden movement. Turned his head a moment too late. Then something had hit him. Cannoned into his ribs and then into the back of his head. He'd gone down, face pressed into the feathers, the gravel and glass, trying not to lose consciousness, pulling himself forward. His shirt had torn. There had been a figure. A silhouette. More of an approximation of a man; a shadow drawn in blurry strokes. It had watched him. Watched him wriggle and crawl. Had he glimpsed his face?

He concentrates hard. The insinuation of a shape above him, crouching, squatting, peering at him as he tumbled down the steps and tried to make his way outside. He'd been muttering to himself. Making an emergency call in his head, thinking he was already on the phone to the dispatcher, listening to her calm, measured tones as he clattered through an empty doorway and fell. He managed to pull himself up only to blindly stagger into another abandoned office. He had turned back. Caught sight of the thing that pursued him and lashed out, hard. He shudders at the recollection of the touch. The flesh had felt like leather.

It takes a moment for McAvoy to step out of the memory and into the here and now. He can't seem to make his thoughts behave the way they should. He drags himself to his feet.

'Stephen,' he mutters. 'He came to take all you have. Came to ensure you're the last of your blood.'

He runs his fingers through his hairline. Feels a fresh ridge of assaulted skin.

The sudden whir of helicopter blades throws great gobbets of sea water and mud into McAvoy's face. He throws up his hand to protect himself. Glimpses the shimmering black fish-leather beneath his nails.

He looks up. The police helicopter is hovering low over the water, its great lights casting butter-yellow spheres onto the hexagonal stones of the sea wall. McAvoy feels suddenly cold. He isn't sure he even wants to know the details. He clamps his teeth, trying to keep his thoughts from overwhelming him. He can't let himself give in to it. There's a tightness in his chest and he realises, to his horror, that he is on the verge of a panic attack. His muscles ache and there is a high ringing in his head. He tries to find Roisin's lullaby. Latches himself onto the graceful eddy of her voice and lets it carry him. He needs her. He's tired of being so sore. Of seeing such horrible things. Tired of being unable to look away.

He sees the lights flash. Tries to focus on the two men in the cockpit of the aircraft that buzzes low over the water. He hears his name. Watches as the lights flash, out across the waste ground, back to where he stands. He turns towards the great broken wasteland of the dock. Understands. The pilot recognises him. They're showing him which way the bastard went.

McAvoy can feel a buzzing in the centre of his skull, like static.

He clamps his head between his hands, trying to squeeze his thoughts into a more manageable shape. He watches the silhouettes of the divers.

He swivels his eyes back towards the Blake building. Forces himself to consider what he had seen. The clammy touch of flesh; the reek of rancid skin; the ugly wounds carved into slow-boiled meat. He breathes in. Sea salt. Diesel. The chemical tang of the refinery. He turns his back to the water.

Fixes his eyes on the light and the tiny, matchstick-like figure who sprints towards Road.

Begins to run.

# 35

*The industrial units between Hessle Road and the
waterfront, Hull
9.37 p.m.*

A harsh diagonal rain is scything down from the dark sky,
cutting through the blurry circles and squares that bleed from
the street lamps and bare windows.

McAvoy feels as though somebody were standing on his
lungs. He skids on a frozen puddle and swears. The scenery
changes around him: the warehouses thinning out, the darkness
becoming denser, picking his way through the rubbish and the
potholes as he goes.

*This is where it happened,* he realises, drawing a straight line
between his suspicions. *Where they killed Roberta. Where they
made the pact that cost them all their lives. All of them. Mags.
Tommy. Rory's old pals. Keeping a promise to a ghost . . .*

He is at the door of the ice-house before he realises: some
deeper consciousness taking the decision for him. There's a car
parked outside. He puts his hand on the bonnet. There is still
some warmth to the metal. He peers through the window. Tries
the handle, which opens with a click. He pulls open the door.
Smells old-lady perfume. There's nothing in the back seat save
a tartan blanket and a blue and white carrier bag. He reaches
into the back. Takes his spectacles from his pocket and uses the
arm to open the bag without affecting the prints. Finds smashed

glass and a broken brocade picture frame. Whatever photo was inside has been removed. He slithers back out of the car and pulls his coat sleeves over his fingertips to open the boot. There's a large plastic container. He levers the lid off. Looks inside.

He closes the boot. There is nothing pastel to his vision, no liminal shading to his senses. There is no dissenting voice. Inside the corridors of his mind a cold gale is howling: slamming shut doors and obliterating the parts of himself that have no part in what he must do. Every rebellious whisper in his skull fell silent the moment that he saw the fragile bones.

*Napper*, he realises. *He didn't dump her in the bathtub but he didn't report her death. Just stole her papers and tried to make sure the secrets died with her.*

He takes off his coat. Removes the lanyard from his neck. Takes off his tie and wraps it around the crooked knuckles of his right hand. The rain soaks through his shirt in moments. He catches a glimpse of himself in the darkened glass of the windscreen.

He cannot announce himself as a police officer. Cannot risk panicking the man in black. He needs to get close to him. Needs to be able to put himself in harm's way.

He crouches low. Pulls open the rusty sliding door. It glides up and over silently. He looks into the small, square space. It's dark. Damp papers cover every inch of the wall. Chandler's notes. Enid's files. The report from the welfare officer at Hesslewood Hall about the little boy they couldn't control.

He lets his eyes adjust. Reads the soggy document stuck to the bare brick.

. . . clear that the time spent in such an extreme state of neglect has had a catastrophic impact on William. He has learned to mimic the behaviour of those other children whom the staff identify as more deserving of reward but it is clear that this is mere simulation. His

333

own nature is impossible to predict. He could as easily decide to parody the actions of an abuser if he believed it would lead to approval. He has begun to demonstrate an unhealthy interest in some of the older female residents and has been repeatedly disciplined for intruding in the female dorms and taking personal items. He seems to have an unhealthy obsession with female hair and reacted with a venom I have never before witnessed when his 'treasure trove' of scraps of female hair was discovered and destroyed. I must think of the other children and insist that he be found alternative accommodation. He has previously developed something of a bond with a former resident now employed as a welfare officer within the Hull Corporation Social Services team. Could I humbly request that Ms E. Chappell be appointed his welfare officer? She has good links with the fishing community and perhaps hard work in the company of decent, reliable men might extinguish some of the fire within him . . .

McAvoy turns from the papers and surveys the bleak interior of the old ice-house: rusting machinery looming from the gloom like the rooftops of a distant city. He makes out the shape of a battered old sofa against the near wall. Shelves to his left, piled high with old glass bottles, rusting tools: a cityscape in silhouette under a thick mesh of cobwebs. He feels a breeze and moves towards it. It's cool upon his face. It carries the smell of the waterfront: a green, brackish scent. He fills himself with it. Catches something else. The flavour of disturbed earth; the fresh-grave pungency of mud.

He moves forward. Sees the light: a soft, yellow haze, rising up from the floor. It's barely perceptible, like flame-coloured spots dancing behind closed eyes after staring too long at the sun. It's coming from the far corner, between the sofa and the wall.

A noise, to his right. Low and muffled; like a baby crying through sailcloth.

He moves towards the sound, the soft pocket of light. He fumbles on the floor, patting damp brick, dusty cement, seeking an edge, a place to put his fingers, desperately seeking purchase. There is nothing to grip. No hidden hatchway. No manhole cover or trapdoor. And yet the scent is richer here, the breeze more keen on his exposed skin. He pats again at the floor. Scratches at a patch of damp grit. The loose stones shift. He pushes deeper, half mad with it now, using his hands as shovels, digging through the earth until his hands touch fabric. He does not stop. Scrapes at the garage floor, throwing handfuls of dirt aside, forcing his hand deeper, his palm pressed against cold flesh. The tip of his index finger brushes the wrinkled flesh of an old throat. He alters his position and starts to dig afresh, pulling handfuls of soil and stone from the floor.

Mags Aspinall. Mags Ballantine. Mags Lowery. Lace wrapped around neck, jawbone, mouth, nose. Stephen Ballantine laid out beside her.

He pushes his right hand beneath the old woman's neck. He anchors himself. Hauls upwards. He hears the sound of falling stones and sliding soil and he is falling backwards onto the hard ground, the old woman frail in his arms, her eyes wide and terrified behind the lace veil. He tears at it with his grimy, bloodstreaked fingers. Hears her gasp and feels her come to life in his arms.

'You're okay,' he says, hoping it is so. 'Just breathe. Where is he? Where is he!'

Behind him, it is as if a photographic negative has suddenly come to life. The shadows rearrange themselves as the figure steps out of the darkness. Knitted grey gansey, dark jeans. Steel boots. His face has no features; just two black holes where the eyes should be. Long black braids hang to his shoulders.

In his right hand he holds a length of cable. A steel hook hangs from it; a question mark suspended in the darkness.

McAvoy has no time to react. He only realises that the killer is behind him when the metal touches his throat. And then he is choking as the steel garrotte bites into the skin beneath his jaw and he is hauled back, his senses transforming into a high-pitched whine as the blood supply to his brain shuts off like a sluice gate.

He feels dead flesh against his face. Smells rotten skin. He seems too high. The perspective is all wrong. The woman on the floor seems too far away. Too small. As if he is rising through a darkening sky, watching stars emerge: bright spots of colour, whirling, blurring . . .

He does not know he has closed his hand around a stone until he has already smashed it into the killer's head. The pressure loosens momentarily. He gasps a breath. Swings again, backwards over his shoulder. There is a sickening thud. He drops the rock. Tries to get onto his knees but the man who holds him is too strong. He twists his neck and feels the metal rip at his skin. He strikes out again, but it feels like hitting a carpeted floor. The man is too strong, too big. He reaches behind him. Feels the leathery surface of the mask. Jabs his thumb back like an ice-pick.

The scream that emerges from beneath the mask is muffled by the leathery folds. McAvoy feels the hands let go of him as his attacker raises them to his ruined eye. And then McAvoy is on top of him, raining down punches onto the rubbery face. A face emerges as the mask is ripped to fibrous scraps.

He slumps forward on the bloodied, semi-conscious body of the thing that used to be Tommy Ballantine.

336

# 36

Dear Aector,

*I've written millions of words in my life. None of them mattered. Not really. But this does. He's coming for me. Billy Godson. He was an orphan. The authorities at Hesslewood never even knew where he came from. His file is a horror story. His birth was never registered. The first anybody knew of his existence is when he was found at some god-awful farm. He was chained inside a hen-house. He'd been there most of his life.*

*When Social Services were called in they found somebody almost feral. Somebody broken beyond repair. Enid Chappell was a Hesslewood girl. She'd fought and clawed her way to a degree and a position where she could help people. She became his welfare officer. Did all she could for him. Tried to heal him with kindness. All he learned was how to give people what they wanted. When he hit puberty his desires became dangerous. He hurt people. Enid spoke to a man she knew. A good man. Rory Ballantine. He took him under his wing. Took him to sea.*

*Billy repaid him by raping his little sister. Ripping her hair from her scalp. That was his first trophy. He has many now. He taunts me with it. I'm so fucking cold and I know he's busted me up inside but he doesn't want me to die until he's taunted me with all his trophies. He has made himself a raven wig from the hair of those he has taken.*

*He's told me all of it, Aector. Told it like he's always wanted an audience. Told me about that night.*

*Rory had just learned he was to be a father when Billy convinced Rory that it was Cowboy Mick Timpson who'd brought the lock of Roberta's 'scalp' aboard, that he'd hurt her. Rory and Gerard beat Mick half to death and he still wouldn't confess to it. It was Napper Acklam who asked what Billy was doing going through Mick's things. They started asking him questions. Started turning on each other. Gerard said they should just destroy it before it brought bad luck on the ship. Held the hair to his lighter and Billy screamed like a dying bird. They knew. They all fucking knew. They beat him until there wasn't much left to beat. Rory tried to stop them. Said he wanted to take him back to Hull. To do things properly. That's when the storm closed in.*

*How did he live? Sheer refusal to die. Billy knew how to endure suffering. He could handle more pain and cold than any of them. He let the sea close his wounds and throw him onto the black rocks on the shore, even as Rory and Mick were drifting away on the freezing seas.*

*A boy found him and brought him home to the last farm at Kalfhamarsvik. Hvalreki, he said. The boy told him other words too. Billy asked that they keep silent about his presence for a time. When they said no, he killed them. Became somebody new.*

*I swear, Aector, Enid thought Billy was dead. She thought Tommy had put a million miles between himself and what happened that night when Roberta tried to tell her boy the truth. But he hadn't. He carried it with him and it fuelled whatever darkness was already there. I saw it in him when I told him who he was. <u>What</u> he was.*

*So much of what happened after Rory's death is a mix of lies and secrets. Enid hasn't ever forgiven herself. Roberta told her about the bird wings at her throat and the boys being raised as twins. Enid didn't believe it. Roberta was grieving. Drinking. She'd lost the one anchor in her world. She'd started seeing demons where there were none. She might even have been responsible for killing Arthur Lowery and Christ knows I don't blame her for that. Enid buried it all deep down after Roberta vanished. It was the only way to stop herself going mad. She tried to live a normal life and to believe Napper when he said that Roberta was too. It was only as she started to lose her mind that she started having doubts. She started seeing things she didn't understand. When I found Enid she saw a chance to make sense of her memories. She had these half-remembered images in her mind – the boy at Hessle-wood, swimming beneath the frozen surface of the pool. A campervan on a clifftop, a sad-eyed girl and two mismatched boys. A patch of disturbed earth in the garden of her friend's house: the patch of paradise where the pret-tiest roses grew. She needed my help.*

*Nobody has needed my help before, Aector. I saw a chance to do some good. To use my last weeks for something impor-tant.*

*I think Arthur Bowbells knew what Mags had done. He saw Billy in the boy's eyes. I think maybe Napper saw it too. Gerard's going to tell, Aector. Find him, please. Keep him safe. The others – they're old, and scared, and they all know that Enid will do what her conscience dictates. Please tell her for me, Aector. Tell her she's a good person.*

*Billy will come for me soon. I have so much to tell you and so little space. I'm scribbling this on the back of the only real piece of evidence that matters – the letter that Roberta planned to give her boys. She was going to tell them everything but she knew the words would stick in her throat. She wrote it down. The letter was still in her coat when the coppers found it in a bin near the ice-house. It slipped into the lining of the great fur thing she used to wear. It was in the police evidence hold for years before her possessions were released back to the family. Mags kept it in her wardrobe for years. Gave it to Enid for her charity shop. It was pure chance that Enid found it. Suddenly everything made sense. When I came knocking on her door, well, I suppose she found somebody to help her. I hope you can get the letter back to her. She wanted to come with me but I couldn't agree to that. She was too fragile and maybe I knew this would be a one-way trip. Try and get this to her for me. It means a lot.*

*As for Billy, he's going to come for them now, I know it. I've set something in motion. He's the closest thing to evil I've ever seen, Aector. He thanked me for the article in CrymeLog: for finding his boy. Without it, his son would never have found him.*

*Aector, there is so much to tell you. So many things I want to share. I've spent the years since last we met trying to put things right. If you ever locate my phone, your name is the password.*

*Everything I know – about this, and so much more, is in there. I'm honoured to have known you. I'm a better man for it. And please, don't grieve. I won't go down without a fight.*

*Yours, ever*

*RC (Sam Marlowe)*

Trish Pharaoh turns the letter. Holds it to the light.

*Dear boys,*

*I wish I could have told you this years ago. I made a promise. I've regretted it ever since. You're not twins. You're not even brothers. Mags gave birth to Rory's twins. Two*

340

*boys. One was stillborn. She buried him on a clifftop, over-*
*looking the sea. Later, Gerard paid for her to build a house*
*there. I have happy memories of that place. I hope you do*
*too. One of you is my son. I gave birth to a boy three days*
*before. On my own, in the outhouse behind the house on*
*Marmaduke Street. I didn't even know I was with child.*
*I'd been raped by somebody I knew, and whose face still*
*haunts my nightmares. They took care of it all. I was to be*
*your aunt. She was to be mother to you both. The memory*
*of what Billy Godson did to me took root in some dark, quiet*
*place. I drank until it became a bad dream, until I didn't*
*know what was real and what was not. Aunt Enid has*
*helped me out of that darkness. I finally remember now. It*
*makes an ugly, horrible sense. The man who did this to me*
*has never stopped. He has mocked me all my life. Together*
*we can make sense of all this. Together we can make sure he*
*harms nobody else.*

*I know it is cruel to share this secret but I have kept quiet*
*for too long. I cannot find peace until I tell the truth. I know*
*you are both strong enough for this. I know it will make Mags*
*very angry and for that I am sorry. Enid wants me to wait*
*but I know the time is right.*
*Roberta (Mum)*
*x*

Pharaoh's sitting in the back of the police car, an aluminium
blanket around her shoulders, Thor's coat covering her knees.
The huge police officer sits in the driver's seat, his head angled
so he can look at her properly. His colleague is busy giving
instructions to the small army of police officers and forensic
staff who are poring over the remains of the farmhouse and the
chamber underneath.

Pharaoh presses her face to the phone. Her eyes are closed
and she's tired all the way through. She wants a cigarette but

doesn't want to put Thor through the misery of telling her she isn't allowed. She says goodbye, her voice catching. Coughs a little before opening her eyes. Thor is holding out a bottle of some plum-coloured liquid. She gives a nod of gratitude. Takes the bottle and gulps down a mouthful. It tastes of cough medicine and bad fruit.

'He is well, your friend?' asks Thor.

Pharaoh looks past him. Hazy green lights are swirling against the clouds. To her right, the mountains are a brooding mass; the muscled shoulders of a giant asleep beneath a thin white blanket. She can understand why the people who found this place believed in magic.

'He'll live,' she says, meeting the big man's eye. 'So will Mags, though she might not be glad about that. She's giving a statement. Telling all. Divers have pulled another body out of the water at the dock. Not much of him left but the wallet in his back pocket belongs to a Gerard Wade – last of the crewmen unaccounted for.'

Thor sucks his cheek thoughtfully. 'This Mags. She killed Roberta?'

Pharaoh nods. 'Says she did but I couldn't say for certain that she isn't protecting one of the boys. Gerard was on his way to confess to it all as well. It's all going to be a bastard to prove, though Mags is getting very bloody chatty since Hector pulled her out of the ground. We know for sure that Tommy killed Enid Chappell, Desmond Kavanagah, Alfred Howe and Bernard Acklam. Probably Gerard Wade too. He certainly got good at it very quickly if he'd never done it before. Whether or not Billy was his father, blood doesn't make you a psychopath. He chose what he wanted to be. Couldn't live up to this vision of Rory that his mum shoved down his throat. I don't know how much he already knew but I think that when Chandler told him that he might be somebody else, that everything was a lie – I think his hold on reality snapped completely. When he

342

discovered Billy, when he learned all the things he'd done – a normal person would be revolted. He saw a fucking role model. Billy convinced him he was a spirit of vengeance; that he was some great Norse warrior tasked with avenging the wrongs against his father. Filled his skull with it and set him on the men who dumped his body in the ocean for what he'd done to Roberta.'

He looks away, digesting it all.

'And Roberta? Rory's little sister?'

'She was a fighter, right to the end. She managed to put all the pieces together – what had happened to her, the lies that had been told. Enid helped her with that. When the drugs were out of her system, when she could finally find the space to breathe – she remembered the boy in her arms. And earlier, that night, when Billy came into her room and took her childhood from her; the shadows on the wall and the fingers making a raven at her throat.' She stares out the window at the cold, white world. Shivers and grinds her teeth. 'She fought with her own mind until she wrestled the memory to the surface. Made herself remember. She confronted Mags. Told her she wanted to tell her "son" the truth. Mags begged her not to. Said it would kill Stephen. Roberta wouldn't change her mind. Eventually Mags agreed but only if she could be there. She arranged to meet the boys at the ice factory that Napper used for his little deals. Roberta had some drinks for Dutch courage. Turned up at the ice factory. Her boys were waiting. She told them everything. What had happened to her. What Mags had done with her baby boy. Told her that they should always view Mags as their mother but that one of them belonged to her.' Pharaoh closes her eyes, imagining how the boys must have felt; to look at their mirror image and see a stranger.

'It ended in violence,' says Thor quietly.

Pharaoh nods, picturing it all. 'There was a scene. Somebody

343

lost their temper. Roberta banged her head. Stephen went to call for help. He didn't ring an ambulance – he rang Napper, out drinking with his old pals. They arrived soon after. By then, Roberta had no pulse. Tommy was gone. They made a decision that would haunt them – haunt them like the thing they did to Billy Godson aboard the *Purcell*. They took Roberta's body back to the place it had begun. Napper told Stephen that Roberta was okay. She'd got a bad head wound but he told him he'd arranged for her to go to a hospital down south. She was going to be okay. Going to have a fresh start somewhere else. Going to start again with a new name.'

'And Tommy?'

'Tommy got on the first ship leaving Hull. Spent the last thirty-five years trying to stay a step ahead of the demons in his head. Wouldn't let himself touch land unless he had to. Worked from ship to ship, reading his stories, remembering the things that were done to him by Arthur Lowery. When Russ Chandler found him he was already broken. I think Chandler saw a story, but more than that he saw a chance to do something decent. To atone. When he found Enid they started something that they couldn't stop. The letter that she found in Roberta's old coat, that was just part of it. All the pieces, all the digging, the stories in the crime magazine and the postcards on the wall – it was a puzzle and they thought they could solve it. All it did was bring a monster into their lives.'

Thor scratches his beard, his eyes briefly reflecting the beam of the lighthouse as it casts great shadows onto the dark road beyond the glass. 'Which one?' he asks at last. 'Which son belonged to Billy?'

'It doesn't matter, does it?' asks Pharaoh. 'Sure, it will all come out at trial. Sure, we'll find out which of them is Billy's and which is Rory's. But I don't fucking care. There's no such thing as bad blood. Tommy didn't have to become what he did any more than Stephen had to try and become this

344

philanthropist to live up to the memory of this man he never knew. We are what we make of ourselves, don't you think? Destiny and fate and all that bullshit – it's all just bollocks made up by storytellers.'

Thor smiles. 'You know of our sagas? All Icelanders love the old tales. Trolls and giants and mighty warriors. They are tales of blood and revenge and adventure. We have such stories in our blood and yet our lives – they are . . . so mundane. All rules and taxes and worrying about whether you have eaten too many carbohydrates or whether you need to upgrade your phone. We are lost, don't you think? The people we admire – the heroes – they wouldn't survive in this world. They wouldn't flourish. Your journalist, Mr Chandler. He became part of his own story. He wanted redemption, I think.'

Pharaoh shrugs. Takes another slurp of spirit. 'Here's to him,' she says. '*Skol*. And *sociable*.'

'He is a good cop, this McAvoy?' asks Thor at length. 'I doubt my boss would do for me what you have done for him. My colleague tells me you have children.'

'Don't make me feel like a twat,' says Pharaoh crossly. She shifts in her seat.

'Tell me about him,' says Thor.

Pharaoh sighs, trying to distil her thoughts from her feelings. Closes her eyes.

'You know when you're walking the dog in the woods and it takes a shit? And you don't know whether you should pick it up and take it away with you? 'Cause you think, what's the point? It's the woods. There're badgers and rabbits and foxes shitting here all the time so why bother, yeah? Polar bears for you, I suppose. Arctic fox. Is that right? Anyway, whatever. Yeah, Hector wouldn't be able to leave it. He'd whip out a carrier bag and plop the shit right in. If he didn't have a bag he'd use his pocket. And if he spotted another shit while he was on his hands and knees, he would pick that up too. And before long, he would be carrying great big bags full of everybody else's. That's Hector. Carrying shit for everybody and nobody even asked him to . . .'

She stops herself. Her joints ache and there is a weight in her chest. She lights a cigarette with an air of 'fuck it'. Pushes the smoke out, long and slow, watching the grey vapour against the purplish blackness of the air. She gives her companion a sideways glance. He's got a half-smile on his face, unsure of what she is saying but enjoying the way she is saying it. Pharaoh turns away from him. Glares back at the sea.

'He keeps shit in his pockets? I hear this right?'

Pharaoh shoots him a hard stare. He's good-looking in a bedraggled sort of way. Beard could use a trim and his hair puts Pharaoh in mind of a blow-dried lion with a ponytail, but he's certainly a pleasant direction in which to point her face.

'No, he doesn't. Not literally.' She sighs. 'Being his friend – it's like watching a wildlife programme. He's this giant fucking wildebeest. Broken leg, lion on his back, guts dangling out of him. Vultures and jackals and half the Serengeti creeping towards him with their mouths open. You're watching, listening to Attenborough, and you're screaming at the poor wildebeest that it's over, give it up, and you know in a moment they're going to have opened his ribs and be munching on his innards. But he won't go down. Instinct, or bloody-mindedness, or hope . . .'

Thor watches her for a while, gazing into her in a way she finds unsettling but not altogether unpleasant.

'Do you have to go back at once?' he asks at last. 'There is much of Iceland to see. Many things I could show you.'

Pharaoh considers him. Wonders if he is being flirty. She gives him the benefit of the doubt and meets his gaze.

'I'm needed at home,' she says eventually. 'Maybe another time.'

Thor smiles softly. 'The offer will always be there.'

Pharaoh feels a sudden burning sensation on her cheeks. She shakes her head, long black hair spilling down to veil her face.

Gives herself a talking to.

*Don't you fucking dare . . .*

# EPILOGUE

It is a cold, bright day. Portly white clouds drift across a water-colour sky like newly painted ships catching the tide.

McAvoy is sipping tea from a takeaway cup while walking down Hessle Road. He's not very good at drinking on the move. Can't seem to make his embouchure fit the gap in the lid. So far, he has managed to scald his tongue twice and cut his lip on the drinking hole. There is a dribble of tea on his front. He has not noticed it yet.

He's not parked far away. Only been out strolling for a few minutes. Already he has been the subject of much interest.

*'Been in the wars, have you?'*

*'I bet we should see the other guy, eh?'*

*'Bloody hell, no means no.'*

It hurts to walk normally. He would like to limp, but he already looks sufficiently careworn to warrant double-takes and backward glances, and he doesn't want to give the Hessle Roaders a chance to add to their repertoire of off-colour personal questions.

McAvoy had managed a smile or two. Even given the odd wink. He can't blame them for looking. A large gauze patch obscures the worst of the livid burn around his neck but there is no disguising the plaster cast on his right hand or the blood that has turned the whites of his left eye a deep red. He had presented a sartorial challenge for Roisin when he emerged from the shower at 6 a.m. She had looked at him like a mechanic sizing up a difficult job, sucking her lower lip and frowning

348

while trying to work out a way to make him look less like he had been brought to life in a Gothic castle through a process involving lightning. There was talk of a polo-neck jumper. Talk of a cravat. McAvoy had politely declined both offers. Eventually she helped him into jeans, round-neck T-shirt, and a zip-up cardigan that he has fastened all the way to his chin.

He passes by the glass front window of Rayner's. Doesn't let himself look inside. He doesn't want to see anybody if he can help it. Isn't ready to talk to Jean yet though he has no doubt she's already heard. The CSIs have already matched the bones in Napper's boot with the samples taken from the braid of hair. The baby laid to rest beside Roberta is a perfect DNA match for Tommy Ballantine, Mags's son. McAvoy had been given the chance to break the news to a half-dead Stephen. He'd declined. Left it to a sheepish and apologetic Slattery to go and tell his friend that he is William Godson's flesh and blood. That Roberta Ballantine was his mother. He wonders whether the knowledge will free him or break him. He's heard people give all kinds of excuses for their terrible deeds but Stephen has a better case than most if asking for sympathy. McAvoy wonders whether the darkness within him was carried in his blood – a legacy of his rapist father – or whether his personality split in two as a consequence of all that he saw and felt and experienced in his messed-up childhood. He grinds his teeth as he considers just how many lives Billy ruined the moment he crept into Roberta's bedroom and made a raven on the wall.

He wonders whether it will leak out. Finds himself wondering whether some historian, sixty years hence, will try to unravel the strands. Whether legends will ever be reverse-engineered into their component fragments of truth; whether some intrigued detective eager to prove themselves will sift through the archives and slice great wounds into the official story.

He walks on. Keeps his head down. An elderly woman is moving slowly past the discount furniture shop to his right.

She's pushing a walking frame on rubber wheels. A ratty collie dog walks beside her, each shuffling forward. The woman does not seem to be gaining much forward momentum, her feet barely leaving the ground. And yet she makes progress. Wherever she is going, it matters to her. McAvoy wants to offer to help but he doesn't know what with. Pick her up and carry her? He offers a 'good morning' and a smile and is rewarded with a series of harsh, high-pitched barks. He rushes on, not sure whether the noise came from animal or owner.

There are flowers adorning the bench at the junction of Boulevard and Hessle Road. Just three bunches so far, but the number will grow. By lunchtime, the brown wooden seat will be overflowing with colours. McAvoy would quite like to stay here to witness it. He reads the card attached to a bunch of pink chrysanthemums. The handwriting is barely legible, the scribe clearly struggling to control the pen. There are three kisses, and a name. Roberta. He shakes his head. Wonders if the tears that stung the writer's eyes spoke of guilt or regret.

He sits down. Watches the world for a while. The smell of fish and chips tantalises him from across the road. He can hear the rumble of tyres from the dual carriageway, muted talk radio dribbling from the cars and vans that crawl along through the last of the standing water. The odd burst of chatter in a foreign language. A tall black woman is pushing a stroller through a straggly gathering of customers looking through the windows at the bakery. A minute goes by.

The woman and child are deep in conversation with a short, plump pensioner in a cheap, dark blue suit, the jacket open to reveal a patterned cardigan and a shirt and tie. He's grinning. Asking after her health. Taking a coin from his pocket to press it into the baby's hand. McAvoy looks away. Doesn't want to intrude upon a private moment; to turn it into some symbolic snapshot of a changing time. He settles back on the bench and looks up at the sky.

He lets himself smile as he hears the rustle of plastic and the creak of the wooden bench. Breathes in. Floral perfume and black cigarettes; this morning's wine and yesterday's deodorant. Feels the warmth of her; her left leg pressed against his right, her arm pushed up against his. They sit in silence. McAvoy does not want to move. He doesn't want to spoil the moment by saying something stupid, or somehow getting it wrong. He'd like to tell her he has missed her, that it has been difficult in her absence. He would like to ask her how much she knew and how much she guessed. He would like to ask her if he has done right or wrong – whether his search for justice for one victim may have caused the deaths of many more.

It is Pharaoh who breaks the spell. She yawns, stretching hugely. Then she squeezes his thigh with a warm, firm hand. For an instant he is terrified; stricken at the thought of what the gesture might presage. Then the hand becomes a claw and sharp fingernails dig into his leg. He yelps and looks at her. She's staring at him over the top of her sunglasses. Her blue eyes are icebergs in a perfect white sea.

She shakes her head. A look passes between them. She folds her hands in her lap. Lights a cigarette and blows a plume of smoke into his ear. When he looks down, she has placed a Toblerone, suggestively, on his knee.

'I leave you alone for five bloody minutes . . .'

I don't normally trouble myself about whether or not people get upset by things I say, or do or write. I'm a great believer that being offended is character-building. But given that a lot of *Cold Bones* is inspired by real events, and occasionally uses real people, I think it should be remembered that this is still a work of fiction. Hull's Hessle Road fishing community has endured unimaginable horrors and it would grieve me if I felt I had misrepresented these proud, formidable people in any way. I have huge admiration for the men who braved the seas and made their city briefly rich – at huge personal cost. I offer my unmitigated respects to the families left ashore; the wives, the widows, the orphans. Thank you for allowing me to paint a picture on your canvas.

DM, June 2018

# Acknowledgements

I would like to offer grateful thanks to the people who gave so generously of their time during my researches for *Cold Bones*. Brian W Lavery, whose remarkable book *The Headscarf Revolutionaries* details life in Hull's Hessle Road far better than I ever could. Alec Gill, whose photographs form an exceptional visual record of a time that could be too easily forgotten, and who schooled me in the many superstitions of this close-knit community. Joan Venus-Evans and the many social media users who were happy to share their memories of growing up within sniffing distance of the fish docks – thank you. Maggie D, your memories of the early days of Social Services were tremendously illuminating. Rebecca B and Lisa C, your guidance on police procedure remains invaluable.

Quentin – thank you for the use of your place in Skagastrond at a time when I really needed to be at the very edge of the world. That particular research trip produced more than just a novel. Yrsa, thanks for showing me how people in Iceland drink on New Year's Eve. Sorry I dropped your pug.

Ruth, thanks for turning seventeen disparate stories into one publishable novel and for forgiving the state of the first draft. Oli, thanks for being my mate. Kerry, thank you for being Kerry.

Elora and Artemisia, you are what love looks like. Despite what I may say, I think of you as so much more than my future organ donors. Honey and Amber, you're awesome and I'm proud to be allowed to pay for your lives. Nicola, you're a more complex character than any I could write but by goodness you're a compelling read. Whatever hair colour you're wearing today, I guarantee you look wonderful.

Most of all, thanks to the people of Hull at the time of the three-day millionaires. To Harry and Rita Eddom, Lil Bilocca, Yvonne Blenkinsopp, Christine Jensen, Gill Long, Mary Denness, Stuart Russell, 'Dillinger' and the countless other everyday heroes from a time that both fascinates and terrifies me.

Finally, thanks to you, dear reader. Aector, Trish and Roisin may take a little while to recover from this one, but they will be back. I hope you'll follow me wherever my imagination takes me next.